# A FEW GOOD MEN

# A FEW GOOD MEN

## WILLIAM OVERGARD

A · THOMAS · DUNNE · BOOK

St. Martin's Press    New York

*Design by H. Roberts.*

Library of Congress Cataloging-in-Publication Data

Overgard, William.
    A few good men / William Overgard.
       p.    cm.
    "A Thomas Dunne book."
    ISBN 0-312-02208-5
    I. Title.
PS3565.V427F48  1988
813'.54—dc19                 88-11585

First Edition

10  9  8  7  6  5  4  3  2  1

*For Herman Hanneken,*
*the real thing*

The people of creed and class,
Of every country and clime
Have paid their respects to the Stars
     and Stripes
At one or another time;
At times they raise trouble among themselves,
And some one must intervene
Then the best man to send, so the president says
Is a United States Marine.

—Private C. Hundertmark
*Recruiter's Bulletin*,
April, 1915


Yes, the Marines are down in jungleland and
they did kill a man in a war, and a great
many people did not know anything about it.

—Major Earl H. Ellis
1921


Come all you yankee dope fiends, come and murder
us in our own land; I am here on my two feet, at
the head of my patriot soldiers awaiting you no
matter how many you are.

—A. C. Sandino

. . . in a special message to the Congress, the President broadened the commitment in the name of protecting lives, loans, foreign investments. . . . He announced that he had authorized the sale of arms to the Nicaraguan army and would enlarge the Marine landing force. The president justified his action in terms that satisfied American interventionists: The intervention was necessary to stop the spread of . . . "communism" . . . and to protect foreign lives and economic interests. Despite testimony before Senate Foreign Relations Committee . . . Congressional criticism of the intervention did not abate even as the Marines sailed for Nicaragua.

—A report of
President Calvin Coolidge's
speech before Congress
January 19, 1927

# A FEW GOOD MEN

# ONE

# Nicaragua

IT was a fact. When the sun rose over Bluefields that morning, warships of the U.S. Fleet were out beyond the bar in the lagoon. It was March 1931 and they appeared overnight as if by magic, conjured up by a force that in a wink of an eye could change the odds in a game already begun. It was as though a stranger had suddenly sat in, laying in a large loaded gun on the table. *Bastardos!*

They were arrayed at about a half mile, anchored in an aggressive position; turrets cranked toward the town; the dots of their bores visible punctuation marks. The ships, serious gray, made of thick iron plates picked out with bolt heads and reinforced by heavy angles crossed by stout cable and stays; the architecture of no nonsense: a space designed to protect and punish. *Putas!*

Two men lay in a tangle of jungle grasses on the bluff above the town. The heat was wet, the sun cooking the Mosquito Coast over a slow burner. One wore the white *cotona* of the country and curiously, a Mexican sombrero. He was Augusto César Sandino, a slight thirty-two-year-old mestizo; fervent messiah of the people and leader of the revolutionaries named after him: the Sandinistas. He was the reason the ships had come to call. As he squinted through brass binoculars, he passionately wished God grant him the power to pull the plug on the lagoon and smash the Yanqui bastards into the mud with a giant foot.

Next to him, hunkered up on one elbow, hat tugged down against the sun was an American, Carlton Wills, a reporter from *The Nation*. During several months traveling with the Sandinistas he had written nine articles critical of U.S. policy and its deployment of "Colonial Infantry"—the Marines. He, too, was dressed as a local, but there was no mistaking the aquiline nose mounted by gold-rimmed pince-nez glasses: the intellectual as a war correspondent.

Neither man carried firearms, although Sandino wore a wicked machete on his belt. They had taken a great risk in being here to greet the ships. It was the kind of foolish gesture Sandino loved; an abstract kick to the imperialist ass.

A sound began that infuriated the gulls. It sent them answering in angry caws, scooting along the puffs of clouds. It was a shrill, high-pitched whistle that trilled, ending in a sudden impatient drop: the voice of the iron ship.

A small boat now set out from the fruit company dock. White and canvas-topped, it cut a delicate wake toward the center ship. Dipping through mild waves the puff of its motor was audible in broken passages, the sound muffled by wind. The warship waited, sending up a curl of smoke from one of the tall stacks, a smudgy reminder that mighty forces pulsed beneath the teak and steel decks. As the boat came alongside and connected, the watchers on the bluff saw figures move up the slanted ladder. At a distance muted colors could be made out followed by lavender.

The American consul Richard R. Kelly was first on the quarterdeck saluting the flag, then the officer of the deck. He was followed by others of his entourage who correctly repeated the ceremony. At the last a young girl in lavender appeared, Kelly's thirteen-year-old daughter, Kate. She was tall for her age, with a figure that might be described as plump, corpulent, or fat. As she stepped from the ladder to the deck, pointing a tiny pump, the officer reached out a hand to assist her. This she rejected, actually rapping it with the tip of a folded parasol. When he drew back in surprise, her head came up and under the picture hat he saw an extraordinary face. It was nearly round and framed in burnt orange curls. The direct eyes under beaded lashes matched the color of the dress. Above, the fine line of independent eyebrows were raised in their own salute. But it was the skin that struck him; as white as could be imagined and lit from within. It was the prettiest face he'd ever seen and it made him smile.

She answered with a tip of pink tongue that might for just a second been poised to push a Bronx cheer. He laughed despite himself and she said, "There's a spot on your fly." He looked down, shocked, and finding nothing, looked up, but she had brushed by him and stood aloof as others were welcomed by the Flag Admiral and his staff.

A tour was conducted down the holystoned deck, pausing under twin 6-inch guns. Barbettes were cranked across the beam; barrels overhung the water and their long shadows fell across the visitors. Spruced gun crews stood at attention, and to the man, watched the plump girl. The consul watched her too, cutting his eyes in the sharp rotation of a signal accompanied by an imperceptible nod, as if this might pull the girl along with the company. But she lagged, staying three steps behind; examining what they didn't, tapping things with the parasol; seeming to indicate by her distance that she was independent of tours. The chief gunners mate (his face still carrying indelible powder marks from the horrific flashback inside the *Missouri*'s number two turret on 13 April 1904), gave figures on the big guns. Eyes glazed over until he talked of shell delivery: destruction. Interest lifted. Just how far would the guns fire, they asked?

"Twenty-two hundred yards, a mile an' a quarter."

"That far!"

"At a fifteen-degree firing angle."

"What kind of hole would it make?"

"Depends on terrain."

"Jungle."

"With a propellant charge of three-hundred and forty pounds an' twenty-eight hundred muzzle velocity—a crater might be gouged eight feet deep an' say, a hundred feet around."

"Really!"

"Some bang!"

"Why don't you shoot it?"

"What?" he recognized the girl's voice.

"Go ahead and shoot, we'd all like to see that."

There were chuckles from the party, and smiling, the flag admiral, David F. Sellers, answered. He was a handsome man with the confidence of the single-minded and used to being listened to. That he addressed a silly child did not deter him. It was a perfect opportunity to line out policy.

"Our guns are never fired for amusement, Miss Kelly, they are only run out after serious provocation—can you imagine the devastation and carnage a six-inch shell would cause to property and people?"

"There's nothing there."

"I beg your pardon?" he said, his smile sliding.

"A mile and a quarter in the jungle is jungle. You could shoot in there if you want to, but it would just kick up the palmettos and bother birds. If you want to impress people and do some good, why not aim it so that you blew a hole just to the side of our house. . . . There below the bluff . . ." she pointed toward the shore and heads turned, ". . . then when the rain filled it people could water their burros and it would make a nice swimming pond."

The gun crew appreciated this, but the officers were less amused and the consul sighed. He knew she was having fun with the admiral. The party moved on. The warship was a good six hundred feet long and after a turn on deck everyone was ready for lunch. Their guide showed them to the forward hatch and they went down stairs he called a "ladder," admiring macramé done by seamen on railings. At the bottom they proceeded in line up a narrow companionway curving with the gentle angle of the ship's counter. At a junction they turned right and the girl left.

She strolled along junior officers' country looking into each open door. Curtains were tied back showing tiny cubicles with tidy double bunks and the few personal items arranged at precise angles. The pervading smell was of diesel oil and fresh paint, and the space had a tightness of air that she imagined the goods in cans must feel. No one stirred, and she was about to turn when she saw a man brushing his hair in the last cubicle. Tall and angular, he bent slightly looking into a metal shaving mirror, trying to tame cowlicky hair that was shaved above his ears: what her mother would have called poor boy's hair. He stopped and looked at her coolly and she was struck by a face like a mask: bronze below, white above; the separation striking a precise line above blond eyebrows. He was no boy, with etched lines and lean, tight jaws, looking like some kind of Swede she thought. His eyes were deep set, pale and blue; eerie against the heavy tan.

"Do you live here?" she said smiling.

"I'm not ship's company." She heard an accent and not a hint of humor. He put down the brush and, tucking a cap under his arm, pushed past her into the companionway. He did not say excuse me. She followed him.

"What do you do?"

"I'm a Marine." She was perfectly aware of this, having traveled all her life in the diplomatic service. She knew uniforms, saw the ribbons and bar (thinking he was old to be a lieutenant, even in the Marines).

"You're one of the ones they sent down here to kill Sandino."

There was no answer and in the next minute he had turned

and preceded her through a varnished door braced by a Marine guard. He was uncovered and they did not salute. Inside, a table was set with snowy linen, silver, and blue-rimmed plates that read U.S.S. *Cleveland*. Black messboys stood waiting to serve while the consul's party chatted with selected ship's officers. "Ah, Mr. Kelly," the admiral said, still cheery, "here's our little ordinance expert." He and the consul walked over to where Kate stood with the Marine. "Have you met Lieutenant Magnusson?"

"Magnusson?" the consul repeated. "The man who killed Charlemagne?"

"The very same," a Marine general next to the admiral said, "not only that shifty *griffe*, but Osiris Joseph up in the north of Haiti. I tell you, then that revolution was dead as last year's love." The others in the party of concerned Americans had gathered around, and Mr. Morris, the United Fruit man, spoke for all of them.

"By God!—excuse me miss—but that is what is needed here! Someone to pass light through this rebel dog Sandino!" This was hyperbole, but the others agreed.

"That we will attempt," the general answered. Each businessman there had a horror story he repeated: how the rebels put the chop to *El Guardia* in the Jinotega department; raids against foreign-owned mines and lumber companies; property destruction, death, terror. The Sandinistas were everywhere and Sandino had become a legend to the Indians.

"Let me instruct you in the way we deal with legends," the general said. "Charlemagne was a legend in Haiti, the *caco* bandits believed him immortal—but then they believe in *vodun* and Mama Drum, the Papa Drum, and the Baby Drum." This got a polite laugh. "When Lieutenant Magnusson shot him up at his stronghold—he brought the body out and it was taken to Cap Haitien and laid in that public place so that the countryside might flock to look." He paused for effect. "Then, just to be sure he stayed quiet and there was no magic in his bones, we buried him under the concrete entrance to the Department Headquarters of the North—now night and day the sentry on Post Number One paces up and down over his head."

They all enjoyed this, laughing heartily. But then, that was why the party had been arranged, so that these American businessmen—mine owners and mahogany harvesters, investors in Nicaragua's future—might see the flag and be calmed. Marine heroes had been chosen to jolly them along with tales of blood and glory against rebels and bandits.

The girl saw that the Marine general was staring at her. He had large moist eyes that didn't blink and a slight smile that said he was on to her. Spare, with sloping shoulders and big hands, he put one out. "We haven't met I think, Miss Kelly, Smedley Butler. I understand you have been instructing Admiral Sellers in proper targets." He leaned closer whispering, "I'll tell you as a Marine, the Navy needs all the instruction it can get." They laughed together and he steered her toward the table. "Let's sit down or these civilians will never begin mess." She sat next to him, impressed. She knew who Smedley Butler was, of course. Lowell Thomas had written a book about him, *Old Gimlet Eye.*

They were all seated and soup came around, onion.

"Thank heaven it's not banana." the General said.

"Banana soup? I've never head of that."

"Oh yes, they get up to that in the Dominican. Actually with chopped-up parrot and bits of monkey tail it's not bad."

He was treating her like a child and she was instantly offended. When you heard that note in adult voices they no longer considered you equal. Kate would not tolerate being talked down to. She had learned through trial and error that if you were blunt—a nit away from rude—they listened to you. If there was anything that confounded the older it was unvarnished truth.

She had been told not to lie so she didn't, not ever. It was a powerful weapon. Her mother said there was such a thing as tact; tact was polite lying that adults got through life with. If an old aunt asked you if her nose was too big you were supposed to say, "of course not." Kate refused to do this and it set her apart. Once she had decided on this personality for herself there was no backing down, and any tampering by well-wishers only hardened it.

She now had the reputation in her family as stubborn, willful—and since she told the old aunt that her nose was not big, but humongous—cruel. They said she would grow out of it, when she became a wife and mother she would soften. She would be no man's wife and the thought of having children made her physically ill. Her mother kept after her about her weight, saying she wouldn't be popular if she was heavy. So she ate. Kate knew she was pretty and could use it to get her way, but refused. Any hint by others that she was being judged by looks infuriated her.

That's what she liked about Magnusson. He didn't look at her twice, barely spoke to her. He was ruder than she was. Kate had been annoyed that the general played foxy grandpa. She didn't want to hear fey jokes about soup—she wanted to know what it was like to be a Marine and a hero. She looked at Magnusson at the other end of the table, noisily eating his soup.

"I guess they don't teach Marines table manners," she said to the general.

"If they shoot well we don't care if they eat soup with a fork."

"How did he shoot Charlemagne?"

He looked up, "Blood and guts, eh?"

"With a rifle or a pistol?"

"Well—Catherine is it?"

"Kate."

"Kate. Magnusson and his Browning man darkened themselves up with burnt cork to look like *cacos* and went to his camp out by Mazaire on the *Grande Riviere*. That night they bluffed their way past three outposts and came to a fire on the crest of a hill. There were two women by this fire and one of them threw an armful of kindling on and it blazed up. When it did a man got up and looked at them closely across the flames. He had a pearl-handled revolver stuck in his belt and wore a silk shirt. Magnusson shot him through the center of it with his service automatic."

"He recognized him?"

"The revolver. It had been stolen from him. So much for flash."

She continued to watch Magnusson through the main course. "Why isn't he more friendly?"

"He's a man of silent habits. Then too, he's a foreigner. A Swede from up Oregon way. He was a raw boy out of a lumber camp when he joined the Corps."

"But he's an officer."

"He was a sergeant when he killed Charlemagne—a captain in the *Gendarmerie d'Haiti*—but a sergeant in the Corps. Colonel Wise recommended him for a Marine commission and the president gave him the Medal of Honor."

In the corner of her mirror at home she had pasted two pages out of the *National Geographic* that showed color pictures of the nation's awards. She saw that the general wore the blue ribbon with white stars. "You won it, too."

"Twice."

After desert she said, "How old is he?"

"Thirty or about."

"That old?"

The man next to Magnusson presented himself. "Lieutenant, my name is Norman Denver." He was large and pleasant-looking with a part in the center of brown hair that looked like it was incised with a razor. He reached his hand across the chipped beef and they shook awkwardly.

"Sir," Magnusson said with his mouth full.

"I'd like to say how much we all rely on you boys down here." Magnusson went on eating. "I tell you we've got one sweet mess up at Rama—I'm general manager of the mill—lumber.

Why I no sooner left for this trip on Friday when Sandino's bunch moved in and took over—shot the place up and terrorized the locals. From what I understand they're camped right on my front lawn. . . ."

"What stand do you favor up there?"

This took Denver back, "Stand? Well, cedar and pine . . . balsa . . . the mahogany has good color but not as dense as Honduras. Is that what you mean?"

"I always liked the way pine chipped out, you could take a piece the size of a pie wedge in two strokes."

Denver smiled. "I take it you were a lumberman?"

"A jack, yes."

"That's interesting—and you left it to become a Marine?"

"No. I cut a fella's hand off."

"Oh."

The consul's house stood on a slight rise out from town under the bluff. The galleries boxing it in on two levels were supported by thin iron pipes and gave it the look of fragility. It was airy, with many louvered windows and gaps in the mahogany floors that allowed the wind to rise from underneath, lifting the sisal rugs on blustery days like magic carpets. This cooling was defeated by a corrugated iron roof that grabbed the sun's heat at first glint and didn't let go until early the next morning. The jungle around the house had been beaten back and held at bay—although it had the look of being ready to spring forward and reclaim lost territory at any moment. Troops of fronds backed by the bayonets of spiked plants waited their chance to jump off.

At one side of the house were several low plaster buildings, edges crumbling, that leaned toward each other for support. They held servants, animals, and a car. The car, a 1927 Packard phaeton, now sat idling roughly on the drive by the open front door. It was empty and the house lights caught the shimmy of its hood and slight exhalation of steam from the radiator. The car was kept running because it had to be cranked to start and the

*Miskito* Indian handyman, Tomás, whose job this was, would only do it once. The crank lever had a sudden reverse snap when the gear was engaged that was more treacherous than the strike of a snake. It had broken other wrists—not his. He sat on the porch steps, hands cupping his chin, watching the car's vibrations, waiting for the moment when the radiator cap would blow off.

In the top, back bedroom, the consul Richard Kelly stood by his daughter's bed. "You were hard on the admiral."

"Did you know the people in Arjeplog, Sweden, eat reindeer meat?" She sat on the bed reading an old *National Geographic*. Her plump legs were cocked up and the tiny, beautiful feet dug into the mattress. He liked the smooth connection of the narrow circle of ankle to the fat, shapely calf.

"You won't get ahead in the diplomatic life that way."

"I'd rather get in the Marines."

"The last time I looked there were no ladies in the Marine Corps."

"Or the diplomatic corps either."

"True," He said, smiling. "With your way of turning a point you should go in for the law." When she didn't answer he asked, "What did you think of General Butler?"

"He doesn't look like a hero."

"No, I suppose not—did you think he would?"

"That Magnusson does."

"Really? Yes, heroes should be angular and modest."

"With bad manners."

Norma Kelly came past the door clipping on an earring. "Come on Dick, the car's going to blow."

"All right." Leaning over he kissed his daughter on her smooth, silky forehead. "Good night, Pudge." She continued reading.

Norma was waiting in the car, shaking in rhythm with its beat. "It's going to go."

He jumped in, put it in gear and accelerated down the drive. "If I can get up a little speed it'll cool down." They ran over a patch of rotten bananas and the rear wheels slued slightly. "Whoops! Just like an icy road."

"Don't I wish! I would give my right patootie to be snowed in now—or on our way to the Army-Navy game—slipping and sliding along the old Storm King Highway above a frozen Hudson. Remember?"

"I remember being numb."

"We were all numb then," she said, laughing.

"The bootleg hooch helped."

"Didn't it ever."

They were silent for a moment passing along dirt roads toward the dim lights of Bluefields. The town straggled along a single street on the lagoon where small boats were pulled up. The tide was out and the smell bad. "Kate was funny with the admiral. He never caught on she was pulling his leg."

"Well, he's dim."

"Norma."

"Beautiful but dumb."

He laughed. "True."

"How was she at lunch?"

"She sat next to General Butler and talked his ear off."

"What's he like?" They were on their way to a late dinner being given in Butler's honor. It would include the businessmen of today's luncheon in from the back country, a bishop visiting the Moravian Mission, and some assorted wives. It was being hosted by Doctor Bruder, who passed for social arbiter in the town of two thousand.

"Oh, he's small, very intense with eyes like a terrier, never blinks—actually she was more interested in a lieutenant— Magnusson—the one who shot Charlemagne."

"That's encouraging."

"That he shot Charlemagne?"

"That Kate was paying attention to a young man."

He looked at her. "He's thirty or so."

"I'm not talking about romance—but at least he's a man and not an animal—a donkey."

"You told me all you cared about at her age was horses."

"That's true enough. If one would have asked me I'd have married him straight away."

"She's just a kid."

"True, but that kid is developing—haven't you noticed?" She held her hands in front of her dress, making rounded motions.

He hated this kind of talk about his daughter and blushed. "Whatever her appearance outside she's still a little girl inside."

"If you could write a tune to that we could get Jolson to sing it." He shut up and she went on. "You know she's going to school in Baltimore this fall, and you can be sure when we see her next summer she'll be a whole different girl."

"I hope not."

"Let's face it, Dick, there's not too much future for thirteen-year-old-girls who want to be Marines."

When the noise of the car passed down the drive, Kate got out of bed and stacked the *National Geographic* atop two dozen others in the corner. The room was whitewashed and furnished simply with foreign service hand-me-downs: a large steamer trunk that had followed diplomatic posting, a green enameled bed with mosquito tenting, and a desk-dressing table. Its top held cigar boxes containing a butterfly collection and spent brass shell casings. Stuck in the mirror frame above it were the color pages showing military decorations and a blurry newspaper photo of Marine Captain Lewis (Chesty) Puller. Sternly facing the bed was another photo, a big sepia reproduction of General John J. Pershing in a fake wood-grained frame. It was the sort of thing suitable for public buildings and had, in fact, been in the consulate in Managua. But the general and his war had gone out of fashion and her father brought it home for her. Although she thought the Marines superior to the Army, she liked the way the visor of his hat cut low across his eyes.

Stepping through the shuttered doors and out onto the

second-story gallery, she leaned against the wavy pipe railing. The chemise she wore caught just the hint of a breeze, puffed out then slacked back, molding against her—and it was true, she no longer looked the little girl. Pursing her lips she made a kissing sound, then called softly, "Calvin . . . Cal!" There was the bray of an answer and she padded along the gallery to the stairs, going quickly down, her flesh gently shaking. Crossing the scrubby lawn on bare feet, she saw the oil lamp was off in Thomás's and Hilaria's one-room quarters. She pictured them and their five children asleep, swinging gently like peas in a pod, in hammocks strung to the ceiling.

At the back was a rough stable tacked together from scrap lumber and roofed with flattened-out Standard Oil cans. At its center in the open half of a makeshift door the head of a white donkey appeared. The moon just clearing the treetops illuminated it, and against the shadows the head appeared disembodied, luminous. Close, the wide brow shaded down to pink between nostrils; mouth protected by a nimbus of fine, long whiskers—and the eyes, large and liquid with a hint of deep blue in the depths of iris, looked out under fringed white lashes. Under each eye was a curious line of black hairs not unlike makeup—a donkey theatrical touch.

The tall ears picked up, flicking toward the sound, and although it had heard the kissing sound, like all white animals it had a tendency toward deafness and saw the girl before it heard her moving softly in the grass. Meeting, she bent down and kissed the soft muzzle, taction like velvet. They blinked together for a moment and she swung the bottom half of the door back on its leather hinges releasing him. Taking down an unraveling straw hat from a nail she pulled it on, pushing the orange-red hair up and under it. The donkey waited patiently until she bucked on a snaffle bridle, then allowed her to mount, her feet nearly touching the ground.

They moved off in a direction they both knew well: across the brave lawn to the frontier of jungle and up the narrow trail to the bluff. Ducking under the palmettos and fronds and onto the suggestion of trail they were instantly sucked in, lost in a tangle of shadows.

On the top of the bluff, Sandino sat next to Carlton Wills, legs drawn up, pad on his knees trying to read the lights from the ships. The night was clear, the sky a dense blue, and the silhouette of the fleet vivid. Each shutter opening of signal lamps reflected on the water of the lagoon was a bright stab, repeating the message. The *Cleveland* was talking to one of the destroyers, flashing out Morse code.

Sandino could get about half of it and even that was quite an accomplishment, Wills thought. To be able to read English from a light blinking Morse code was not easy. But Sandino had a facility with languages and he was determined to understand. If he missed a word he got angry.

Wills had written in *The Nation* that he was born angry. The bastard son of a modest Spanish landowner and his Indian serving girl, Sandino grew up privileged, near Granada. His father educated him and used the family influence to get him a job. But the anger exploded in a senseless argument at eighteen and he shot and killed a man in a gun battle. On the run through Central America and Mexico he worked as a clerk and later as a mechanic, where he became involved with a labor union and first heard the word *syndicalism*.

In Tampico he got caught up in the socialist-nationalist ideology of the Mexican Revolution and was instructed to properly hate the *Yanquis*. In those early years when he talked with fire about a leader emerging from the mixed-blood masses— his people—a man with a machete who would rid Central America of foreign exploitation, he was talking about himself; fusing his hostility against the Nicaraguan elite, Americans, and capitalism into one cause—his.

In 1926 he was back in Nicaragua working for an American-owned gold mine in the department of Nueva Segovia near the

Honduran border. Here it came together and when he had saved
enough money, he personally armed a band of twenty-nine men.
They began by attacking a government outpost and then marched
overland to the port of Puerto Cabezas to meet the Liberal leaders
he supported, Sacasa and Moncada. The two were puzzled, they
had never heard of him, he was not one of their established
caudillos. But he fought well against the government troops and
advanced to general. Two years later when his heroes caved in
and the Peace of Tipitapa was signed he rejected them all, fading
into the mountains with his Sandinistas. They would continue
the fight against the new Díaz regime, the Marine-led *guardia*,
the U.S. Fleet, and President Herbert Hoover. At this point he
was the *only* rebel anyone had heard of.

Wills had written what he thought was a fair description and
appraisal:

> [Sandino] . . . is short, under five feet, weighing
> about 115 pounds. His face shows a strong crossing of
> Indian and the Spanish aristocrat; it is straight-lined
> from temple to sharp-angled, firm jaw. Curved
> eyebrows are high above black eyes without visible
> pupils, eyes of remarkable mobility and refraction to
> light—quick intense eyes. Despite a serious demeanor
> he loves jokes and puns.
>
> He is extremely optimistic and possesses the ability
> to convince others of his most fantastic schemes. It also
> must be said that although he feigns modesty he can
> be vain and sophisticated, believing his wisdom
> infallible and will not tolerate subordinates of
> outstanding ability. His slogan is *The Welfare of Our
> Fatherland*, stressing his championing of the peasant
> class.
>
> When he speaks he comes alive . . . *I will not
> abandon my struggle while even one gringo remains in
> Nicaragua; I will persevere as long as my people are*

*denied even one right. My cause is the cause of the people, the cause of the other America, the cause of all oppressed peoples.* He lacks the polish of elocution, but is expressive, vehement; says what he feels—sometimes even what he doesn't feel. Here he is the Creole type one hundred percent—the talker with the dash of swagger, macho. A self-made icon.

"Queef? What is queef?"

"Quiff—women—they're talking about going on liberty—women."

"Women?! What the hell is this navy?!"

"Signalmen do that," Wills said, "when the official traffic is slack, and on late watch they talk back and forth to each other about personal things—like *telegrafías*," he said, smiling.

Sandino's wife, Blanca, was a telegraph operator. "I want them to talk about military things—that is what I want to know."

Wills was thankful they didn't. It was very tricky being a correspondent; walking the line, remaining neutral. After all he *was* an American, and more relevant his professional ethics would not allow him to help César read military messages. Not that he was neutral about his political directions, he had made that clear in his articles. Like Sandino he had picked up his socialist credentials in Mexico. As a young correspondent covering the American seizure of Veracruz in 1914 he'd been shocked by Woodrow Wilson's imprudent use of force—*the thinking man's president indeed!* When the Pershing Expedition crossed the border to punish Villa in 1916 he had already begun to speak out against intervention.

"These ships were here in nineteen-ten."

"Yes." They had been over this many times.

"Then just two years ago we had this town, had these *costenos* tied up. That same one, *El Cleveland* came down and ordered us out. Amazing isn't it, that a foreign ship would sail in your harbor and order you out of your town?"

"Well on the east coast they're partial to Americans, people get upset when you disrupt their jobs at United Fruit."

"That's what comes of speaking English here, they don't even know they're Nicaraguan, it's a whole different country when you cross the *cordillera*. But don't tell your readers that," he said, smiling.

Wills first met Sandino in 1928 at San Rafael de la Torre, sent on by Froylán Turcios, one of Sandino's admirers in Honduras. The general's bride, Blanca Arauz, had served them coffee and they talked far into the night. He had immediately been struck by his inspirational, hypnotic quality and then thought him a man utterly without vices, with an unequivocal sense of justice and a keen eye for the welfare of the humblest soldier. He blushed now at the purple prose. Their friendship was sealed when Wills asked Marine General Feland why they insisted on calling Sandino a "bandit" when he was obviously not one. The general replied that the word "bandit" was used in a technical sense, meaning, "member of a band." Wills wanted to know if that meant John Philip Sousa was also classified a bandit.

Since then he had seen the flaws, been shocked when after a job interview with Sandino, the body of Roy A. Johnson, a soldier of fortune, had been found hacked to pieces of a Marine patrol near Quilali. He knew now that the man could be savage as well as just.

Wills looked at his watch. "If we're going to get picked up on the river road we better get started."

"Not yet." And he continued watching the lights. The signalmen were now discussing local prices for "around the world."

Calvin carried Kate up the bluff trail in small assured steps. Tomás said donkeys had built-in scales, that they would only carry so much weight and no more. She wondered when she would be too much. Calvin had been a birthday present two years ago. A tiny white thing just born, so little she was able to lift him in her arms and swing him to the sun, bringing the jenny anxiously braying. When he was old enough, Tomás taught her to ride, steering with gentle taps of a twig at each side of the neck for direction. Her father called this the "Levantine manner." Then she took to riding Calvin to school at the Moravian Mission and some people were amused, the Chinese merchants hiding smiles at the sight of a fat girl on a donkey. The others—mestizos, Caribbean blacks, and Indians—were puzzled. Why would the daughter of a rich *Yanqui* ride on a burro when she could ride in a machine?

The *norteamericano* concept of pets was not understood. Animals were eaten or made to work. Dogs, if they were to escape the pot, stood on the roof and barked. Interbred, they all looked alike with the long legs and splotchy coats Mexicans call *Esquinkli*. They were unfriendly, wary of the town boys who carried rocks in their pockets. Kate had once seen three men walk along the road carrying a large dog by his ears and tail. They thought this very funny and could not understand why she was furious. It was their idea of fun with a pet.

As the trail grew steep she felt guilty and got off, walking behind Calvin, letting him lead. The narrow path here hugged the bluff on one side, dropping straight off on the other into the jungle. The climb was only a hundred feet or so but its reward was the best view in Bluefields. From the top you could see the shape of islands in Mosquito Gulf and to the north the Escondido River flowing into the lagoon. In Lord Nelson's day the Dutch pirate Blauvelt escaped British frigates up this river and they couldn't follow because of bad lee shore. The town was named after him, corrupting Blauvelt to Bluefields. Picnics were held on the bluff and fireworks on the Fourth of July. For a reason no one knew—perhaps soil or rock conditions discouraged jungle growth—the bluff grew just rough grass. It projected out into the lagoon like a fat slice of green coconut cake, its scruffy triangle visible for miles at sea.

Kate came here often with Calvin, but not at night. Her

parents never would have approved of that—but she wanted to
see the lights of the ships. As the donkey came around the last
bend they came in view. Looking across the prow of the bluff the
ships were perfectly lined up *and the lights were flashing!* The
next second Calvin snorted and figures rose out of the grass at the
edge of the bluff.

Wills was up first, with Sandino unwinding himself from his
concentration on the blinkers. "Somebody just came up the trail,
César—a woman." He spoke in a steady voice hiding the sudden
alarm he felt. Mesmerized by the lights, they had been caught
out.

"Speak to her, don't let her get away until we speak to her!"
Saying this he shifted to a crouching position and slid the
machete out of its holder. Wills saw the move and hurried
forward faster than he should.

"*Buenas noches, senorita!*" Against the dark backdrop of the
jungle the figure in white, hat pulled down, appeared to be a
native woman.

Kate had not at once been alarmed, assuming these two had
also come to see the lights. But they had reacted so quickly on
seeing her—then the moon showed the shine of a naked blade.
She grabbed Calvin's bridle and turned him back to the trail.

Wills began to run now, and thinking she might be a Carib,
spoke English. "Please! Don't run away—" but the woman was
on the donkey and began to ride off. He increased his stride,
running hard, heart pumping, panting and closed the distance.
As she turned down the trail he reached out and made a grab for
the donkey's tail. The moment he touched it the animal kicked
straight back, raising both legs off the ground. Wills had not
thought this possible but the burro had done it, lifting the weight
of the woman up as the hooves came back. He caught the edge of
the blow in the midsection, knocking him flat and taking his
breath.

Sandino was up and running. The only chance of catching
her now was to cut across the bluff and slide down the steep hill

to the trail below. Reaching the bank he jumped and descended, digging in with his heels, catching at the brush to keep upright. Chopping out with the machete he tried to whack a path ahead, then stumbled and fell. Stopped by brush, he struggled to his feet and went on. Now the cut of the trail was visible below and there was the woman riding the burro toward him. Both were pure white and seemed for a moment like an apparition appearing magically out of the night. Before he reached the trail she flicked the animal and it increased tempo, tiny hooves flailing out, brushing past just as he reached them. "*ALTO!*" he made a grab for the bridle but was off balance and they got by. He shouted "*ALTO!*" once more, then swung the blade.

It struck the right rear leg, chopping through the bone and taking it off cleanly. The burro dropped instantly, pitching the girl over his head. She hit hard at the edge of the trail, tumbling over, rolling down the bank. The animal began a hideous, shrieking bray, the intake of breath between each ghastly whinny like a pump pushing out the next. Sandino stepped away from the thrashing legs and in four strokes took its head off. Then he went after the girl.

At the top of the trail, Wills heard the horrific braying of the burro, the muffled chops—and silence. He got up painfully and, holding his stomach, went down the trail. He found the animal, head separated from its body, two white pieces that inexplicably reminded him of a donkey costume he'd once seen at the Artists and Models' Ball at the Knickerbocker Hotel in New York City.

The trail was empty. He stood and listened, steam rising from the burro, the buzz of night insects in the air—then he heard a sound. Looking over the bank he could make out the white, twisted figure of the woman lying in the tangle of brush below. Sandino stood over her, machete raised.

## TWO

# Bluefields

A S the consul and his wife proceeded up Bluefields's main drag, Norma Kelly wondered if there were another town anywhere quite as out of it. Fiji maybe, or Casper, Wyoming. On one side the place clung to the narrow edge of the Mosquito Coast, cut off from the interior by a solid weave of swarmy jungle. On the other it was cut off by the immensity of ocean. There were no roads to speak of, only rivers. Managua, the capital, was 250 kilometers away in nearly a direct horizontal line but it might as well be on the moon. Travel was vertical: up and down along the coast, or endless on the river. Bluefields, with its two thousand people, was the largest town. *God!*

When she'd married Dick, a career in the diplomatic service seemed romantic, a free ticket to the marvelous cities of the world. Because he had fluent Spanish he'd been shunted to Latin America. So far they had Panama, Antigua, Teguicigalpa, and now Bluefields. At the rate they were advancing they would retire upon reaching Tierra del Fuego. And the people here didn't speak Spanish after all, hating the real Nicaraguans on the west coast who reciprocated by calling them *los morenitos*: the little brownies.

If boredom went with the territory so did fear. The sheer hostility of a place where it was always wet—the rainfall was a world record—hot, and things with lots of legs scurried up the walls was unnerving. It was not a place people *should* live. Ye gods, fence posts sprouted green shoots and cleared areas were overgrown in days. Driving along this verdant mass, the lights of the town pitiful against the hovering jungle, she felt the apprehension that was always with her: the feeling that something was wrong. Then they were at Doctor Bruder's house.

If the lights at Doctor Hinrik Bruder's place were brighter than the others in town, so was his attitude. Unlike Norma he had found a home. In 1920 he took over the practice from his predecessor, Doctor Humberto M. Sanchez, when the latter followed the Army of the Revolution into the mountains and didn't return. Sanchez, one of the important political Mena family, had been commissioned surgeon-general to the rebels and died of God knows what during the campaign. Friends and Liberals in the town thought him a patriot and a hero. Doctor Bruder thought him stupid. As for himself he'd had enough of sacrifice for one's country on the Western Front in 1914. He had come to the Mosquito Coast he said, for the weather. When people found that hard to believe, he asked if they'd ever wintered in Rügen, his hometown on the Baltic Sea. He doubted if he would ever get warm enough.

He was a small energetic man with a shaved head and a Kaiser-Bill spiked mustache. A good GP, he had made a real effort to improve the awesome infant mortality rate when he first came out. Trying to get them to keep the flies down, he bought screening and went around to instruct the Indians in using it. But instead of installing it on doors and windows they made fishing nets out of it and toys for their children. He shrugged and after a while gave up. He now preferred to minister to his white patients. Unmarried, he lived with a handsome young mestizo he was training as an assistant.

What he liked to do was entertain, even though guests were the same few people who made up the foreign colony and knew each other as well as their own backsides. His house in the center of town was a handsome old English Colonial, reflecting a time when the British Lion protected the Mosquito Coast. At the second-story level, open colonades piercing thick walls allowed a view that looked out toward the lagoon, and tonight, the ships.

When Dick and Norma Kelly arrived (parking the Packard on a hill) they found the party arranged under the colonades and Smedley Butler the center of attention. Celebrities were rare in Bluefields; someone remembered Douglas Fairbanks, Sr., had once come ashore from a yacht and stayed nearly an hour but that was about it. Tonight the business and foreign service people in white dinner jackets, wives in nearly identical silk prints, were gathered around the general, thrilled to be in the company of someone they'd actually heard of.

Butler was at his best in a crowd of admirers; Lowell Thomas said he had "pepper, virility, swagger, and dash" and he did. Wearing a white mess jacket with the rosette of the Medal of Honor in his buttonhole, with his unblinking eyes shining, he kept them amused. Dick Kelly hurried over to stand next to him, for besides all his charming attributes, he was provocative— famous for putting his foot in his mouth. But it was going well. A large Southern lady vowed they had met the last time he was there in 1910—and he gallantly agreed, making her seem like an old friend although he had no idea who the woman was. When inevitably the talk turned to the continuing epidemic of revolution the consul sighed.

"The only thing that changes is sides—and if we're lucky— their underwear," General Butler said, "When we came down here in ten, Díaz was running the revolution and was in trouble. The government forces had the rebels bottled up in town and were ready to pounce—so we were ordered to go in and 'neutralize' the situation. It didn't take a ton of bricks to make me see Washington would like Díaz to come out on top."

"Now, General . . ."

"Dammit, Dick, I'm telling this! When we landed in Bluefields I sent for the government generals and said, 'You want to take the town? Fine. But we're neutral and no shooting, some of our people might get pinked.' They were puzzled, 'How can we take the town if we can't shoot?' 'That's your problem,' I told them. Well, they thought about it and agreed: They wouldn't shoot if the rebels would disarm. 'Oh no,' I said, 'I'm not worried about them—they'll be shooting *out*—but you people would be shooting *in* and one of us might get hurt.' Oh hell, they said and pulled out."

There was a laugh and Doctor Bruder, who liked to think he was an amused observer of American foreign policy said, "So neutralizing the area let your man win?"

"Let's just say that Díaz was head of the La Luz mine and our secretary of state at the time, old Philander C. Knox, had stock in it."

"General, that was hearsay, it was never proven."

"Neither was the virgin birth." Doctor Bruder laughed at this and Dick kept a tight smile.

"There's never been any question we support legitimate business down here . . ." the consul said, ". . . that's progress—and certainly our job is to protect nationals . . . however, our main purpose is reform—to see proper elections are held and . . ."

"Let me instruct you about elections, Consul. When I was in Haiti there were two candidates, Doctor Bobo, a redheaded Negro the American government didn't think would do, and our man, Senator Dartiguenave. When the National Assembly met to vote, Marines stood in the aisles with fixed bayonets until the man selected by the American minister was made president."

"If pressure is applied, then it's to protect the people from anarchy and scoundrels—we're trying to make the world safe for democracy."

"Can you whistle that?" The general said, having already heard the same tune from Mr. Wilson. "Maybe you people at State are, but I've spent my life making the world safe for American investors and corporations."

There was some amused hand clapping for this and the general moved away with his admirers. Glasses clinked and cigar smoke drifted seaward. Norma stood next to Dick, amazed. "I can't believe it—is he drunk?"

"Hardly, as police chief, he once tried to drive the bootleggers out of Philadelphia—and in fact later on had a full colonel under him—a friend—court-martialed for drunkenness."

"But how does he get away talking like that?"

"Well, his father was a congressman—Thomas Butler, chairman of the House Naval Affairs Committee until he died in twenty-eight."

"That explains it."

"It cut both ways. They made a lot of enemies at the State Department and in the Corps. Despite the fact that he was a proven hero—a real hard charger—he couldn't get a combat command during the big war. He spent his time at Brest fighting the mud. They called him 'General Duckboard.'"

"What's he doing down here if he's got the State Department's nose out of joint?"

"Officially he's not here. Admiral Sellers commands the Special Service Squadron and General Feland the Marine Brigade. They shunted him down here—on me—to keep him from riling the anti-interventionists at home until this thing quiets down."

"So he's getting a free trip, like an old actor on a farewell tour."

"These people here want to be reinforced, they approve of what he says—they like him."

"You like the old windbag, too—I can tell!"

"Well he is an original, and plain speaking is a nice change from my job."

"Wash your mouth out with soap."

"It's sad, Norma, here's a man who in the best traditions of the old Marine Corps was a legend—now they're embarrassed by him. This is his last hurrah, when he goes home it will probably be to retirement."

Norma had enough of the general. She checked out the room.

"Where's that lieutenant Magnusson? I wanted to get a look at him."

"I don't see him."

The bar at the *Hotel El Tropicale* was about the best Bluefields had to offer the tourist. Its decor was done in the mistaken idea that gringos were crazy about monkeys. Because live monkeys would be trouble, the manager hit on the idea of using dead ones. Several dozen were shot in the jungle and the best of the lot stuffed by a local taxidermist and mounted in lifelike positions overhead, tails nailed to the rafters. Lieutenant Magnusson was sitting under one at the moment, stretching out a rum swizzle when a languid woman sat on a tall stool next to him. She was Carib with a brightly painted face and amazing drawn-on eyebrows that curved halfway to her ears.

"Whooee! Mon it's hot!" she said, and began to flap a yellow cotton skirt up and down. Wearing no underclothes, the action of the air caused the considerable hair on her pudenda to rise and fall like a wheat field on a windy day.

Magnusson finished his drink. "I'd get that thing mowed, lady, if you want the breeze." He laid a coin on the bar and left. He didn't insist on subtlety in his whores but did like a hint of make-believe. Besides he sure didn't want a hair in his cocktail.

Outside the hotel, he lit up a cigar and strolled along the

waterfront. A campaign hat of the Montana peaks variety was tilted forward over his eyes and the summer service khaki gave the appearance of a sharp press despite the wet heat. He was tall and thin to the break of heavy shoulder, and from the rear had a tight, box-shaped ass much admired by the ladies. The strong odor of tobacco helped mask the smell of low tide but annoyed the dozing pelicans, and they flapped up, resettling on other pilings. Magnusson looked to the lagoon, reassured by the lights of the ships. He had forty-eight hour pass before reporting to the *guardia* and as usual was uncomfortable with leave. It was his Swedish nature to be uneasy unless on the job. This work ethic and the fact he wasn't a drunk or a gambler had got him ahead in the Corps and saved him a lot of money, half of which he sent to his Uncle Arnie and the kids. That he had become an officer in the Marines never failed to amaze him: it was good fortune he could hardly have expected as an immigrant with little educa-tion. Just twelve years ago he was content to be a logger in an Oregon lumber camp. He would still be there if he hadn't cut off his uncle's hand.

They were starting to cut on a big Douglas fir using razor-sharp double-bladed axes when his uncle inexplicably reached across the tree. The swing of his ax had already begun and he chopped Arnie's hand off at the wrist, also cutting his Longine watch neatly in half on a forty-five-degree angle. In the hospital his uncle was embarrassed and apologetic. He'd thought he'd seen a penny on edge in a crack in the tree and in a reflex action, reached for it. Magnusson didn't say it, but he wished it had been at least a half dollar. He went back to the tree but found no coin. Then, his uncle always had been an impulsive man.

Impulsive or not, he had brought him over from Sweden and sponsored his stay. Worse, he had a wife and kids Magnusson now felt responsible for. Fired out of the camp for "carelessness," he got a ride down to Portland to look for work and when nothing better turned up, joined the Marines at seventeen.

Although recruiting standards had gone up from the days of

wholesale enlistment of immigrants when Commandant G. F. Elliot instructed, ". . . don't send me any more Poles if Americans are available," the recruiter liked Magnusson's size and cool. When asked if it would bother him to kill a man, he replied sensibly, "It would bother me a lot more if he killed me." He was a born Marine.

In training with the old Advanced Base Force at League Island Yard a live grenade was dropped on a field exercise. When the others froze, Magnusson whacked it a good hundred yards down-range with the stock of his Springfield. The captain told Colonel Wise it was as fine a drive as he'd seen down any fairway, and if there had been a cup there the man would have had a hole in one before it went off. Colonel Wise dined out on the story and remembered the Swede. As for Magnusson he was fined for improper use of a firearm.

By 1919 Magnusson had campaigned in Haiti and was one of the sergeants selected for a captain's commission in the *Gendarmerie d'Haiti*, a police force to be administered by the Marine Corps to fight the *caco* bandits. The same gift for language that hurried his English along helped him learn the local French patois. It was highly corrupted and so dense with root words from Africa as to be nearly untranslatable. But he had an ear for it and eventually could shift his inflection to match the village he was in. It was this skill that got him past Charlemagne Peralte's *caco* sentries and allowed him to shoot the man through his silk shirt. That's why he was in Nicaragua now. His old mentor, Colonel Wise, the man who had recommended him for a commission in the Marine Corps and the Medal of Honor, had recommended him to kill Sandino.

As he passed a brightly lit shamble of a two-story building with a discreet sign that advertised: HOUSE OF JUNGLE JOY, he heard the charge played on the bugle. In the next instant it was choked off and the sound of angry shouting began on the second-story front. Next came thuds as a scuffle could be heard progressing along an upstairs hall, then a series of skipping clumps as a body hit each step on the way downstairs. Magnusson had reached the sagging front porch when the front door was batted back and a huge black woman threw a boy down the three steps—or so it seemed. When the "boy" sprung back up, still holding the bugle in one hand, Magnusson recognized him as a Marine from the *Cleveland*. He wore only the dress pants of his uniform held up by nonregulation red suspenders and shoes without socks, the laces tangled.

The woman had turned to go back inside but the bugler ran up the steps and kicked her in the rear with such terrific force, planting a footprint on her dirty shift, that she knocked the front door off its hinges. Howling in surprise, she backhanded him with fingers full of rings, sending him into several rickety chairs and over the railing to land once again at Magnusson's feet. The latter removed his cigar and said, "Do you know that's a woman your fighting, Music?"

"Dammit sir! She insulted my mother!"

"Oh," Magnusson said, and helped him up. "Here, let me take that." He relieved him of the bugle. When the boy charged this time she was ready, legs braced and fists cocked. However, one pendulous breast had come adrift and hung outside her shift. He leaped for it and getting under her guard clamped his teeth into it, locking his arms around her waist. She screamed in pain and began pounding him on the head and shoulders with her fist in the erratic beat of a tom-tom. But he hung on like a bulldog and they circled the porch like two berserk dancers, slamming into the building, rattling the glass in the windows and shaking the gas lights. Then one of her feet went through the porch floor, and she fell back taking out the railing and hitting the hard-packed dirt of the road with a resounding smack. At last it was quiet. The bugler remained on top, teeth still locked on her breast while she blew a noisy breath riffling his curly hair—out cold. He looked almost peaceful, as though about to nod off. Finally Magnusson said, "I think you took her out, Music."

The bugler roused himself and stood shakily up, wiping his

mouth. "Well sir, by Jesus, you have to draw the line with these people."

He was very young, looking thirteen or fourteen but Magnusson guessed sixteen, no doubt lying about his age to get in the Corps. He had black curly hair and even with his battering, the angelic face of a choirboy. One of those tough Irish kids who spent his life getting in fights because he looked pretty. In the Marine Corps the bugler was called "Music Boy" or just "Music" and also had the dangerous job of runner in combat. Magnusson handed him back his instrument. "Let's go down to the *guardia* and get you toileted up."

They walked on in silence, then the boy said, "She called my mother *madre de puro*, sir, whore-mother!"

"*Puro* means chaste."

He stopped. "But I thought it meant whore!"

"*Puta's* whore."

"Is that right?! Maybe I should go back and say sorry . . ."

"I wouldn't," Magnusson said, steering him ahead. Then after another few yards the boy caved in, collapsing on the road and curling up. When he didn't respond, Magnusson picked him up, hoisted him on one shoulder, and continued.

The barracks of the *Guardia Nacional* were in what had once been a Seventh Day Adventist foundling home until the Catholics and the Moravians won the battle for homeless waifs and froze them out. There was a soggy playing field behind the low rambling structure that now served as a grinder to teach the *guardia* recruits close-order drill. By the bare bulb above the entrance, Magnusson could see a Krag rifle leaning against the door jamb. The sentry was down at the far end of the building with his back to him, talking to a girl. Magnusson picked up the rifle and still carrying the music boy, walked through an empty orderly room, kicking the door open at the other end.

A captain sprang up from behind a desk, service automatic aimed and cocked when Magnusson threw the rifle at him and shouted, "Present arms!" He caught it correctly.

"Jesus, Mag!"

"It was stacked by the door."

"God damn it! Somoza!" A heavy mestizo in sergeant's stripes came in and the captain tossed the rifle at him. "One of your people is out there fuckin' the duck! Kick his hemorrhoids into his tonsils, put him on report, and you stand his watch!" The sergeant went out taking his time. "Christ!" the captain said, sitting down.

Magnusson lay the bugler in the corner and sat facing the desk. "That one of your hand-picked noncoms, Charley?"

"The only thing he ever picked was his ass. His uncle's a big politico."

"I'm glad to see your reflexes are still top-notch," he said, nodding at the gun in Charley's hand.

He placed it on the desk top. "Reflexes hell! That's fear!"

"You were never afraid of a thing in your life." Like himself, Charley Edd had been a sergeant of Marines, a gun pointer on the old *Washington*. They went back a way together.

"Well I am now." He smiled for the first time. "I hope you're here to relieve me." He was a big man with a fringe of red hair and generous features; large ears and nose mitigated by a thin line of a mouth and eyes of the right "plainsman squint."

"Not exactly, I've got a job to do for Wise. It came down from Eighth-and-Eye.

"Christ, you're going after Sandino!"

"You don't think that's a good idea?"

"This is not Haiti—there have been ten mutinies in the *guardia* since I've had the duty, Mag—seven good Marines have got the chop from their own troops."

"Not in this department."

"Not yet. But that scissor-bill outside is a good example. It takes all you can do just to keep them from selling their weapons and equipment—let alone rob the locals or fall in with the politicos. I've had it with being a policeman in jungleland. We ought to all get out of here. When I get back to Diego I'm retiring out."

"Come on."

"Listen, my wife's brother Oliver has a Buster Brown shoe store. I'm going in with him."

"Well you should know about feet."

"They've got an X-ray machine in the stores you stick your foot in and you can see the bones and whether or not the shoe fits. I tell you its amazing! He's letting me in on the ground floor and eventually we'll expand—have a chain . . ." There was a groan from the music boy on the floor. He rolled over pressing his nose up against the wall, snuffling. "Is he unconscious or asleep?"

"I'm not sure."

The consul didn't see Tomás standing in the street below until General Butler tapped him on the shoulder, pointing it out. "Is he one of yours?"

His heart immediately constricted. How long had he been standing there? Looking up, waiting to be noticed. "What is it Tomás?" The Indian spoke a missionary English-Spanish but his answer couldn't be heard over the noise of the party. Glasses clinked and the shrill laughter of the ladies ballooned out, pushing at the air between colonades.

"*Quiet!*" The general shouted and it stopped instantly. The guests looked around, frozen, offended by his no-nonsense drill-field voice. Norma, talking to Doctor Bruder, broke off and ran to the railing to stand with the consul and the general. *It was about to happen.*

"Say it again, Tomás!"

"The burro ees chopped. Dead."

"What? I don't understand—you mean in the stable?!"

"No, een the trail up . . ." and he used his hands making a slice then patting them flat. "Before ees flat."

"The bluff? It's on the bluff . . . but . . ."

"*Kate!*" Norma said in a chilling voice.

"Tomás! *La niña?!*"

"*Se fue.*"

"Gone?" The consul couldn't comprehend this, how could she be *gone?* "Gone?! Where?!" The Indian shrugged his shoulders, and he was uncertain what to ask next, afraid of the answer. Next to him Norma seemed in shock, mouth open, face ghastly white.

"Is your car here?" the general said, in an urgent but controlled voice.

"Yes . . ."

"Let's go." Taking Norma's arm he steered her, silent, through the stunned guests. Dick followed carrying an empty cocktail glass.

"What's happened?" Doctor Bruder said, catching up to their stride. "May I help?"

"Get your instruments and meet us at the car." And the general was out the double doors, towing Norma down wide stone steps, her high heels clicking, the consul running behind them.

In the street they crossed to the Packard, parked on a slight incline to facilitate starting. Dick got behind the wheel and Norma slid in beside him while the general used his command voice to try and get the Indian in the back. He'd never ridden in the big car, and balked.

"*Ahora!*" Norma issued the single shrill word and he climbed in. A minute later Doctor Bruder came running out of the house wearing a Panama at a rakish angle and carrying the over-the-shoulder bag he took on emergencies, although he had no idea what this emergency was.

"If this is a broken leg let's hope it's not compound," he said in his cheerful, Teutonic way.

All aboard, Dick let off the brake, coasted with the clutch in, then popped it. The car started with a roar, faulty muffler booming between buildings on the narrow street. "Stop at the *guardia!*" The general shouted over the noise. Dick looked at him quickly, *guardia*?! He could still not get a grip on what had happened, believed it had to be a mistake, that Kate would be there when they got home. . . .

"Stop!" He slid the car to a halt at the turn in to the *guardia* compound. A sentry was under the bright light of the *comandancia* uneasy at the sudden appearance of the big Packard. The general leaned over the backseat, and laid on the horn causing everyone to jump. Then standing, he shouted, "Get the Commandant out here on the double!" Puzzled, Sergeant Somoza brought his rifle to the ready as Captain Edd and Lieutenant Magnusson cleared the door. Squinting down the road to where the car stood idling in a haze of exhaust smoke, both recognized Butler's alert figure standing up in the backseat.

"Yes sir!"

"Is that you Magnusson?"

"Yes sir!"

"You and Edd gear-up and fall in!"

"Aye aye!" They both turned and ran back inside.

The consul was appalled at what was being put in motion, refused to accept that it was this serious. "Wait a minute, General—isn't this overreacting? Why not wait until . . ."

"No," the man said flatly.

Edd opened the arms locker and took out a Thompson submachine gun, stuffing four one hundred-round drums in a canvas carrier. "Expecting an attack by hordes, Charley?" Magnusson said, taking down his personal Springfield sent on from Panama.

"No, I expect to have to defend myself from old Gimlet Eye—he may call for volunteers."

"True." Magnusson hooked up a web belt with a side arm and grabbing two bandoliers of cartridges followed Edd into the C.O.'s room. The stomping of feet had roused the music boy and he pushed himself up on wobbly arms. "Whu . . . ?"

As Edd and Magnusson came by, each grabbed an arm and jerked him to his feet, continuing out the door. "File to the front,

Music!" Double-timing it to the car, his feet barely touching the ground, they jumped him up on the running board and with Magnusson holding him, the car lurched off in gear sending mud flying and the roof dogs barking.

They tore off down the street: armed men on the running boards, a general, a doctor and an Indian in the backseat. In the front seat, the consul looked at Norma next to him. She stared straight ahead through the windshield, eyes dry, face fixed in the same awful suspension of fright, the look he'd seen on her face when she'd asked the Indian about Kate.

"Norma . . ." he said above the noise, ". . . Kate could have gone for a walk—hidden from Tomás—at her age girls do foolish things, things that are unthoughtful and scare you—I'm sure she's all right."

"No . . . no she's not." It was said with such conviction that for the first time the consul believed the worst, too.

At the house the car turned up the drive, skidded on the patch of greasy bananas and bumping past the outbuildings jolted to a stop behind the stable. At the entrance to the bluff trail, Hilaria came up in the lights, standing with her two oldest half hidden behind her skirts. She held a torch, its smudgy smoke drifting straight up into the windless night, the flickering glow drawing bugs in a fluttering halo. The consul jumped out of the car hurrying the Indian along. "Show me where the donkey is! *Rapido!*" he said, pushing aside the fronds and moving toward the trail.

"Wait a minute, Dick," the general said, stopping them with his voice. "Let's be smart. Magnusson will go ahead with the Indian as guide. Edd, you bring up the rear and the rest of us will make up the file." He looked closely at the music boy for the first time. Caught in his scrutiny, he came to shaky attention, still bare-chested, pants supported by red suspenders, and shoes with no socks. "Is this man in condition to do us any good? Where's the rest of his uniform?"

"At the House of Jungle Joy I expect, sir." Magnusson

answered. "He was on liberty and defending his mother when called to duty."

"It was a misunderstanding, sir," Music mumbled.

"*Let's go!*" the consul shouted, out of patience, and they all turned toward the trail. The doctor shifted his bag for the climb, resigned but not happy with the prospect. The general laid a hand on Norma's arm.

"Mrs. Kelly, why don't you stay here? Those shoes are not fit for the field. . . ."

She pushed past him, following her husband. The general sighed and lighting off a torch fell in with the doctor. The music boy followed, still not quite sure where he was, puzzled how he could have arrived from atop a wet whore at the Jungle Joy to the deep woods. Edd, the realist, fell back to have a clear field of fire so that if he had to shoot he wouldn't hit children, women, civilians, and old generals.

After twenty minutes of a hard climb, they found the white burro on the trail and stopped breathless and shocked. Its luminous body, parted as it was from the head, seemed obscene in the torch light and for the first time Norma broke down. Leaning into Dick's arms she let out great gasping sobs that stood the hair up on the music boy's neck. The onslaught of insects flying and crawling taking charge of the donkey's carcass actually moved it, caused it to undulate. Before long the large animals on clawed feet would arrive to drag the remains into the jungle. Already a dozen different eyes glowed in the damp night; the music boy, head rotating, could see their reflection. He was a city dweller from a family of masons in Boston, and his first year in the Corps had been spent at sea; ships company aboard the *Cleveland* where you slept in a nice hammock and it was nothing special to have gedunk—ice cream—once a week.

The Indian, Tomás, sat hunched near the animal holding a ragged hat he flicked out at the bugs while the doctor leaned over the carcass. "Machete," he said, adding, "very clean." Nobody needed to be told this.

In the next minute there was a regular footbeat and Magnusson jogged down from the trail above, campaign hat cocked over his eyes, swinging the rifle easily. "I circled the bluff, sir," he said reporting to the general, "no sign of Miss Kelly. People have been up there—the grass is matted—but I understand it's a popular lookout."

The general examined both sides of the trail. "We'll break up in two parties and begin a search. Edd . . ."

"Ees her hat," Tomás said, giving the hat a timid swing.

The consul broke gently away from his wife and stepped over to the Indian. He took the hat. "That's right! Where did you find it, Tomás?!"

"Don there." He pointed at the sharply inclined bank breaking on the right of the trail. The consul immediately started to climb down when he was stopped by Tomás's voice. "No, *jefe*, two men take her."

The consul was stopped cold, foot poised, ready to step off the bank. He cranked his neck around. "*What?* What did you say?" But Tomás did not repeat it and the consul said it for him, loudly, "*Two men took her?! What two men?! Where?!*" He was in front of Tomás now, hovering, knowing if he lost his temper the man would never talk. He took a deep breath, quieting down. "You saw them, Tomás? *Tomás?!*"

"Hilaria."

"*Hilaria!* My God!" He ground his forehead with his hand, "Why didn't she tell us down there!" But he knew the answer, they hadn't asked her. "Where did she see them?"

"*Atras* . . . behind the buildings—to the road."

"Were they locals? *Aldeanos?* Someone you knew?" At the beginning of the questioning, the others had stopped and listened to every word, felt the consul's frustration of trying to pull a sentence out of the Indian.

"Sandos."

"Sandos?" the general asked, looking around at Edd. "Sandinista, sir," he answered. "It's what they call them locally."

"Would they know?"

"Oh yes."

Back at the car the general stood talking to Captain Edd and Lieutenant Magnusson in the glare of the headlights. Norma watched them with the consul waiting to be told what to do. *Then this is what it is,* she thought; *what it comes down to: my husband juggling issues for the State Department, dealing in abstract political ideas, talking of saving democracy—and finally the point is: can it save my child? Who cares what side the rotten bastards were on, Sandinistas? What does that mean to me? Who would hack a donkey to death and take a thirteen-year-old girl? Is this war? Politics? Ideals?*

Just hours ago she had thought of the general as a fool, an old actor who bragged about what he had done because he couldn't do it any more. Now . . . looking into his face she saw confidence, unhesitating authority, the ability to *act*. No matter that he had swagger and contempt for civilians, at this moment he *was* acting, and she believed that he, these men, would risk their lives if need be to get her daughter back. It was *not* politics or ideals to them, it was what they did, they were Marines, and she had to hope they would do it better than the other side.

Doctor Bruder sat on the running board examining his feet while the music boy leaned against the side tire mount, sleeping on his feet. Captain Edd, uneasy now that he had been pulled away from his post as *guardia jefe* was anxious to get back. "With your permission sir," Edd said to the general, "I'll fall back to the barracks and turn out the men." He looked at his watch, "by zero-five-hundred we can have a party ready to move out."

"You do that, Captain, but I'm afraid you'll have to walk back. I intend to press on immediately in the car."

"You're going after them *now?*"

"That's right. It's been a little more than three hours since this incident took place—they're on foot, we still have a good chance of overtaking them if we move now." Edd and Magnusson looked at each other.

"If they're Sandinistas, sir, they will surely have horses or a vehicle up the road."

"Well then, by god, let's go! Let's catch them at once! The daughter of the American consul has been taken and I don't intend on waiting to get her back!"

"Go with them," Norma said, volunteering her husband.

He looked at her, "Yes . . . I'm going with you, let me drive!"

"Of course. Do you have any arms?"

"Wh . . . why a shotgun."

"Get it. . . . Mrs. Kelly would you instruct your people," he said, nodding at Tomás and Hilaria who stood apart watching, "to get us all the water bags you have—and gasoline."

"Food?" she asked, galvanized by the assured tone.

"No, we won't be gone that long. If we can't get the dogs in the next twelve hours or so we won't get them at all." When she looked stricken he said, "But we will get them—and remember, this an important person they've taken—they are not apt to harm her in any case." This was nonsense but because it was said in such a positive manner, Norma believed it, and for the first time began to recover from the shock. She hurried off toward the house herding Tomás and Hilaria along.

The general turned to the doctor, who continued to massage his foot sitting on the running board. "You'll, of course, want to come. Despite what I told Mrs. Kelly there's a chance the girl will be hurt."

"Yes," the doctor said, "I would guess so." He had listened to this as he had to his old commanders in the Great War plan attacks with outrageous confidence. Using bodies as numbers they sent men out of the trenches stumbling across no-man's-land into the machine guns, while he waited at the medical station with his saws and instruments to untangle what pieces of the bodies were left. For him the order to go into combat was a move toward population control.

Edd and Magnusson stood to one side quietly talking, backs

to the general. "Does he have any authority for this, Mag? I thought he was on a goodwill tour or something."

"He is a general, Charley, and he's right, we've got a shot at catching them. Once this goes through the command wringer they'll be gone."

"If they've faded into the jungle you're not going to catch them in this big heap."

"I don't think they have. Where could those two make the closest hookup with the rest of the troops?" Magnusson took out a much folded map and rearranged it to show Bluefields, on twelve degrees latitude. "Where's that bunch that has everybody in a swivet?"

"West of here, a column came in and shot up a sawmill and a couple of mines—then helped the local Sandinistas roll up Rama."

"Rama . . ." Magnusson moved his finger along the map starting with Bluefields. "That's up on the Escondido River about . . . thirty-five miles. They'll have to go down the road here to where it connects with the lagoon to take it—that's what they're going to do—I'll bet on it." He refolded the map and put it away.

"Admiral Sellers is not going to like this."

"Look, I'm detached and at the whim of a crazed general," he smiled. "If we can catch them before they get on the river we'll be back tomorrow night."

Edd had been in the company of heroes many times and in the company of cowards as well. And the thing was, the roles could be interchangable. What made men like Magnusson unique was that in the face of death they didn't blink; they never believed for a minute they wouldn't come through; they were smug about immortality, as sure they had it as a congregation of Holy Rollers. Curiously, the ones he knew who were live heroes: Smedley Bulter, "Chesty" Puller, and Magnusson—had come through harrowing episodes time after time. It seemed if you hesitated you died.

"Oh," Magnusson said, "you'll have to cover for the music boy—tell Sellers the general insisted on his personal runner."

"I hope he can play something besides that horn." He handed over the submachine gun and satchel of drums. "Good luck, Mag." And he started off at a trot toward the road, glad to be out of it—not for him the posses, the unstructured command. He didn't like any of it. What he would like was a Buster Brown shoe store in downtown San Diego with its own foot X-ray machine.

Minutes later they were all in place in the car, water and gasoline lashed to the running boards, weapons at hand. The Packard had been reluctantly cranked alive one more time; the big V16 engine churning away, tappets dancing noisily; faulty exhaust sending back a pulse of shaky timing and dirty carburization. The consul was to drive with Magnusson in front and the music boy between them. Eyes half closed, head bobbing, he shook with the idling of the car. In the back, the general sat in the center next to the doctor who lit off a giant Joya de Nicaragua cigar, and the Indian, Tomás, squeezed in the corner, eyes darting wildly. The general gave the command, and they moved out and down the drive, once again sliding on the rotten bananas.

Norma stood by the house in her torn silk dress and run-down heels watching them go—then just before they turned and were out of sight, General Butler raised a walking stick he had picked up and pumped it twice in the air in sharp salute.

Hilaria appeared behind her and said under her breath, "*Vaya con Dios.*"

"And the U.S. Marines," Norma added.

# THREE

# Banana Town

IT was a whirring sound, a cadence of clicking, then shaking—movement that brought nausea. Coming back to consciousness Kate felt numb, then gradually a tingling of fingers and finally an urgent telegraph of distress: aches, bruises, abrasions; signals from a dozen points. And a headache—a headache that increased its tempo with awareness.

It was dark and she lay on her back feeling a hammering at her spine, the rush of movement. Above her head a canopy held taut by bows flapped and danced. And there was a smell—the sickening smell of rotten fruit. As yet she remembered very little of what had happened, her father by the bed . . . a dream quality of moving along a moonlit path . . . riding . . . *"Calvin!"* She said this aloud and pushed up on skinned elbows. A man knelt next to her shifting his balance with the jarring floor. Kate realized then she was in the back of some kind of truck and now made out sounds of tires on a dirt road. At the back of the truck, outside the flap of canvas the sky was lighter and she saw its reflection in glasses close to her face.

"Are you feeling better?" A hand moved a canteen into her line of sight. "Water?"

"Calvin . . ."

"A friend? Your brother?"

"Donkey!"

"Oh."

"We were riding!"

He moved the pince-nez up the bridge of his nose and an odd fluttering tick occurred with his eyelids. In the half-light the outline of very straight features had a regularity that announced Anglo Saxon as certainly as the texture of hair and blush of skin. He was young and self-important.

"There was an accident. . . ." Carlton Wills thought of himself as a tough no-nonsense journalist. His articles were meant to wake up complaisant Americans. He had aimed devastating attacks at business men and politicians—State Department lackies and the military. He was a man who would not give a journalistic inch to anybody. But here and now he could not tell this young, fat girl her animal had been hacked to pieces. When they discovered she was not a native woman, but redheaded, young and white, Sandino wanted to leave her, moving up the angle of hill to the trail. Wills could not permit this and with great effort carried her up on his back. He was seriously concerned about her condition but Sandino was not moved. Wills knew his attitude was formed by Latin disapproval; what was a young girl doing out at night alone—unescorted? This suggested that her family: a father or brothers, were not protective and made her unworthy of his further concern.

"The burro . . . fell and broke his leg . . ." Wills heard himself say. "I'm very sorry. . . ." The girl lay back and covered her eyes crying softly. "The only humane thing to do was . . ." But he couldn't say it. Reluctantly Sandino had helped carry her down the trail. When they came by the galleried house at the bottom, Wills wanted to leave her on the porch. But Sandino refused. If she were to rouse and give the alarm while they were on the crucial lagoon stretch of road to the river they would be trapped. It was harsh, military reality but at least consistent. They compromised, agreeing to take her along to the river and leave her at the United Fruit Company.

Struggling down the road was not easy; she was heavy and the two men, very conscious of propriety, had to deal with underarm grips, leg holds, and a shaking of nubile flesh that was disturbing. Then they began to giggle and at the meeting place opposite a cut in the roadside bank they collapsed laughing like schoolboys. "Jesus!" Sandino said, "it is like carrying a sackful of Hello!"

"Jell-O," Wills corrected, and they both burst into laughter again. It was this lapsing back into juvenile behavior that had drawn them together in the first place. Sandino especially enjoyed bad jokes and puns, and Wills's only real weapon against him was not to laugh.

But he was still concerned about her condition. Wills checked her breathing and rolled back her eyes. But this was even more unsettling and he had to hope she would come around. She was not quiet and the—moans and long sighs—were eerie in the ditch beside the lonely road.

They were to be picked up at two o'clock but nearly an hour later Wills was still checking his wristwatch. With Latins he was never sure if they deliberately didn't show up on time or really couldn't be bothered with appointments. At three there was a distant whir he recognized, and minutes later an old chain-driven Reo truck slowed. It had no doors and the hard rubber tires were chewed off at the edges. The driver stood, a foot on the running board, steering with one hand, peering at the roadside.

"Look at this," Sandino said, "our standing army." He climbed the bank raising his hand and the man stopped, leaving the truck running. There was a muffled conversation and he finally got down and walked with Sandino to the ditch where

Wills waited with the girl. When he saw she was white he turned back shaking his head. "He is afraid to take her because she is white—what do you think of that, Wills?" He raised his voice, "All right, we'll leave her. But first get out of that cab and let me run over her until no one will know who she is. Wills! Lay her out on the road!"

After that, the driver, who had no sense of humor, let them load her in the truck while he sat sullenly in the cab.

This man, with other Sandinista supporters at United Fruit's big consortium was a mestizo from the North, and had helped smuggle them aboard the company's steamer at Rama for the trip down to Bluefields. The return plan was to be a reversal. The steamer was due to leave that morning.

Sandino and the driver got in front and Wills sat on the floor of the truck bed with his back to the cab watching the girl. Once again he had to reinforce his position to himself: As a correspondent his job—like the paper he wrote on—was to be blank, impartial, a recorder on which the events occurring were carefully transcribed. He had no part in their happening—well—he had run after the girl, scared her; he was involved in what happened. And certainly as a human being he would not allow her to be endangered because of him. But, once she was delivered into the proper hands, his responsibility ended.

Sandino pushed back the burlap curtain that separated the cab from the truck bed. He smiled. "This comrade recognized the girl. She's not a young nobody after all—he says she is the American consul's daughter."

The loaded Packard, with its full complement of rescue party, bore on down the lagoon road as fast as conditions would allow. On one side the tepid water lapped at the road bank and on the other merged into a swamp that spread out for miles seeping into the jungle. There were no crossroads or even canoe paths through this tangle and the only firm ground was ahead at United Fruit Company.

The big car was a double-cowled phaeton; the rear passengers were provided with a second windshield. This sent the wind buffeting over heads and provided some protection. The canvas top had long since disappeared along with the shine of the paint: a deep red body set off with tan fenders. Gas cans were lashed to running boards next to huge spare tire mounts and on the driver's side to the upright stanchion of a powerful searchlight. In the back, yet another spare tire was chained on the removable leather trunk. Water bags had been looped over the drum headlights to tend the faulty radiator. On the top of its chrome-plated shell, in front of a Motor-Meter that registered engine heat—a winged lady leaped forward to point the way.

There had been little talking since leaving the consul's house. The recent partygoers recovering from the rapid events that had propelled them from the cocktail hour to the rescue sat lulled by the car's motion. The Indian, Tomás, squeezed to his side and gripped the cowl, head bent into the wind, hair streaming back. In the front seat the consul drove with a heavy foot while next to him the music boy slept, head jerking in kinetic movement. Magnusson, rifle angled at his side, submachine gun on the front floorboards, watched the road against ambush.

But there was none and the road curved in with the lagoon to make contact with the estuary of the Escondido River. The long dock of the company was visible first, then the smokestacks of the mills against the night sky. Below them, arranged in neat rows, were the red roofs of company buildings and workers' houses. To the left, strung out along the bank of the river was the sprawl of the native town, masts of fishing boats crossing in slender silhouette. Behind this, rising from the cut of the river were the low hills of the Mosquito Coast, faintly purple in the light.

"Where to first, General?" the consul asked, slowing.

"Straight to the manager's office, Dick, let's get a briefing." The consul had been here many times and continued without pause up the one street through an open metal gate and past identical houses to a large central building. It stood under the spread of thick mango trees and he stopped in front of the wide porch. Once again the general leaned over the seat and sounded the horn. This sent a jolt through strung-out nerve centers and the music boy jerked awake so violently that his curly hair hit the back of the seat. "Whattza!?"

The strident tone was repeated at one-second intervals and sent the town dogs howling from rooftops. A minute later lights came on, the front screen banged open, and a man came out on the porch pulling on a shirt.

"What in hell?!" When he saw the car full of men, guns, and an erect figure in a white dinner jacket standing in the back, he could not fail to be impressed. He recognized the consul. "Is that you Mr. Kelly?"

"Yes Mr. Elcon . . . sorry to wake you . . ."

"Are you in charge?" the general asked.

"I'm the assistant manager—Mr. Morris—the manager is down in town at some party for a general."

"We've just come from there Mr. Elcon," the consul said.

"Is that right?"

"Two men we believe to be Sandinistas have taken the consul's daughter," the general continued.

"Is that right?! I'm surely sorry to hear that, how . . ."

"Never mind how, *now* is the question. It's likely they've come this way to go up river to Rama. We mean to stop them."

Mr. Elcon had walked down the steps to the car and took note of the armed Marine officer and the other odd individuals. "Well, the only way to get up river is on the *Banana Queen* and she's not going." He was a slender, stooped man with a slide of belly toward the pear shape.

"Your talking about the company steamer?" the general asked.

"Yes sir, Mr. J. M. Cochrane, the captain, said he won't take her back up there till the shooting is over. They holed his stack."

"There's no other vessel?"

"Plenty of fishing boats, but they won't tack up against the tide until it drops off tomorrow morning."

"All right, we must assume they still are here!" He tapped the front seat with the walking stick. "Magnusson, seal off this road behind us—Elcon, get your people up, see what you can find out, then order a house-to-house check. We will proceed to the river and stop all traffic." The assistant manager thought there was a lot of assuming going on but he had spent his working life being bossed by people just like this huffy bird.

Magnusson clicked the door open and hefted up the submachine gun from the floor. "Fall out, Music." They walked to the back of the car with the music boy trying to get his feet to cooperate, still feeling the full effects of a killer hangover. They stopped and Magnusson elevated the gun. "Have you been checked out with this weapon?"

"Ah, no sir." He shifted the bugle from hand to hand.

"And stow that horn! You're not going to be tooting anything up here—although it's my guess your breath is more deadly than this weapon."

"Yes, sir!"

Magnusson continued in the aggressive rote of the drill instructor. "Listen up! This is the bolt, it is pulled back to engage the cartridge, as so—next, safety off . . ." He thumbed it. "You pull the trigger as so," indicating this with a pantomime squeeze of the forefinger, "and the weapon fires." He reversed it and put it into the music boy's hand. The boy fumbled and nearly dropped it. He saw that NAVY was stamped on the side.

"Is that all, sir?" he asked dismayed.

"If you have to fire, fire slowly, the locking mechanism is questionable." He pointed down the dark road. "Position yourself there . . . where the road squeezes in by the gate and stop all civilians coming out—until ordered otherwise."

"What if I have to shoot?"

"Unlikely, but don't overreact—and watch it, these weapons tend to climb and you may trim the mangos."

As Magnusson returned to the car, the general was saying to Mr. Elcon, ". . . as we didn't catch up to these people on the road then we must assume they have a vehicle."

More assumes. "The only one who has a private automobile here is Mr. Morris—a Ford—and he took it into town to that general's party."

"You have trucks?"

"Oh yes, Reos and some Mack Bulldogs down there at the garage," he said, pointing at a distant roof, "but I would know if anybody took one."

"Magnusson, come aboard. We'll check. Elcon," he said, fixing him with a gimlet eye, "Get on with it! Get your people roused up!"

"Yes sir." He leaned in. "Sorry about your girl, Mr. Kelly."

"Thank you," the consul said. Eyes averted, he put the car in gear.

"Get going Elcon!" the general repeated.

"Yes sir." But he stood watching as the car drove off down the street, remembering the girl's red hair and that white skin.

"Dick, stop at the truck garage."

The doctor was jerked awake by the sudden start of the car. "Odd," he yawned, "I dreamed I was back in Rügen, skating on the frozen Baltic—it was so cold I shivered in my sleep . . ."

"I envy you," the general said, mopping his face.

"That must be it." They stopped in front of a large corrugated metal shed at the very edge of the company road. Beyond was another metal gate and the first straggle of native shacks.

Magnusson got out, and holding the rifle at the ready, went around a stack of bald tires chained to a tree. The garage doors were open and the interior dark. Cautious as always, he waited until the consul backed the Packard around so that its headlights suddenly illuminated the space, sending shadows stretching to the angled roof. Inside he made out the shapes of a dozen trucks lined up neatly to the right side. From the raised hoods several were under repair. The floor was covered with engine parts and mechanics' tools. It seemed unlikely to him anyone would fail to lock the doors. He walked along the rows of trucks feeling the hoods of those not under repair. The last, under a swag of chain hoist, also had its hood up, but as he turned he felt the heat of its exposed engine on his back. Beyond was a small door opened to a rectangle of lighter sky.

Kate leaned against the rough wall boards, legs pulled up, head resting on crossed arms. She felt sick and could not comprehend why she was here. The one with the glasses said they were going to find a doctor but how could he be in this place? The room was totally bare; a shack. Through the cracks in the floor she could smell the slime of low tide and hear the complaining of boats as they adjusted to it. Two men sat by the half-open door talking in low murmurs. Then in a flash she remembered being on the bluff and a man running toward her . . .

"Don't do this, César, it's wrong, a mistake."

"Who says that? You or your Uncle Sam?"

Wills tried to hold his temper, remain impartial, serious. He lined out his objections as though at a debate. "I have spent a great deal of time instructing the people of the United States in your cause. You have sympathy, you have become a symbol of intelligent opposition to intervention—the hero of a just cause—if you persist in taking this girl hostage all that will change. Americans will no longer care whether your politics are right or wrong, they will only know you have kidnapped a young white girl."

"Ah," Sandino said, obviously enjoying the moment, but what if that young white girl embraced the cause?"

"What are you talking about?" Wills said, exasperated. He had experienced these daydreams with Sandino before. Sandino had the maddening habit of introducing a piece of fantasy into a rational discussion, throwing everyone off while he imagined a fanciful situation aloud, hinting it was some kind of inspired notion.

"If this daughter of the American consul was to speak out for the revolution—the people, what a thing that would be. Right? Then they would listen."

"That's not going to happen."

"How do you know it? If we take her with us, show her what it's like to live as a dog in your own country—guide her, then when she goes back she could tell them."

"If she goes with us there is a very good chance she could be killed."

"Then whose fault will it be? Tits for tat!" he said, laughing.

Wills knew this would get nowhere. If Sandino seized on an idea it had to be carried out no matter how self-destructive. If you disagreed with him he was all the more sure to go ahead. Wills blamed himself; he'd handled it badly not taking the time to play word games or make jokes—but he was truly concerned over the girl's condition, her fuzzy reaction.

"We must find her a doctor."

"A doctor? *She* needs a doctor? Can you guess how many women, girls in this place have need of a doctor? Can you guess how many can afford one? This girl is too fat, that is what the matter is. We shook up her butter and she curdled a bit."

"This is no joke, César, I must object most strongly, morally and professionally."

"Really? Is that right? Morally like a priest? I thought you were here as a reporter to get a story. If I need a conscience then I will talk to Jesus. I am told in your songs he loves me."

Perversely Sandino cut to the bone. Wills *was* a reporter—not a moralist—and what a story this was! The firsthand account of the kidnapping of the American consul's daughter by a rebel he'd made famous. It would not be confined to *The Nation* or the back pages of dailies; it would be front-page worldwide news. Well, he had registered a serious, strong protest, but Sandino was right when he said he was a reporter and his job was to gather news. On with it. If he stayed here and they went without him who would look after the girl's rights then? Who would be best suited to assure her safety? "When we get to Rama, I must insist she is looked at by a doctor."

Sandino laughed. "What she'll want is a big meal."

"Then I must choose the menu," Wills said, smiling, playing the game.

The driver came down the river road hurrying to slip back into his company house next to his sleeping wife. First he had to close and lock the garage doors. He should have done that when they arrived but he was too anxious to get rid of the girl. *My God! An American girl!* What a damn fool thing that was. It was fine to support the Sandinistas, especially if they happened to be winning—but risking his job, or even his life was another thing. A mechanic as well as a driver, he had no trouble taking the truck but if he had known what was involved he never would have agreed. If his wife found out she would kill him. She hated politicos of any stripe. "What revolution gets you," she said, "is shot."

He was suddenly aware of lights ahead and his heart jumped. They came from a car in front of the garage. In the next moment a soldier was in its headlights. The driver turned around, and keeping in the shadows, ran for his life.

"One of the trucks has been used recently, sir. And a door's open at the back." Magnusson said, moving quickly out of the light.

"All right!" the general answered, "Let's begin a search." He stepped over the Indian, curled in his corner, and out the rear door. "Dick, does this spotlight work?" he asked, tapping the huge drum lamp on its stanchion with his walking stick.

"Yes, I believe so."

"Then turn it on and move the car at a walk up the road. As

you go, shine it back and forth. We will precede you. The doctor and I on one side, Magnusson and the Indian on the other. Did you bring a weapon?"

The consul reached in the seat beside him and produced a double-barreled shotgun.

"It will do, but do not shoot unless fired on or at my command. Come on, doctor."

The doctor got out, tugging his bag over his shoulder. "Nobody told me I was joining the infantry."

"At your weight you can use the exercise. Magnusson! Get the Indian going and lead off on the right. House-to-house search with one man covering the other." Magnusson thought this was amusing; his ass was going to be covered by an unarmed Indian. "How about you?" the general asked the doctor as they walked ahead of the car. "Have you got a weapon?"

"Of course." He produced a Luger from his medical bag. "If I have to shoot I'll do my best to wound at a spot that will be within my skills to mend."

"Good thinking."

The big searchlight blinked on with an immediate drain to the battery, causing the headlights to dim. The consul directed it by the chrome handle to fall just ahead of the general and the doctor. They swung open the company gate and he followed with the car, creeping along behind them. To their right was the first shack, perched on pilings above the river bank, spindly legs braced against a slide into the water. Small boats and *pipantes* were drawn up and the rotting ribs of wrecks showed at the mud line. The pull of the tide was evident in eddies around these obstructions.

"Interesting," the doctor said, "the minute you leave the company town the standard of living drops to zero. There's not a screen on a single door or window, garbage laying about and pools of stagnant water.

"Predictable," the general answered, turning down the bank to step on a rickety catwalk leading to a shack door. The minute he rapped on the door a large dog appeared on the roof and began to bark. It arched its back and leaned over the edge showing its teeth, barking in sharp snaps. The general ignored it and rapped again with the walking stick, shouting in English, "Official! Open up!" The door cracked, showing the frightened face of a sleepy man. The general put a leg in the door, and bending at the waist, looked around the small room. A woman and child, eyes wide, clutched at one another in a hammock. Behind them the searchlight of the car penetrated the cracks and knotholes of wooden walls, sending a frightening set of slotted shadows beaming across the room. "Excuse me, madam." He saw a collection of pitiful possessions: carefully folded clothes, a table with a tattered scarf and a blue magnesia bottle with a flower on it. A cross on the wall was made of wooden matches, and next to it, a large 1928 Standard Oil calendar showed a sepia photo of downtown Managua. There was no place to hide anything. "We are looking for a redheaded American girl. Have you seen such a person?"

The man was speechless, astounded and offended that this American in a white jacket should appear in his house. He could only shake his head. The general backed out. "If you see her report it at once!" He pulled the door shut and went down the catwalk to the road. As he did the dog followed on the roof barking. When they reached the low side of the shack next to the road, the animal leaped.

The doctor and the consul yelled a warning at nearly the same time, fumbling their guns up. But the general had seen its movement and jumped back. The dog lit at his feet and teeth bared, lunged again. Before it could close, he jammed the walking stick down its throat. Pushing sharply forward he pressed its head to the ground and stood on its neck with the heel of his shoe. There was a gargled yelp and the frantic flop of legs, but the general put his weight on the foot and after a brief struggle the animal grew quiet.

Caught in the circular beam of the searchlight, the consul

thought he looked an actor on stage. Like the others he had stopped, arrested at the speed and coolness the general had shown in dispatching the dog. He stood now looking down at it, rubbing his formal pump gently across the motley fur. "I'm sorry he did that . . ." he said, ". . . I like dogs. At home I have a bulldog named Jiggs."

"They're coming right down this road!" The driver caught his breath, gulping air after the run from the garage. "Look for yourself . . . you can see the lights!"

"How many?" Sandino said.

"A car full of heads, one soldier for sure with a hat and a gun!"

"An advance guard then."

"A posse," Wills said. "We were probably seen at that house below the bluff."

"What are you going to do?!" the driver asked, his voice rising. "The steamer will not leave until tomorrow. . . . maybe not even then!"

"True, if we wait we're going to be trapped."

"What about the jungle?"

Sandino looked at him as if he were simple. "Without weapons or guides? No, we counted on the river and we must use it." He went out the front door and stood on the warped angle of a tiny porch overhanging the water. "There are no other boats that could take us to Rama?"

"No," the driver answered, sticking his head out the door, "Not until the tide changes." A hint of dawn was beginning and as the sun sent rays under low clouds, angling them across the hills, the first stab of light caused a reflection on the river bank at the end of the native town.

Sandino brought out the brass binoculars. *"There!"* he shouted, "see that? A power boat! I can see the shine of a white cabin!"

"That's the company survey boat. They have been taking readings all month for a channel to be dredged."

"The boat runs?"

"Every day, but . . ."

"Perfect. We'll take it, come on!"

"But . . . it's the *company boat.*" The driver said, horrified.

Sandino stopped. "Did you hear that Wills? It's a company boat, our hard luck. He leaned in to the driver, "Who in the hell do you think we're fighting in this revolution? Do you think United Fruit has a dispensation from the pope?!"

"But they won't like it."

Sandino laughed out loud. "I give up. Here is the backbone of the country—our standing army—telling me the company won't like it!" He smiled without humor, showing his teeth. "Enough jokes, company man, who drives this boat?"

"A pilot."

"Where is he?"

"He sleeps on board—the engineer is up at the company house."

"Better and better! Have you guns?"

"Only two old handguns . . ." He recoiled at the suggestion of violence.

"Get them." Posing as refugees to board the steamer at Rama, they'd been carefully searched and bringing weapons along was made impossible. He turned to Wills. "This will work. We escape and with the company survey boat at that."

"They will follow in the steamer. Look, Cesár, I have a sensible idea. Let me take the girl and meet this rescue party. It will give you time to get away—a trade."

"Ah, my friend, what sacrifice!" He made a kissing sound. "But then I would owe you a favor and how could I repay it?"

"You could make me finance minister when you become president." They laughed over this.

"No, let's continue as comrades. I enjoy your bad jokes, and besides, you may get the chance to die with me. Would you want to miss that?" Wills did his best to smile.

The driver returned, brushing dirt off an oilskin bag. Sandino cupped his hands. "Come on! Come one!" Two old handguns were unwrapped, thick with grease. One was a large chrome-plated revolver with a long barrel and small handle—a Spanish make, probably left over from Commodore Dewey's time. The other, a Mexican copy of a frontier Colt, was even more of an antique. It had a crude hand-checked grip and a stamp under the cylinder: REMINGTON, indicating the kind of ammunition it would accept. "Look at this! I'll bet that old walrus-face Teddy shot at the Cubans with it!" Sandino handed it back to the driver. "You carry it . . ." he wiped the grease off the other pistol and gingerly held it up, squinting down the sight, looking in the chamber and counting four shells. "Are these more shells?"

"No."

"Just as well, it would probably explode. Besides, this looks formidable and in the end that is what is important."

"At least in the ends of Wagnerian sopranos."

"Exactly," he said, laughing. Tucking the gun in his belt he put on the Mexican sombrero and scooped up his shoulder pack. "Forward, comrades." He moved toward the street door, pushing the driver ahead of him. "Let's go, company man—bring the girl, Wills, and try to keep the jiggling of flesh down."

Kate had listened to rapid exchange of Spanish between the three men, catching only bits and pieces. Her mind had cleared and with it a realization that something was happening beyond her control. She had lived all her life in the diplomatic "trunk," and knew many of the dangers involved in being a political expatriate—had, in fact, been warned by her father that his job carried the privilege and hatred of representing Uncle Sam.

Wills came over to where she still sat, back to the rough wall. He leaned down smiling, noticing the brightness of her eyes and for the first time the pretty face, dirty as it was, framed in a tangle of orange curls. "Feeling better?" he said in English.

"Who are you?"

"Wha . . . ?" This took him aback, coming as it did when there was no time for gracious explanations.

"Tell her," Sandino said from the doorway.

"Carlton Wills—I'm a correspondent from *The Nation*. "I . . ."

"You're American?"

"Yes . . ."

"Who's that?" She pointed at Sandino. The driver stood behind him, and speaking no English, he watched mouths.

"Introduce us, Wills."

Wills stood up. "This is General Augusto César Sandino— leader of the Defending Army of the National Sovereignty."

Sandino swept off his Mexican sombrero and bowed. His small, compact frame bent gracefully in a deep sweep, the hat fanning the dirt off the shack floor.

"That's *Sandino?*"

"Yes."

There was a pause. "He's not much, is he?"

Mr. Elcon and his crew had joined the general's party. A dozen or more formed up behind him looking as a piece in baggy cottons and straw hats, some showing weapons. The assistant manager had strapped on a large holster with a flap that concealed a Smith and Wesson pistol he had been unable to find the bullets for. "These are Conservatives, sir, *costenos*, who hate the guts of Sandos and the southerners, so you can be sure they will persevere."

"Fine," the general answered, "there is no finer motivator than hate." He raised his voice to the level of oratory. "Men, we are mounting a search party for the young, defenseless daughter of the consul. She is somewhere in the town abducted by communist cowards who would use a girl to further base political motives." When the proper degree of suppressed Latin indignation was heard in macho rumbles, the general switched to basics.

"All right! Split up in squads and search every house! *Consul*, keep the car and light moving up the road! *Magnusson*! Take command of the group on the right! I'll head up the left flank."

They moved off, the workers delighted with the authority to break into houses and terrorize the occupants. It was a time when duty could be done and some old scores settled. Soon there was the sound of door pounding, shouts, protest, shrieks of women— all accompanied by the incessant barking of the dogs. Mr. Elcon didn't like it at all. He knew how easy it was to set off the poor. They hated the company workers for their jobs and accepting the Yankee dollar. It would be very simple for this thing to accelerate into a riot. Before he turned out the men, he called Mr. Morris, the manager who was staying the night at the *Hotel El Tropical*. He was told to go ahead—let General Butler take charge. He hoped the man knew what he was doing.

A dozen shacks down the road, Sandino prodded the driver ahead. The girl's indifference to who he was smarted and he took it out on him. "Come on company man, move!"

"I don't think this is a good idea, General . . . if I am seen with you, then my job is lost and what use will I then be?"

"What use will you be dead? Show us to that boat!" Kate was close behind him, boxed in by Wills. They moved along the river road staying in the shadows of the shacks now that day was breaking. She could see a bright light just up the way and hear the shouts and barking dogs. Was that her father with a Marine rescue party? If she shouted would they hear her over the noise?

"Please don't do anything foolish, Miss Kelly," Wills said, as though he had read her mind, saw in the look past his shoulder her intent to act. "Whatever you think of Sandino, he is capable of getting us all killed rather than give in."

"What are you doing with him? You're an American!" She tried to keep her feet, stumbling along in the half light bunched up between the men.

"I'm a reporter—an observer . . ."

"Does that mean if I'm shot you'll observe me?"

The shacks began to thin out and a low flat dock of logs came in sight. The survey boat was tied to one end of its pilings. The road ended ahead and terraced ramps reinforced with squared mahogany logs led down to the dock, stacked with crates and oil barrels.

"There is the boat," the driver said. "I will leave you now . . ."

"Oh no! We're going to need you and Teddy's old gun—come on." Behind them the search party had moved close enough to hear distinct voices, a shout, the slam of a door.

The pilot was aroused by the sound of feet on his deck and the sway of the boat. He pushed up from the bank in the tight forward cabin and in the next instant a flashlight was shined in his face.

"Wha . . . who is that? Get that damn light out of my face!"

The light was lowered and he saw a man framed in the oblong of the open hatch above him. "You! Up here and start this motor—now!" The barrel of a long gun was visible in the light, and he swung his legs out of bed, going up the three steps to the enclosed helm of the boat. Dawn was up and he could see others, one with a gun and his face covered with a bandanna and a man with glasses standing with a fat girl.

"Who thinks he has the right to board a company boat and point guns?"

"See those lights up on the river road?" Sandino said, pointing. "If they find us your company boat is going to be shot to pieces and none of us will leave it alive—now start the damn motor!" The voice was calm and serious, the eyes under the sombrero level. The pilot reached over and made sure the brass shift lever was in neutral, then pulled the starting lever.

The Packard had backtracked and the general stood with Mr. Elcon and Lieutenant Magnusson near the company gate.

"We've been up the street and back, General, with no luck. They're searching the last shacks before the dock."

"What dock is that?"

"We keep the fuel down there for . . ."

"*Listen!*" Magnusson's voice cut through Mr. Elton's sing-song. "What's that?"

All talk ceased. Heads inclined and there was a pause in which breathing could be heard, then—a sudden rumbling spurt of engine noise, stopping, and the slow motion crank of a heavy starter. "What *is* that?" The general wanted to know.

"Sounds like the survey boat kicking over," Mr. Elcon said uneasily.

"*What?*"

Magnusson leaped to the running board of the Packard, the consul still at the wheel engine running. "*With your permission, sir.*"

"*Proceed!*" the general snapped. Then turning to the assistant manager. "You told us there were no other power boats capable of going up river!"

"But that's the *company* boat!" Mr. Elcon said, dismayed.

The consul lay on the throttle, tearing down the narrow street, going airborne over thank-you-ma'ams, coming down with the heavy whomp of solid chassis; skidding, taking out the irregular fences; hopping the wheels around in grooves that sent rocks flying like shrapnel.

Aboard the survey boat the dual ignition got in synch and the big engine throbbed with a regular beat, sending out an exhaust of smoky puffs. But alongside on the dock, the driver was having trouble untying the lines. Wearing the bandanna over his face and holding the gun in one hand he could not get the knots undone. "*Hurry up for God's sake!*" Sandino shouted from the deck. Above the engine sounds he heard another high-pitched one. Then, on the river road he saw the flash of a car between the shacks. He reached over the side and whacked the lines with his machete.

The Packard slid to a stop at the terraces leading down the dock and Magnusson saw a neat white boat move away. He leaped off the running board, kept his feet, and hopped down the steps, rifle held as balance.

The driver felt he had done his duty to his Sandinista brothers and his duty now was to get out of there. Swaying up the ramp to the dock he saw the big car stop at the top of the road. In the next second a soldier jumped down with a long rifle, and taking the steps two at a time shouted at him. He kept going, continuing to wag the old imitation Colt as a warning, thinking to put the soldier off until he could break free. Then the unexpected happened: It fired.

Running, Magnusson was aware of a man dodging along dockside pointing a handgun. "*Alto!*" he shouted, "*Alto!*" but the man continued on to his right and the covering of stacked crates. Then, there was the sound of a shot, a puff of lazy smoke, and the limp trajectory of a round that barely made it past his head, thudding audibly into the mahogany step. Magnusson dropped to one knee, tightened the sling with his forearm, and carefully aiming low, squeezed off one round from the Springfield. There was a clack like the slap of two boards together and the man dropped with a grunt, holed at the upper leg.

As Magnusson came by him, the man gripped his bleeding leg and kept repeating, "*Soy un hombre de la compañia!*"

"*Consul!*" Magnusson shouted back to the car, "Man down and wounded!" He went on. The survey boat was now midstream trying to correct for the river tide and sort out directions. He squatted, a firing position he preferred, raising the bar on the sight. It was not a difficult shot, one he had made many times competing with Marine rifle teams. At the stern of the boat he saw several figures; to the left and clear, a flash of red hair—the girl. Standing next to her a man had his back to him. When he turned, the shine of his glasses were lit by the dawn's early light. It was a perfect target.

He squeezed the trigger.

# FOUR

# Escondido River

ADMIRAL Sellers came up to the bridge of the *Cleveland* where the flag staff watched the landing of a company of Marines on the Bluefields dock. Commander Swayzee, second in command of the Special Service Squadron, lowered his binoculars and saluted. "Marines away, sir. We have a signal from Captain Edd that the *guardia* is formed up and the bull trains ready to shove off." The plan was to cut across on the overland trail, the "Walker Track," to Rama and intercept the Sandinistas before they could get away into the mountains. With luck they would make contact in three days. The town and sawmill were still occupied by rebels and the owners were putting pressure on Colonel Matthews, the *guardia jefe*, to free it up for business as usual. What stuck in the admiral's throat was the way they were doing it—in ox carts!

Here he sat on capital ships with enough combined firepower to blow the top off of Rama and he couldn't use it. The warships could not get over the bar and up the river. Ox carts in the twentieth century!

The communications officer stepped up to the admiral and Commander Swayzee. He had been reading the flap of yellow and red flags from the beach along with the chief signalman and handed over a clipboard with an amended transmission. It contained all the messages received so far. "Here is the dispatch to Com Eleven. I'd like to get this on the keys. Will you authorize release to the press, sir?"

Admiral Sellers read it. "Affirmative, but take out any mention of Butler. He's not officially here." This was the only thing that made the day bearable. Admiral Sellers despised Smedley Butler.

The primitive bull carts were drawn up along the grinder under trees, the heavy animals standing nearly motionless, yoked in pairs. The drivers lounged nearby smoking and talking to friends, regarding the Marines with amusement or downright comtempt. Since Sandino had come down from the Isabelias' to the coastal plains the bullwhackers had to be paid double, in gold, in advance. The trainmaster, Lieutenant Polansky, another ex-sergeant of the U.S.M.C., could rant and rave, as he was doing now, but they still couldn't be shouted into policing the equipment, keeping it clean, oiling the harness. Brigade orders said the locals must not be manhandled, and treated with due respect. Captain Edd would have liked to plant his respect up their backsides with his boot. But the carts were crucial, for they were carrying eighteen-hundred pounds each of heavy ammo, supplies, and gear up the joke of a trail.

At one angle of the grinder was his *guardia* company with Somoza and Lieutenant Castuno walking the ranks and bullying them into shape. They wouldn't have looked too bad except for the adjoining Marine Corps company. It did Edd's old Marine heart good to see the condition of gear, spit-shined shoes, and everything in its place. A young lieutenant who looked straight out of Annapolis brought the company to attention with the sharp snap of rifles.

He saluted and Edd returned it, still feeling the deference of an enlisted man despite his *guardia* rank. "All right, Mr. . . ."

"Delware, sir."

"Mr. Delware, put out your files alongside the train. Keep the machine gun squad by their weapons." The Heavy machine gun, three Lewis guns, and a Stokes mortar were established on the carts. "The *guardia* will make up the advance party—they know the trail. Stay in line and relay all messages to the main body."

Whistles blew and the first platoon swung out ahead of the Marine column, moving on the dirt road of the "Walker Track" that would become a trail, then a path and finally a compass direction. Whips cracked, drivers yelled, and the patient oxen heaved, breaking loose the wheels, pulling in their slow, even stride. The audience of local loungers livened up and the young boys ran alongside the big wooden wheels, throwing pebbles at the animal's haunches. Mothers screamed, drivers cursed, and the town dogs began their cacophony of barking howls from the roofs.

At the back of the *Comandancia* under the arches of a loggia, Norma Kelly watched the column march off. *It's the second time in as many hours I've seen men go in search of my daughter,* she thought. The size of this group awed her, that all this was put in motion for her child . . . still, her hopes lay in those few men who had gone before; she heard the confidence in the general's voice, saw the eyes of Marine who had killed Charlemagne.

"When the sun reflected off his glasses, I recognized him sir, and pulled the shot."

"Who was he then?" the general asked. They stood on the steamer dock with Dr. Bruder and the Indian. The search had been called off and the sleepy workers returned to their houses. The consul was driving the assistant manager up to the company hotel to pick up the captain and the engineer of the *Banana Queen*. Her great hulk loomed over them, providing shade from the early morning sun.

"That's just it," Magnusson said, rubbing the back of his shaven neck. "I don't know. I've seen the man or his picture somewhere—he was white."

"You did the right thing, Lieutenant. He may be another hostage, and God knows we don't want to shoot one of our own."

"What about the girl?" Dr. Bruder asked, relaxing back on a cargo sling. He had the ability to find comfort in the meanest surroundings. The Indian looked up at the steamer wondering how many paddles it would take to move it without its engine.

"I saw red hair."

"But not Sandino?"

"Not that I could tell." The wounded driver had been carried to the company dispensary in the Packard. The first thing he told them was Sandino's name. He didn't know the American but had recognized the consul's daughter. Despite the pain he was mostly concerned about how the day's action would affect his job.

The Packard bumped on the dock, returning with the captain and the engineer. They were not happy. Mr. Cochrane, the captain, stepped down, buttoning a vest up in spite of the heat. He spoke for both of them. "I have stated that I would not take my boat up to Rama until those shooters were out of there. The company, I thought, concurred." He looked at Mr. Elcon, sitting up front with the consul. He shrugged.

The general smiled pleasantly. "Surely you would not want to see this young girl harmed for lack of aggressive pursuit."

"Faint heart never won fair maid," the doctor quoted in a tasteless simile.

The captain shot Dr. Bruder a serious look. Mr. Cochrane was a pristine man with small features whirled to the center of his face by the centrifuge of age. Religious and exacting to a fault, he could not tolerate these drinkers still in dinner jackets telling him where his duty lay. "Is it your purpose to risk the lives of many and sink the company steamer so that amateurs may charge around playing hero? This is a job for the military."

"I *am* the military," the general said, not smiling. "And I tell you this steamer is leaving now and there will be *no* delay about it. Lieutenant Magnusson, escort these patriots aboard!"

"Note this, Elcon! This fool is threatening us!"

The consul got out of the car. His appearance was disconcerting: white dinner jacket splattered with the driver's blood, tie long since gone, and the blue of his beard—an Irish legacy—heavy and in need of shaving. "Captain, I'm sure General Butler is only expressing his concern over my daughter's kidnapping. As her father I must add to this—and ask you to please help us."

There was an awkward silence and finally the captain said, "Very well, as a Christian and a father I can understand." He turned to the assistant manager. "Mr. Elcon, please let it be recorded that I protest." He went forward in his stiff gait toward the gangway followed by the engineer, Mr. Wayne Cott, who appeared to be his complete opposite: loose-limbed with an amused smile and rumpled clothes. He mimed crossing himself and raised his eyes to the sky.

"Thank God for Christians," the doctor said, "without them there would be no real villians left."

"Amen," the general amended.

The survey boat, *Chiquita*, was a double-ender built of Port Offered cedar in Buffalo, New York, in 1925. It had been shipped down to New Orleans by rail, then brought across the Gulf of Mexico and Caribbean to Bluefields. The pilot, Bayardo Arce, had been hired for his skills in navigating the Escondido but no one was paying him extra for being shot at. He had personally heard the bullet go over his head, fracturing the windshield and sending quarter-inch glass shards into his hair. The American it had been aimed at stood next to him at the helm. Aft of the twenty-eight-foot boat, the bandit talked with much hand waving to the redheaded girl. It was raining lightly, and ahead the river disappeared around a kink in the bank—they had left the pull of tide behind. He glanced at the American out of the corner of his eye. The man had a nose like a toucan and if he realized the bullet was meant for him, he didn't show it.

"You people are going to get into big trouble taking this boat. It belongs to the company."

Wills smiled. "That's been pointed out. Please understand I am American and a correspondent. I had nothing to do with taking the boat. I am not a rebel—I report on them for an American magazine."

"What's this? Bandits have their own *annunciadors* now?"

"Just drive." Wills was trying to listen to the conversation between Sandino and the girl—Kate—over the noise of the engine. She had proved a surprise, not in the least intimidated by César. In fact, she had begun by insulting him and kept it up. She sat on the low gunwale combing her hair with a comb borrowed from him. She had washed her face with river water and looked fresh. Sandino, gun in his belt, sombrero tugged down against the wind, leaned in and gestured with his hands.

"What I am saying, Miss Kelly, is that we bring you along to see what is happening to us—the poor ones who don't own mines and saw mills and . . ."

"What you're doing is kidnapping me." Kate continued combing, not bothered by the rain.

"Look! Understand that this is a great opportunity for your country to know us through you. . . ."

"What they know is, that you're a man who kills people to get his own way—they'll come after you. The Navy and the Marines will get you."

He smiled. "They have been trying to do that for five years."

"But this time they're sending just *one* man to do it personally."

Despite himself, Sandino asked, "What are you talking about? How do you know this?"

"Because I met him—a Marine lieutenant named Magnusson. He's the one who killed Charlemagne in Haiti and now he's coming after you."

Sandino knew about the *caco's* leader's killing, but up to this moment it had never occurred to him that a great nation would send *one* man after him. That thought was more disturbing than fighting the whole Marine Brigade.

Kate flicked the handle of the gun with the comb and he jumped back. "He was carrying a gun just like that in his belt and Lieutenant Magnusson and another American crept right up to his campfire disguised as natives. Then he shot him dead in the center of his silk shirt." Pointing her finger she said, "*Bang!*"

He jumped again, "Don't ever do that again, or by sweet Jesus, I *will* kill you!"

"Just try!"

He turned in a fury and walked back to where Wills stood with the pilot. "That girl is . . . crazy!"

"Well, she's a redhead," Wills said.

In the next instant she was over the side of the boat in a large splash and swimming away. The pilot had kept in close to the lee shore and it was less than twenty-five yards. "*There she goes!*" Wills shouted and handing Sandino his glasses cleared the gunwale in a flat jump.

"Boy! that is something!" the pilot laughed, "The girl has real pepper!"

"*Slow down and back up!*" Sandino shouted.

"Easy, easy—in time, I run this boat." He pulled the long brass shift lever back. The engine was a Sterling Petrol and the manual shift lever went through a slot in the deck of the transmission.

"*You run this boat the way I command!*" Sandino knew what the problem here was—he had lost respect because of the girl talking back to him.

The pilot smiled. "You're going to shoot me? Then who will run the boat? Do you know how to get through the sand banks?"

Sandino drew the gun and took one step, slamming the long barrel down on the man's right hand where it gripped the wheel. He broke two fingers and the pilot screamed in pain. "I don't have to kill to get you to run this boat. There are many ways to do a thing."

At four in the afternoon they at last pulled away from the dock. There was a husky hoot on the whistle as paddlewheels dug in and the *Banana Queen* moved into the mainstream. In the engine room, Mr. Cott tapped at the gauges. Steam pressure: forty-six pounds—near the optimum of fifty, vacuum twenty-eight inches. Beside him the huge three-ton piston was stroked nine feet by the vertical "walking" beam, transferring power to Morgan paddlewheels. The black gang handfired the boilers, the day was glorious (despite a mean temperature of 106 degrees in the engine room), and God was in his heaven. The engineer was a happy man and began singing at the top of his lungs, *"Don't bring me posies when it's shoesees that I need!"*

Forward, the Packard was lashed down and secure, its winged lady pointing toward the bow. The doctor was slumped in the backseat, sleeping while the Indian had gotten his courage up and sat behind the steering wheel, twisting it with the boat's direction. The space the car took up had once been a promenade deck when the boat plied Lake Champlain in her glory days. It had been removed along with the one aft to make way for extra cargo and heavy machinery.

When Mr. Elcon asked the general why he wanted to take a motorcar into the jungle, the general replied that few things would strike fear in the hearts of your enemies like the unexpected. Mr. Elcon agreed that seeing a Packard where even the donkey had trouble maneuvering would surely cause speculation as to one's sanity.

"Exactly! The most terrible thing a soldier faces is the possibility that his foe is crazy."

"You don't have to worry then," the assistant manager said,

not without a smile. He'd grown fond of the prickly old devil. Anybody who could give Captain Cochrane a hard time was not all bad.

On the hurricane deck, the general went past the oiled wag of the "walking" beam and down the ladder to the cross deck. The consul leaned on the rail watching the riverbank slide by. The general was worried about him. He had hardly said two words on the trip and that was not right for a man in the political business. He did look more presentable; the bloody coat had been discarded and his dress shirt was rolled to the elbows, a straw hat in place. He turned and the general noted that the shadow of beard was now inking itself in.

"Oh, General . . ."

"We're on our way, Dick, we'll catch up to them shortly."

"I . . . wonder if this is the right way to go about it. Might the fact that we're pressing Sandino cause him to do something . . . desperate?"

"Who knows what a dog like that will do in any event? When the challenge is thrown down and the fight begun then you must press in on your opponent without let up. What is the alternative? That we withdraw and allow him to dictate his own terms? That could last months—a year—and in the end—to my thinking—the outcome would still be in doubt."

"Yes, I suppose you're right . . ." He turned back to the river view. "But it's hard to think rationally when a child's life is at stake."

The general put his hand on the consul's shoulder. "Dick, I hope you don't think I'm being the cold-hearted old militarist. I have three children of my own you know, and one of them is a baby girl. Nothing is more dear to me."

"A *baby* girl?"

"Born in Olangapo, the Philippines. Named Ethel Peters after her mother, but we call her 'Snooks.' The biggest fellow in the 2nd Regiment was named Snooks, and since our baby was the smallest, the men called her Snooks also. I gave a

Thanksgiving dinner for Company E and she was carried in on a pillow as guest of honor. She's a born Marine, but talk about cute, with dimples and a mouth like a Kewpie doll."

"How old is she, sir?"

"Twenty-seven."

"Oh."

"Married a Marine lieutenant last March."

"Oh."


Wills was a strong swimmer and he caught up to Kate as she struggled up the gluey river bank. The jungle here came right down to the edge of the water, overhanging it with a twist of vines on trees that reached out. He got hold of one chubby arm and pulled her back. "Miss Kelly . . . please . . ."

"*Let go!*"

She swung with the other arm but missed and he edged her out into the river, swimming backward. "Don't be . . . foolish . . . we're a good ten miles . . . from Bluefields . . . you can't get through that jungle . . ."

"*That's what you . . . think!*" She squirmed, but he had her gripped under both arms and kicking with his feet made their way to where the boat idled.

With Wills pushing and Sandino pulling they got her over the low freeboard of the boat and on the deck. She knelt on her hands and knees breathing hard. When Wills climbed over the gunwale Sandino was screaming at the girl, out of control. "*What do you think you're doing you fat bitch of a girl?! You will not act like that here!*" He jerked her up by her hair, holding the gun in his other hand.

Wills had seen Sandino in these murderous rages before and it was frightening. "Wait a minute, César . . ." He stepped forward and Sandino turned and swung the long barrel of the gun in a flat arc, slamming it in his stomach. He fell back with a grunt.

"*Shut your damned mouth you* gringo lombiz—*you fucking writer!*"

Wills smiled, holding his stomach and speaking in a hoarse whisper, "Are you using fucking as a verb or an adjective?"

Sandino didn't hear him and shoved the girl ahead of him across the deck past the pilot nursing his broken fingers. A narrow hatch led down three steps to the crowded cabin and he pushed her through it. She crashed to the deck banging up against the V of bunks. "*From now on you'll be treated as you deserve!*" He slammed the hatch shut, locking it. "*When we get to Rama I've got just the one to show you discipline!*"

Kate lay on the floor and began to cry. But first she stuffed the hem of her wet chemise in her mouth so they couldn't hear her.

Lieutenant Magnusson and the music boy sat on the fan tail watching the chimneys of the United Fruit Company fade. The paddlewheels of the *Banana Queen* created a double wake that came together in a roiling of water that sent up bottom weeds, sand, and dead fish. The music boy had been allowed to sleep off his hangover and looked alert enough now. He'd found a shirt, and a red bandanna was twisted around his head to keep off the heat. A tumble of black curls protruded from the top and bounced in vibration with the boat's engine. The bugle was looped over his shoulder and the Thomson submachine gun and its sack of drums was close at hand. Cleaned up, Magnusson thought he looked even younger—like one of the cherubs you saw on church ceilings blowing a long trumpet for God.

"Sir—do you think I'll get back on board the *Cleveland?* In his tone Magnusson heard anguish. There was nothing worse than suddenly being separated from your ship or station. "I was working on this yarn-holder for my mother. The quartermaster—Henny?—was showin' me how to carve it outta fish bones. He'd made them from whales as a boy on the Atlantic Grounds. I'd sure hate to lose my start."

"If you don't get back, your gear will be shipped on."

"I'd like my mother to have it by Christmas—she cried about a week when I joined up at fifteen."

"Why did you join at that age?"

"Well, there was trouble with a girl . . ."

"Oh . . ."

"I don't mean like that . . . although we done a lot of that, too—no, she wasn't knocked up, she was Polish and my people being Irish had a fit—but not as bad as the Poles—they came after me. The hell with it I said, and joined."

"That seems an extreme thing to do to stay away from the Polish."

"That's what my mother said."

"How did you take up tooting?"

"The union band. My old man and all his brothers are masons—ever see the Custom House in Boston?"

"Hard to miss."

"My people built that—oh yes."

In his time, Magnusson thought, he wouldn't have dared say two words to an officer. But then he'd been an enlisted a long time. Maybe it showed.

"I sure hope I can get back to the *Cleveland*—what would you say my chances were, sir?"

"Well, can they replace you? Any other tooters on board?"

"No . . . only a bosun striker that was pretty good on the pipe."

"Then I wouldn't worry. Bosuns are a cocky bunch, thinking they've got the only real seaman's work. Blowing a horn would seem like a pussy's job to them."

"That's comforting to know sir," the music boy said, with an irony beyond his years that was lost on Magnusson.

As the survey boat continued up river, Wills stood at the helm with Sandino and the sullen pilot. Nothing had been said since the rage but Wills could tell by Sandino's expression that he was feeling guilty and in control of himself. "Why would she act like that?" he finally asked.

"Well, César, she has been taken against her will."

"No, I mean the personal insults, the wild behavior—this is not the way women and girls should act with men."

"She is an American. Women there do pretty much as they please—they vote, smoke in public, and change husbands when they feel like it."

"That is not right. Women were meant to be wives and mothers."

*The Latin bill of rights*, Wills thought. "Forgive me, César, but you really have not had much experience with North Americans . . ." Sandino looked at him sharply. ". . . I'm not talking about Marines and politicians—the interventionist—I mean the *people*. They are diverse and independent."

"My brother Sócrates lives in Brooklyn."

"Then you should visit him. You have to remember that most Americans were pleased with themselves and their country—at least until the Depression."

"How can they allow their troops, these pirates, to come here and kill us?"

"They believe it's for your own good," Wills said, smiling, "Americans were optimistic about their success, convinced it would work for everyone—that's where the trouble started—they wanted to spread it around."

"Manifest Destiny."

"Yes, the belief that their system would work even if forced down others' throats. Missionary zeal."

"We've had our fill of those."

"I don't mean the Gospel of Christ, but the gospel of progressive reform. The secular modernizers chomping at the bit to transplant what they think of as American democratic political institutions, technology—business practices to poor nations. These missionaries believe that it's their duty to spread the advantages of the United States to others—to make their lives richer."

"And they do this with guns."

"That's where the perversion began, enforcing their convictions—and investments—with the Marines. They could not believe others did not want what they sold. But you have to understand, César—like this girl, there are many kinds of North Americans and they are not all bad."

"The ones I fight are."

Wills sighed, feeling a real sadness for Sandino—a pity because he did not understand any more who he was fighting than his enemy did. He was a simple, honest man, a brave patriot who had one compelling mission, to drive the yankee soliders from his land. After that his plans were vague, a mystical vision of an Indo-Hispanic Latin world of brothers living in communes. There were sharks swimming out there in the political waters, left and right, who would gobble him up once his purpose was served.

"She called me a shrimp—what kind of an insult is that?"

Wills thought fast. "At home the shrimp is considered very good inside, but with a tough shell that must be peeled off."

"Hmm. I don't understand why she doesn't like me. I have always been popular with females." This obviously bothered him.

At dusk they approached Rama. It began first with a sprinkle of huts and natives waving from the river bank—villages at the edge of tree-eater, Rama-America Mills. Then a swing of bank and the panorama of industry sprawl, the lumber mills with their stacks of wooden buildings; two-storied, stilted, long sheds—domed head-rig houses staved and banded like giant pickle barrels. Above, the vertical fingers of many smokestacks were smokeless against the sky.

Behind the clutter of mill and town was the green sweep of forest: cedar, pine, balsa, mahogany, stretching out on the Moquito Coast basin. Great swathes were cut clean, angling up toward the curve of distant mountains, the land reduced to stump farms, tended by squatters and tolerated by the company. The town was built right on the river with the manager's house the most prominent; two-storied and constructed in the traditional way with wide verandas and the overhang of a tin roof. From a distance, lights could be seen in the windows and surrounding it, the fires of the Sandinistas.

As the dock came up, Wills asked, "How long will you stay?"

"Only a few days. It is a good place to announce to the world that the American consul's daughter has joined our cause."

"I can't write that," he replied, smiling.

"It will be my official communique—you can equivocate in *The Nation* and confuse the issue, but what is said first will be believed."

"What will you ask for her return?"

"We are not asking for anything, she's come to us to learn."

"That's not true." Wills was not going to give in on this point.

"It will be."

"What did you mean when you said you would give her over to someone here—for discipline?" He knew he was pushing it, but would not allow the girl to be misused.

"Why *Capitán Sangre*, of course!" He burst out laughing. "César . . ."

"Admit it, who would be better?"

As the boat touched the dock, lines were caught by eager soldiers, shouts went up, and they could hear gunfire being let off at the campfires around the manager's house in their honor. "Let us hope the manager's wife has made us some fresh *Gjetost*."

"*Gjetost* is never fresh," Wills said, allowing the subject to be changed. "That's the idea."

"But the manager's wife is," Sandino said, making a kissing sound. "I have a little surprise for her," he added mysteriously.

"Really? What?"

"Wait and see. They went ashore leaving the consul's daughter locked in the cabin. Before he stepped off the boat, Wills said to the pilot, "I'll ask somebody to look at your fingers."

"*Chiga tu madre!*" The man snarled and Wills shrugged, continuing on.

Still soaking wet and shivering despite the heat, Kate looked out the narrow porthole and saw the two men enfolded by back-slapping comrades. Her view included the dock and beyond—a large house ringed by campfires. At a second-story balcony she made out the tall figure of a woman in black.

Karen Sven stood at the upper veranda watching the two approach. Hearing the gunfire she knew it must be Sandino and was relieved. There were more than a hundred men camped around the house, some of them right up on the lower veranda and under the house itself, raised as it was on poles.

A lot of drinking went on, but so far there had been no real trouble; it just seemed to make them sleepy. That first terrible night of the attack with the hideous rattle of gunfire and the hoarse shouts of men, she had also heard the screaming of women and was sure rape must be occurring. But now there were many town women living right with the soldiers and she couldn't be sure just what had happened. They had left her alone, thank God. Although the oafs stood on the porch and openly looked through the windows, they hadn't come inside the house. This was because of Sandino's protection. She had heard him tell the soldiers that she was the manager's wife, a decent woman, and must be respected. She reciprocated by pulling the frightened servants together and cooking a real *Norge* meal, drawing on stores from home. It was surprising to find General Sandino was educated and even had a sense of humor.

Karen had done her best to appear unattractive. Dressing in a bedroom hung with blankets over the windows, she dealt with an unfortunately large bosom by painfully strapping it down with yards of cotton batting. Tall and thin, the awesome frontage and a slope of bottom had been assets turned liabilities. The bottom was disguised with a full skirt and searching through a closet still hung with the odds and ends of another's severe wardrobe she found a loose, high-necked blouse. The long hair, white-blond was braided tightly, thick as rope, circling her head like a saint's halo. The face with its shine of good bones, full lips, and tilt of eyes was more difficult. She wore no makeup and did her best not to smile.

It had been a nightmare worrying that someone—a servant, one of the mill workers who remained, would give her away. If that happened her life would be a hell. If she could just hold out for a few more days they would be gone. She prayed to God that before that they wouldn't find out that she wasn't the manager's wife at all, but a whore he had brought all the way from a bordello in Storyville, New Orleans.

For Kate it seemed they had forgotten her. She had been locked in the cabin of the survey boat for hours. Did they intend keeping her in this cramped space with no food or water and a filthy toilet? She still wore the wet chemise and it stuck to her, clammy as glue. Finally she took it off, wringing it out the best she could, and hung it on an electrical cord to dry. There was nothing to cover herself with besides an oily piece of canvas. At that moment the door opened and she snatched the canvas up.

"Hey, what's this? You going to show us your *cuerpo*?" A woman appeared above her at the top of the hatchway. She had a wide, flat face with odd splotches of freckles and kinky hair the color of rust sticking straight out from under a battered Mexican sombrero. "Put your damn clothes on! These hombres see all this fat shaking and they go fockin' crazy!" Kate put on the wet chemise and came on deck.

"Who are you?"

"I am goddamned Captain Sangre, that's who I am. Who are you, some kind of a redheaded woodpecker?" She was Kate's height, stocky and dressed in a dirty shirt, long ragged skirt and run-down boots. The shoulder strap of a Sam Browne belt cut across the divide of loose breasts, connecting with a worn holster belt containing a large automatic with silver-embossed grips. She reached over and got a grip on Kate's arm. "Come on, let's vamoose."

Kate jerked her arm back, "I can walk by myself!"

The woman regripped and raised her other hand. "Behave, niña, or I'll knock your fockin' teeth out!" Kate shoved, and the hand came around slapping her hard on the side of the face. She went down pulling the woman with her and lashing out with her feet, knocking the sombrero off. Sangre grabbed her legs, rolled her over, and slammed her head just once on the deck. Then, pulling the captured arms back, she jerked her to her feet.

The soldiers on the dock enjoyed this, and as the dazed girl was marched ashore they laughed and offered lewd comments. Captain Sangre answered with a lewd Mexican gesture. Winding their way around the campfires, past the sprawl of equipment and sleeping men, they came to the manager's house and ducked under the porch. Ponchos had been tied to provide shelter on two sides and a tattered blanket had been laid down over the damp ground. Bedrolls, bags, and a scarred saddle were piled in a heap and an oiled Winchester carbine hung from a nail on the pole supporting the house. A large black mule was tied to the same pole and just outside the corner of porch a young girl with greasy hair sat back on her haunches cooking in front of a small fire.

"Bad luck, Chula, we have another damn hole to stuff." She shoved Kate down and flopped next to her, back against the pole. "No more fockin' around, huh, woodpecker?" She pulled off her boots, digging her filthy bare feet in the dirt.

Kate was furious, near crying, squeezing her mouth shut to keep her chin from quivering. She glared across at the woman who glared back. Kate prided herself on unyielding resistance to any bullying, including well-meant criticism. She thought it praise when her father called her stubborn as a mule. She was independent and unwilling to give an inch to any man. But in this dirty vulgar woman she was up against a role reversal she didn't understand. Kate had fantasized herself a Marine, to wear the uniform, march to bands, flags flying—to be as brave as General Butler or Lieutenant Magnusson—to be a hero. But was this awful person what it meant to be a woman and a soldier?

Maria Antonia Anayamontes was born in 1901 on a miserable horse ranch in the state of Chihuahua to a half-black, Yaqui Indian mother and a Mexican-Scottish father. At twelve she ran off to the revolution following that old cattle rustler, Pancho Villa. As a young girl living on the fringe of the army she was no different than the other camp followers who went with their men, breast-feeding babies, cooking on the march, and sometimes fighting alongside the army.

Then at the terrible slaughter outside Celaya when Villa's cavalry was chopped to pieces by Obregon's machine guns she became famous. Caught up in the fury and bloody tumble of horses and men she picked up a fallen rifle and charged the chattering guns on foot, rallying others to break through the barbed wire and destroying two guns and their crews. This would have gone unnoticed but for a picture restaged later by *New York Times* photographer Edwin Casserine. It showed a young girl in a huge hat and crossed cartridge belts standing legs astride a dead soldier. The barrel of a machine gun was turned to the sky and her rifle was held victoriously aloft. There was a look of such savage joy on her face that it stunned readers.

Carlton Wills, there with Huerta's observers, had seen the picture and written about rebel girls, *soldadera*. They called her *la Sangrienta niña*, the bloodthirsty child, and he shortened it to *Capitán Sangre*, Captain Blood. She was elevated to a symbol, a totem, and when Villa rode into Mexico City in 1914 next to Emiliano Zapata she was with them. In that famous picture she can be seen to the right of Villa, smiling her savage smile. By the end of the revolution she dressed the part, playing it to the hilt.

Sandino had spent all of 1930 in Mexico and when Wills came down they took the train up to Guanajuato, Mexico, to see *Capitán Sangre* at the ornate *Teatro Juarez*. Her act included a halting narration of the Battle of Celaya complete with a real horse on stage. During the singing of *Adelita*, the horse broke wind at such length and volume there was intense fanning and muttered consternation. Wills and Sandino thought it probably the single funniest thing they had ever seen. They invited her to dinner, and after much wine, Sandino joked that she should join his army. To his dismay she accepted.

Things had not gone well for her since the revolution. The promised job with the government had proved impossible: She couldn't read, write, or stand to be indoors. Later, drinking heavily and married, she shot her sixty-one-year-old husband to death over the meaning of the word *ilustre*. That night in Guanajuato, Captain Sangre told Sandino she was only meant to ride and fight and brag. Certainly no one doubted her ferocity or skill as a soldier. And she was not dumb—if she now appeared the clown—she had drawn the caricature herself.

Battered and exhausted, Kate began to drift off to sleep despite herself. As she did she was vaguely aware of footsteps and the sound of music overhead in the house. Then there was a prolonged scream that snapped her eyes open.

# FIVE

# Rama

ABOUT halfway through dinner Sandino began to talk about the church. Up to this point the conversation had been light, an amusing account of their escape from Bluefields, leaving out, Wills noted, any mention of the consul's daughter. They were seated at a table in the dining room of the manager's house, a rather gloomy space with heavy mission furniture done in the Gustaf Stickly style. Lights had yet to be restored—the engineer had left with the other refugees—but the table was pleasantly lit with candles.

Karen sat at one end of the table, Sandino at the other. Wills found himself opposite Colonel Pedro Altamirano, his least favorite dinner companion. Better know as Pedrón—"Big Pedro," he was a man who had spent fifty years in banditry and guerrilla warfare. Huge and ferocious, the sight of him alone was enough to inspire quaking. During the 1928 elections he had roamed the polling places personally killing Liberals and terrorizing voters. In every respect the antithesis of Sandino, there was an indissoluble bond between the crude, illiterate bandit and the articulate revolutionist. Wills found this tie inexplicable, but there was a simple, sinister explanation, one that Sandino did not care to let out, certainly not in *The Nation*—he needed Pedrón to administer Sandinista justice.

Returning from Mexico in 1930, Sandino had found it necessary to tighten control of the guerrilla zones he operated in. He began with the carrot: authorizing the firing squad for any merchant who refused to distribute medicine or salt among the poor. The stick: if any of the poor refused to accept this handout, they were also to be shot as traitors. His men circulated gathering "taxes" from rich landowners and the middle class, taking what supplies they wanted but carefully leaving IOUs. Protests could be addressed to Sandino and he sometimes scaled down his demands so as not to drive the "taxpayers" out of his area. He tried to strike a balance of terror and fairness that would maintain the cooperation of those under his administration. However, for the uncooperative, or any who assisted the hated *guardia*, there were the terrible *cortes*.

*Corte* was a word he loved, meaning either "courts" or "cuts." Pedrón devised the punishment. At the bottom of the scale was the common *corte de chaleco*—vest cut—the traitor's head and arms were lopped off with a machete and a thoughtful message carved on his chest. Next, the simple *corte de bloomers* in which the victim's legs were chopped off at the knees and he was left on the trail to bleed to death. But for the real offenders there was the sophisticated *corte de cumbo*—gourd cut. Here an expert machete man sliced off a portion of the victim's skull, exposing the brain and causing the loss of equilibrium and hours of agony and convulsions before dying. Just the thought of this created converts. Pedrón also had his playful moments and bodies were left as warnings with the "tie cut," in which the throat was cut and the tongue pulled out the slit—and the familiar "cigar cut," in which the penis was chopped off and put in the man's mouth.

Sandino's only private comment on these hideous mutilations had been: "Liberty is not conquered with flowers and for this reason we must resort to the *cortes*." In fact, the official seal that was on the letters he wrote showed a Sandinista beheading a prostrate Marine with a machete. Then, too, he had executed a number of his own officers and at least two generals. Hence, the need for an enforcer—as he said, "I am the arm and Pedrón is the sword—or in this case the machete."

Curiously, Pedrón was thought of as a patriarch among the troops and called "Papa." He usually campaigned with his entire family, his fat wife Maria and sons and daughters who served as aides and advisers—he was surrounded by his family and joked that they were "his bodyguards." On this expedition they had been left behind in southern Jinotega where he headed up the First Column. His territory included the departments of Matagalpa and Chontales to within sixty miles of the east coast. But General Blandó, leading the Sixth Column on the Mosquito Coast, had gotten himself killed at Logtown and Sandino asked Pedrón to temporarily assume command for the Rama attack.

Tonight he was beautifully dressed in an olive drab uniform with the black and red colors of syndicalism at his cuffs and collar. Above the table he was resplendent in gold rings and chains; below, two large handguns were at his hips. He was obviously enjoying his role as bachelor and his eyes never left the hostess. Wills wondered if she were dessert.

"The church in Mexico clearly feels itself independent of government." Sandino went on, "Why that old rascal the archbishop of Mexico publicly repudiated Mexico's new constitution! Can you believe it?! So much for sweating and dying and the revolution! When President Calles reacted by deporting foreign-born priests and nuns, the church went on strike—strike! And for three years no services have been held. How's that for retribution? No more getting up for mass or telling your sins to a fat, foreign cleric."

Wills couldn't see where this was going. He knew that

Sandino was a practicing Catholic. Once bragging that he had paid for a Virgin of May Mass for the entire troop. As he went on talking, conversation became a one-way dialog. Karen kept her tight smile and Pedrón kept his eyes on her, his smile faintly crocodilian.

"Being Catholic has become a dangerous thing. The *Cristos* in Jalisco and Michoacán go around shouting, '*Long live Christ the King*,' and dynamiting trains. Killing Christians! The government counters by carrying out a scorched-earth policy and shooting everybody wearing a cross. It's a contest to see who is the most brutal." He took a long draught of wine and Wills could see his eyes shine.

"It makes you wonder if there is good in anybody. In Mexico City nuns are not allowed to wear their habits and it's very odd to see them walk down the street, these pious women, these 'Brides of Christ' with their short hair and long dresses. You feel as though you were witnessing something indecent. Oh you can't miss them, even without the clerical veil they never raise their eyes . . . can you blame them, married to a Holy Ghost—eh Karen?" he said, laughing.

She was startled, "Why I . . ."

He talked over her, "Who is to say that our mothers and good wives—like yourself—are not just as noble? If there is no purity and sacrifice among women then who can we look up to? Pedrón"—switching to Spanish—"did you know that Karen stayed behind to protect her husband's—the manager's—property?"

Looking at Karen, "That's right. He is where . . . ?"

"Bluefields," Karen said in a small voice. Pedrón remained unimpressed.

"Yes, and rather than desert the company house—take the boat downriver with the other mice—she stayed bravely here—inspiring, no?" There was a pause while Sandino filled his glass again. "But I've talked too much. Let's have some music. If there's one thing I miss in the jungle it is music—God I'm sick of the sound of birds and monkeys."

Sandino got up and went to a sideboy where a wind-up gramophone sat. Squinting over a rare cigarette, he sorted though a pile of records. "Ah, here's one, *Desencuentro*—a tango." He held it up. "The words say, 'Your luck is so bad that when you want to put the last bullet in your pistol into your head—it won't fire—Ha!" He laughed and put the record on, winding the machine up, dropping the needle and releasing the scratchy but compelling music of the tango. Then going around the table he bowed and presented himself to Karen. "Shall we?" he asked, gesturing with his hand.

"I'm sorry, I don't . . ." she replied, but he took her wrists and pulled her to her feet.

"Of course you do." And locking her in the studied position of the tango, they swung awkwardly into the dance. Wills was amazed. He had never seen Sandino pay this kind of undignified attention to a woman, let alone dance with one. Pedrón livened up and clapped loudly with the music. Around they went in an exaggerated style, Sandino mugging for Wills. The *bandoneons* wailed, violins squawked, and when at last the song ended, he bent Karen abruptly in a low dip. There was silence as Sandino kept her pressed on the floor, the only sounds the needle hopping in the same groove and their breathing. Finally he laughed and straightened.

"Thank you . . ." she said, starting to pull away, but his hands remained around her narrow waist.

"Oh," he said, eyes down, "a button is loose . . ." And taking hold of the bottom of her blouse, he suddenly jerked up, ripping it open and sending the buttons flying like shot. She gave a startled cry and pulled back, but he had both hands under her arms, thumbs hooked over the wrap of cotton suppressor. "What's this? Our manager's wife has been wounded in action?" Gripping the wrapping he pulled it straight down and her breasts sprung free, showing the marks of the cloth.

*"Stop it! Stop it!"* She beat at him with her fists, but he contained her easily.

Shocked, Wills got to his feet, convinced Sandino had gone mad. *"César! What are you—"*

"I told you I had a nice surprise for our manager's wife, Carlton? Well, I'm glad to report that she is not married to the man after all—I knew she had better taste." She struggled, twisting, but he held her, one arm locked under the circles of breasts. Pedrón was whooping with delight.

"What?"

"That's right, one of the crew on the boat downriver told me that the captain—an old blue nose—refused to take the manager's woman because she was a common whore brought here from New Orleans. You think I'm making this up? Ask her."

Karen had given in to his strength and was crying now. "Please don't hurt me . . ."

"Hurt you?" Sandino sounded offended. "We're going to put you back into business. We have a whole army of bored men out there—paying customers. Tell me, Wills, how much would you say the yankees here pay for our girls?"

"César—"

"No, let's be fair—we do not requisition things without paying for them in our Revolutionary Army—would you say fifty cents in your money was right? No? Too high probably. Twenty-five cents would put her within the price range of our poor soldiers."

"I hope you're not serious, César."

"Oh yes, very serious."

"She's a white woman . . ." This was a mistake.

"Really? I hadn't noticed, I thought she was just a whore. But then—can a whore be choosy, even if she's white?"

"What I meant was—"

*"Enough!"* he shouted, showing his teeth. "If this woman had told me what she was in the beginning, it would have been different—but no, she chose to make a fool out of me, pretend

she was the Virgin Mary. I do not take that lightly." He turned to Pedrón, who was enjoying the spectacle enormously. He hadn't understood the English but knew exactly what was going to happen. Sandino spoke to him in Spanish, "Why not be the first to plow our lady's trough? She might as well start at the top of our troops and work down—so to speak."

As Pedrón came around the table Karen twisted free and stumbled for the door. Lunging out, he grabbed for the skirt and caught the hem. It didn't tear but instead slowly came down. She fell to her knees and he hauled her back, working the skirt down around her bottom until it jerked free. Then, roaring, he slapped her hard, leaving an imprint of red fingers. She staggered up naked, trying to run and began screaming.

At sometime after midnight the *Banana Queen*, lights out, approached Rama-American Mills. One mile ahead, a turn in the river would present a view of the town and main mill buildings—it would also present a view of the boat. The engine reversed and the boat backed water, the ten buckets on each paddlewheel digging in as they churned up their own personal maelstrom. The moon, fragmented by clouds, reflected on the white, roiling wake.

Captain Cochrane had insisted on blacking the boat out several miles upstream and keeping to the main channel. Whatever could be said of his disposition, his navigation was first-rate. Shoving up the window of the wheelhouse, he shouted down at the rescue party standing on the forward deck next to the car. "This is as far as I go!"

Below, General Butler examined a large company map of the mill and its ancillaries, identifying landmarks ashore. The music boy held a flashlight and the others gathered around. "Those shapes on the right are stacked logs—so this must be what they call a 'cold deck'—where the logs are sorted for the mill . . . docking is indicated." He turned and shouted up to Cochrane, "Put us alongside that dock over there . . . so we can unload the Packard."

Captain Cochrane leaned out the window. "You are out of your mind! That is just a mat of logs lashed together—they float on the river. They won't hold an automobile!"

"Why don't we find out? Kindly put us ashore!"

Grinding his teeth, Cochrane gave the orders to Engineer Cott and the boat crept cautiously ahead, nudging into the log dock. At its bump the logs swayed and dipped and the engine stopped. In the silence, two company deckhands jumped to the logs and secured lines to spikes driven into the wood.

The Packard was unrigged and a ramp extended to the log dock. The original sharp bow of the *Banana Queen* had long since had been built over, forming a squared-off prow to allow for straight-on loading and unloading. The consul sat behind the wheel and adjusted the spark and choke while Tomás cranked the big car over. When it started in a noisy explosion of the faulty muffler, he adjusted the mixture until the engine vibrated at an acceptable level. The general stepped up to the driver's side.

"Dick, we will follow on foot to keep the weight down. When you hit that dock give it all its got—don't bog down."

The consul took off the brake, firming up. "Yes sir." Ahead he could see the undulating effect of the logs on the river. Fortunately he faced them horizontally rather than on end, so there would be some traction. The dock extended about fifty feet and was chained to tree stumps on shore.

"Here goes!" he said. Gunning the engine, he bumped up on the ramp and started down. The minute the wheels of the car came onto the log dock it shipped water and went under. Lines from the boat became taut, straining against the weight with a distressing sound. On deck the rescue party could actually feel the bow dip.

"*Gun it!*" Magnusson shouted. "*Gun it!*" And the consul did, spinning the back wheels on the ramp and jumping forward. But once up to their hubs in the water they began to slip, then slide back.

"All hands—*Push!*" the general commanded, and they ran

down the ramp and onto the submerged end of the dock. With Magnusson and the music boy on one side, the general and the doctor on the other, and the Indian at the back, they all heaved.

From the wheelhouse Cochrane shouted at the deck crew, "*Stand by to cut the bow lines!*" But he knew if they did that, the boat would surge backwards and with the swell it caused and the car would surely slide off the log dock, taking everyone with it.

"Heave!" the general shouted, "Heave!" But the car seemed to stand still, slowly losing ground, the spinning wheels churning up foam. Then the Indian, Tomás, got his back flat up against the rear spare tire and bracing his feet on the prow of the boat straightened his legs. At last they moved, gradually the tires gripped, and the car accelerated ahead—fishtailing and bumping off the log dock on to the bank where it dropped with a whomping sound.

In the wheelhouse Cochrane said in English to a pilot who understood none, "Crazy—just crazy. They got it ashore—but there is no way in the world they will get that automobile back on board."

The general looked at his watch and shouted up to the captain. "Give us three hours—we'll be back at zero-four-hundred—before dawn."

"I'll tell you this fairly, sir," Cochrane shouted back, "if my boat is fired upon at any time I shall immediately make steam and leave the area."

"When I see the consul's daughter, I will give her your news!" And the general turned back to the others. They stood around the car hands on knees getting their breath—except for the doctor who seated himself on the running board examining his wet shoes.

"Will you look at these? I bought them in Berlin in twenty-eight—they were advertised as dancing pumps for fairy feet."

"Do you suppose we were heard?" the consul said, doing his best to keep the car on a low idle, the pop of exhaust echoing across the water.

"No doubt," the general answered. "The map doesn't show any company housing—but there must be locals about."

"Rama Indians, sir," Magnusson added, "But I don't think they'd run a mile to the Sando camp to tell them we arrived."

"That's true," the consul said. "There're not many Rama left—they were hunted out. At this point they must be wary of any soldiers."

"Well, soldiers are rarely popular in anyone's home town." The general spread the map on the car hood, the music boy again holding the flashlight. "Do we understand the action? We move with the automobile to the closest point possible to their camp. Lieutenant Magnusson will scout ahead and endeavor to locate Miss Kelly. When he does . . ." He held up a brass flare gun taken from the *Banana Queen*, ". . . he will signal us and we will charge in with the Packard, creating a diversion. Hopefully he will be able to bring her out and join up." They all looked at Magnusson and he knew exactly what they were thinking. He was going to pay the price of fame: Here was a man who had bluffed his way into a notorious bandit's very campfire, shot the man, and brought the body out through hundreds of his fantastic followers. Still, he'd five years in Haiti to bone up on the language and bluff the locals.

"I have to tell you sir, my Nicaraguan is not perfected. If I ask these local people questions they will know I'm not one of them."

There was a silence and the consul said, "Take Tomás with you—they will accept him and he can ask around."

"Are you volunteering him, sir?" he said, smiling.

"Yes."

The general laughed. "Sounds like the way we do it in the Corps. All right! Let's go." And they piled in the car and pulled away. The path they traveled contained iron tracks for a donkey truck used to haul out logs. It was overhung with low branches that created a tunnel effect, flapping against car and riders. Moving parallel with the river they went nearly a mile, then coming around a curve, the few lights of the town came in view. Ahead was a clearing that stretched down to the river dock. The manager's house was set back on a slight rise boxed in on three sides by the buildings of the mill. The open space facing them was the camping grounds of the Sandinistas and their fires could be seen smoldering. "Looks as thought they're bivouacked around the main house as per Mr. Elcon." The assistant manager had come up with the intelligence gathered from the returning mill personnel.

"Look out!" Magnusson said, and, reaching across the startled music boy, shoved the wheel over. They bumped off the tracks and stopped in thick brush, the car stalling out. At the end of the treeline where the tracks of the donkey train curved off into the head-rig house, two figures could be seen crossing the path.

"Women!" the consul said, under his breath.

"Judging from the hat, one is a Mex."

After the riveting scream from the house above her head, Kate had no trouble staying awake. No one else paid it any attention and with all the noisy carousing going on in the camp no one had probably heard it. She was handed a plate of some kind of bean mess and a stack of tortillas. As hungry as she was she couldn't eat it. Captain Sangre examined her wooden plate, shrugged, and threw the beans back in the pot. "How did you get so fat anyway? Hey, you better keep those tortillas to wipe you ass on, kid. They got no paper in this fockin' place." Then she flopped down, put her back against the pole, and uncorking a bottle of wine, took a deep drag. When Chula, the young cook with the greasy hair finished cleaning up, she cuddled next to her and they shared the bottle, looking across at Kate.

"What did you want to get mixed up with this bunch for?" Captain Sangre asked her.

"I had no choice—they kidnapped me."

"What? Come on!" she laughed, "Hear that Chula? They're

kidnapping fat girls now! Hey, Sandino told me you were a new recruit for his army."

"That's a lie! I wouldn't be in any army who had a little shrimp like that for a leader."

Sangre thought this was very funny and laughed a long time over it, repeating it in Spanish to Chula. Then they settled back to their drinking and conversation dropped off. Several times soldiers came over and, squatting down, whispered in Sangre's ear, gesturing at Kate. This made her very uneasy and when one leaned down and quickly tapped her head she jumped back and swung at his. Sangre grabbed his crotch and twisted. He howled in pain and, she shouted *"Pendejo!"* after him as he hobbled away.

"God damn it! I'm sick of this fockin' around!" Getting up she searched through the pile of gear and sailed a ragged straw hat at Kate. "Put this on! But first tie up the hair or I'm going to cut it off!"

*"They're not going to rape me!"* Kate shouted.

"Rape? Hell no, it's that red hair—they want to touch it for luck . . . but who knows with these horny hombres—maybe that is next." She drew a pair of loose, pajamalike pants from the pile. "Here put these on and hide that fat ass."

The pants were spotted and wrinkled but Kate took them gladly. Turning around she pulled them up and shoved the chemise inside. Then, tying up her hair with a thong, she pulled the hat down. *Now I look like all the rest of them*, she thought.

Pedrón Altamirano caught Karen on the stairs to the second floor. But trying to hold her with one hand and get his gun belt and pants down with the other was tricky, and she got away. Running up the steps and into the bedroom she slammed the heavy door, throwing the bolt.

Wills and Sandino sat at the dining-room table drinking wine and listening to Pedrón pound on the door. There was the tension between them that sex always introduced. "Tell me,"

Sandino said, "why is it that a woman who takes hundreds of men to her bed for money will suddenly behave as a vestal virgin?"

"Women are odd, I suppose even whores like to believe they have a choice when it comes right down to it. Some even believe they have rights," Wills said, smiling.

"Spare me. When a whore takes up that life she gives away any rights. There are only good women or bad."

Wills thought this odd moralizing coming from Sandino. He knew for a fact that he had a mistress, Teresa Villatoro. When she had been hit by shrapnel and a small piece of her skull removed during surgery, Sandino had this bone fragment mounted in a ring of San Albino gold and wore it faithfully. So much for taste.

Sandino smiled. "Why this sudden concern over women? Are you their crusader? Do you have a wife or sweetheart waiting to be defended?" He knew the answer to this.

Wills caught the inflection and stiffened. "I am not their defender, or their abuser. Does that make me a *maricon*?"

Sandino twisted the bottle, spinning its bottom on the table and began to speak in a formal way that made Wills instantly regret taking offense. "In Granada when I was a young student I had a friend, Mario, I thought highly of. We were inseparable. Then one day at a local place I heard another person I knew make a joke of our friendship using that word you just spoke. I went home and got two guns from my father's case—I was afraid this person would not be armed. At that local place I cocked the guns and gave one to him, asking him to repeat what he had said in front of the others. This fellow went very pale, laughing and saying it was nothing—a little joke, not to make a thing of it, forget it. But no, I couldn't do that because I knew he meant it. He was jealous and thought to insult me. 'Come outside,' I said, 'or be shot here.'

"So we went outside on the street and he pleaded, saying we were old friends, that our families were close—that we had known each other all our lives—we were brothers. I told him I would count to three and fire, and he better do likewise. He began to cry, saying he would not shoot a friend and held the gun at his side. I counted to three and shot him. Several times I believe." He unstopped the bottle and poured off a glass.

Ah *maricon*, Wills thought *the love that dare not speak its name in downtown Granada*. He had heard other versions of this duel, but was touched that Sandino had made this one up so that he wouldn't feel insulted. He was a sensitive friend.

Upstairs Karen Sven sat on the bed shaking. The hammering on the door continued and she knew that although barred, it would only be a matter of time before he . . . and all the others got in. Coming to Jungleland had been a terrible mistake.

She had met Mr. Denver at the parlor house on Basin Street. He was a big, good-looking man who wanted straight missionary style, no whip work—*le vice Anglais* as they called it. He was there three times a week and had a sad story. Working for a big lumber company in Central America, his wife had contacted a terrible fever. She nearly died and was recuperating in a sanitarium at Westwego nearby where he visited her once a year on leave. He was very lonely and offered Karen a good deal of money to come down to the lumber town with him for a few months. He painted a tropical paradise—exotic birds, orchids, moonlit rivers. Bored, she said yes. Fool, Nell said.

At sixteen Karen was in the Storyville section of New Orleans working for an old madam named Nell Kimball. She got a job there first as a maid after being put off a train on the way to Galveston in the company of a known gambler. He gave her Nell's address and nothing else before deserting her.

Nell did not push her into the life. Quite the opposite; good maids were harder to find than whores. But Karen could not fail to see the money that passed hands and the lazy luxury the girls lived in. Having sex with strangers seemed no less unpleasant than emptying slop jars and washing out the monthly rags the girls threw under the beds. There was Venice glass over old-fashioned gas jets, lots of red velvet drapes, and good food cooked "Jim Brady" style as Nell called it. The wine came in dirty bottles with the right labels and the girls slept till noon. Finally Nell took Karen on, she said, because the whores were getting skinnier. Due to the times, they wanted Kellerman types she wouldn't have used used as rat bait in the old days. She could use a featherbed girl, one with some bulges, knobs the boys could get a grip on.

Karen had been at the manager's house in Rama a month when he went up to Bluefields with others to meet a famous general. The day after he left the rebels attacked. She rushed to the banana-boat dock, packed and ready to be evacuated with the other refugees. But the damn religious madman of a captain barred her way, saying he could take no whores on his boat. Humiliated, she was left at the dock—trapped.

She got up from the bed and began to dress, picking out sturdy clothes—a whipcord jacket and skirt, lace-up boots and a tie-down hat. Then taking only essentials, jewelry, and money, she placed them in a game bag. The bag, like the clothes, had been bought for hunting. She had never hunted before in her life but it was something Mr. Denver liked to do and she was glad now he had insisted on buying the clothes and teaching her the rudiments of shooting. From the back of the closet she took out a 12-gauge pump shotgun, a light seven-pound Remington he said was just right for her. She loaded it with five shells, put on the safety, and laid it along with a bandolier of other shells on the bed. Cracking open the shutter she looked out at the campfires of the soldiers. Later, when the men slept she would get away. At the river an Indian could be paid to paddle her downstream to safety. If anyone tried to stop her she would shoot.

About midnight Kate began having stomach cramps. She hadn't eaten and knew it was from all the river water she had swallowed. "*Sangre*! I have to go to the bathroom!"

"What . . . ?" The captain slept in the corner with the cook in a messy pile of bedding.

"*Now!*"

"God damn it!" When she got up, Kate was embarrassed to see she wore only a shirt and the girl, Chula, nothing.

"What you think I'm kid nurse?" But she pulled on a skirt and boots, untying a rope she'd put on Kate's ankle. "Around here you got to learn to hold it."

"I can't! Hurry!" Grumbling, Sangre took the carbine and a short-handled shovel, pushing Kate ahead of her.

"Come on then before you fill those pants of mine." They went across the campsite passing sleeping men to a place just beyond the campfires. Sangre handed her the shovel.

"Out here in the open?" Kate was shocked.

Sangre laughed. "What'd you think? We got a big toilet with a pull chain?"

"I'm not going here in front of everybody!"

"*Jesus!*" She slapped her side in exasperation. "I thought you had to shit now! Come on then! *Jesus!*" They moved toward the edge of the trees crossing the donkey path.

Magnusson waited until the distant silhouettes of the two women moved on, then he quietly got out of the Packard, handing his rifle to the general in the backseat. He hated to leave it and depend on just his service automatic, but if the girl was injured or unable to walk he might need both arms and the fireman's carry. The general passed over the flaregun. "We'll wait for your signal. Good luck." Magnusson wished he wouldn't talk so loud.

The others looked at him, weapons ready, and he wondered if they were thinking the same thing: what chance had six men to break into an armed camp of a hundred to rescue a girl of whose exact location they had no idea? Surprise, the general said, was their only real weapon. He'd heard that before. These Sandos were not untrained troops: They had fought a successful guerrilla campaign for five years.

He tucked the flaregun in his belt, put on the Indian's Nicaraguan rain cape, and replaced his campaign hat with a straw one. He gestured at Tomás to follow and tapped his automatic. The Indian raised his shirt, showing a large nasty knife at his belt. At least he wasn't a pacifist. Moving on the path to the edge of the tree line they stopped and, hunkering down, looked across the clearing to where the Sandos camped around the house. There were other mill buildings crowding it— Magnusson recognized the familiar domed shape of the head-rig house and could see long open sheds with the dark shapes of machine planers and edgers. To reach the house—and he believed this must be where the girl was—he could approach from the back, keeping to these buildings until the last minute. He tapped Tomás on the back and the Indian moved into the clearing while he waited.

Walking in a submissive slouch, Tomás went past the sleepers and toward a fire blazing near the front of the house where men could be seen drinking by its light. Others shuffled around the camp—women, a man making water against a fire— and no one paid him any mind. There were coughs, snores, and a distant laugh.

At a respectful distance from the drinkers at the fire he sat down. When they looked over he took out a few wrinkled *cordobas* the consul had given him and laid them on the ground. One shook the bottle, Tomàs nodded, and it was passed over, the money gathered in. They went on with their conversation, ignoring him. He had a hard time with their mountain accents but understood they were sentries, that was why they were awake. They talked of ordinary things, sharing the bottle, until another man came down from the house carrying a long rifle. Handing it over to his relief, he began to tell an amazing story. Through the window he had seen one of their chiefs chase a naked white woman up the stairs! When they doubted this he went into details, saying her skin was as bleached as cotton with hair only a white woman would have. She had locked herself in the bedroom upstairs and right now the colonel beat on her door.

And if they didn't believe him listen! And it was true, they could hear a distant sound of pounding.

When Pedrón Altamirano grew tired of beating on the door, then kicking it, he went down the stairs and past Wills and Sandino still sitting at the dining-room table. They looked at each other as he disappeared into the kitchen, then returned with the long iron bar used to move the stove. He went past them without a word and up the stairs. At the door he jammed the end of the bar next to the jamb and began to pry.

Inside Karen heard the sounds of the door being forced. Putting on the bandolier of shells, she picked up the pump shotgun. When the door frame began to shatter she took off the safety and aimed at that spot.

Magnusson listened to Tomás's halting story in Spanish and found it hard to believe they could be lucky enough to find the girl right off. He was a seasoned pessimist and was suspicious when things went right. Nevertheless, he sent him back to the car to tell the others and began to flank the house via the buildings. The look and smell of the lumber mill brought back his logging days in Oregon—and just for a second he thought about cutting Uncle Arnie's hand off.

Moving from building to building he made it to a small stable about fifty feet from the house. Should he dash or stroll across that open space exposed to the camp? The stroll was less suspicious but—the difficulty was resisting the impulse to run. But he did, and reaching the back stairs, went up wondering how he would locate her exact room.

The bedroom door remained solid but the jamb shattered near the lock and when the end of the bar wiggled in Karen fired. The heavy door withstood the shotgun blast but pellets exiting through the crack Pedrón had opened stung his arm, and he jumped back with a startled grunt. Then he reached for his belt gun. The sound of the shotgun had given Magnusson direction, and at that instant he kicked the full-length shutter open and shoved his service automatic into the room. Startled, Karen swung around from the door, leveling the shotgun.

*"Don't shoot!"* Magnusson shouted.

"What?" She was puzzled by his odd appearance; the Nordic features and *campesino* clothes.

"Lieutenant Magnusson, U.S. Marines—excuse me, ma'am," he said, looking around the room, "do you know the whereabouts of a Miss Kelly, the American cousul's daughter?"

"Who?"

"She's a redheaded girl about thirteen—fat."

"There's no one here like that—what accent is that?"

"Swedish—are you sure? We . . ."

"Thank God! I'm Norwegian!"

Pedrón unlimbered the large handgun and began firing through the door. The thick wood slowed the slugs down but they tore long splinters out before running out of spin.

"I think we should get shut of this place, Miss." Magnusson said, directing her toward the window, then drawing his own automatic, and firing several rounds through the door for effect.

At the sound of shots Wills and Sandino ran up the stairs. The sentry came through the front door and Sandino waved him off.

"Back to your post! We'll take care of this."

"It seems the manager's whore is defending her rights," Wills said.

"I'm impressed," Sandino answered. Ahead, Altamirano stood to one side of the door as return fire came through, slapping up against the opposite wall. "Pedrón! Don't you think this is an excess of seduction?"

"The bitch is shooting at me! First with a shotgun, now with a pistol!"

Outside the window on the second-story veranda, Magnusson paused, and holstering the automatic, took the flare gun out of his belt. "You've come just in the right moment!" Karen said, panting with excitement.

"We're here for the consul's daughter . . ." Leaning out

over the rail, he pointed the brass flare pistol up. "You haven't heard of her kidnapping?"

Puzzled, "No, they—Sandino just came back today. It wasn't mentioned."

"You know Sandino?"

"I was held here against my will . . . I'm a . . . friend of the manager."

"Oh." He fired the flare.

The camp had begun to stir, hearing the firing from the house, and when the red flare went up, exploding in a star burst over the mill they were stunned. If General Butler wanted surprise he got it. Seeing the arc of unexpected fireworks overhead in the middle of the night was a real eye-opener.

The rescue party saw the flare from the donkey path. The Packard had been started and moved up to the end of the tree line, pointing toward the approach to the camp and house. Minutes earlier Tomás had loped up and told them the girl was discovered. He was now standing on the rear bumper and hanging on the spare to be clear of the field of fire. Weapons were ready. *"Load!"* The general commanded and there was a variety of odd caliber clicks. *"Forward!"* And the consul let the clutch out, sending up a shower of gravel.

The doctor, unable to resist, shouted, *"Charge!"* And they did, roaring forward, headlights and spotlight on, the powerful car winding out in the gears straight toward the enemy. Standing in the front seat, legs braced, the music boy leaned over the windshield and fired in the Thompson submachine gun; spraying the ground ahead, the bright copper jackets hopping up and over his shoulder. In the rear seat, Doctor Bruder emptied the double-barrelled shotgun, then the Luger, firing out one side while the general fired Magnusson's Springfield out the other. The noise was horrific, with everyone shouting at the top of their lungs; Irish and German battlecries, rebel yells—and from the Indian hanging on the back, a Miskito *zagareet*.

The startled Sandinistas scrambled up, tumbling over each

other to get out of the car's path. There were shouts, confusion, and the panic of the unexpected—a motorcar, lights full on, guns blazing, driven into the center of a sleeping camp. But they were quick to recover. Ambush was a jungle game they understood and return shots were heard. But to shoot at the car meant shooting into their own people, and the crossfire was wicked, causing more damage than the attackers. On the deck of the second floor veranda, Sandino, Wills, and Pedrón lay flat out watching the car plow through the camp, skid, turn, and running parallel to the house, blow out the windows and shred the drapes. Next to Wills's ear, Pedrón pulled the trigger of his big pistol. Fortunately the gun was empty and produced only clicks. Below them a man dashed out from the house towing Karen Sven.

*"There he is!"* the consul shouted as Magnusson came up in the headlights followed by a strange woman with a shotgun. He slowed and they jumped to the running board. *"Where's Kate?!"*

*"Not here,"* Magnusson said. Gritting his teeth, the consul swung the wheel over and they slid around in a U-turn, heading back toward the donkey path.

On the veranda, Sandino stood up watching the car escape across the clearing unhit, then turn into the tunnel of trees that marked the entrance to the donkey path. As always he was cool in action. "Pedrón, get down there and stop our people before they all kill each other. Then move out after that automobile!"

"Where could a car like that come from?"

"From the river—there's no road—they must have brought in by boat. *Get going!*"

"The *Banana Queen,*" Wills said.

"Yes."

"There may be other troops."

"No, they would have used them instead of these few mad men."

"That's the same Packard that chased us at United Fruit."

"I think so."

Two hundred feet from the donkey path, Captain Sangre

had sat dozing while Kate suffered diarrhea in the bushes. As the captain nodded off she thought she heard a car motor idling—a ticking of valves—but knew this was impossible. Then, there was the scream of an engine, exhaust booming, and Sangre's head came up as a big car, lights on, guns firing, drove straight into the camp. She lay flat, carbine cocked, listening to the car's noisy passage, the scattered return fire—saw it slow by the house, then turn, going full blast. Keeping low she ran to the brush at the side of the donkey path and got into position. Seconds later the car came past her in a flash of headlights, people on the running board, a man clinging to the back. She rolled over onto the path, brought the carbine up, and fired, jacking the next shell in.

The shot hit Tomás in the back just under the right shoulder blade and he fell hard to the road. *"Stop!"* Magnusson shouted and the consul locked up the brakes, sliding the car. Before it stopped he was off and running, crouching low as the next round smacked into the spare on the rear. *"Cover me!"* But General Butler was already standing straight up in the backseat, sling adjusted, firing at three-second intervals down the path.

As his shots sent up dirt, clanging off the iron rails, Sangre rolled off the path into the bushes. She saw a man run from the car bending low, then pick up the one she had hit, put him over his shoulder, and run back. She tried one more shot but had to pull back, pinned down by the accurate rifle fire from the car.

Magnusson lifted Tomás gently into the backseat between the general and the doctor and hopped on the running board next to Karen. The car moved off more slowly now, as Dr. Bruder sorted through his medical bag. "The bullet's gone clear through his chest," he said, pressing a bandage against the ugly wound, where bloody foam bubbled up at Tomás's each breath.

The consul was sick with disappointment. They had failed to rescue Kate, and Tomás was badly wounded. He would have to go back and tell this to Norma and Hilaria. In the end, if Kate survived, it would probably come down to humiliating negotiations and ransom.

He remembered thinking that the trip to attack went very quickly, while returning it seemed to take forever. At last the trees began to thin and there was the clearing with the stacked logs of the "cold deck." Then the river came in view as well as the floating log dock. The consul hit the brakes without putting the car in neutral and it shuddered to a stop, stalling out. The *Banana Queen* was not there.

They sat in silence, the only sounds the raspy breathing of the wounded man, and from a distance the shouts of men moving up the donkey path after them.

## SIX

# Walker Track

"*HELEETE ockfå!*" Magnusson said aloud in Swedish.

"I agree," General Butler added, standing in the rear of the car.

"How could Captain Cochrane leave us, General?" The music boy wanted to know, near tears.

"Well, he has his rules, priorities, and . . ."

"No balls," the doctor said, holding a compress to the Indian's wound.

"Exactly."

"What's the matter?" Karen looked from face to face, seeing frustration and anger. She believed she was saved and in the hands of the U.S. Marines.

The general turned to her, smiling. "The steamboat was to have waited here for us—have we met?"

"Ah—I'm Karen Sven . . . a friend of Mr. Denver—the

manager." She stepped off the running board and the general got out of the backseat.

"You're Swedish?"

"Norwegian." She looked at Magnusson who was listening to the sounds of pursuit from the donkey path.

"Delightful accent. Tell me, Miss Sven, you saw nothing of Mr. Kelly's young daughter?" he said, indicating the consul.

"No, no—I told this officer, Sandino had just returned and there was no mention of a white girl."

"Sir . . ." Magnusson said.

"I know, we haven't much time. Get out the map." He paused, "I assume none of you want to wait here and give yourselves over to these people—I doubt if you could expect much in the way of accommodation after our drive through town." There was silence. "All right! Lieutenant, take the music boy and dispute that path until we get coordinated."

"*Aye aye!*" He shucked the rail cape and limp straw, adjusting his campaign hat to the right, hard angle. "Music! Bring the Thompson and drums!" And he jogged off with his rifle, the music boy lugging the heavy gun and sack of drums. Karen looked after Magnusson, thinking: *could there be anything more thrilling than the fair Viking warrior burning with the ambition to kill something?*

The map was spread on the ground and the consul held the flashlight while General Butler ran his finger along the line of their position. "There are certainly no roads to speak of—what's this?" he said, tapping a dotted line.

"A logging road," the consul said, "what they used to call the Walker Track. It's a rough trail now used to pull the logs out of the basin by oxen."

"The connection is right here." He raised his head to look at a gap in the stacked logs where a trail was visible as it cut into the woods.

"Yes, but full of stumps and holes, impossible to drive over in a car. During Walker's time they tried to lay down a rail bed through to Bluefields to bypass the river, but today the only thing that can make it are oxen or very stubborn mules."

"Sounds like us."

"Not *us*—if you don't mind—we'll remain," the doctor said. "Give me a hand and we'll lay Tomás on the level ground." They did this, putting him down and covering him with his rain cape. "There is no way this man could survive the trail you describe."

"Will he survive Sandino?" the general asked.

"Probably not, but it's the only chance he's got."

"You could leave him. No one would blame you, he's not a white man."

"No."

The general didn't argue. "Very well."

"Wait a minute," the consul said, "are you sure you want to do this? The Sandinistas have a reputation for shooting prisoners."

"They wouldn't dare. I'm a German national and a doctor. After that mess we created back there they will have need of me . . . oh." He took his Luger out and handed it to the consul. "You'd better take this or they'll get the idea I'm belligerent."

As Magnusson and the music boy entered the tunnel of trees that canopied the donkey path, the moonlight faded. "How many drums?"

"Three left, sir, I did a hundred rounds on the Sandos."

"One of them includes tracers. There should be a tape on the bottom noting this."

"I can't make it out in this light, sir."

"Feel for it!"

"Well, yes, this one seems to have a sticker on it."

"Load it." There was a stumbling pause, a fumble of drums, and the solid clack as it was fitted. "Do you know that any one of those sounds would get you killed instantly in a real war?"

"Isn't this a real war?"

"This is an exercise. Now—get over on the other side of the road and wait. When I signal, fire a five-second burst waist high, then fall back fifty yards."

"How will I know fifty yards, sir?"

"When you hear them shooting back."

"Oh." He crossed the path, laying down in the ditch beside it.

*May God protect me from the VD and tooters*, Magnusson thought. Ahead he could hear the advance party of Sandos. They were coming at a trot straight up the path rather than by slow infiltration of the dense woods at each side. Shame on them. He signaled the music boy and there was a maddening pause while he noisily pulled back the bolt and fumbled the safety off. Finally he fired. Every third shot was a tracer and its bright flash stitched a line down the center of the road illuminating figures in an eerie strobe-light effect. Magnusson fired at the images, knowing that the chances of hits were slight but better than finding a target in the dark. The flash and noise of the submachine was vivid, then suddenly broke off.

The music boy got up and ran. True to Magnusson's word, return fire began at about fifty yards and they both dove into the ditch breathing hard. "What now, sir?" the music boy asked.

"They will infiltrate the woods and attempt to flank us."

"What will we do sir?"

"If we don't talk, we may hear them before they're on us." After that conversation dropped off.

Captain Sangre and Kate walked back to the camp. The captain was jubilant. "By sweet Jesus I got one! I saw him fall! That son of a bitch is fockin' finished!" Kate, weak and exhausted after the bout with diarrhea could not understand what had happened. There was gunfire, the roar of a car, and when she crawled out of the bushes, it was over. Now as they came into the camp she saw the wounded cared for by women. There were bloody rags, screams of pain, and bodies laid out, waxen. For the first time she broke down and began to sob.

Sangre put an arm around her. "Hey, come on kid, don't do that—this is war—what do think, somebody is not going to get hurt?" Kate was appalled. *Had this happened because of her?* She had never seen wounded and dead before and the reality profoundly shocked her. She had no way of knowing that most of the casualties and all the fatalities had come from their own gunfire.

Chula appeared, dodging through the confusion and Sangre turned as she threw her arms around her. *"Gracias a dios que estas bien!"*

"Come on, cut it out!" Sangre said, unwinding her arms, but pleased. "If we're not careful these people will think we're fockin' homos or something!" They burst into laughter. Kate saw Sandino and Wills standing in front of the house talking to several men and she turned in that direction. Sangre hauled her roughly back. "Hey! Come on! Don't try that escaping shit again!"

Sandino listened to the runner. What was left of the company had made contact with the Yankees on the donkey path. Firing was heard and Pedrón Altamirano would press ahead. The survey boat had been sent around the bend and reported no steamboat visible.

"Then how did they get that car up here?" Wills asked.

"There is the Walker Track," Sandino answered, "I took it myself in twenty-eight after the raid on Chilamate. But I can't believe a motorcar would make it through." He waved his hand. "Enough speculation. We've got to quit this country." He had been frustrated in announcing to the world his recruiting of the American consul's daughter into the ranks of the revolution. Overzealous *campesinos* had cut the telegraph lines and no one was capable of putting them together again. Whatever the size of the force attacking them now, a large one would be arriving in days or even hours. "It's time to get back to the North and reform. Are you joining us, Carlton?"

"What about the wounded?"

"We will take ours as always. But these locals, Indians, and Caribs will want to stay here with their families. When the *guardia* get here they'll have medical people." Both men knew the *guardia* had the reputation for shooting prisoners, wounded or otherwise. Their medical solution was euthanasia.

When Magnusson and the music boy loped into the clearing they found the Packard started and waiting. Behind, firing could be heard from the donkey path after a final ambush. The general was in the backseat with the Norwegian and they both slid in front next to the consul who immediately put the car in gear and moved off. Magnusson saw the doctor wave, settling in beside the Indian.

"He's opted to stay with his patient," the general said. "We've found a trail that may take us out of here and back to Bluefields. That's it I believe Dick." And the consul proceeded cautiously, putting the big wheels on the beginning of the Walker Track.

William Walker was an American adventurer from Tennessee who had been brought into Nicaragua in 1856 by a revolutionary faction and at first supported by Cornelius Vanderbilt's Accessory Transit Company. His military successes made him president of the country, and one of the shaky schemes he became involved in was a proposed rail line that would parallel the river and open up the interior. By the time he had been deposed (he reintroduced slavery in 1857) and executed in Honduras in 1860, the money had run out and only a crude trail had been cut where the road bed was to be.

It was as advertised. A deep groove gouged up the center from hauling logs, matched by depressions on each side from hooves of the oxen team who did the hauling. Boxed in by tree stumps, it was impossible to turn around once committed. Added to that were rocks, holes, sandy stretches, and several washouts. The rescue party had lurched and bumped less than a mile when the rear tire blew. The music boy looked over the side of the car at the flopping flat. "Holy moly! How long will that take to fix?"

"Just as long as it takes you to do it," Magnusson replied.

Pedrón Altamirano came cautiously into the clearing at the head of his depleted company. The first thing he saw was a man in a white dinner jacket smoking a cigar. He was actually waving at him. When he got closer he saw another man on the ground.

"I'm Dr. Hinrik Bruder," the standing man said in a no-nonsense professional voice. "This man is badly wounded and needs immediate aid." When Pedrón kept staring he went on, "I am a German national and a neutral—now please have two men make up a sling so that we may carry him to cover."

Pedrón looked down at the Indian and back at the doctor. "What?"

This time the doctor was stern. "The man needs help!"

Pedrón leaned over the Indian and saw his eyes flick back at him. "You're right." And placing the barrel of his pistol between Tomás's eyes, he pulled the trigger. There was a muffled *whomp* and the Indian's head jumped several inches off the ground.

"*By God!*" the doctor let out, taking a step back. Turning, Pedrón shot him in the face. He'd meant to hit the fat cigar but the man moved and the bullet entered his cheekbone. He went down clutching the wound, feet frailing. Stepping over him, Pedrón shot him twice more in the left lapel of his dinner jacket. "Jesus!" he said laughing, "Look at those fucking shoes.!"

A scout came back and reported finding tire marks leading up the logging trail. Pedrón knew the Walker Track from the escape he and Sandino had made in 1928. He also knew it wouldn't take long before the motorcar was bogged down and they would catch up.

On the morning of the second day Captain Edd thought they were on schedule. The column had moved with the speed of the oxen and that was ten miles a day, twelve in some stretches. They should be within striking distance of Rama this afternoon. He was having coffee with the Marine officer and gunnery sergeant around a damp fire, as a gray dawn filtered through treetops. It was raining and they sat silently, listening to the men grouse as they turned to. Clothes hung out to dry from yesterday's march were soaked and many men had blisters.

"Damn!" Corporal Wiener said to a young mortar man, "You told me your friggin' shoes fit! What do I have to do for you people, fit 'em myself! A blister on a man's foot comes right back to the platoon leader! If you straggle, you dumb bastard, the friggin' Sandos will chop both feet off; then, by God, you can bitch about blisters on your stumps!"

"What the hell are we doin' here anyway?" the company intellectual said, water streaming off his hat to a faulty poncho, "Do you read the papers? This guy Sandino is some kind of a hero according to *The New York Times*. We're the oppressors— us! State Department troops sent down here to harass patriots."

"They got the hairy-ass part right. What kind of a lousy war is it where you walk around in a bunch of God damn wet bushes? The place smells so foul a good fart is a treat."

"Who said it was a war, dickhead? France was a war, with swell roads you could ride on, and if you got your ass shot off, at least it was another white man doin' it!"

The sergeant stood up. "Excuse me sir, I'll get these sea lawyers under way." And he broke into their discussion. "All right, you people get your gear together and police the area! First platoon fall in behind the Guardeeah and knock off the shit about why you're here! What difference does it make? You're here, ain't you?"

Listening, Edd related to the puzzling question. He had wondered many times why he was there. But the sergeant's reply was the right one, and deep thinking in the ranks only led to drinking. Lieutenant Delware was obviously embarrassed that his

men proved less than enthusiastic about motivation. As they got
up he asked, "Any chance we'll make contact with the rebels
today, sir?"

"Possibly, if they've got their lines out."

"Some action might raise the men's spirits."

"Maybe we'll get lucky," he answered, hardly concealing his
sarcasm.

Captain Edd went ahead of the advanced column of his
*guardia* on the point. This was against the rule books, but he
personally had to know what was happening first. At his side
several machete men cautiously walked the edge of the trail.
They would chop into the bush in the event of an ambush. The
narrow trail through the matted jungle was made for ambush.
There was no way to secure flanks and actually, the advance
guard *expected* to be ambushed; that's why they were out in front
in the first place.

A weapons squad of Marines was next in formation and
behind them at two hundred yards was the first platoon. Bringing
up the rear was the ox train flanked by the second platoon, acting
as train guard and reserve. Edd followed the 2nd Bridgade's
standard practice of meeting ambush with overwhelming automatic weapon fire. They had the edge there and approaching any
suspicious slope or turn in the trail he intended to call up mortars
and blast away. God help the innocent who happened to be in
range.

The music boy changed the rear flat with difficulty. While
Magnusson ran back down the Walker Track to provide a rear
guard, the music boy and the consul jacked the car and removed
the spare from the right fender. The lug wrench kept slipping but
they managed to get the big red wheel and tire off, flopping it
aside. The rain didn't help.

In the backseat, General Butler held an umbrella over
Karen Sven. "Are you anywhere near Vendel, Miss Sven?"

"What?"

"It's in the East-Swedish province of Uppland, I believe."

"No, no, I'm from Norway—Oslo—right in the city . . ." She was looking back up the track and waiting for Magnusson to reappear.

"I read in the *National Geographic* about a magnificent helmet found there—an outstanding example of Viking craftsmanship."

"Is this all the Marines?"

"I beg your pardon?"

"I thought with United States Marines there would be more."

The general laughed. "We've never had enough, but yes, this is the complement—Mr. Kelly, of course, is with the State Department."

"But is that all to fight against Sandino?"

"For the moment," he said, smiling. "There was no time to put together a proper unit. We hoped to catch up with him before he reached his troops."

"But we *are* going to get away—they won't catch up to us will they?"

"No, of course not." He smiled reassuringly.

The tire was changed and the jack wound down. "Shall I put the wheel back in the side mount, Mr. Kelly?"

"No, no!—Let's go!" And jumping in the car, he laid on the horn. The music boy flopped the flat and wheel out of the way and went around the front to crank. A minute later Magnusson jogged back.

"Any sign of hostiles?" the general asked.

"Not visually . . . but I heard them coming up . . . at about two hundred yards."

"That close?"

The music boy cranked the car over, jumping back from the evil crank in the nick of time and climbed aboard next to Magnusson. They went slowly with the rain adding to the difficulties. The grooves cut in the track by the ox cart proved too wide for the Packard wheels and the ones made by the oxen too narrow. As a result they slid back and forth between the two, fighting to move ahead. Lugging the car in low gear caused the engine to heat up and the rain pelting the hood turned into steam. The consul could see the Motor-Meter on the radiator cap climbing to the red mark.

"We're going to have to stop and put in some water!" he shouted, "If it goes dry and the engine seizes up the car's finished."

He stopped again and the music boy hopped out, ran around to the front and flipping the cap up with his bandanna, stood back while the steam geysered.

"I always wanted to visit the Drottningholm Court Theater," the general said to Karen, "I understand all the original eighteenth-century stage machinery is still in working order. I've had an ongoing interest in the drama," he paused, laughing, "but then my critics have called me an actor."

"Why are we stopping?" Karen asked, looking behind them.

The music boy unhooked one of the water bags from the headlamp and poured it slowly in the radiator as he'd been taught by his father who had a Model-A Ford truck. "I hope this cold water doesn't crack the cylinder head."

"So do I," the consul answered. "Come on! That's enough!" Replacing the bag and clicking back the cap he got in, and they started off again.

Two of Pedrón's scouts running ahead on the point saw the rear of the car as it disappeared around a bend in the track. Both raised their long rifles, and stopping to brace, fired.

"You were close on the distance, Lieutenant," the general said as the shots sang by, "but I'd say they're less than a hundred yards now." The car came up a slight rise and the consul increased the speed. Then ahead, he saw a large tree stump directly in the middle of the track. It had been cut off at about eighteen inches from the ground. Carts would pass over easily and the oxen could go around it, but would the Packard clear it? The consul felt he had no choice and went ahead. In the next instant there was a jarring stop and they were thrown forward as the oil pan sounded its distress and hung up on the stump.

Captain Edd heard the distant shots and held his hand up. When there were no more he pondered. The shots were too far away to have been fired at them . . . then at whom? A hunter? Possible. A distress signal? Doubtful. He called over a runner he'd trained up. "Captain's compliments to Mr. Delware, and will he send up one mortar?"

The runner repeated it as he'd been taught to. "Capitáns compleemeents to meester Deelware and weel he send up *uno* morteer?"

"Go!" Edd slapped him on the back and the kid ran off flat out. If he had a few more like that, Edd thought, he could make up a squad.

There was no time to try and lever the car off the stump or assess the damage—there was no time for anything now but to stand—or rather lay and fight. They piled out of the stricken car with General Butler opening the rear door politely for Karen Sven. "Miss Sven, I suggest you lie under the car for the time being. Perhaps you might avail me of the pump gun. If we can get the dogs to come close enough it will be handy."

Numb with fear, Karen crawled beneath the car and put her arms over her head. The music boy got behind the right rear wheel, laying out the last two drums for the Thompson on top of the sack. The consul was instructed to lie under the front of the car (next to Miss Sven) and direct his double-barreled shotgun up the road. Magnusson had fired two accurate rounds from his Springfield and driven the scouts back. He knelt now by the left rear wheel, adjusting the sling in the way a violinist must keep tuning between selections.

The general strode up and down beside the car, shotgun

under one arm, walking stick in the other hand. "These fellows won't be foolish enough to come straight down that road. No, they'll flank us at about a forty-five degree angle for maximum cross fire . . ." He pointed off to the left with his stick. ". . . about there I'd say . . . and over there . . ." indicating the right. "How many yards would you say we can expect engagement, Lieutenant?"

"Possibly as close as a hundred, sir."

"That sounds right. Music, sell those two drums dearly, no sustained bursts." The music boy was astounded the general knew how much ammo he had. He'd never seen him as much as look his way.

A sound of chopping could be heard on both sides. "That's the machete men," Magnusson said, "the Sandos can't get up on us without them—when they stop—look out!" At that moment they did, and there was scattered fire coming in high and trimming the trees on the other side of the track. "Hold your fire—they're going to move up." Another pause and renewed fire, this time slamming into the tree stumps and one round thudding into the side of the car.

"All right, Music, show them we're lively," the general said. And he let off ten rounds as instructed, causing the firing to drop off as heads ducked. "On the right Lieutenant!" and this was followed by more staggered rounds clipping the trees and winging off the metal wheels. From his position under the car, the music boy could see the general's legs pass by as he continued pacing.

"Pardon me, sir—but shouldn't you, ah, get down?"

"No I've learned better son . . . at Guantanamo during the Cuba War . . . went in there with the Eight Ohio—the president's own regiment . . ." *My God!* Magnusson thought, *he's going to tell a story!* "Our officers were Civil War veterans, men who had been at Bull Run, Antietam, Chickamauga— battles like that—some even were sharpshooters with Farragut at the capture of New Orleans . . ." The story broke off as Magnusson returned fire on the right. The consul, overanxious, swung the shotgun around and let off both barrels. The effect was lost but relieved his tension.

". . . the war was still on and my second night there, Captain Goodrell took me for a round of the pickets. He was sixty-one years old then with a bushy beard like they all had in those days and still a captain . . ."

"*On the right!*" the general suddenly shouted. And the music boy traversed the submachine gun, cutting brush horizontally. The rebels had spread out and established a skirmish line.

". . . we walked along for about a mile—it was night but with a moon that flooded the whole bush with silver—the stone and cactus seemed more real than by daylight. Every few minutes the captain would stop and point out a good place for an ambush, and I tell you I saw a Spaniard behind each palmetto. Then, zing! a bullet—the first ever shot at me—whizzed past my head with a sickening sound.

"*On the left!*" he shouted. Magnusson responded and hammered out four fast rounds resulting in a scream. A terrible sound.

". . . well I sprawled flat on the ground, panting with fright. Captain Goodrell looked down at me with his hands on his hips. 'What in hell is the matter?' he said. 'It was a bullet,' said I, and he looked at me for the callow youth I was. 'Well, what of it?' I got up shamefaced and we walked on. At last he said, 'Butler, you came to the wrong place if you didn't want to get shot at. During the Civil War every man except me in the Tenth Iowa got killed, sitting, standing or laying flat, so in the end it don't matter.' And that's been my guideline."

The firing had slacked off and Magnusson noted, "I guess they didn't have time to bring along automatic weapons." No sooner was this said than a heavy machine gun commenced, chewing up the edge of the track and sending splinters flying from the stumps.

"Hotchkiss," the general said.

\* \* \*

The mortar crew had come up and Captain Edd hunkered down with Corporal Wiener. They had moved forward several hundred yards and the firing was loud now. "Quite an exchange, sir," Wiener said.

"Yes, but by who?"

"It wouldn't pay to mortar the wrong bunch I guess."

"Here comes my intrepid scout." Sergeant Somoza panted up the track, fanning himself with his hat and collapsing beside them.

"It's a big car . . . on the . . . trail."

"Dark red?" Edd said, "With two—*dos parabrisas?*"

"*Sí*, they are attacked from both sides—company strength."

"Damn! That will be General Butler and the posse."

"I can go into battery right here, sir!" Wiener said.

"Set up! Somoza, you and Castuno get our people moving, flankers out and wait for the barrage." He tapped the runner who knelt by his side. "Compliments to Lieutenant Delware, and bring up the first platoon." The runner repeated the message and took off. Edd turned to the Marine weapons squad kneeling behind him. "Let's go! Sergeant! Deploy your section and make up a firing line on contact! Put your gun to the left of the trail!"

As they went forward Wiener got the trench mortar in action. A shell was dropped in, coughed on ignition, and was away in a steep trajectory, whistling up and arcing down to burst in the jungle. It sent up palmettos and vines, started the monkeys howling and the birds lifting off in clusters. He twisted the traversing screw and got off two more, keeping three in the air at once. They exploded in a nice pattern, ripping up the jungle. "Damn trees!" he said to the other gunners, "Takes up all the fragmentation!"

"Yeah, but we ought to be able to burn their little brown tails, Corp."

"You got that right, blisters."

When the first mortar rounds dropped, Pedrón knew his company was going to be overrun and he moved fast pulling back. Machete men whacked away in a frenzy to cut paths to the Walker Track so they could break free before the heavy weapons came up.

Julio Lopes decided to wait. It had been maddening to fire at the car and get no hits. A crazy man walked up and down on the other side of it and he had not been able to put a bullet in him. His life was charmed. Julio was an eighteen-year-old who had been with the rebels three years. A local boy from Las Perlas who had been radicalized after spending a year in prison for pissing on the altar of *Templo de San Diego*. He was considered a marksman by his fellows. At a distance he saw a squad of men run up the trail toward the car led by a big yanqui officer. This was a target he couldn't miss.

"*Marines!*" the consul shouted from under the front of the Packard. Karen Sven uncovered her head and looked up for the first time since the shooting began.

Dispersing his squad to the right, Captain edd jogged up. "You people look like you're in need of the Automobile Club."

"I just happen to have my card," the general answered. Raising up from his position at the left rear wheel, Magnusson put his hand out. Smiling, Edd reached for it and in the next instant the front of his shirt blew out. Magnusson caught him as he fell, letting him down gently to the ground. Over Edd's shoulder he had seen a puff of smoke coming from the jungle and without hesitation ran toward it. Julio saw him coming and fired again, but put off by his aggressive charge, missed, and jumping up, plunged back through the machete path. Behind him, Magnusson broke his way through the undergrowth with his rifle. Thorns tore at him and branches slapped back but he kept on. Breathing hard, Julio didn't dare look back—if he could catch up to the others they would turn his pursuer. But he had waited too long, and there was a sound that seemed to explode in his ears and he pitched forward. Magnusson came up and saw his shot had entered between the youth's shoulder blades, exactly where Edd had been hit.

When he got back to the car Edd was laid out, dead in his *guardia* rig; native-tailored breeches and cordovan leather putties. He was on his back with the big expansive face turned to one side, looking surprised but smiling. Magnusson knew it was maudlin, but he couldn't help thinking of that Buster Brown shoe store and the damn X-ray machine that let you look at the bones in your foot.

The firing up the Walker Track had been audible in Rama at the manager's house, and when Sandino heard the sound of mortars he knew time was running out. His baggage had been collected and he strapped on a handsome handgun presented to him personally by President Gil of Mexico. He and Wills were waiting when the first troops staggered in an hour later with Pedrón Altamirano.

"They're right behind me, César, maybe a half hour," Pedrón said. "There are three companies with mortars and automatic weapons."

"All right. Pedrón, order the locals to leave their weapons and fade back to their homes. Your regulars will have to get into the jungle and keep moving toward Chilimate. We'll reform at Santo Tomas. I don't think the Yankees will puruse them once they've taken the town."

"You want me to lead them?"

"No, Captain Dez Sancho—I want you to come with me. Take only what you can carry and meet us at the dock." Pedrón saluted and immediately began shouting at the men, directing them toward the river trail that led west. Sandino and Wills walked toward the dock, Wills carrying his recovered portmanteau and tiny *Blickensderfer* typewriter. "You're joining us then, Carlton?"

"Yes, my apartment in Manhattan is sublet until the end of the month." They both laughed, and passing down the slope past the wounded, saw Captain Sangre and Kate.

Sandino shouted at her, "*Sangre!* We're leaving now on the

boat! Come along and bring the girl!" At the dock the chastened pilot stood holding his hand. His fingers were bandaged but the throbbing told him they were infected. "Is the boat fueled?" Sandino asked.

"Yes."

"Then get on board and start it up. We're leaving." He did as he was told and a minute later the engine ground over and the thump of exhaust echoed across the water. Pedrón came up, carrying a U.S. government issue backpack. At the moment it was filled with *Cordobas*, an extra pistol, and an engraved silver cigarette box the manager had won skeet shooting.

"Captain Dez Sancho will lead the company, César, they are to avoid engagement and push for Chilimate then Santo Tomas."

"Good. We will take the river as far as La Libertad then cut across on the road to Acoyapa and up past Lake Nicaragua. I have an appointment in Managua on the thirty-first."

"With your dentist?" Wills asked.

"Something like that." Captain Sangre arrived towing Kate. Behind her the cook, Chula, was loaded with baggage. "Come aboard with Miss Kelly, Sangre," Sandino said, as he and Wills climbed over the low freeboard, "but leave your servant and the baggage here. There's no extra room in this small boat."

Sangre was horrified. "But, General, I . . . I can't leave Chula behind!" she pleaded, throwing her arms out in theatrical supplication, "She is more than a cook—this girl is like my sister!"

Sangre insisted on talking in English that sounded like the dialect routine of a vaudeville comedian. Sandino was amused by it once, but not any more; it grated on his nerves. She said she couldn't understand Nicaraguan—that was possible, there were five languages in the country, Miskito, Ramas, Sumo, English for the Creole population—and of course, Spanish. He spoke very clearly in Spanish. "I am giving you an order. If you choose to disobey it—then stay behind and deal with the Yankees—but we are going—*now!* Wills, help Miss Kelly on board."

Sangre looked at Sandino for a long minute then turned to Chula, explaining softly in Spanish. There were screams and wails as she clung to the captain's neck. Sangre disengaged her and got aboard.

Wills offered Kate his hand, but she shook it off and went to the stern of the boat and stood by Sangre watching Chula. She was sprawled over the discarded junk; a worn saddle, tangled blankets, and serapes tied to hold cooking pots. Laying her head on the saddle she wailed.

As the boat pulled away from the dock, Kate saw there were tears in the captain's eyes. "I'm sorry . . . Sangre," she said, using her name for the first time.

Sangre turned and looked at her. "Why?"

"That you . . . have to leave Chula behind."

"You want to take her place?"

Behind them the rear guard began to burn the mill. In 1928 Sandino had laid out his tough new policy in a letter to the La Luz and Los Angeles mine owners:

> My dear sirs; I have the honor to inform you that on this date your mine has been reduced to ashes . . . everything North American which falls into our hands is sure to meet its end. In this way the Marines will have no excuse of coming to Nicaragua to protect American property . . .
> I am your affectionate servant,
>
> A. C. Sandino

And it was true, before the intervention, Nicaraguan generals on both sides had carefully avoided damaging U.S. property, but now the capitalists were paying the price.

So were the workers. The local English- and French-speaking blacks had been imported from the West Indies for this work since the turn of the century. Others were brought to the Mosquito Coast as slaves in the 18th century by English settlers.

Those who mixed with the native Indians were called Creoles. Their descendents got along well with the pure-blooded Indians and together they shared a dislike for Spanish-speaking Latinos. As they watched their jobs go up in smoke they were bitter. The world depression had hit the export industries in Nicaragua and they considered themselves lucky to be employed. They knew nothing of politics and war and stayed away from both sides in the constant turnover of revolution. When Sandino romanticized his Indo-Hispanic nation of the future he took no account of that part of the population who actually believed their lives *had* improved because of foreign industry. These people had no intention of going back to skinning crocodiles for a living and actually felt nostalgia for the good old days of the Mosquito Kingdom, when they were under the protection of the British Empire.

Lieutenant Magnusson and the music boy came in on the point with the Marine weapons squad and discovered the bodies of Doctor Bruder and Tomás. Both had received *cortes*, Bruder the "cigar" and Tomás the "tie."

"Oh . . . oh . . ." the music boy said, and turning his back was sick.

"Pedrón," the Marine sergeant said, switching a plug of tobacco from one cheek to another.

"I thought he was up north in the department of Jinotega."

"Maybe, but this looks like his work. The guy's a real artist with the machete or the straight-edge cutache."

"Christ!" a gunner said, putting down a heavy Browning, "Lieutenant Pennington over at Matagalpa gets his picture taken holdin' a cut-off gook head and it shows up in every paper in the friggin' world. Now you know you sure ain't gonna see pictures of these two in any papers."

"Maybe showing a guy with his own dick in his mouth ain't too good for circulation."

There was a distant rumbling sound. "What's that?" the gunner shouted, picking up his weapon.

"The survey boat!" Magnusson answered on the run. He was already off and jogging down the donkey trail hoping for one more shot. This time he wouldn't pull it no matter who showed up in his sights.

# *SEVEN*

# La Libertad

THE *guardia* was the first into Rama with Lieutenant Castuno and Sergeant Somoza leading the advance force now that Captain Edd had been killed. While Castuno deployed the men to pick off stragglers and press the retreating Sandinistas, Somoza walked among the wounded looking for old enemies. Stopping at each man he mentally made a note of his face for future reference. Most were strangers from the North, with the occasional local. He stopped at Alberto Clemento. The man was educated, a teacher in Bluefields at the Moravian Mission who propagandized for the Marxists. He had been arrested several times.

"Well, Alberto, you poisoned minds in town, you stinking communist—what do you teach in the jungle? Huh? How to kill your countrymen?" Clemento looked at him dully, the pain from a stomach wound taking all his energy. Somoza cocked his automatic so he would hear it and shot him.

From the top of the slope a native corpsman, trained by the

U.S. Navy, shouted down, alarmed, "What happened, Sergeant?"

"The fool tried to pull a weapon!" The corpsman knew better but he kept his mouth shut. Like most of the men he was wary of Somoza, aware he was related to President Moncada's foreign minister, Anastasio Somoza. Besides, with Somoza walking ahead of him, his patient load would drop off dramatically.

The Packard was hauled off the stump by Marine muscle and towed backwards down the Walker Track by oxen. Because of the heat, the bodies of Tomás and Doctor Bruder were buried quickly. A Moravian minister, a missionary with the Rama Indians, conducted the services. After the Marines had moved in and the area was secured, General Butler, Lieutenant Magnusson, and the consul stood next to the smoldering remains of the manager's house. Magnusson had raced down the donkey track, but by the time he reached the dock, the survey boat was around the bend.

Lieutenant Delware came up with orders from the telegraph. The lines had been repaired and the orders were plain. There was to be no pursuit of the rebels. Once the town was secure and the mill restored to its owners, the *guardia* would be left to garrison it and the Marine Company returned to their ships at Bluefields. The signal from Admiral Sellers also advised that "attempts at the rescue of Miss Kelly by private individuals could not be supported by the U.S. Military." Until word from the State Department, he further strongly advised the American consul to return to his post. General Butler was not mentioned nor the music boy (because of a communications garble, no one knew his whereabouts and he had been listed as Absent Without Leave); Lieutenant Magnusson, on detached duty with the *guardia* was *Jefe Commandante* Matthews's problem.

"I am not going back until I make contact with my daughter," the consul said flatly.

"Good for you, Dick, we're all committed to that. Magnusson?"

"I have oral orders from Colonel Wise to find and kill Sandino, General. I go where he is."

"Eyewitnesses reported seeing Sandino leave on the survey boat with a small party that included a young white girl," Delware said.

"What would be his direction?" the general asked.

"There is a tributary of the Escondido—the Mica—that goes west to La Libertad. From there you can make connections to a road and the rail line north," the consul answered.

"That sounds right—" He looked at his watch. "What time does the boat arrive?"

"At dusk, sir—so they say."

The *Banana Queen* had been turned around at United Fruit, in Bluefields. American personnel of the lumber mill were put on board and ordered back to Rama and to get the place humming. Nearly two weeks of production had been lost— thousands of board feet plus the fire damage.

"Well," the general said, "It will be nice to see Captain Cochrane again."

The rescue party stood on the dock as the *Banana Queen* puffed into sight. They had spent the invertening time being refitted. The Marine Company got together a uniform for General Butler; shirt, pants, leggings, and a proper sidearm. Tugging down a campaign hat, he looked his old aggressive self. A company wag had cut out stars from the top of a ration can and attached them to the collar of the shirt. The General was pleased. The music boy, because of his munchkin size, had to make do with a hat, underwear, and socks. The consul kept what he had, adding a pair of lace-up boots donated by the company store.

For Karen Sven it was a shocking thing to find the house she had just left in ruins. All her clothes had been burned or looted. She had decided to press on with the rescue party, hoping to reach Managua. She was not going to stay another day in this horrible place. The problem was the bluenose captain. He had kept her off the boat before—would he recognize her with her hair up and in the rough hunting clothes?

The *Banana Queen*, backing off paddlewheels and maneuvering, docked bow forward. Lines were put off and the engineers and mill personnel came off carrying their luggage. Wives and dependents would not be allowed in until things were back to normal. Fortunately for Karen, Mr. Denver, the manager, had been detained in Bluefields with the start-up procedure and there would be no confrontation. She had left a note pinned to the wreckage of the house thanking him for a nice time.

After the surge of passengers going ashore Captain Cochrane came down from the wheelhouse and stood blocking the gangway, arms folded. "I hope you people don't think I'm going to turn around tonight and take you back to Bluefields."

"No," the general said pleasantly, "You're going to take us upriver to La Libertad. That is where Miss Kelly has been removed to."

The captain was dumbfounded. "By the good Lord sir, you have to have the nerve of a crazy man! There is no way this boat moves from here in any direction but east!"

"Oh I think it will if commandeered." And they started forward.

The captain knew the town was under military command and seeing the general in uniform shook him. The company depended on the Marines for protection and in policy did all they could to support them. He wavered, then saw Karen.

"I have no recourse if forced by armed men to take you— but I will not permit . . ." he said, pointing at Karen, ". . . that whore on my boat!"

"*What?*" The general said, "WHAT?" and charging up the gangway grabbed the captain with such force that his cap flew off. Holding him by the front of his shirt he swung him around. "*You dirty dog of a yellow coward! You dare speak like that to a lady?*" Cochrane struggled but the general held him in a powerful grip, pushing him down the gangway. *"You pusillanimous poltroon! You snake's scrotum! A low polecat of your stripe, with the diseased mind of a flea, does not deserve command of a garbage scow! OFF JACKANAPES!"* and saying this, kicked him hard in the rear, knocking him to his knees on the dock.

Cochrane scrambled up sputtering. "By sweet Jesus! I'll see you . . . and this bunch of . . . adventurers in jail!" And he lurched off to telegraph the company.

The general bowed, "Miss Sven, please forgive that unpleasant scene. The man is obviously deranged. Take my arm." As they came aboard the *Banana Queen*, the general spotted the engineer watching from the cross deck. "Mr. Cott, who is second in command here?"

"That would be the mate, Ramrez."

"Then please relay to Mr. Ramrez that he is now captain. My compliments and will he get under way at once for La Libertad?"

"Aye, aye," the engineer said, smiling. He might never live to see his pension but by God, he had seen Mr. Cochrane kicked flat up his stiff ass.

"Let's get the car aboard and tied down," Magnusson said, shaking his head over the dramatics. "Mr. Kelly, if you will back it on please."

The consul smiled, "If the old girl is willing." They had taken to calling the car Fidelia, in short for the Marine motto: *semper fidelis*, always faithful. The abrupt meeting with the stump had dented the pan but the engine seemed intact, and the pistons still had clearance. Spark plugs were cleaned, oil was added, and that was it. There were more than two dozen bullet holes in the body and the front windshield was shot out. The rear one survived because it was laid flat. Fortunately the tires hadn't taken any hits and there were two spares left.

As the consul backed it on board, Magnusson noticed he was letting his beard grow. It was one of those inky black jobs that made the owner look like an anarchist. He turned to the job at hand, shouting, "Music! Get the gear loaded!" and walked forward to supervise the deck gang lashing down the car.

The music boy looked at the pile of gear. It had multiplied—duffle bags, backpacks, guns, ammo—the case of drums for the Thompson alone weighed a ton. He looked around for help and seeing local loungers, tried his Spanish, "*Hey you seenyoors!* Vamoose over here and el moveo the el baggos onto the el boato!" They stared.

The survey boat proceeded upriver. It was narrower here, and small boats were seen, pirogues loaded with fruit and trade items—whole families going to town for market. As they got closer to La Libertad and away from the coastal plains, the *Montañas de Huadi* rose on one side, the *Sierra de Amerique* on the other. Ragged villages appeared, farms stretching to the rises. Nearing populated areas and *guardia* control, Sandino stood with the pilot to make sure he stayed on course and there was no funny business. Below in the cabin, Pedrón snored, and behind him, back against the gunwale, Sangre dozed, her yap shut for once. The girl sat at the stern, hand trailing in the water. Wills was next to her, hopefully to prevent another swimming espisode.

Wills took a draft from his canteen and offered it to Kate. She shook her head. "Are you feeling all right, Miss Kelly?" She looked wan, and it occurred to him she had lost weight. The activity and poor food had thinned her considerably. When she didn't answer he went on. "I'm sorry to put you through all this—but those people who attacked us were after you."

"Good," she said.

"Do you think it worthwhile to kill and wound many people to try and take back one girl?"

"I think it would be fine if they wiped out the bunch of you."

"Is that what they taught you in Sunday school?"

"They taught me to do unto others as they do unto you." He smiled. "Do you believe in God?"

"Yes, and the U.S. Marines." She smiled back for the first time.

"You really are the little *militis*, the daughter of the regiment."

"I'm the daughter of the American consul and when he catches up with you it's going to be too bad."

"Kate, can't you understand that nobody wants the Marines and the Americans here?"

"Then let them stop burning things down and kidnapping girls."

"It's the only way they can fight back at the people who exploit them—the foreign companies backed up by your Marines."

"Are you telling me people don't have jobs in the banana factories or whatever they are trying to burn down? Were they better off before living in the jungle and eating monkey meat?"

"What good does it do if the companies take all of the money out of the country?"

"Didn't they put the money in to start with?"

"My God, she's a capitalist, too!"

"So what? I'll be what I want to and you and that shrimp are not going to tell me what I can be! I know there are poor people here—I can see, but what makes you think you can change that?"

"Because we are fighting for . . ."

"These people are always fighting among themselves—don't you read the papers? I thought the Marines were here to stop that—to let somebody be president longer than a couple of weeks."

"Look," he said trying to simplify for a child. "Think of the American revolution—Americans fought against an exploiter—Great Britain, to have the right to decide their own fate. In fact—Sandino has been compared to George Washington." Modesty forbade Wills from mentioning it was one of his articles that suggested it.

Kate laughed. "If he's George Washington I'm Betty Boop."

Eyes closed, Captain Sangre listened to this—as much as she could catch. Wills was a big talker, but it had been his talk (and writing) about her that made her Captain Sangre. She began to understand that the fat girl was someone important—that she had been kidnapped. No one (except the girl) told her that. In fact they told her nothing. Since the humiliation of today—of leaving Chula behind—she began to brood. She did not want to admit out loud she had been playing the fool, that in this army she was not consulted; did not have a command—*not even a squad*—kept around to provide jokes for Sandino and Wills— those two were closer than flies on shit—and although no one could doubt Sandino's bravery she brooded about his sense of humor at her expense.

She had realized in that moment on the dock when their eyes held, that he did not like her—wished to be rid of her. Then, a thought occurred: If this fat girl was so important then she must be worth something. If she could just find out to whom, and for how much. . . . she would have the fat girl, money, and the last laugh on those two funny boys.

It was nighttime as the *Banana Queen* continued upriver on the Mica, snaking past the same twists and turns of river the survey boat had passed hours earlier. There was no traffic now, pirogues had been drawn up on the banks and Indians sat at cookfires watching the great white boat slide by lit at dozens of windows. It was an amazing sight for them; nobody could remember seeing this big a thing on the river at night.

In the wheelhouse, captain elect, Ferman Ramrez couldn't remember it either. The *Banana Queen* stayed out of these waters—especially at night. The last thing he could have imagined this morning when he kissed his sweet wife good-bye was to be in command of this boat. He was a mestizo, and the company advanced only white men to captain. The general had been firm; they were to proceed, and in the dark, at whatever maximum speed possible. No time was to be lost in rescuing the American girl. Ramrez had two men on the bow watching for snags, floating logs, swimming boas, or God knew what. He stood in the wheelhouse next to the native pilot, both of them straining their eyes ahead and praying.

Below, at one end of what had been the saloon, the rescue party enjoyed the first sit-down dinner in three days. The cabin carried some remnants of former glory: a worn Brussels carpet and paneling of butternut and cherry carefully installed by Vermont ship carpenters; stenciling still decorated the ceilings and most of the etched glass was in the windows around the oval of skylights.

The sensation of the evening was Karen Sven. She had been given the captain's cabin and used his small shower tub to bathe and wash her hair. That hair, loose now and hanging to her waist, was something to behold. A natural pale blond-white, it gleamed in the cabin lights soft as the moon's rising. She had allowed herself modest makeup and discarding the rough hunting jacket found one of Captain Cochrane's dress shirts in the closet. It was a bit small and showed her figure nicely, unbuttoned to a hint of glorious cleavage.

The men in the party had not realized what a beauty she was—and she had contrived that—but now she was after a different effect. One that might stir Lieutenant Magnusson. He had grown in her mind to a knight in shining armor, or closer to home, a Viking warrior—a hero who dashed in to save her at the last possible moment. The trouble was he paid her little attention, never meeting her eyes and aways seeming to be listening or looking elsewhere. She smiled at him down the table and as usual he missed it. For her even the curious bronze face and white forehead had appeal—reminding her of the war paint of wild Indians.

The conversation was lively and neutral, staying away from the events of the last days in respect to the consul; keeping his mind off his kidnapped daughter.

"I found a six-month-old newspaper in my cabin," the general said. "It seems there's a new college craze for swallowing goldfish."

"Well, I knew there were breadlines at home," the consul replied, smiling, "but that seems a bit desperate—besides as a college boy I remember hating fish."

"Did you go to college, Lieutenant?" Karen asked.

"No ma'am." Magnusson's conversational skills were monosyllabic.

"Neither did I," the general filled in, "went into the Marines at sixteen."

The music boy perked up, "Is that right sir? So did I—was that the legal age then?"

"No, seventeen. I lied about my age, telling them I was eighteen. When my father heard this he said, 'Son if thee is determined to go, thee shall go, but don't add another year to thy age. Thy mother and I have only been married seventeen years."

They laughed. "My father talked like that, you know, we are Quakers."

"Really?" Karen said, "I thought Quakers were against war."

"We are—but then who isn't? My father believed in a strong defense so the other fellow would think twice about striking you. He was a congressman and once after making a speech advocating a good-size navy an angry pacifist said to him, 'Thee is a fine Friend!' and he answered, 'Thee is a damn fool!'"

They laughed again and the consul changed the subject. "This weather must seem perverse to you, Miss Sven."

"Oh yes, I do miss the cold, everything then seems cleansed—held in suspension when frozen—time stands still while you move outside of it."

"Very poetic," the general said.

She blushed. "No, no! I just meant there is a . . . hush about winter, no buzzing sounds of insects or the pounding of rain—nature is so noisy in this country."

"Although I've heard the ice crack on the Hudson," the consul said, "and it sounded like the shot of a cannon."

"Yes . . ." They were all looking at her and she knew each was thinking: what was she doing in Rama at the manager's house? If she was not his wife or related, then what? They wouldn't admit it, but Captain Cochrane's name-calling had shaken them. A cloud hung over the rising moon. No one of them would have been impolite enough to ask, so she spoke up.

"I had always wondered about the tropics, being from the North. The palm trees and bright birds of the travel posters—but didn't believe I would see it. Then last year I met Mr. Denver where I worked. He was such a sad man, his wife being sick for so long—and he was lonely. Right away he asked me to marry him—to come live here. I said no—there was no romance between us . . ." She paused, looking at Magnusson.

"But he persisted, telling me I should at least come down as a guest and see the marvelous lush things of the jungle. So I did, but I did not love him and could not stay. I was packing for home when Sandino arrived."

They were relieved and sympathized. Agreeing that to a man of Cochrane's rigid strictures, an unchaperoned woman in a man's house could only mean one thing.

"What was Sandino like?" the consul asked.

"Very formal and polite at first . . . obviously a man of intelligence—but wound up—like a key had been turned and you waited for the springs to fly out. Unpredictable, I would call him." To say the least.

"There was another man with him, wearing glasses—a white man?"

"Yes, an American."

"What was he? What did he do?"

"A writer I think, but he did not confide in me. He did not like me I think." They found this hard to believe. "I do not think he liked women."

There was an embarrassed pause at this, then the conversation changed to lighter subjects. When someone asked what she worked at in New Orleans she playfully answered, "Ladies' underwear." They thought this very amusing.

The consul had listened to her story with interest. He remembered meeting the manager's wife several years ago, but he had not heard she was dead.

The engineer, Mr. Wayne Cott, joined the party and brought with him a bottle of *vino de coyol*, a drink made from the sap of the local coyol palm. Glasses were produced and toast drunk to Captain Cochrane's absence. Although the general upheld prohibition in the U.S. he was not there now and certainly could not pass up such a worthy toast. No one would call him a bluenose. Talk went on, and about ten o'clock Lieutenant Magnusson excused himself to have a cigar on deck. Karen took this opportunity to turn in. They stood as she went out, grateful to have had such a beauty to dine with.

On deck, Karen followed the cigar smoke and found Magnusson at the rail. "Lieutenant . . ."

He turned, surprised to find her so close.

"I have never thanked you properly for my rescue." She said this in Norwegian.

"Why, ah, you understood we came there to find the consul's daughter?" He answered in Swedish.

"Yes, but you defended me and brought me safely out. You are a brave man." He stammered, but she went on. "I'd like to thank you in the way I know best." She turned and crooked a finger.

Puzzled, he followed her and they went around the curve of the stateroom hall to the captain's cabin. Opening the door she stepped in and when he hesitated, crooked her finger again. Inside the tight space she began unbuttoning the shirt. "When Captain Cochrane called me a whore he was correct—not a common one I'd like to think—but a whore. In fact I'm considered to be quite clever by those who know the business."

Magnusson's mouth fell open and the cigar went dead. When her breasts were shook loose all aquiver he could only stare. Dropping the skirt and step-ins, she turned back the sheets of the bunk, carefully remade. "Now I'm going to get in bed. If you have no moral or medical scruples please join me—I'd like to pay you back for your trouble."

He stirred himself, tossing the cigar out the door, closing it, and shucking off his shirt and pants in a heat. She was amused to see his body was as white as hers and with just the face, hands, and wrists tanned, like a mask and gloves. "I wonder if I could turn out the lights?" he said, before doffing generous khaki shorts. She knew then what kind of liberated fellow he was.

He slid in beside her, tentatively slipping his arm around her waist, feeling the weight of one glorious breast on his chest. "I . . . don't know what to say."

"I was hoping you would say nothing."

He began quickly as other hungry men had—men who went for long intervals without a woman. The first time was over in seconds, then with scarcely a pause he was ready again. Each time the act grew longer and finally was stretched to multiple pleasure. She whispered no sweet dirty nothings in his ear or made any move that might be considered "French." She sensed that he wanted his whores "decent." There was no moaning and only a mutual gasp at the last coming together. Then he slept. As she lay awake next to him she thought: *Here I am the good Swedish wife lying beside my good husband. He works in town (at what?) and I keep house, care for our children, and tend the garden. We grow old together and wait for visits from our grandchildren. Would I like that life? No.*

When he woke long before dawn, she woke with him and they lay silent. Then he said what she knew he would, in almost the exact words she had heard many times before. "I . . . don't understand why a girl like you would want to be a . . ."

"Whore?" She answered as she always did. "Because it pays well and I enjoy it."

"But to go with any man . . ."

"Not any I disapprove of. They come to me rather than their

dull wives or girlfriends out of desire and admiration. I am paid for handsomely—certainly better than those poor wives they hold in chattel."

He listened but heard none of this. "Surely most women want to get married, find a descent husband. If you're a . . ."

"Whore? Listen! One of the problems in brothels is keeping the girls from running away and getting married! I don't mean to pimps and gamblers—respectable men; bankers, lawyers— upstanding citizens were forever stealing our girls. Whores make good wives.

"Let me tell you about respectable and decent. I was brought over to this country when I was fourteen by an aunt who worked for a rich family. What they did was buy me. I worked as a maid at the meanest possible jobs. They lived in Albert Lea, Minnesota, in a big turreted house on a lake. I had to clean that house seven days a week, twelve hours a day with Sunday morning off for church. The family barely spoke to me, when we met in the hall I was expected to keep my eyes down as a sign of respect.

"Only the grandfather treated me as a human being. He was an elegant old man with beautiful manners, a widower. Secretly he taught me English and we played cards together. I grew very fond of him and on my fifteenth birthday he bought me a pretty pearl ring and took me to bed. He was a gentle lover and it was wonderful to have someone care for me—I was very lonely.

"But the bitch of a wife—his daughter-in-law—found out about us and I was literally thrown out in the street the same day with a few miserable belongings. My aunt never again spoke to me. There were other jobs with 'respectable' families, but by then . . ." nodding her chin at her chest, ". . . these had come in and husbands and sons of the household were hard to hold off. At a Norwegian dance I met a handsome fellow who told me he was leaving for Galveston where he was an oil man. I asked him to take me with him, saying I'd saved enough to pay my way.

"He was a gambler and thrown off the train at New Orleans for cheating—me along with him. He'd spent my money and all I got from him was a madam's address on Basin Street. I began as a maid and graduated to a whore."

He turned on his side, and face to face they kissed. She liked that. "That was a hard way to begin in this country," He said hesitating, "But for a Scandinavian to be a . . ."

She laughed out loud. This was finally what bothered him, not the sinning, the dissolute life, the high-daddy hilarity—but the fact that she was a countrywoman—a Scandinavian. His national pride was hurt. "Don't you think there are any Swedish whores?"

"Maybe, but the girls I've seen were all tough as mongrels."

"You've never been to a first-class place. Nell ran a strictly white whorehouse, the fairer the girl the better—well not true— she did keep a few really beautiful mulattos, what they call *metisse* or *negrillonne*, but if they couldn't pass for Spanish or Chinese she wouldn't have them."

What he found hard to accept was Karen's matter-of-fact attitude. He had never heard a woman talk openly about this. The whores he went with babbled about bandleaders or kittens they had as pets. If anything personal came up they got coy or belligerent.

She saw his look and sighed. "As a matter of fact when I get back I'm no longer going to work at being a whore."

He brightened. "Really?"

"I'm going to be a madam. That's where the money is."

"What?"

"It isn't easy to run a profitable house, you know. You've got to be sharp and keep an eye on everything. Linen is a big item, a house can go broke if that isn't watched—and of course the girls make or break you. A lot of them are what Nell called 'rabbity'— a little crazy upstairs. They need a firm hand. She used to fine them, or if they really got out of line let Harry the houseman work them over—but not to cause bruises—that may sound mean but a lot of them are wild and if they go off the deep end can do a lot of harm. We had a Jewish girl from a good family who was the wildest thing in Storyville—then one night she hit a man over the head with a chair and hung herself in the attic. If a house gets a reputation of having girls who don't act right with the customers you might as well close.

"Then, too, there's dealing with the police and politics—no one can stay open without bribes. You've got to have a strong man around, someone who can deal with the roughneck customers and protect the madam." Kate looked at him. He'd gone back to sleep. Leaning over she kissed his sweet Viking nose. "That's where you come in lover," she whispered.

La Libertad was a market town built on what once were the prehistoric remains of an ancient civilization. It was filled with overgrown mounds and the ruins of monolithic statues of men and gods, the tumble of temples and tombs. There were piles of earthenware bowls and vessels that the current inhabitants helped themselves to for everyday use. Who these ancient people had been no one knew or cared, and including the standing walls of once great buildings they put up shaky stalls for animals and goods. The market had grown to enclose a city block, partitioned with tin and wood and covered over with a patchwork of brightly colored tarps. Under these, sellers squatted bargaining with buyers.

The market extended down to the dock where the survey boat tied up. The river dwindled away beyond here and this was the last stop on its highway. The unloading of goods was ongoing; with the Indians carrying up homegrown produce from pirogues, and commercial boats unloading the city-made goods they in turn would trade the Indians.

Sandino wrote out a note and a messenger was found among the dockside boys to carry it. "There is a stable in the old town that can be trusted to bring us transportation." he said, and they waited, he and Wills with one foot up on the gunwales as a bar rail, watching the hustle of merchandise. "Even the most primitive Indian will trade a beautiful handwoven rug for a piece of city junk," Wills said.

"They have to be taught values."

"No matter, this instinct of man toward bad taste is irreversible."

"Bad taste was invented in Great Britain and America during the industrial revolution."

"So was socialism," Wills said. Sandino didn't laugh.

An hour later two vaqueros rode up leading horses and several mules. Gear was loaded and they mounted up. "Damn!" Captain Sangre shouted, putting on her spurs and clanking the enormous rowels. "This is more like it!" Being of the late Poncho Villa's army she considered herself a cavalryman first. When she tried to help Kate up on a small nervous horse, the girl shook off her hand.

"I can ride!" And climbing onto the Spanish saddle with its *rosaderos* and rigging ring under the fork, she thought of her donkey Calvin—no saddle for him, remembering she had named him after President Coolidge and thinking of his soft nose and tender eyes. It seemed a long time ago she rode up that trail to the bluff.

Wills was concerned about the pilot. His hand was swollen three times its size and the man was feverish. Sandino sloughed it off. "He can find medical aid here—besides he's lucky we don't shoot him. Come on, Saint Wills!" he said, laughing.

They were off riding through the marketplace, through crowds that were almost totally Indian; past open stockyards where cattle were slaughtered and *cargadores* staggered across the road to butcher shops carrying whole animals on their backs. Wearing canvas capes with hoods to keep off the blood and hair, they cinched broad belts to the last knotch against rupture, walking like automatons.

The old town was several miles inland and from there a trail that was almost a road led between mountains. No cars or trucks were seen, only the dust of animals and the occasional cart. As they went on with the two vaqueros leading, the trail was marked with more ruins, some hundreds of feet long built of cut stone that must have been brought from great distances. Wills had seen ruins like these all over Mexico and Central America. It was humbling to think that the people of those great civilizations had vanished without a trace. Some called them Aztec *chontal* or *bravos* but these words meant barbarian, wild. A curious name for a people who lived in fine buildings while most of the world squatted in caves—so much for leaving your mark on the tide of history.

By midafternoon the mountains opened for the slope of a valley and shapes of cattle grazing were visible; black spots moving on the high grassland. Sandino turned the horsemen off the main trail and into the unmarked entrance of a ranch. Fencing stretched for miles with no sign of buildings.

"You haven't heard of Plutarco Heran del Sancho?" Sandino said, riding up besides Wills.

"Is he as long winded as his name?"

"Oh yes, a real Spaniard with an ego that a peacock might envy. But he is a patron and we must have a few of those along with the humble Indian. He was a friend of my father's in Granada and seriously sunk in that quicksand of conservative politics. He's in exile now on this ranch with its thousands of *manzanas*. Hard luck, eh?" he said, laughing, "If he went back they would shoot him. He's one of the few big landowners to support us with his name and money."

"Why?"

"So that we might tumble his enemy President Moncada out of office. Plutarco is the kind of man who would pour gasoline over himself, light it, then grab hold of you if it were the only way to get revenge on an insult."

"I understand."

A walled hacienda came into view under the shade of a huge old Zapoté tree. They went through heavy wooden gates with bronze nail bosses and a *mascarone* knocker in the shape of a bizarre Moor's head. Inside, horses clattered onto a stone courtyard and Plutarco Heran del Sancho waited. He embraced Sandino as if he were his son and shook Pedrón's hand, whacking him on the back, aggressive and snappy as a terrier. Wills saw that he was tiny, with dyed black hair and goatee, an old man dressed in the fashion of years ago. His nose was extraordinary, a hook of aristocratic aloofness last seen in Renaissance paintings of the Spanish court. He was obviously proud of this break and when introduced made comparisons.

"I like your friend's nose, Cesár. Though not as august as mine, it shows *aristos* were in the woodpile." They laughed and he led the three men into the house going under monastic archways and down corridors that were austere, the rough brick painted white. Ceilings were timbered and the decoration religious. Ornate crucifixes and sad-eyed saints looked out from niches. Wills recognized fifteenth-century della Robbia sculpture and a reliquary containing God knows what old hank of hair or pawned-off bone. It was a house with the split personality of conquistador and padre.

The group at last reached the dining room which had all the charm of a monks' refectory, burdened with outsized furniture and a terra-cotta floor that clacked underfoot. "You are just in time for *la comida*," their host announced, and they sat down to *sopa de ajo* between elephantine candelabra with enough candlepower to have lit the cathedral at Seville.

Kate and Captain Sangre were not included in their host's plans or even introduced. They were led by servants to a square, solid room behind the kitchen that would double as sleeping room and cell. That was fine with Sangre, to hell with the funny boys. She had watched carefully as the horses were taken through doors a few yards away to an outside stable built against the wall. Once the door closed on the room, she flopped on the bed and digging her spurs into the end board, ran the rowels up and down to create a pattern. Then she came to the point. "Who are you, kid?"

Kate sat on the only chair next to a rough, round table that showed use as a cutting board. "What do you mean? I'm Catherine Kelly . . ."

"Who is you . . . people? You . . . papa?"

Kate looked at her closely, wondering at the sudden interest. "He's the American consul at Bluefields."

"Ah . . . so that's it! You think he's got money to get you back?"

"We're not rich if that's what you mean." She did not mention that her grandfather, a Boston Brahmin, famous as the man who had the Grapenuts sign removed from the Common, was very rich.

"Come on! You telling me you papa would not buy his little *niña* back?"

"I don't know."

Sangre lowered her voice. "Listen, how would you like me to took you out of here—back to papa?"

Kate's heart jumped. "Would you?!" Then thinking it over, she said, "Why?"

"Because I'm sick of these guys . . ." She swung her legs off the bed and shucked off the boots, tossing them in the corner with a clang of spurs. "We think about it, huh?" Standing, she pulled her shirt, then skirt off. Kate was appalled. She was naked. As she flopped back on the bed, her breasts slid to both sides like flapjacks and the curious rusty colored pubic hair stood like steel wool. "Jesus, that shitty horse they give me had a short leg—my back is killing me—do me a favor, kid?" There was a silence. "Rub my back will you—be a good *niña*." When Kate didn't answer, she went on in an whining voice. "Come on! If we're going to be *compañeras* we got to help each other." She turned over. "Just a little rub."

Reluctantly Kate got up, moved to the bed, and began tentatively rubbing her back. "Ahh, that feels good—a little lower—now grab my ass and knead it like you were making dough for tortillas—you do me and I'll do you . . ."

* * *

At the end of *la comida* and over light claro cigars, Sandino made his pitch. Wills had never seen him in the role of fundraiser and he and Pedrón listened along with Plutarco, twirling cigars. "As you know, patron, I have spent the last year in Mexico enlisting support and recruiting military men for our cause. I have personally talked to President Emilio Portes Gil about munition deliveries we can expect . . ."

Wills knew the answer to that: none. Gil had given him the runaround. Sandino had decided to travel to Mexico when things began to turn sour internally for the Sandinistas. His chief foreign representative, the poet Froylán Turcios, had resigned over a dispute in policy and suggested that the Sandinistas withdraw to Costa Rica and surrender their arms for amnesty. Sandino was insulted, claiming North American money had seduced him and decided on his own trip abroad to rally support.

". . . we discussed a hemispheric conference to be held in Buenos Aires inviting the United States, with myself representing Nicaragua. The purpose would be to demand Indo-Hispanic sovereignty and independence of our race—equality with the North Americans. And of course the complete withdrawal of all Marines on our soil. This was received with enthusiasm by my supporters there."

In Mexico three groups fought to direct Sandino: the moderate, Dr. Pedro José Zepeda who urged a broad front of all anti-imperialists; the radical APRA whose Peruvian leader, Esteban Pavletich, preached racism and social revolution; and the communists, represented on the general's staff by Agustin Marti.

"I don't like this talk of communism. Next you'll want to give the land away." Plutarco said, frowning.

"I've told you of my policy there—I do not approve of agrarian reform in Nicaragua; there is plenty of unused land. The key is the colonization of our vast wilderness into cooperatives like my Indian ancestors did at Guiguili . . ."

"These communists will take you over." When Plutarco got hold of a point he hung on.

"No, my motto is 'Neither extreme right, nor extreme left, but the United Front.' Nevertheless—the organizations on the left make us think—those who preach determined social doctrines point the way. You must have complete confidence in the direction I follow, it is for good of all of us, rich and poor alike."

"I heard the communists in New York exhibit your brother like a circus freak."

Sandino did his best to smile. His half brother, Sócrates Sandino lived in Brooklyn where he worked as a carpenter. He had lately been addressing rallies and signing his name to newspaper articles in conjunction with a Comintern branch of the All American Anti-Imperialist League. "Nonsense, he just tells Americans we're not against them, but the policies of the government—and he raises money for medical supplies." He also infuriated the American Legion Wills thought, smiling.

"I don't like it."

"Listen," Sandino said, "doing his best to be patient and hold his temper, "last year the communists accused me of betraying the party and taking a bribe to exile myself to Mexico— that shows you how we get along. And how could I betray the party when I don't belong to it?" Shaking his head he continued, "Their boss Gustavo Machado raised one thousand dollars for our cause and delivered it here to me in person—after taking out his expenses we were left with two hundred and fifty dollars." He laughed. "Do you think I am going to be bought for that paltry sum?"

"You are called a communist these days if you pick your nose with your left hand." Pedrón said in his inimitable style.

"I can say my talks with President Gil were of great importance for the future of our country and the Sandinistas."

Wills knew better. Portes Gil had offered Sandino only political asylum in Mexico. After conferring with the American ambassador to Mexico, Dwight Morrow, and assuring him

Sandino would not be allowed to set up a base of operations or come to Mexico City, it was arranged he should stay in Mérida, on the Yucatán Peninsula. He was kept there cooling his heels for six months before the interview. Sandino knew then he could expect nothing but lip service from the Mexicans. They had been scared off by the American oil companies. He was alone.

"I don't trust the Mexicans," Plutarco said, "They were here before the North Americans invaders you know." *My God!* Wills thought, *he's talking about 1822 when that crazy old royalist Iturbide declared himself Emperor Augustin the first and annexed Nicaragua for a year.*

Sandino rolled over this. "The U.S. is tired of fighting us. Their own senators Borah and Ladd support a movement of trade unions and university people that demand Congress renounce military occupation as a tool of foreign policy. Liberals like Inman and Waldo Frank are behind us—ask Wills."

"Yes," Wills said slowly, being dragged on stage, "I believe the U.S. means it when they say they will pull the Marines out after next year's elections."

"Once they go and the *guardia* loses its backbone—how long can they last? We press them now everywhere with raids and provocative acts." Wills noted he didn't spell these out as extortion, terrorism, and kidnapping. He certainly wasn't going to mention the consul's daughter to this good family man. Sandino knocked his cigar ash off in a dish decorated with a polychrome of the baby Jesus.

"What is needed is an attack on the capital. We will strike Managua." His listeners were stunned. "On March thirty-first I will rendezvous with Angel Ortez in Managua. He will bring up three companies by train, burst on the city, attack the presidential palace, and be back on the rails before the Marines can react."

"With a little luck," Pedrón said, "we can shoot off Moncada's balls—if he's got any."

Plutarco liked this a lot. He hated Managua as much as he did President Moncada. In the old days Granada had been the

Conservative capital; and Leon, the Liberal one. To put an end to the bitter internecine fighting, Managua, then much smaller than either city, had been made the official capital.

It was ironic, a cliché really, that the date that Sandino had picked for his great blow would go down in history for an entirely different reason.

Kate jerked back from the bed as Sangre grabbed her. There was a scuffle and they went down on the floor, Kate scratching and kicking. "God damn it kid! I'm trying to be nice to you!" Twisting her leg, Sangre shouted, "You are some kind of crazy *niña!*" Scrabbling for a weapon, Kate caught hold of one of Sangre's discarded boots and swinging it, clipped the captain's head with the spur. She broke loose, clutching the spot. "*Ahooo! Jesus!* Look what you did!" Showing blood on her fingers she exclaimed, "That's not funny!"

She jumped at her again and this time Kate slammed the spur into her back. Sangre got hold of her wrist and finally shook loose the boot, but now there was pounding on the locked door and shouts. Sangre gave up. "It's nothing! Go fock yourself!" And she sat back on the bed, pouting. "Don't think I'm taking you anywhere you bitch!"

Sangre remained sullen during a terrible meal of beans and boiled plantains and went to bed still naked. Kate tried to stay awake sitting on the chair and leaning against the wall. Next she was awakened very late by the captain, fully dressed and carrying the carbine and her pack. "Shut up!" she whispered fiercely when Kate opened her mouth. "We're going!"

Foggy, Kate followed her through the empty kitchen where they picked up a cheesecloth sack used as a strainer. Outside it was dark with the stillness before dawn and the house showed no lights. Sangre was hunched over, and working a cobblestone loose, dropped it in the sack. At the open gate to the stable a man leaned against its arch, hat bent flat on one side, sleeping on his feet. Sangre hit him hard and he fell, his neck twisted at an odd angle.

They picked three horses, saddled two, and put their gear on the third. When they let the others loose the animals immediately broke for the remuda, five miles up the slope at the line camp. Sangre and Kate led the horses in a wide loop of the hacienda and mounted down the road. Swinging a leg up and spurring the horse, the captain shouted, *"Brava! Viva el Capitan Sangre y valiente niña! Apretado! Rapido!"* It was the first sentence in Spanish she'd ever heard her complete. Kate mounted her own horse, and kicking it ahead, rode after Sangre into the night. The sounds of hooves and wind tearing at her hair thrilled her. At last she felt free.

Wills was awakened before dawn by sounds in the courtyard. He dressed and went down to where men stood by the stable gate. Another man lay on the ground, his head bloody. "He's dead," someone said, "his neck is broken."

"Who were these people?" a thin voice asked. And Wills made out Plutarco in an odd dressing gown.

"The girl was the American consul's daughter. . . ." Sandino answered. Plutarco stiffened at this, and Sandino hurried on, "We had hopes of converting her to our cause—she was not held for ransom—no—the Mexican was watching her."

"I told you not to trust Mexicans."

Pedrón looked over his shoulder toward the slope of mountain. "What about horses?"

"It will take time to get them back."

"Damn!"

"Did this Mexican know of the plan to attack Managua?"

"I don't know," Sandino said honestly.

Plutarco heaved his small shoulders. "Come with me." He led them along the wall to a shed. It was unlocked and the doors pushed back. In the dim light Wills made out the shine of a grill. "A Hispano-Suiza," Plutarco said, laying a hand affectionately on a shiny fender. "I bought it in Barcelona years ago and used it when I lived in Granada; here it gets no use. Take it—you should be able to catch them and continue onto the city. Raul will drive and bring it back—it is as much as I can do." There was a sigh that reverberated. Wills had the feeling the old man would have as soon lent his wife as the car.

Rolled out in the open the automobile proved to be an enormous old boat of a machine, the body a coupe de ville for formal town use. It was black and dark green with huge polished wheel disks. An hour later they were ready to roll, gear aboard, Raul driving, and another vaquero squeezed in the front of the open chauffeur's compartment. He held a Mauser rifle with a telescopic sight. In the back under the enclosure of a drop top, Sandino and Pedrón sat on mohair with Wills facing them uncomfortably on a jump seat. As they pulled away, Wills could see through the portholes of rear windows and there was the old man watching them go—forlorn, no doubt with a tear in his eye.

Sangre pushed all night and it was only when the sun rose that the horses were allowed to rest and drink at a small spring. "Where are we going?" Kate asked, sore and dead tired.

"To the city. We get in touch with your papa and he pays me for my trouble—maybe give me a medal too," she said, laughing. "Then I go live with the Yankees—yes, and get in the movies with Tom Mix and guys like that." She had it all figured out.

Looking at her, Kate wondered if things were any better. She had helped her get away—but this woman was wild—crazy, and something else she didn't want to think about. At least with Sandino you knew he was smart—educated. Would educated people kill you as quick as dumb ones? She felt—well, sorry, for Sangre, felt a sympathy for her. Talk about exploitation, she had been treated by Sandino as an inferior and a joke.

They rode on leisurely and at about noon, saw a dust cloud behind them. There were few travelers on the lonely road and Sangre knew this kind of dust didn't come from animals. They began to gallop but in minutes the cloud was closer and they heard the sound of something mechanical. "Shit! They got a fockin' automobile!" And she spurred the horse toward the rise of mountain on the right, grabbing the reins on Kate's horse and pulling her along. "Come on! *Apretado! Rapido!*" If they could get up in the rocks she would have a chance. They let the third horse go and climbed, animals fighting to get a footing. The landscape here was huge boulders tumbled on each other in ancient upheaval and worn smooth to take on the gray tone of elephants—the kind of ground Sangre was used to fighting on in Mexico. There could only be a few of them and they had to come to her. If she couldn't pick off a couple of funny boys and the pock-marked moose, she should give up.

Below, the car came to a sliding halt and Sandino leaned out the rear window pointing at the horses clattering up the slope. "Get the Mexican!"

The vaquero leaned the Mauser on the edge of the windshield, sent the bolt home in an oiled clack, and aimed very carefully through the telescope sight. It seemed a long minute— then he fired, the sharp slap of the shot echoed through the mountains. Sangre's horse dropped and she went over its head onto the rocks. She rolled and came up to a sitting position holding her leg below the knee. It was broken. Struggling to control her own horse, backing and prancing, Kate got it snubbed down and jumped off. "*Sangre!*" Running to her, she tried to help her up. "What's the matter?"

"I broke my fockin' leg! That is what's the matter! Shit!" Reaching over she pulled the carbine from under the dead horse and using it as a crutch pushed herself up. "Give me a hand, kid, God damn it!" As they moved in behind the closest cover of boulder, shots rang out, clipping the rocks, sending off the smell of flint. But this was for effect; those below were being careful not to hit the girl. Letting herself down against the warm face of stone, Sangre groaned and lying on one side, held the broken leg stiffly out. Cocking the carbine, she fired five quick rounds, jacking out the cases. She could keep their heads down for a while but this was it. The end. Without the freedom to move around, stalk, ambush, they would get her.

On the road they had scrambled out of the car and over the side of the bank where the mountain dropped off in gradual descent. Wills heard the bullets *whang* in, glass tinkling and the plunking sound as the Hispano was holed. Next to him, Sandino shouted at Pedrón, "Get in behind her! Climb up and come down from the top! We'll keep her busy!" Pedrón raised his eyebrows in the classic "who me?" expression but checking his pistol, went. *What it came down to,* he thought, *was cajones. If yours clanked you went. All right, let them see a man at work.* The fact that he was setting out to kill a woman and perhaps a child didn't occur to him.

"You know how to shoot, kid?" Sangre said, taking the big automatic out of its holster. It was an early 1900 model Colt with showy silver grips embossed with the Mexican eagle and snake pattern. She cocked it, handing it over. Kate took it, her hand dipping with the weight. "No! No! Use both hands! Jesus! It's ready—go ahead shoot! See if you can hit one of those bastards!" Kate closed her eyes and pulled the trigger, aiming in the direction of the road. Sangre ducked as the shot hit the rocks below, ricochetting in a noisy echo. "Jesus! You are going to kill both of us! Open you damn eyes!"

Kate had not been afraid to fire the gun, and in fact felt the power that was transferred. When Sangre handed it over she had said in effect: *we are now really* compañeras. *It may be too late but at the last I trust you sister.* The next time Kate fired the gun she would keep her eyes open.

Panting, Pedrón leaned against the boulder and caught his breath. He had kept low under the cover of the road bank until he could cross over, then worked his way up the mountain. He was above the two now and could see the shadow of a gun barrel curving along the rock. Taking his boots off, he moved closer like the old Indian he was, careful not to disturb stones underfoot. He was from the North and, like Sangre, used to fighting in the mountains. Leaning over the face of a smooth boulder he could see the top of her miserable rusty head. Bringing the big handgun up and over, he rested it on the stone and took time to aim.

*Damn!* Sangre thought, *an automobile!* Why hadn't she thought of that? Because she was dumb, that's why. A stupid girl who never learned to read or write or think about things. She should have looked to see if the big car was there—then put it out of order before they left. Shit! She took off the sombrero and wiping her head, laid it aside. This was her last day on earth, hiding behind a damn rock defending a redheaded kid you couldn't even pet. Well good-bye redhead! Good-bye funny boys! Good-bye revolution!

She had one thing she was taking with her, one day before the machine guns of Celaya—the day they followed her into the snouts of those guns and killed them—the day she stood on the pile of dead shouting her little lungs out holding up a rifle she could hardly lift and heard them shout back, *"SANGRIENTO NIÑA! SANGRIENTO NIÑA!"*

She moved at the very last as if by some instinctual warning. But Pedrón fired, dropping her with a shot through the head. The rifle clattered down the mountainside, bouncing, then finally falling free. Then it was quiet.

Pedrón waved his bandanna to let them know below that he was all right and not to shoot. Moving cautiously he found Sangre slumped over in the bright ring of blood. But the girl was not there. He listened, heard a rattle of rocks, and found her trapped between boulders. As he came toward her she raised a gun. He smiled and said in Spanish, "Hey, little one, be careful—let me help you—no one wants to be hurt." He said this in a cooing, soft tone, moving forward, left hand held out.

When he was less than three feet away she shot him.

# EIGHT

# Managua

THE *Banana Queen* nudged up to the market dock at about dawn, pushing fat sides against the trade boats and sending out waves that rocked nesting pirogues. Those who were about at that hour were amazed. There had never been anything her size this far up river. When they began to unload the automobile, crowds gathered, people sending for friends and relatives who had never seen one.

The survey boat was highly visible tied up among the local craft, and General Butler gathered the consul and the music boy together on the forward deck as they docked.

"Where's Lieutenant Magnusson?"

"I don't know, sir, still sleeping?"

"Odd, he's always the first one up. Well, come on let's get over to that boat."

They found the pilot, Bayardo Arce below in the cabin being tended to by an old Indian woman. Although in a great deal of pain he was anxious to talk. "That bandit Sandino took my boat, he and a big soldier they called Pedrón."

"My daughter," the consul asked, "a redheaded girl about thirteen?" The interview continued in Spanish.

"Fat? Oh yes, she is something—below Rama she jumped over and tried to escape—but they brought her back."

"Is she all right? What's her condition?"

"Well, they knocked her around a bit, but she took it. That girl has pepper." This was commendable but hardly reassuring.

He heard nothing of their destination, only that horses from a local stable had been sent for and he personally saw them leave, riding through the market.

"It was reported there was a white man with them—he wore glasses."

"Yes, and called himself a reporter—I don't know his name." He grimaced as the Indian woman placed his hand in a mash of herbs. "When you find that bastard Sandino, I hope you cut his balls off!"

"We were thinking more of his head," the general said, smiling. "Get well."

The car was loaded when they returned and Karen Sven sat in back ready to go. "Well," the general said, tipping his campaign hat and joining her. "You certainly look fresh this morning. I trust you had a good night's sleep?"

"Oh yes, I find a boat very soothing."

"It's the rocking motion."

"Absolutely."

"Come on, Music," Magnusson said, smiling. "Let's go."

The music boy found the smile puzzling. The lieutenant had loaded the baggage himself. "Yes sir."

"There's nothing like a congenial dinner party and a good night's sleep to sharpen one's resolve," the general said. They all agreed and the consul put the car in gear, driving carefully through the crowd of Indians. Their faces showed absolute wonder at the miracle of a motorcar. Little children ran alongside, pushing their fingers in the bullet holes in the car's side, while their elders debated the vehicle's manner of power: saying it rode the trail like a canoe so then it was oared by hidden spirits under its bottom—that the noise came from these spirits exhaling. It was awesome.

"I don't know that a second coming could be any more enthusiastically received," the general said. "Let's hope He arrives in a Packard the next time." Sitting in the back with Karen, he was warmed by her sexual glow; noticing the difference in her attitude and that of Magnusson. It wasn't that they looked at each other, rather that they didn't. He was an old hand at observing beautiful women and if they couldn't fill his arms, well, he was glad they filled the arms of those he approved. *Amor proximi.*

They pulled up at the stable on the edge of town. From the interior of a dilapidated barn came the clang of a hammer on an anvil. "I'll ask, sir," Magnusson said, getting out of the car.

Inside it was gloomy and he walked toward the glow of a furnace. A blacksmith stood in front of it, bent over, shaping a shoe on the horn of an anvil. Magnusson was aware of others in the barn, several men in the dress of vaqueros. Reaching the blacksmith he said in his most courteous Spanish. "Forgive my intrusion, sir, but I would like to ask, is the renting of horses permitted here?"

The man kept his head down and continued hammering. Finally Magnusson leaned over and took hold of his wrist, using leverage to hold the hammer on the anvil. "Perhaps you did not hear me?"

There was a shifting of the others, a creak of leather, the tinkle of a spur. Then a loud metallic *clack*! They stopped. Silhouetted in the sunlit doorway was what appeared to be a boy holding a machine gun pointed casually at the ground. In the silence that followed, Magnusson released the blacksmith, then turning his head, spit on the hood of the furnace. The sizzle was audible as he walked out.

"These people are not friendly, sir." Magnusson said. The music boy held the Thompson as he got in, then jumped to the running board as they drove off.

"It's obvious," the general replied, "that Sandino found comfort here."

"Well," the consul added, "we have to remember that even if they don't support him, he is Nicaraguan and we are not."

"I can live with that handicap," he answered dryly.

They passed out of the town, paths merging into a road that led toward the mountains. Donkeys and ox carts straggled by. "One of the advantages of a primitive country is the lack of roads. We don't have to worry over which way to go—there is only one way."

"Which way is that?" Magnusson asked, putting his arm on the back of the seat and sweeping his eyes past Karen back to the consul at the wheel.

"It leads over the mountain and to the lowlands at the edge of Lake Nicaragua. From there the road goes to Tiptapi and Managua."

"I'll tell you, sir," the music boy said, depressed at the sight of so much open space, "mountains must be good for somethin', but you sure aren't going to step up to a rock and get served beer or a plate of corn beef."

"That's hard to argue with," the general answered.

Sandino and Wills made their way up among the boulders behind the two vaqueros. They passed Sangre's body and found Pedrón higher up, twisting a bandanna around his bloody left arm. "The little girl shot me," he said, laughing. "Please don't tell the troops." Wills climbed up to help him, tightening the cloth to stop the flow of blood and taking off his belt to make a sling. "Tie it in tight," Pedrón said, gritting his teeth, "I think the bone is chipped."

Sandino examined the girl. She lay to one side, back against the rock, head on her chest. "Is she all right?" he asked, cradling her head.

"I hope not," Pedrón answered. "She was ready to pull the trigger again when I clipped her. I tell you, she's a piece!"

There was a shudder and Kate threw her head back, jerking away from Sandino's touch in a spasm. "You're all right . . ." he said, smiling, trying to soothe her.

"Fock you!" she answered in a voice that sounded remarkably like Sangre's. He was shocked and stood up stiffly.

"Get down to the car! I can't believe you're the daughter of the American consul."

"And I can't believe you're the son of anybody," she snapped, working her jaw.

Sandino turned away, furious. He caught Wills's eye and if he had smiled, made even the most feeble joke, Sandino would have shot him on the spot. They went down past Sangre, head dipped to the pool of blood, arm thrown back as if in a dancer's bow. Kate passed, eyes averted, Sandino, Wills, and Pedrón behind her. The vaqueros stopped to remove her spurs and gun belt. Going through her pack they took the small amount of pesos, several medals in a narrow boxed closed with a rubber band, and earrings made of silver and turquoise.

On the road they got in the car, with Wills and Kate on the awkward jump seats facing Pedrón and Sandino. Sandino kept his head turned toward the window, tense and aloof. Pedrón smiled, amused by a little girl who had the nerve to shoot him at three feet with a big Colt automatic. "I think you didn't want to kill me, *niña*," he said in Spanish. "How could you miss at the distance?"

Kate answered in her stilted Spanish, "Because bad man, the gun was too heavy to point between your eyes!"

He thought this very funny and laughed aloud, and alone.

As the car droned on, dust sifting in the windows with sudden swerves around rocks, Sandino regained control, at last speaking in his most formal English to Kate. He had still not given up his idea of reforming her to the cause. There were very few people he had been unable to dominate if he put his mind to it, and he would not let this little girl treat him without respect. Patience, he knew was less expensive than force. He tried again. "You must understand that you are involved in an important time of Nicaraguan history. If events are harsh, then this is necessary to bring about change. Our cause . . ."

"Your cause is you!" Kate said, eyes squeezed together, a flush of red rising on her cheeks. Sandino noticed for the first time that cheekbones were visible, that the face had begun to change to an almond shape from the round. She was still a child but there was that about her now called, *feminina*.

"If you mean am I more important than a dirty Mexican woman, you're right." He had leaned in to meet her hate, finding the beautiful lavender eyes disconcerting at this range. He was famous for staring people down, but she didn't blink.

"She was brave! A hero! And you let them kill her up there like she was . . . nothing! Let these . . ." she said, gesturing at the two in the front seat, "take her pitiful things."

"Would they look better on a coyote?"

"Her medals would." Silence.

Wills was getting very uneasy. Both he and Sandino made the same mistake treating her as a child. She was precocious, intelligent with a maddening way of turning your point against you, and an independence he had seldom met in adults. It was a poor simile, but she was like a fighting cock that couldn't be stopped unless you killed it. Watching her with Sandino was disturbing because her emotions were totally revealed and he tried to hold his back; be the teacher; the mentor, and in the end was forced to leave logic for a shouting match.

Wills touched her arm and she shrugged it off, eyes still locked on Sandino's. "Kate, Sangre was under César's command—she deserted and took . . . a political prisoner . . ."

"Is that what I am? Really?! I'm thirteen years old and I'm a political prisoner? Are you saying that you two came all the way to Bluefields to capture me?"

"No, what I . . ."

"As I remember I was riding Calvin up to the bluff to watch the ship's lights and you were there—doing what? Spying on them? Then you chased me and Calvin, and broke his leg . . ." She turned and looked at Wills, her expression changed. "He didn't break his leg . . . *you killed him!* Is that right? I should have known! Who did it, you? No, you wouldn't have the . . ."

She turned back to Sandino, but he had broken off the confrontation and was looking out the window. "It was him! Of course—he killed him! He could do that!"

"Kate," Wills said, "it was necessary . . ."

"Why? Because he was a political prisoner who was running away?" Sandino kept his profile toward the window, tapping his teeth with his fingernail. "Magnusson's going to get you," she said, "But if he doesn't, *I will.*"

It was a child's silly, empty threat, but it raised the hair on Wills's neck.

The consul was able to make good time driving the Packard; twenty-five, sometimes even thirty miles an hour. They had passed the huge ranch of Plutarco Heran del Sancho noticing only the cattle grazing on high slopes. The farther they went, the fewer travelers they saw. And when they passed an old man leading a donkey and wearing a sombrero, Magnusson shouted at the consul to stop. Leaping out he ran back catching the donkey's bridle before it could be turned off into the rocks. "Don't be afraid, father," Magnusson said. *Afraid?* He was indeed afraid. Earlier he had heard shots on the road and hiding, saw men and a machine. Later when they left he climbed up, found the body of a woman, and had taken her clothes and hat. And here was a soldier asking him if he was afraid. Ha!

"I like your hat—it came from the head of a Mexican, I think."

The old man kept his face ducked, trying to smile back, and said nothing. Magnusson hung on to the donkey. "Look, father, keep your hat, it suits you—but tell me if you saw others on this road riding in the company of a girl with red hair?" He shook his head and Magnusson went on patiently. "Think hard, now. These people have taken our daughter and when we find and kill them we will bless those who help us—Heaven help those who don't."

"They rode in a machine like that," the old man said at last.

"What? An *automobile!* Are you sure?"

"Oh yes, it was black and had a square top with heads in it." He would not be likely to forget seeing two machines in one day. It was a thing that would never happen again in his lifetime.

"Thank you!" Magnusson shouted and running back, jumped in the Packard. "They've got a car! The old man saw it!"

"How . . ." the consul wanted to know.

"No matter!" the general said. "*Let's go man!*" The car was put in gear, accelerating up the grade on a series of switchbacks that climbed the last mountain before descending to the plain. The gears wound out, whining, struggling to pull the weight of the passengers and gear. The Motor-Meter began its trip to the red and the music boy pleaded, "Please, Fidelia! Don't do that!"

"Look!" Karen shouted. But Magnusson had already seen the dark spot of a car as it came in view on the opposite side of the mountain road, a mile away.

They were seen at the same time in the Hispano-Suiza. "A car!" one of the vaqueros shouted.

"The Packard!" Wills said, leaning toward the window in the backseat.

Kate straightened. "Magnusson! He's coming after you!"

Pedrón pushed between them and shouted through the roll-down divider at the sharpshooter in the front seat. "Can you hit them?"

"I don't know, *jefe*," the man said, laying the rifle along the back of the seat. He aimed past the driver directly across to the other car. "It's nearly a mile . . ." Leading the car, he waited until the crosshairs of the scope lined up and pulled the trigger.

"*Jesus!*" The driver, Raul, jerked forward as the gun went off in his ear and the car swerved.

"Look out!" The road was narrow with no guardrails or shoulders and a drop meant a fall of hundreds of feet to a dry wash of rocks below.

In the Packard they heard the shot. "He's still too far to hit us," Magnusson said, unslinging his Springfield and adjusting the sight. This particular rifle was called the "Special Target" and had been hand assembled and finished for shooting competitors in national matches. He thought highly of it.

The Hispano began to fall behind on the steep rise. It was a good ten years older than the Packard and underpowered for the weight it carried. When it came in view on the next switchback, Magnusson tightened the sling on the rifle and braced himself against the stanchion of the rear windshield. "The yardage is within reach now." He could make out the driver and sharpshooter in the chauffeur's compartment.

"Be careful for God's sake!" the consul said, "Kate's in that car!"

Magnusson did not have to be told. He had never in his life let off a weapon unless the target was clearly sighted. But he understood the concern. At that moment there was a shot from the other car, close this time, coming in a foot over their heads. They ducked but he paid it no mind, concentrating; relaxing but not relaxing, leading the target, compensating for the cars movement; waiting for that split second when he was locked in. *There!* He fired.

The sharpshooter lurched back as though kicked in the head—which in a sense he had been. The thirty-ought-six "spitzer" projectile entered just under the brow of his right eye. His head banged back against the door sill and his eyes looked up at the sky.

"Damn!" Pedrón said, "That was some shot!"

"Magnusson!" Kate shouted.

Sandino leaned forward. "Faster!"

The car lugged up the incline at what seemed a snail's pace.

"My foot's to the floor, *jefe*! There's too much weight!"

"Somebody's going to have to jump and lighten us," Pedrón said, laughing.

"Who's going to be first?" Kate asked, smiling and goading Sandino.

"Push out the shooter," Sandino said in a matter-of-fact voice, shocking her as he intended. The driver reached over and opening the right-hand door with one hand shoved him out. He hit the road sending up a puff of dirt then bounced and flopped back, limbs at all angles.

The road had straightened out as they approached the summit and the Packard was only minutes behind the Hispano and gaining.

"*We're going to catch them!*" The music boy shouted.

"Once they get over that hump and start down it's going to depend on driving," Magnusson said. The consul was a skillful driver. Thanks to his wild college years and a Jordan "Playboy," he had developed this skill racing on frozen lakes near Amherst College. He swerved suddenly around the body in the road, brushing the mountainside and returning to the center track.

"Terrible," the general said, looking back. "What kind of a military man would treat the body of one of his men like that?"

Pedrón loaded his big revolver, holding it between his knees. Then leaning out the left window of the car, he held his wounded arm in, and rested the gun on the S-shape of the landau bar. The front end of the Packard was only a half dozen lengths away coming straight at him. He fired, first hitting the radiator, then aimed for the left front tire.

"*Down!*" the consul shouted, but Magnusson stayed up, sighting his rifle along the hood of the car. At this angle he could only see the arm of the gunman and didn't dare shoot through the back of the car for fear of hitting Kate. If he shot the tires out there was a chance the car would go over the side. At that point

Pedrón's last shot hit their front tire and it blew out in an explosion louder than the sound of the gunfire.

The car crossed up and hopped sideways, slamming into the mountainside in a hideous sound of scraping metal, then bounced back, skating to the edge of the road, kicking rocks over. The left rear wheel was actually skipping down the bank, while the front end set up a shimmy. For a second it seemed they must go over, following the falling rock into the gorge below. The passengers were thrown from one side to the other and Karen's scream changed pitch at each reversal. The consul fought it, elbows held straight out, gripping the fat wooden wheel, refusing to give an inch. Gradually he kept it on the edge of the road and came to a shuddering stop with the wounded wheel hanging out over the drop.

Ahead, the rear of the Hispano with its two round carriage windows disappeared over the summit as surely as if it had dropped off the earth. It was quiet now with only the sound of the water from the holed radiator piddling on the ground. They were all thinking nearly the same thing: The rescue attempt had failed. Once Sandino reached the city and was swallowed up the only way they would see him was when he arranged it.

Sabar Manzanares put together the train ride. Nervous and efficient with bottle-bottom lenses set in wire-frame glasses, he looked the clerk—which was exactly what he had been when he met Sandino in 1926. One of the original group that had marched off to take Puerto Cabezas, Sabar was also one of the few in the new army that understood dispersement and complications of supply rate. Sent ahead to deal with the railroad contacts, he dressed as they did, in a pongee suit, tie, and wide Panama; meeting with them in cafés and brothels, listening and soothing. The railroad was managed by an American company, J. G. White, and they had to be careful—but after all, it belonged to Nicaragua. He understood their fears and carried a large suitcase full of *Cordobas* to smooth these away. Despite the ferocious reputation of the Revolutionary Army, a great deal of business was done with bribes as well as guns. Certainly the officials he was dealing with were patriots, men of the right political party, but they were also businessmen, and where there was risk there should be reward.

There was only one public railroad in Nicaragua, Costa Pacifica, and it ran from the port of Cortino up near the Honduras border, past the main cities of León and Managua to end at Granada 400 miles away. It was a left-handed legacy of Cornelius Vanderbilt's Accessory Transit Company, having originally been formed in the 1850s to transport American Argonauts by ship to the California goldfields via Greytown on the Mosquito Coast. From there American passengers were transported across the country in a series of stagecoaches, then lake steamer to the Pacific Coast where another ship took them to California. With the success of this rapid transportation system, the railroad was eventually built connecting the West Coast cities.

Sabar arranged for an old engine, an expendable wood burner, to be shunted onto a siding outside of Cortino. There, coupled to three boxcars and a caboose it waited out of sight amid the deserted buildings of a cement factory. Troops infiltrating down from Ocotal would be loaded on the night of March 30th. Then the train would be put on the freight line and given a highball straight through to Managua for the attack the next morning.

There were problems. Because they could not trust the yard personnel at Managua to turn the engine around, it would have to *back* to Managua. When Sabar told this to Angel Ortez, the troop commander, he shrugged. "If we're seen, then they'll think were going in the opposite direction." Miguel Angel Ortez y Guillén was Sabar's opposite—dashing and a romantic with flowing blond hair and features that suggested an Anglo-Saxon strain in his background. He was one of Sandino's most aggressive officers, popular with the men and actually admired by the Marines and *guardia* for his courage and military ability.

Dapper as always, he wore polished cordovan puttees and a broad hat rolled at the sides. He was one of those young men from a good family attracted to the revolution for adventure. If he had a weakness it was leading a complicated love life with a wife, mistress, and girlfriends.

"What I'm concerned about is Cesár. Where is he?"

"Coming up from Bluefields."

"Is he still traveling with that hawk-nose who writes?"

"As far as I know."

"It makes me very nervous to read in the papers about battles I haven't fought yet. What's to prevent this American from leaking plans of our attack on Managua? If the *guardia* is waiting, they will fry us like *chicherones*."

What worried Sabar was *would* Sandino be waiting? If the trucks to transport them to the presidential palace were not there, they would be trapped. "Don't worry," he said, sounding unconvincing.

"Tell me not to breathe."

The troops under Angel Ortez's command had begun to straggle in several days ago, camping around the train while refitting went on. Sabar had managed four Lewis machineguns and one trench mortar brought over by a defecting *guardia* crew. There were ammunition and rations to be loaded, even the luxury of medical supplies.

"What's this?" Angel asked, "Bandages? We never had those before—does this mean someone might be hurt?"

"They came from the American Red Cross."

"I knew those Yankees loved us after all."

On the night of the 30th, the boarding began, the troops laughing and shouting with the relief of getting under way. The engine was stoked and fired, valves were opened, and they began to chug down the line in reverse, pushing the three boxcars and caboose ahead.

Officers were quartered in the caboose and had the eerie sensation of being at the back of a train rushing forward with only a few inches of wood between them and whatever they might meet. A headlamp had been rigged and brakemen stood on each side step clinging to handgrips, lanterns ready to signal the engineer at any obstruction ahead on the track.

"I always wondered what it felt like to be shit and going down the toilet," Angel said, "this is it."

Standing on the little front porch as the train raced into the night, Sabar did not answer. He could only hope, once again, Sandino would be waiting.

Something else was waiting, and at about 4:30 A.M. on the 29th the citizens of Managua felt the first tremors: a slight shaking of cups and plates that popped eyes open all over the city. But it passed and they went back to sleep. To live in this city was to live with earthquakes and eruptions. Managua was squeezed between two lakes and a half dozen volcanos, some of them active. There were people still alive who remembered the horrific outbreak of eruption and incessant rumbling of earthquakes in 1885. Ash showered down as far away as Mexico and the entire population fled the city while the *infernillos* emitted sulphurous vapor and smoke, lighting up the landscape with bluish flames.

As the Hispano-Suiza traveled through the night of the 29th, the most awesome of the volcanos, Momotombo, came in view across Lake Managua. It rose straight from the plain, startling viewers with an uneasy sense of the supernatural. Its smooth conical sides somehow suggested a monstrous breast punched through the earth's crust. The poet Rubén Darío wrote that it was "bald and nude," a slumbering, sinister she-colossus.

They saw it from the unimpressive town of Tipitapa on the south bank of the river that was its namesake. This *rio* linked Lake Managua with Lake Nicaragua during the rainy season. It was here American secretary of war Henry L. Stimson's shaky peace settlement was signed in 1927. Only fifteen minutes from Managua, it was one of the outposts of the government army defending the capital. But as they went by the *guardia* barracks appeared unmanned.

"They've been ordered down to Masaya," Sandino said. Wills looked at him, wondering how he could possibly know this. "General Irias is making a feint with the third column to draw them off. He'll be noisy and keep them occupied on the thirty-first."

"You will still have to deal with Marines and *guardia* in the city—after all César, that is their headquarters."

"All the better, if the people know that we can strike right under their noses, then we have won. At this point one thing is very important—the Yankees must acknowledge once and for all that we are not bandits, but the Defending Army of the National Sovereignty."

"Maybe one of the reasons they won't acknowledge it, is its length. Americans tend to fall asleep in the middle of long titles."

"They will be awake on the thirty-first."

Although the road here was still dirt, it seemed a superhighway compared to the mountain road, and they made good time. Approaching the outskirts of Managua, Sandino went on speaking quietly in Spanish to Wills. Pedrón had moved into the front seat with the driver and Kate slept curled up next to the window. The two men sat in the back rocking with the gentle motion of the car.

"This is what I ask you to do, Carlton. When we get to the city please arrange a press meeting. Can you do that? It is time to announce our intentions regarding the consul's daughter." He nodded toward Kate. "It's been four days since she joined us and the world holds its breath." He smiled.

Wills took his time answering. "I can approach Gabry Rivas at *La Prensa* to select the right people—foreign correspondents. This is going to be dangerous to do in Managua, César—I hope you have a safe place picked out to hold the conference."

"I was thinking of The Grand."

"César . . ."

*El Grande* was the only first-class hotel in the city. It was downtown overlooking Laguna Tiscapa and the presidential palace in what was considered the most desirable area—where the wind blowing off the open market and poor section went in the other direction.

"No, I'm serious, it's the perfect place, central to newspapers and elegant enough even for you. Check in and later Pedrón and I will smuggle the girl in. Oh, and be sure a photographer is there."

Wills shook his head. Whatever could be said of Sandino he certainly had skills as a publicist. "I hope you're not going to persist in the business of presenting her as a convert?"

"I'll tell them what I told you, that she is being given a tour of our country to better understand the necessity of revolution— that we demand no ransom, only understanding."

"All right, you say what you want, and I will report it. But it must be understood that I will be allowed to file my story ahead of the others?"

"Of course," he said, tapping his teeth, an annoying gesture he had developed lately. "I'm also going to announce the raid on the presidental palace."

"You are joking now."

"The timing will be tricky but if the raid begins as the conference ends, it should make a stir."

"To say the least."

As the car entered the city of Managua they came round through the lakeside district. In the middle of the last century the rich built homes here at the water's edge. They were done in the French style popular then, with mansard roofs and the filigree of iron work made in Albany, New York, and shipped down as ballast in banana boats. The houses still showed French elegance despite vivid colors the French would have sniffed at—and there was a tone, a quality of worldliness not visible in the rest of the city. But it was changing. The poor were nibbling at the corners. It was necessary now to construct walls topped with broken glass and hire private guards.

The Moncada regime blamed it on rebel elements and the

rebel elements blamed it on the president. The journalist Belausteguigonitia said of him, ". . . Moncada with his air of an old Bacchic faun, lover of good wine and bad women . . . his life has a bit of everything, something of the fox if certainly nothing of the lion . . . now he builds some school or hospital but the poor people say under their breath that first he made them poor . . ."

Even Lake Managua, along with its Siamese twin Nicaragua, linked by the delicate cord of the Rio Tipitapa, was changing. Larger than Delaware and Rhode Island, together they were the only freshwater lakes that accommodated both the maneating shark and the crocodile. The Managuans loved them, calling them the sweet sea, but the sweet sea was beginning to smell. Moncada said it was progress and his enemies called it exploitation.

Turning off into the heart of the city they became entangled in a crosshatch of streets that only Sandino could navigate. Wills thought he recognized a familiar baroque church and the blocklong colonaded building that had been a colonial landmark; now a market. As Sandino instructed the driver, the car began to be noticed. It was not the sort of machine you saw often and it turned heads. The people up at that hour gawked as they passed.

"This damned capitalist's wagon is a liability now," Sandino said, "Raul, as soon as you drop us off, turn around and get out of the city."

"Yes *jefe*." But first Raul was going to find an automobile shop to patch up the bullet wounds. There was no way he could take this machine back to Don Plutarco with a single dimple on its tender skin. He was directed down narrow side streets until they came to a two-story garage painted a salmon color. It carried the sign, LA BUEN TONA—BASURA CARRETERA. The horn sounded, doors were pushed aside and the Hispano drove in, parking by several big trucks. These were the vehicles that would carry the troops to attack the presidental palace.

"Well I always knew you had a sense of humor, *jefe*," Pedrón said, getting out of the car and sniffing.

"What better than these to carry us to the palace of the president?"

A fat man came down wooden stairs from the second floor and embraced Sandino. This was Hector Balcazar, a cousin who had for years been one of his contacts in Managua. "César! General Sandino! Please come upstairs where the air is better." They went up the stairs arm in arm. "I am sorry about these trucks, but nothing else was possible. However we were able to recruit drivers from among the union men—good revolutionaries."

"That's fine, Hector. Is there a phone here?"

"Oh yes." They went in a balcony room that was fitted with dirty glass windows that overlooked the garage.

Sandino paused and called down at the others. "Pedrón, bring Miss Kelly up here. Carlton, you'd better start for the hotel. I'm afraid I can't offer you any transport. As you saw, taking the Hispano would cause comment and these trucks are not quite chic enough for The Grand." Waving, he went in the door and it closed.

Pedrón opened the back door of the car for Kate. "Come on *soldado*, we've arrived at the perfumed gardens."

Kate got out, sleepy. "What's that awful smell?"

"Garbage," Wills said.

Up the street, José Saltillo had been going to work when he noticed the Hispano-Suiza turn in the garage. He recognized it. As a mechanic in Granada years ago he had seen the car many times. He wondered if that old devil Plutarco was in town and if the police would be interested. Informing on the rich gave you a warm feeling inside and sometimes a few *cordobas*. He would receive neither. By this time tomorrow he and 1,450 of the city's population of 35,000 would be dead.

Today they were just getting up, asking each other if they felt the tremor of last night, and being reassured by the old myth that the big earthquakes came 100 years apart. It was not time yet. They talked about the continuing depression and worried about their jobs—if they had one, and very few gave a thought to Sandino or the Marines. The fighting had gone on five years and they were bored. He was a hero to the foreign press and student radicals.

It was Holy Week and many planned trips to the mountains or the seashore. The popular American minister Hanna and his wife had already left to spend the Easter holidays in Guatemala. Sandino might also have been shocked to find out that a great many of these city people actually liked Americans.

Wills checked in *El Grande* about noon. It was a hotel that prided itself on being *modernismo*. Built in 1905 in the Art Nouveau style of the time, exterior balconies undulated in waves across the six-story facade and inside, sculpted plaster curved to meet sensual woodwork in rounded-off shapes—there was not a straight line in the place. Unfortunately, the spatial effect was spoiled by an overlay of heavy drapery and the ubiquitous palms.

The desk clerk explained that although the hotel was fully booked, there was a suite available on the sixth floor. Wills knew why. In an earthquake town you could always find space on top floors. When he had cleaned up and changed into his seersucker suit, he walked around to the offices of *La Prensa*. These were on a large square that had been called *Xilloa* and was now renamed for Vice President Salzar. Entering the building and going though the newsroom was heady after his rural interlude. Newspaper offices smelled the same the world over and the sounds of typewriters, phones ringing, and urgent voices soothed him, even if slowed to Managua's tropical beat.

He was shown into the office of the editor by a pretty, modern woman in bright lipstick. Gabry Rivas was a reserved man with a great deal of presence and a reputation for fair-mindedness that was rare in the political capital. Wills personally liked him; his only affectation seemed to be combing strands of hair straight across his bald head in a style Wills punned as *hairpursuit*.

They shook hands and sitting under a noisy ceiling fan talked general news for several minutes. Then Wills came to the point. "Gabry, I can present you with a big story. One that will guarantee headlines around the world."

"Shirley Temple will visit?"

"Nothing that sensational. No, this is something else entirely—it requires secrecy and security. I must have your word that you will follow instructions as to the time and place of the interview."

"I see, yes certainly you have it." Gabry knew exactly who was involved. After all it was no secret that Wills had been traveling with Sandino for months as his stories in *The Nation* plainly showed. He knew him to be an accurate, if pedantic reporter of integrity. "What is it you want me to arrange?"

"The reporters. Your people of course, and a few foreign press—no more than say, eight in all. Have them stand by here, and I will call you later today as to when they will be picked up— it may be very late."

"The interview will be in the city?"

"Yes, I can tell you that."

"Very well." And they went over the reporters to be selected. When this was finished, they talked of news from the United States. Gabry, much more current that Wills, cheerfully reported continuing stock market disasters, Legs Diamond's shooting in a place called Albany, and a new song craze called Heebie Jeebies. He asked what a Jebbie was.

As Wills rose to leave, the editor shook his hand and smiled. "Well Carlton, it looks as though you've become something of a press secretary." Wills didn't like this a bit, but smiled back.

Outside, the tension of the last days, culminating in this last piece of suspense—the secret news conference—hit him. There was something else, an uneasy sense of it not being right. Guilt? The editor's words had stung. Had he become Sandino's mouthpiece? Was his integrity compromised in putting the story before everything?

Walking back he came by the *Campo de Marte* at the bottom of Tiscapa hill. This was the headquarters of the Marine-led Guardia Nacional—the very people who had been chasing them the last four days. He stopped. There was no question that he had the right to protect the source of his information, but did he have the right to jeopardize the consul's daughter while collecting it? This continued to rub his conscience. When this story came out how would his colleagues feel about him? He thought he knew.

*All he would have to do is walk through that gate and discreetly arrange that the Marines and* guardia *be waiting at The Grand to take Sandino and rescue Kate after the conference. Not only would he save the girl, he would have an even bigger story.*

The Packard ended up on the edge of the road, left front tire hanging over the drop. When the rescue party gingerly piled out they found it a wreck. The right side of the body was smashed in, permanently wedging those doors shut and the rear fender was pressed up against the tire. It had been necessary to climb over to get out, with General Butler helping Karen Sven. As Magnusson and the music boy stepped around front to look at the blown tire, the radiator finished its last piddle.

"Damn!" the music boy said, "I believe *Fidelia* has been killed!"

Magnusson bent down and looked at the tire. It was shredded and the wheel bent. "Get the tools and let's change this."

What that means, the music boy knew was, *you* get the tools and *you* change the tire. But he got them, and balancing precariously over the edge of the drop, began to work the nuts loose.

The consul walked up the road until he found a dead limb from the *quebrancho* tree, called the "axbreaker" by the locals.

Coming back, he got it wedged under the fender and began to pry it away from the wheel. The general and Karen looked on. "Does this automobile belong to the government, Dick?" the general asked.

"Yes sir," the consul said, grunting.

"That's good, it would be a shame if it were yours."

Karen was watching Magnusson and when he leaned over the edge to give the music boy a hand in pulling the wheel off, she said, "Oh! Be careful!" He frowned and she bit her lip. The wheel broke loose and they let it fall free, dropping a hundred feet, bouncing up, and continuing on in a series of clattering hops until it bottomed out, thudding into the hard packed stone of the wash. They watched its descent, each thinking, "That could have been me."

"Can we start the car now?" Karen asked.

"I'm afraid not. The radiator won't hold water," the consul answered. ". . . however if if we can get it to the top of this grade, we can probably coast down to the main road. As I remember there's a village there."

Magnusson looked to the top. "That's a good two hundred feet at about a three-percent grade."

"Then let's get to it men," the general ordered cheerfully. "Miss Sven, can you drive?"

"No, I'm afraid not . . . but I think I could steer if that's what you mean?"

"Fine. Let me help you in, and while you guide the car the rest of us will push it." He helped her over the door and she climbed nimbly behind the wheel. The front end dipped toward the cliff side but if she felt it she didn't react.

The men got behind and began to push. It was deadly hard work and with the combined effort of all four the car barely moved. Every few feet the music boy would block the rear wheel so they could rest. It was hot even at that altitude in the mountains and sweat poured off them. At last, only yards from the top, it didn't seem they could go on. Too exhausted to even talk they sat in the road, backs against the car, lungs heaving, breath coming in hoarse rasps.

When they had rested, Karen got out, and standing by the driver's open door, put one hand against the side mount the other on the steering wheel. "Let me help—I can push and steer too." Nobody argued, and when they began this time—with her extra effort and less weight—it was just enough to make the difference.

Sooner than expected the Packard crested the grade and began down. Karen just had time to get to the running board and into the seat. *"Oh! Oh! How do I stop it?"* Magnusson was off and running, arms and legs pumping out his last bit of energy, shoes slapping the road, then he took a jump to the running board and a tumble over the side into the front seat where he reached down and pulled on the brake. He was finished, head flopped back against the seat, mouth open gasping for breath, eyes closed. She kissed him.

"I knew you would save me!"

At the top of the hill the consul smiled and said, "I'd say he earned that, sir."

"By God, I'd run down the hill barefoot for another like it," the general answered.

The music boy came puffing up behind them. "What happened?"

The ride down was an anticlimax after the ascent; a series of soundless swings around curves, the wind blowing back and cooling the exhausted pushers. Then the road began to level off, showing a broad green plain, and beyond through the haze, the twin peak outlines of sinister volcanos on Ometepe Island, Lake Nicaragua. The tin roofs of a village appeared ahead and a real road, with an occasional appearance of a truck among the carts. The car came to a final, silent stop about a mile from the closest building and the music boy got out. No one had to tell him who was going to walk that mile and look for help.

"Try and arrange for someone to tow us," the consul said, "I seem to remember a garage or blacksmith shop up there."

"Yes sir." And taking the water bags he set off.

When they next saw him trudging up the road an hour later there was no sign of a team of oxen following. "Damn!" Magnusson said, "I should have gone, he didn't bring a tow." When he got close they saw his jaw was bulged out and he was chewing vigorously.

"What about the tow, Music?" Magnusson said, annoyed.

"Won't need it, sir," he replied, talking around the object in his mouth, "I met this English guy at the cantina and he showed me where to pick these." He held up several leaves.

"Gum copal," the consul said.

"If you chew it up, then spit in the radiator it will plug up the leaks—so he says."

"Disgusting!" Karen said from the backseat, turning her face away.

The general opened the left-hand door. "Miss Sven, why don't we retire up the road while the expectoration is applied?"

Magnusson, the consul, and the music boy stood in front of the car chewing and spitting in the radiator. When the last leaf had been masticated the consul gagged, "My God that's the worst thing I've tasted, including cod liver oil and tapioca!"

"It should work." Magnusson was trying to move his mouth. "It's got my lips stuck together."

Water was poured in and like magic, the leaks stopped. "Would you look at that?!" the music boy said, "Damn! When I get home I'm going to manufacture it and make a fortune—I could call it 'SpitStop'!"

With a hundred good chewers you ought to be able to turn out ten gallons of the stuff a day," Magnusson said taking a big swig of water.

"Count me out," the consul added.

They traveled on; around the edge of the lake through a dozen small villages and by late afternoon entered Managua. At over thirty miles an hour the front end set up a shimmy, but even so they made good time, arriving some ten hours after Sandino.

"What next?" the consul asked.

"Well, Dick, we will want to contact Colonel Matthews at the *guardia* for help in locating Sandino. Since the American military has indicated lack of support for our rescue party, they are our best hope. However, before we do that I suggest we check in a hotel."

There is only one first rate place, *El Grande*, sir."

"Fine, only the best is good enough for us," he said, smiling at Karen.

Checking in to The Grand they were told the same story given to gringos and the unwary; the hotel was booked and the only rooms left on the top, sixth floor.

"Just right," the general announced, "I prefer the view. We'll want a nice single room for Miss Sven here—Lieutenant Magnusson, you and consul can double up and I'll take the music boy in with me as factotum." He chuckled. The music boy knew what that meant, he was going to be a butler as well as tire changer and machine gunner. It looked like he would never blow the bugle again.

They went up in an elaborate cage elevator and stepped off at the sixth floor into a long hall. The walls curved up to a ceiling plastered in the soft swirls of Art Nouveau. In wells down its length lighting fixtures with many stained globes were hung by chains. As they walked along the tile floor, the fixtures began to sway, tinkling.

"Oh!" Karen said. "Are they supposed to do that?"

"Not unless we're at sea," the general answered, feeling the deck beneath him move.

"Earthquake," the consul said, suddenly pale.

Across town at *La Buen Tona*, garbage garage, the glass in the office partition started to rattle. Hector Balcazar, the old earthquake watcher, got up immediately and started for the door. Sandino reached out from his chair and caught his wrist almost casually.

"Where are you going, cousin?"

"I thought I'd step outside for a . . ."

"You can do it here in your pants," Pedrón said, laughing.

Kate looked from face to face, feeling the room shake.

"What is that?"

"Nothing," Pedrón said, "Don't worry about it. They figure the big earthquakes come about a hundred years apart—the next one is not due until nineteen eighty-five."

It was March 30, 1931.

# *NINE*

# March 31

ARRIVING at *El Grande* late in the afternoon of the 30th the rescue party was exhausted. After their horrendous day, the brief shake was nothing. Each member swore they were going straight to bed. Karen Sven waved good-bye at her door saying she would welcome the motion of an earthquake to rock her to sleep.

General Butler surveyed his room, and once the music boy adjusted the furniture to his liking, settled in at a three-legged Art Nouveau desk and wrote letters. The first was to his wife Ethel, then "Snooks" and her new husband, finally the boys; Smedley, Jr., and Tom Dick. Inspired, he jotted a note to Lowell Thomas asking how their book was doing, suggesting he was involved in a chase after Sandino that might make an article for *Collier's* entitled: "Short Revolutionaries I Have Known." He chuckled, ready for dinner.

"Time to fill up the cracks," he announced as the music boy supervised the serving by two waiters. Looking at the chicken molé he segued into a story. "This reminds me of Haiti. The big Marine event of the sixteen season in Port au Prince was Littleton Waller's appointment to the rank of brigadier general. We all wanted to honor the old boy—our commanding officer—so we arranged an eleven-gun salute from the fort on his birthday party. We had invited fifty guests—the president and his cabinet—the white community too . . ." He tucked his napkin in and commenced eating. "At midnight when the first gun went off we all stood with our new brigadier as his personal flag was unfurled and the band played, 'Hail to the Chief.' We waited a long time for the next gun and at number three they stopped altogether."

Butler was a democratic officer and not above talking to an inlisted man while he ate. The music boy shifted from one foot to another, nodding his head. "Well," he continued, "three guns in the middle of the night is an old Haitian signal meaning revolution is beginning—and everybody began to get nervous. So I rushed over to the fort and found the *gendarmerie* were warming the gunpowder in frying pans before each shot. It was damp from the rain. 'Dammit, men,' I said, warm enough at one time to finish the salute! I went back to the gala and about an hour later there was this terrific explosion from the fort; I mean the whole ammo dump went up, sending off what looked like fireworks— pinwheels and rockets. Everybody assumed the effect was planned and began clapping. I joined in with them."

The music boy laughed with him and at last the general retired to his bedroom. "You're set for the night, Music?"

"Oh, yes sir, they've put a cot up in the pantry."

"Good enough, time to pipe to the hammocks—reveille is an hour before dawn as usual."

"Yes sir." He waited until the door was closed, counted to one hundred then went out the door, down the lift, across the hotel lobby, and into the Parrot Bar. As he came in, a girl who looked like Lupé Velez said, "Hey sallour want to have the good time? Huh, babee?"

"I'm a Marine," the music boy said, smiling.

"Sheet, I know that—I juss wanted to see eef you was payeeng attention."

"Listen, baby," he said, sweet talking her, "what I got for you already stood at attention and saluted."

In the room he and Magnusson were sharing, Richard Kelly could not sleep. He wanted to talk, feeling guilty about Tomás's death and now that they had lost Sandino's trail, worried sick they would not find his daughter, Kate, in time. "I tried to call my wife . . . Norma, but I couldn't get through. You'd think Bluefields was on the moon—no, I probably could get through to the moon." There was silence and just when Magnusson thought he was drifting off, the consul said, "You know, when Kate was born I was disappointed. I've never told anyone this—but I wanted a boy. Maybe she sensed that. Have you ever met a little girl with such, well, fierce bravery? No, of course not, you don't know her. I used to think it was stubbornness, refusing to cry and terrorizing playmates with dangerous games . . ." He lay on his back looking at the ceiling, talking in a monotone.

"I was proud of her bravery—but it made me uneasy— where did it come from? Me? Hardly. Who knows? In a litter of pups who can say which will go to ground . . . a poor analogy, but you know what I mean . . . and independent, it could be maddening. She has no instinct for tact—none, says out loud what she feels—tells no lies. That's what we're taught isn't it? Ah, but who practices it? Then this mania about the military—the Marines—did you know she has a picture of General Pershing over her bed?" There was no way Magnusson was going to comment on this.

"It's sad, perverse I suppose, there's no place in our society for the militant woman—the female warrior. What good will it do her to be fierce and brave?"

"Well," Magnusson ventured, "it might do her some good in the fix she's in now."

The consul turned his head toward him. "That's what worries me. Latins have rigid ideas about women. How are they—Sandino—going to understand a thirteen-year-old girl who behaves like she has equal rights?"

He broke off and Magnusson was afraid he was going to cry. He had no real experience with children or parents and didn't know what comfort he could offer. Finally he said, "Sir, I wish I could tell you that we will find your daughter alive and well. I can't. As far as worrying about it; we will or we won't. Tomorrow I am going to get up and go after her. You can count on that."

If he expected assurances or sunny forecasts from Magnusson he wasn't going to get them. But neither did he get doomsaying. The man was not to be stopped. It was as much as he could hope for.

It had been difficult for Magnusson to stay awake. Lying in bed with his head propped on his hand listening to the consul he kept dozing off, and jerked awake once putting his thumb in his eye. Only the shimmering image of lust kept him going. Finally, the consul slept and he got up, dressed, and slipped outside carrying his shoes. The hall was empty and semidark, tile cool on his feet. Walking quietly, he got past General Butler's room to Karen's door, its curved frame and Art Nouveau panels were set in the plump plaster as though pressed in dough.

He tapped lightly and there was a long wait. Finally the door opened a crack. "Is that you, Lieutenant Magnusson? Is something wrong?"

"Oh no, I just thought . . . well . . . maybe I could come in . . ." He smiled nervously.

"Do you think that would be proper?"

This stopped him. She appeared to have been asleep and from what he could see had a sheet pulled around her. "Proper?" She had been in his mind all day; all through the hectic, dangerous day—a memory that popped to the surface and made him smile: the image of a finger beckoning a slide into bed—the glorious heft of her in his arms. It had made today disappear. He thought only of last night. It didn't occur to him that she wouldn't be waiting for him.

"Don't you think it possible to be a whore and proper?"

"Why, yes, yes, of course . . . but on the . . ."

"On the boat I told you I was repaying your bravery. I did that. I may be a whore, but I am *not* promiscuous."

That stumped him, then it slowly dawned that a speech was expected. In the past he had very little to do, emotionally, with women, but he did know that "going to it" wasn't enough. You had to talk to them. That's what had been so wonderful about Karen, she seemed to understand his shyness and had gone about the thing with so little trouble. He made up his speech. "I'd like to say . . ."

"Yes?"

"That I . . . enjoyed your company."

"Thank you." She started to close the door. "Good night then."

"Ah! And I would like more of it in the future—your company that is."

The door opened and she smiled. "Well then, let's have a new beginning. We must get to know one another—but not at midnight."

"No?"

"And not without your shoes."

"Oh." He looked down.

"Tomorrow perhaps you could call and take me to lunch—or what they call it here."

"*La comida.*" Tomorrow he expected to be off on Sandino's trail, whatever direction that led. "I don't know if I can make it tomorrow."

"When you get back then. Good night." And this time she did shut the door.

Magnusson put his shoes on and walked back down the hall feeling frustrated and puzzled. A game was being played and he didn't know the rules. But he did know he wasn't getting laid tonight.

Karen went back to bed feeling pleased. She had expected

Magnusson tonight, fell asleep waiting for him. But if they were going to have serious relations, and that was what she wanted, then he would have to be brought to halter. She was not a whore for nothing and understood that with men if they didn't pay for it one way or another, sooner or later they did not value it. He would have to understand from the start she was valuable, a treasure.

She had brought her own money out of Rama and would stay in Managua while the lieutenant chased around after Sandino. He would be back. In the meantime it would be a chance to have a new wardrobe run up by an inexpensive seamstress. The worst was over. She had imagined hell as a place where she would be gang-raped by brutes and that had almost happened. But thanks to her viking warrior . . . there was a roll to the bed, a dip that ended in a shake, and the rattle of the water carafe next to her bed. "Oh!" she said aloud, then unaccountably giggled, thinking that if God could have managed that during her time in bed with Magnusson, he would be her slave for life.

Magnusson didn't feel the quake descending in the lift. In his agitated condition it was likely he would not have noticed it in any event. Reaching the lobby of the hotel he crossed into the bar. Despite the *modernismo* pretentions of *El Grande*, the place was decorated for tourists. Rather than the dead monkey motif of *El Tropicale* in Bluefields, this one had live parrots. As Magnusson slid up on the bamboo stool to the bar, a large green and red parrot on a hoop perch tilted down and squawked in his ear.

"Let me tell you," he said to the bartender in English, "If that bird does that again I will squeeze its neck!" And he held up his hand in a claw grip. "Be warned!"

The bartender, a city man used to dealing with gringos smiled smoothly, "Ah, *señor,* thess ess the beautiful bird of our land . . . like your eegle."

"Are you comparing this monkey-eating, beak squawker with *my* American eagle?"

"No, no!" he said, retreating.

"Bring me a God damned bottle of pisco, *pronto!*"

In a palm-swagged corner of the bar, the music boy sat with the lady who could have passed as Lupé Velez. The management did not allow whores in The Grand, but this one was an exception because invariably, she was mistaken by tourists for the Mexican movie star. "Hey!" the music boy said, "There's Lieutenant Magnusson, my officer! Come on Lupé!"

The music boy had been lulled by Magnusson's smile and easygoing ways of today. He towed the slinky girl across the empty room and pushed up against the bar. "Sir, I'd like you to meet this lady—doesn't she look like Lupé Velez?" The girl hit a pose.

Magnusson took a large quaff of pisco and examined her. "She looks like shit."

"Sheet?! *Sheet?!*" Lupé said.

"Sir, I don't think that's fair. Look at her profile . . ."

At that moment the parrot bent down and screeched.

Magnusson's arm shot up and grabbed the bird by the neck and the squawk died in its throat. The bartender leaped to the rescue. "Don do that to Sando!"

"*Sando!*" Magnusson shouted and began to whack the bartender over the head with the parrot, feathers flying. "*I'll give you fucking Sando!*"

In the lobby two *guardia policia* looked up at the racket and quickly crossed over to the bar. As they did, the lift descended and Carlton Wills stepped out.

The train stopped just outside of Nagarote about thirty miles from Managua. It was a dark, deserted spot in the countryside with only a watchman's shack and water tower against the night sky. The sleepy watchman was surprised to find three boxcars full of troops armed to the teeth, but he smiled, anxious to be of service. He brought out lanterns and offered to help water the old side-valve locomotive. The officers were welcome to the poor comfort of his shack.

"Do you have a telephone?" Sabar Manzanares asked, knowing the answer.

"Ah, no I am sorry—but there are wires." He smiled and pointed overhead at a tilted pole carrying three lines.

"I'll get the artist," Angel Ortez said. This was Pedro Alzuma, a former lineman for Bell S.A. He was the only man in the entire Revolutionary Army who had skill with mechanical communication equipment and was treated like a maestro. They kept him away from combat and out of danger, allowing his wife and young son to travel with him. He was a jewel.

Pedro arrived and buckled on his pole-climbing spikes. "Is this going to be a problem?" Sabar asked, giving him the opportunity to be important.

"No, no, a whistle." and digging in the pole, he started up.

"Look at that!" Angel said, "Goes right up like a squirrel!" he said, shamelessly patronizing the man. "Me, I'm afraid of heights."

"Amazing," Sabar agreed. Pedro clipped on the line and gracefully dropped down a dialer. Sabar took it, kissing his fingers to their star and dialed his way through the maze of Managua connections. Finally a voice came on the line he recognized. "Is this my friend from the mountains?"

"Sabar! Where are you?"

"Nagarote. Is everything ready?"

"As planned. The trucks will be in the freight yard. Look for two swinging red signals one mile in from the Managua cut off. Load and proceed to the palace. I will be waiting. It should take you no longer than one hour. If turned back for any reason reform at the train. Arrive here no later than five ten. Sunrise is at four thirty-six."

"All right . . ." He glanced at his watch. "It's one now, that will give us good time. Anything else?"

"Tell your people to look ferocious, the press will be watching. *Adios!*" And he hung up.

Sabar let Pedro reel the phone up. "What did he say? Is everything ready?" Angel asked.

"Yes . . . he joked that the press would be there—you don't suppose he arranged it?"

"With César I would not be surprised if Movietone News awaits." If their comrade had one annoying flaw it was this business of advertising himself. There had been several occasions when it came close to disaster. Behind them the watering of the locomotive went on in pulsating gulps and men climbed down from the boxcars to urinate against the tracks. Laughing and playing grab ass, they acting as if it were a picnic. Sabar watched them, wondering how many would be up to games on the way back.

"All right!" Sandino said, putting down the phone and taking on the excitement of impending action. They had been sitting in the stale office all day and into the night, smelling garbage and listening to his cousin talk about the earthquake of '85 as his grandfather remembered it.

"Thousands of people were killed," he went on, "more than eighty percent of the population. Those who survived went away from the city as far as they could go—to the oceans, to Honduras, Costa Rica even—ten years later they still hadn't returned. Ten years! But then new people came who did not remember and slowly the city was rebuilt. The Grand Hotel is put on the spot where the old inn was swallowed up. Right on top of what those book people call the fault."

He sat tense in the chair, his ass barely touching it. Pedrón thought he looked like a runner who would bolt at the sound of a starting pistol. If he clapped his hands the man would be down the stairs and out the door like a cat with its tail on fire. He turned, Sandino was addressing him. "You arranged things at the hotel?" He knew this but wanted to hear it again.

"Yes, *jefe*, there is a back entrance with a freight elevator. I told the boy who runs it that my patron wished to bring his sweetie up to the top floor and paid him to look the other way."

"Hector . . ." He was watching a glass of water on the desk, had the liquid moved? "*Hector!* What about the drivers?"

"In the cantina up the street, César, at your word I will summon them."

"Not yet, we don't want them waiting around at the freight yard causing interest. Give them a good hour to get there. They should start from here about three—now, I'm going to call Wills and tell him to pick up the journalists. It is time to set things in motion." He looked at Kate, asleep sitting in a chair, head up against wall. Then we will put the girl in Hector's car and start for the hotel."

The minute he got his car back, Hector was going to pack up his wife and children and drive to the coast.

"You brought the uniforms?"

"Yes." He indicated a cardboard suitcase.

Sandino dialed The Grand and was put through to the wrong room. It rang a long time and finally a sleepy woman's voice said, "Å *fan!* then in bad Spanish, "Hello?" When he didn't answer she said, annoyed, "Lieutenant Magnusson? Is that you? Hello?" He hung up shaken. *Magnusson?* The name the girl kept throwing at him—was that possible? Had he misunderstood? The woman spoke with an accent—a familiar accent.

"Is something wrong?" Angel asked.

"No . . ." He called The Grand again and asked for Carlton Wills, saying he had been connected with the wrong room. Then a smile in his voice, he wondered if he might have the name of the woman he had just awakened by mistake—so that an apology might be offered in the morning.

A pause. "Miss Sven, sir, a foreign lady who checked in today."

When Wills came on the line he said one word, "Now," and hung up.

Putting the phone down, Wills guessed that must be the most succinct conversation he'd had with Sandino; dramatic as usual and sounding nervous. He was annoyed to have to stop working. It was the first time in days he'd had a chance to be alone and write. He was typing out the story of tonight's interview with Kate Kelly in advance. He had lined out the backstory, laying on the color, and would fill in the concluding events when they happened. That way he would be able to file his story long before his competitors. He got up from the tiny *Blickensderfer* portable, sighing. He straightened his tie and put on his jacket, then went down in the lift.

Crossing the lobby he heard a ruckus in the bar and saw two *guardia policia* heading that way. Stepping quickly to the desk he was told the car would be out in front in a moment.

When the *policia* saw the troublemaker was a Marine, they slowed down and broke out in grins, speaking English, "Hey! Lieutenant! *Compañero!* Glad to see you're haveeng a good time! That ees owed to us soldiers, eh? Bartender, make sure thees fine fellow is treated with respect!" The bartender, his hair full of feathers and parrot shit, smiled weekly.

Magnusson looked at the two and calmed down. As a Swede and an officer he had never acted like this in public. He could only put it down to a crazed sexual condition. He carefuly laid the battered parrot on the bar and taking out his pigskin wallet removed five U.S. dollars, placing them on top of the bird.

"See that he gets a nice funeral."

The bartender brightened and one of the *policia* said, expanding his arms, "See? Deed I say ees a real gentleman— thees officer?" Looking over his shoulder, Magnusson saw a man pass through the lobby wearing pince-nez glasses on a hawk of a nose that preceded him like a prow. In the next instant he was out the street door.

"MUSIC! *Where's the car?*" This startled everyone and they stepped a foot back.

"Why . . . in the basement garage, sir . . ."

"*Get it! Bring it around front!*" And he pushed through the tight group into the lobby.

"Now, sir?"

"*NOW!*"

He knew that face instantly. Having had a man's face in the

sights of your gun, you tend not to forget it. Stepping outside he resisted the impulse to rush up and grab him, pound him into the pavement. That wouldn't lead to Sandino.

Wills had ordered a large, eight-passenger car from a funeral establishment. It was an old Hupmobile, tall enough to enter in a top hat, with a rear compartment big as a Pullman. What appealed to his sense of drama were fringed curtains that could be pulled down all around for privacy. Perfect for this occasion. The driver, formally dressed, bowed. He had already been carefully instructed on the night's moves: A gambling party was arranged at The Grand later, and it was necessary to throw the local bribe-takers off until the rendezvous at the hotel. He got in and the ponderous vehicle moved off at a stately roll.

*"Damn!"* Magnusson said aloud. Where was the music boy? They were going to lose the sword-bill! *"Damn!"* He should have laid hands on him! Grabbed him! Then the Packard hove in sight, taking the corner from the garage ramp and pulling up in front of the hotel in a rattle of suspension. He jumped aboard before it stopped. *"Let's go! Let's go!"* Lupé was in the back seat, "What's she doing here?"

"Somebody had to adjust the spark and choke while I cranked sir."

*"All right!* Box the square!" The Hupmobile had turned right, around Salazar Square—he was sure of that, *"Damn!"* If the car went up a dark side street they would never find them. But it hadn't. The tall car was parked in front of the offices of *La Prensa* just across the square from the hotel. "Stop!" Magnusson jerked the lever of the hand brake and the rear brakes locked up, sliding the Packard to a shuddering stop. "That's it!"

"Can I ask what, sir?"

"That car, the funeral wagon."

"Oh."

"It's the bird I took a shot at on the survey boat—the one with the nose glasses. He got in that car."

This enthused the music boy. "Is that right, sir? *Damn!* And he's parked in front of a newspaper office—the pilot was right!"

Magnusson looked at him. He had been part of that interview. "Right about what?"

"He said the man was a reporter . . ."

"*Wills,*" Magnusson said, slapping his thigh. It clicked in place. He knew he had seen the face before! It was the reason he hadn't shot the man. Now he remembered where; Colonel Wise had shown him a copy of *The Nation* with an article about Sandino. Carlton Will's picture accompanied it, all glasses and nose.

"What do we do now?"

"Wait."

"Shall I turn off the car?"

"No, no!"

"But the radiator . . ."

"Hey," Lupé said from the back seat, "Haf one of you guise got a Luckee?"

Ten minutes later seven men came through *La Prensa*'s front entrance and got in the car. The fringed curtains were pulled down and the car moved away.

"What do you make of that, sir?"

"Follow them."

Lupé leaned on the back of the seat. "Ess one of you guise goeeng to geeve me a smoke?"

They followed the Hupmobile for the next half hour. Down the curve of narrow streets, around dark squares, looping the city in what seemed in a large circle. There were no street lights and the fronts of the stone buildings were slick from a light rain, windows opaque, only the rare flicker of light seen. They passed the occasional lit cantina and *guardia* kiosk but it was a city where the sidewalks were rolled up early—and there were few sidewalks except in the rich district—others made do with cedar logs sliced like cucumbers and placed where a mud hole threatened to envelop a passerby. Plants and weeds pushed up in every open space; lush palms bending their fronds over the street;

vines entangling telegraph wires. Flowers bloomed wild in the meanest neighborhoods and everything made for a sense of disorientation: Newark, New Jersey, in Jungleland. Few cars were out, and it was inevitable that they would be spotted.

Wills sat in front with the driver, the newsmen in the back on black mohair seats. Besides the man from *La Prensa* and the big South American dailies, there were stringers from London, Paris, and Rome—all Latins. Wills had not invited *The New York Times*—he would break the American story himself. There were seven in all, some smoking, all looking sleepy and bored. Wills tried to keep their interest with a backstory about Sandino's year in Mexico. Then the driver leaned in, speaking low. "There is a car following us, *señor.*"

Wills head snapped around. "Are you sure?"

"Oh yes, it would be hard to miss on these empty streets."

A thought immediately struck Wills. "Can you tell what kind it is?"

The driver glanced in the outside rearview mirror. "A Packard I would say."

There it was. The worst that could happen. It didn't seem possible that the same car, the one that had hounded them from Bluefields could still be out there. But he knew that was it—that General Smedley Butler and Lieutenant Magnusson—aggressive, uncorruptable, men he had never met, were pressing on. There was no way to get in touch with Sandino and no way to stop the forward motion of events, moving now like that freight train of troops toward the city. He took out his wallet and removed several bills. "Is there a way of losing that car?"

"Oh yes," the driver said, smiling.

Ten minutes later when the music boy turned one more corner in the labyrinth of the poor section, the Hupmobile had vanished. Ahead was a rabbit warren of narrow alleys leading between miserable housing. *"Which way did they go?"* Magnusson shouted.

"I don't know sir."

"Find him!"

"I think we'll be lucky to find our way back."

"Didju say Luckee?" Lupé asked from the backseat. "I'll haf one."

Pedrón pulled the Ford around to the back of The Grand hotel and Sandino got out, keeping a grip on Kate. It was dark with only a bare red bulb above the metal rear door. Smells of cooking odors and trash came up. If the front of the hotel was *modernismo*, the back was fifteenth century. "Go ahead and clear the way—and don't forget the bag." Pedrón walked up to the door carrying the cardboard suitcase and rang the night bell. It opened, showing the face of a young man with a bad complexion dressed up in the white jacket of the hotel. He tried to look past Pedrón but the pressure of a Angel's hand on his narrow chest pushed him back. They stepped inside. "I told you my patron does not wish to be discovered," he said, smiling, "this is what I want you to do. Go over there," pointing to the far end of the interior, "and turn your back until we're in the elevator, will you do that?"

"But I must run it."

"No, I will manage."

"Then who is to bring it down?"

"We will let it stay up until we're ready to come down."

"Oh no! The management would never allow that, it might be needed!"

Pedrón moved closer, not smiling now, the jacket of his coat open to show the handle of a large revolver stuck in his belt. "Haven't you been paid? Is there something more needing to be done?" The boy turned around and marched where Pedrón had indicated, his back to the elevator. Pedrón gave the high sign from the door and Sandino took out a large pocket knife with a stiletto blade, snapping it open so Kate could hear it. Since Sangre's death there was no longer any pretense of civility between them.

"Listen to what I am going to tell you. If you in any way call out or speak even in a small voice I am going to cut you. Not kill you, cut you. I will push this blade into your soft parts as many times as it takes." This was recited in a quiet matter-of-fact voice that chilled Kate. "Now let's go in and do not give me any trouble."

*Give him any trouble?* Kate thought. The knife had her respect. A gun was somehow abstract, promising what couldn't quite be imagined. But a knife—everyone knew what it felt like to cut yourself.

Pedrón ran the lift, fumbling the circular lever at the sixth floor until he finally got it stopped a foot from the floor level. "All right!" Sandino said, "Enough! Let's go!" Pedrón stepped up to the hall, checked it, and went across to Wills's door, opening it quickly with a key. He gestured and Sandino hurried Kate into the small vestibule and through a large room with windows overlooking the street. "In there." He indicated a bedroom on the left. "I want you to put these on," he said, tossing clothes from the suitcase on to the bed. "There are people arriving who will be concerned for your well being and I want them to see you are not harmed—yet." He gestured toward a bathroom, "And take a bath, you stink." With that he went out, closing the door.

Kate looked at the clothes. There was a skirt and blouse of dark green khaki with a bandanna in the syndicalist colors. A uniform? There also was a wide leather belt and boots that actually fit. Was she supposed to looked like them? Why? She went in a bathroom tiled in black and white squares and shucked off her filthy clothes. Turning, she caught sight of herself in the heavy door mirror. She was shocked. It was the image of a girl she did not recognize. Not eating, diarrhea, and the nervous fear had changed her radically. She had planes, angles; showed ribs, *ribs!* A real waist—and a bosom that seemed bigger by contrast. It was an eerie sensation, suddenly finding that other body under the old one; she had peeled off the fat like stepping out of a winter coat. The person who looked back at her was not a child. She ran the hot water and climbed in the big claw-foot tub feeling if not better, different. If they killed her now she would die thin.

In the living room of the suite, Sandino took another uniform out of a grip and began to undress. "I want to tell you some good news," he said to Pedrón.

"You've sent for whores?"

"Close—Karen Sven—the manager's girl is in the hotel. Right here."

Pedrón's eyes widened. "How could that be?"

"I asked myself the same question. The answer is obvious. Those people in the Packard managed to make the city as we did—there is only one good hotel in this town and they are in it."

"The others too?"

"No doubt. It's like fate isn't it, that we should all end up here together?"

"Better, it will give me another chance at that big blond—as you say it was meant to be. If we should happen to run into the others—let that be too." Pedrón smacked his fist in his hand. "This is going to be a good night." He turned to the window looking across the roof tops toward Laguna Tiscapa and the presidential palace. Lights uplit the pretentious facade reflecting arches in the lake. "There it is," he said, laughing. "Our future home." Then there was a ripple across the lake, a wave that traveled the length of water, spilling over at one end, like a tipped saucer. In the next instant a tremor rattled the windows. This one lasted longer those that went before. "Ha!" Pedrón said, "I bet cousin Hector is shitting tamales!"

After an hour of cutting back and forth through a complication of alleys and backing up from dead-ends, Magnusson had to admit they were not going to find Wills. He blamed himself for not grabbing him when he had the chance—he blamed himself—but that did not improve his disposition. "Back to the God damned hotel."

"Ah, do you know which way that is, sir?" The music boy hated to suggest he had not been keeping track of the lefts and rights but that was the truth.

"You don't know?" He started a slow burn, but before he could explode, Lupé piped up.

"I know."

"Great, Lupé!" the music boy said, twisting around, "Where?"

"Furss I geet a fokeeng Luckee."

The music boy shook out a pack and handed one over the seat. "All you gotta do is ask."

The funeral Hupmobile arrived at the rear of The Grand, parking next to the Ford sedan. Curtains up, the reporters were amused to find themselves across the square from where they began.

"It was necessary to be sure we weren't followed," Wills said, hoping to God they weren't. When they discovered the freight elevator was stuck on six and they would have to walk up, the company was less amused. Wills insisted on it. Seven known reporters trooping through the lobby would not go unnoticed. So they climbed, puffing and complaining up narrow back stairs, exiting on the sixth floor and clumping up the hall to Wills's room. By now they were wondering out loud if the trip was worth it. Stepping through the vestibule to the living room they found out.

The interior had been arranged like a stage set. A desk had been pulled around to face the arch of the doorway, silk lamp shades on its polished top tilted up for dramatic effect. Sitting in their half moon arc Sandino was in the full uniform of a revolutionary general, dark green with silver stars embroidered within wreathes on the taps of an open collar. The loop of a bandanna in syndicalist colors looped his neck and a gold watch chain stretched between breast pockets. Behind and to his right, Pedrón stood in the at-rest position, colonel's eagles on his collar tabs, the visor of his cap square across hidden eyes. Behind them fixed to the blinds was a large flag divided vertically into red and black sections. In the red section was the curious design of a white skull with crossed rifle and sword beneath—a witty reference to that old Dutch pirate, Captain Blauvelt who had pulled the British lion's tail at Bluefields.

"Please sit," Sandino said, and they lowered themselves onto a collection of chairs arranged in front of the desk. Wills smiled at the lighting, straight out of a Von Sternberg film. He had never seen Sandino in any kind of a real uniform and thought he looked . . . bigger—wondering if he was sitting on a phone book.

"You know who I am," Sandino said without preamble, and began an oral history of the Revolutionary Army and its aims. This was all old stuff and the reporters knew it by heart. They patiently sat through half an hour of it, then when he paused for breath, the *London Times* man jumped in.

"What about Catherine Kelly, the American consul's daughter? The AP ran a story Monday that she had been kidnapped by your people." Others spoke at once, echoing this.

Sandino waited until this outburst subsided. "She was not kidnapped, she has joined us."

This went down hard. Nobody could believe it for a minute. "Let us see her then!" they said, "Let *her* tell us."

"Very well, Colonel, bring in our little comrade." The room got very quiet as Pedrón crossed over, went in the bedroom and closed the door.

Kate looked up from brushing her hair, surprised to see Pedrón also in uniform. "What is this? What game are we playing?"

He came close to her speaking slow in Spanish so she would understand him. "Hear what I say. When you go into the other room you will see a young man sitting in the center of chairs. He has thinning hair and a high, smooth, forehead. If you give us any of your trouble, if you are disrespectful to General Sandino, I will shoot that young man in his smooth forehead. Do you understand? Do you believe me?"

She thought Pedrón a brute and sometimes a clown, but she knew he was capable of anything.

"Now, when they ask your condition—say it is fine—because it is. When they ask if you've joined our army say yes, that it is true." She frowned. "Is that much to do to save a hole from entering a young man's forehead?" Straightening, he put his hand on the door knob. "Remember."

When she came in the room the reporters didn't recognize her from the picture AP had on the wire service. This girl looked older and was not fat. Only the hair described as red, fit. But they knew from experience about newspaper pictures and believed it was her. There was excitement seeing her in the uniform of the revolution; something extraordinary was about to happen. The *London Times* man had been selected as spokesperson. He smiled, "Are you Catherine Kelly, daughter of Richard Kelly, the America consul?"

"Y . . . yes." Her eyes went past him and instantly found the young man in the front row. As Pedrón said, his forehead was smooth and high. Her eyes focused on it.

Sandino had deliberately waited until the last possible moment to have Pedrón coach Kate. Reasoning that if he gave her time she would know they were bluffing—know they wouldn't dare shoot a reporter in front of others. What he was looking for was good reviews, not a massacre.

"Are you all right, Miss Kelly? Have you been harmed?"

"Uh, no." She stared at the young man's forehead. Puzzled, he looked behind him, then turned back smiling uneasily.

"General Sandino has just told us that you have joined him of your own accord—is that true?" Tension in the room tightened several notches, reporters leaned forward, cigarettes clenched in teeth, smoke hanging at eye level. Next to her, Pedrón shifted his weight, hip against hers, resting his hand on the hilt of the revolver, tapping the butt with a pinky ring. Time seemed to hang.

"Is that true?" The *Times* man repeated. "Have you joined his army?"

"No." Letting her breath out and taking a quick step to the

side, she stood in front of the young man. "I wouldn't be caught dead in this shrimp's army."

The Packard pulled into the basement garage of The Grand, coming down a spiral brick ramp between mushroom columns and heavy undercrofting. Originally designed for horse and carriage it was a tight fit and the music boy turned the car at the bottom so that it faced the entrance.

Magnusson climbed over the jammed right-hand door, got out looking surly and walked up the ramp toward the street level. Lupé linked her arm through the music boy's and they followed. "I hope jus guise are goeeng to buy me a dreenk?"

"Sure," the music boy winked, "Something with a banana in it." Then, looking up he said, "Is that thunder?" In the next instant they were knocked to the ground as it pitched, fell away, and began to roll. No more timid window rattling—this struck with the hideous rumble of earth shruging off discomfort—that very earth always firm underfoot—a place that comforted feet, gave them a point of reference. It was as though an earth mother sleeping forty miles down in her mysterious fault had grown annoyed at elbowing slabs and turned over, pulling the earth's cover with her.

It continued in a rise and fall that built to a shuddering heart-breaking shake, then subsided, followed by the thunder of buildings falling. Heavy unmovable blocks of stone—moved. The fronts of buildings sheered off in splintering twists of wood with the ripple of tin roofs lifting. The foreground music was tinkling, as windows, dishes, glasses—anything vulnerable broke; plaster Marys carrying baby Jesus; saints bobbing their heads off. Crosses with the Savior nailed to them, let him go.

They lay on the basement floor clutching as paving stones that moved under hand. Holding their breath at each succeeding rumble, praying it would be the last—then there was another, the build-up, the earth's nod, shake, roll, bricks shucked off columns and rained down. Now, a different sound, the shriek of a population screaming at the tops of their lungs. The initial tremor couldn't have lasted more than a few seconds, some swore a full minute, but enough to topple an entire city.

When it at last was stable, Magnusson pushed up under the bricks and ran through the dust of masonry up the ramp toward the entrance. The basement garage had surprisingly supported its ceiling, the heavy mushroom columns and Gaudilike complex vaulting, a precursor of modern "egg shell" concrete techniques, flexed and gave with the earth's movement. Only two of the columns had failed, one of them dropping a single brick from twelve feet on Lupé. The music boy still held her hand and when he felt no response rolled her over. That single brick had fractured her skull. The eyes looked at him with a question. Laying her gently down, he followed Magnusson.

In the street it was bedlam. The six-story facade of the hotel with those undulating balconies that critics likened to nervous waves had crashed into the street as their beach. The whole front of the building had come down, sheering off and leaving the rooms exposed like a hive. That top sixth floor shunned by earthquake experts held, while the other five in the center of the building collapsed in on themselves, taking on a curious hourglass shape. All down the block, around the square, was the rubble remains of what had been a business district. There were no recognizable landmarks, the church towers had been shaken away and only low irregular mounds of tumbled stone and brick made up a skyline. Rich and poor had been made equal in a one minute revolution. Flames could be seen in the night. Fires were already beginning that would destroy what was left of the city and in the end kill more people than the earthquake.

There was no way into the churned mess of the hotel and Magnusson began to climb up the outside, using the exposed pipe and wire as handholds. As he went he shouted down at the music boy, *"Try and get the car out!"* Climbing the open front of the building gave him the eerie sensation of passing by the compartments of peoples' lives—of spying on private things. In the exposed rooms bodies lay revealed in grotesque positions, some folded into beds compressed flat with the ceiling for covers—in others, people still in their nightclothes stood stunned, looking out the open vista to a street vanished in a sea of rubble. He shouted to them to climb down, but they didn't see or hear him.

At the sixth floor he climbed up onto the tilting floor and made his way down the hall, stepping over tile that had been popped up in orderly rows. At the twisted wreck of the elevator shaft he saw a man waiting as if he expected it to arrive. He was covered with a dusting of plaster but appeared all right.

"I'm Salvador of the *London Times*," he said, "Do you know what's happened?"

Magnusson shook him hard. "You'll have to climb down— hurry!" He could feel the floor shift under his feet, saw tiles begin to slide as the building moved slightly to the left. Ahead the figure of General Butler appeared buttoning up his shirt. He was dressed, campaign hat in place, in complete control of himself.

"Good to see you, Lieutenant. The music boy?"

"Downstairs trying to free up the car."

"Good man. Let's look to the consul." They found his door jammed, but the two of them got it wedged open and pulled him out from under a tangle of bedding and plaster lath. He was shaken but whole. "I'll get him going—find Miss Sven!" Magnusson was already off and running down the long hall. As he went sounds became more ominous; a strained creaking of beams under terrific pressure—a squeak as nails pulled themselves out and bolts sheered off. At any minute he expected the top floor to go, dropping to join the rest of the hotel in the street.

Karen's room was at the end of the hall and when he reached the door opening he found no door. And in fact, no room. Leaning out over open space, he looked down to where the remains had broken off and tumbled in with the rest of the rubble. Fires lit the pile with a flickering glow and the arms and legs of several bodies stuck out at odd angles. He wondered which were hers.

## TEN

# Rail Yard

AT just before sunrise the rebel train approached the
outskirts of Managua. By now the excursion atmo-
sphere had evaporated and the troops sat silently in
their boxcars rocking with the motion of the train.
There was little talk, a lot of smoking, an occasional nervous
cough; a nose blow; the click of rosary beads.

In the caboose being pushed straight into the night, the
officers saw the skyline of the city, church spires picked out
against the first orange streaks of a predawn sky.

"Look," Sabar said. A half mile ahead on the track the
pinpoint of a swinging red light was visible.

"Good!" Angel Ortez answered, "For once they're ready—
let's hope that the . . ."

The car suddenly dipped, dropping as though on a grade,
then came up rolling from side to side. They were tumbled to the
floor, and Sabar remembered thinking, *We've been derailed!
Ambushed!* But the ambush was by nature and the cars rode

tracks that undulated, twisting like snakes. The engineer hit the brakes too fast and they locked up. The heavy old locomotive began to slide, sending back sparks and when the brakes finally grabbed, the cars were pulled sharply back, bucking with the clacking sound of couplings taking up the slack.

After they stopped and he pushed himself up, Sabar looked down the track and had the eerie experience of seeing the rails twist, rising and falling like they were rubber. The two brakemen riding each side of the caboose were gone. Had they jumped? Next, he heard a rumble as boxcar doors opened and the men leaped out and began to run. Angel was out of the caboose heading them off; herding them back.

"*Where are you going?* Hey! Slow down! Come on back, it's only an earthquake!"

*Only an earthquake! My God*, Sabar thought, *a second ago when he looked there had been Managua—now, there was rubble.* A landscape wiped out as though by the swipe of a hand. A sound came up that sent chills up his spine; the screaming of people audible miles away. Angel ran back alongside the train. "I've got them calmed down." And it was true, Sabar heard the men laughing now, joking that they weren't running away, just charging into battle.

"Talk about luck!" Sabar said, "in another hour we would have been in the middle of that! It's amazing the train stayed on the tracks. We'll still be able to get out of here and back up the coast."

"Sabar! Don't you see what this is? A great opportunity!"

"For what?"

"To take the whole damn city!"

"Angel . . ."

"Listen! What's to stop us? The *guardia* and Marines are going to be knocked out! With three hundred armed men we can move in and take control!"

Sabar looked at him, shaking his head, "And then what will we have?"

"Why . . . Managua . . ."

"What you'll have is a city of the dead, a place full of corpses. You want to do something that would really be heroic? Then let's leave the weapons here and go in and help those poor devils—pull them out from under the buildings."

Angel drew back, offended, "They're the enemy!" he said.

The rescue party pushed their way across the square in front of what had been their hotel to the *guardia's Campo de Marte*. The old buildings had been thoroughly shaken and the attached *Academia Militar* collapsed in on itself. At the end of the street the twenty-five-foot stone walls of the penitentiary lay in a pile. The surviving *guardia* and Marine personnel had been reassembled in the square. A temporary headquarters was set up under a tent and the bustle of reorganization went on. There was no telephone service and runners dashed in and out, threading between mobs of the dispossessed each with a plea for help. An officer in the uniform of the *Jefe Director* stood at a shaky card table dealing with total confusion.

General Butler presented himself, and *Jefe Director* Matthews raised his eyebrows at the four of them: the general in his homemade stars; Magnusson and the music boy in mismatched uniforms and a wild-eyed man with a black beard. "Smedley— Who in God's name are these people and what are you doing here?"

"Chasing Sandino, Calvin. This is Lieutenant Magnusson, the music boy, and Dick Kelly—the American consul at Bluefields."

They shook. "Oh yes, of course, sorry about your daughter—sir, rotten business. I thought Admiral Sellers sent a Special Service Force up to Rama after her?"

"Yes, we made connection," the general answered, "but Sandino got away with the girl—here we think. You haven't heard of him?"

"No and at the moment, I'm afraid he's the last of my

worries. Smell that? The dead. They've already turned in this heat. If we don't get them burned we're going to have a major epidemic going for us."

Behind him, *guardia* and Marines hefted barrels of fuel oil up on a surviving Model T truck. Orders were to recover bodies where possible and bury them. The others—and there were hundreds tangled in the ruins—were to be burned where they lay. The fires that had begun within minutes of the first quake now raged out of control and to be trapped in a building meant being burned alive. Civilians and the military worked at pulling people out, but conditions were appalling. Refugees clogged the streets, streaming out of the city, and movement against this human tide was impossible. Smoke from the fires hung low over the rubble and this desperate mob, blackened by the smoke, surged blindly ahead. An occasional shot could be heard as *guardia policia* executed looters on the spot—but even above the roar of the fire and buildings falling, the prevailing sound was the wail of the mob. Of the original population of 125,000 only 11,000 would remain the next morning. Later the Marines would be accused of deliberately burning the city, but the fire needed no help.

A large black Buick appeared like magic in the square. Red light on, siren sounding, it expertly dodged the wreckage, rolling over what it couldn't go around. Pulling up to the HQ tent, the driver, a square, muscular Marine, jumped out and elbowed his way through the crowd. Chest shoved out in exaggerated posture, his campaign hat was fastened under the jut of an undershot jaw that looked remarkably like a bulldog. He stalked into the tent and snapped a salute at *Jefe Director* Matthews that blew papers off the card table.

"Sir! I would like to report three companies of rebels outside the city, armed and provocative!" He spoke with a Southern accent.

Matthews sighed despite himself, "Is that right, Captain?"

"The peckerheads fired on us sir." He gestured at a fat man

who had got out of the car and was leaning against a fender mopping his brow. "The *Jefe Politico* and I were driving in from Jinotega when I spotted them in the freight yards disembarking from boxcars. When I approached to question intent, they opened fire."

"We don't need any more aggravation at this point—they will have to wait their turn to be dealt with."

"I believe these people to be Sandinistas, sir . . ."

"There it is," Magnusson said to General Butler, "Sandino's in town to hook up with an advance party."

The captain's eyes cut to the right, looking under his brows at Magnusson. "Mag?"

Magnusson had recognized him instantly and watched with amusement as he plowed into Matthews. "That's right, Chesty." And he headed over to shake hands.

He had met Chesty Puller in Haiti in 1918, both serving as sergeants in the *Gendarmerie d'Haiti*, and anyone who had met Chesty was not likely to forget him. Fearless and aggressive to a fault he was now in command of the famous—some said, infamous—Company M, the most successful of the *guardia* formations, and had just won the first of five Navy Crosses.

"Captain Puller," Magnusson said, "you know General Butler." Of course he did, for Butler was the officer who had created the *Gendarmerie d'Haiti* in 1915.

"Good to see you, sir."

"Lewis." There was a coolness between the two that had to do with style. They were very much alike. The Marine Corps had a legacy of flamboyant leaders; "Hiking Hiram" Bearss, "Whispering Buck" Neville—even "Sunny Jim" Vandergrift and scholarly "Uncle Joe" Pendleton had their mild eccentricities. Those who kept track of such things were betting that "Chesty" Puller would take the title "irrepressible" from Smedley Butler. Up from the ranks and already a captain—a grade ahead of Magnusson—he was a comer. If the good Lord would provide a couple of decent wars he would make general. Not only did he have Butler's color, but he was already known for putting his foot in his big mouth.

The general turned to Matthews, who had gone back to matters at hand, patiently explaining to the *Jefe Politico* why he couldn't detail men to guard his father-in-law's house. "Calvin, this bunch at the freight yards may have arrived to link up with Sandino—I suggest we be allowed to reconnoiter."

"Smedley, I can't spare a single man—we're in the middle of a catastrophe!"

"True, but if these people chose to attack now—you'd be in the middle of two catastrophes."

Matthews looked at him, wondering just what authority he had. No word had come down that he was officially supposed to be in the area—still, Butler outranked him. If rebels did attack and he was not prepared . . .

"Let me put together a short squad, sir," Puller said, pushing in. "With General Butler's group we could make a nice showing."

"All right . . . no more than a squad, keep a line back to HQ, and for God's sake, don't aggravate matters!"

"I'm going to need more transport sir."

"We've got a car, Chesty," Magnusson said.

"Great! Get it around here while I recruit!" And Puller was off, already collaring two Marines off burial detail. "You and you! Come on! I'll give you birds the chance to make your own stiffs!"

*Jefe* Matthews went back to his catastrophe, hoping the three companies of rebels would keep Butler and Puller off his back.

Angel Ortez put out pickets and had the three companies in position, using the boxcars as cover. Sabar was furious that they had fired on the Buick. "That was a stupid thing to do!"

Listen! When the *guardia policia* drive at you with a red light and siren going, you react!"

"Then at least your sharpshooters could have hit a car as big as a moose! Now they'll get back with word that we're out here!"

"Do you think at a time like this they could find the people to attack us? We could take the city ourselves with this three companies!" Nervous and snapping, they had argued about continuing the raid, with Sabar finally prevailing. In a revolutionary army that depended on headlines, it would not be good press to launch a raid on a population knocked to its knees by an earthquake. They agreed to wait and see if Sandino could break free of the city. But it was one thing to go forward into action and another to squat in a freight yard waiting. The engineer wanted to leave at once and had to be forcibly induced to stay on the job.

But they were good friends and calmed down, Sabar sitting on the caboose step while Angel Ortez smoked, leaning against the car. Looking beyond the crosshatch of tracks to what once was Managua was unnerving. Fires continued and smoke drifting across the sky darkened the sun. Awful sounds could be heard in the distance, but in the rail yards it was quiet. The train crews had run away.

"Where was César calling from, Sabar?"

"He wouldn't say on the phone—probably from the cousin's—Hector's."

"The one they call 'Shivers.'" And for the first time since the quake they laughed together.

"It's hard to be related to a hero and be a coward—it takes a lot out of you." There was a long pause, after this. Then, he said, "Shall we set a deadline?"

Sabar nodded, "Give him another hour."

"It would be ironic if it all ended here." Sabar refused to speculate on this.

When the front fell off The Grand, it had been as though a black curtain came down, lights went out, and the night sky presented itself as a wall. In the first nasty moments of the tremor the real danger was from furniture. The sound of heavy bookcases and cupboards crashing over was daunting. Loose objects became missiles and a reporter was brained by the lead base of a gooseneck lamp as it slid off the polished top of the desk. When the initial shock wave slacked off and they lay where they had been tossed, the sound of a piercing scream continued. Sandino looked at Kate next to him, then realized it was coming from one of the reporters. They were now aware of a swaying motion as the building moved from side to side, balancing on the axis of its own squeezed-in center section. At this point those who could scrambled up and made for the door.

"Wills . . . are you still with us?" Sandino said, trying to make him out in the semidark.

"Yes . . . I believe so." And a figure rose from the floor dusted in plaster and resembling a poorly made statue.

"Pedrón, bring the girl—there's nothing more to be done here, we can leave."

He reached out to help Kate and she batted his hand away. "Get away!"

He jerked her up. "Come on, *soldado*, I'm just trying to be nice."

"Then jump out the window!"

In the hall they found the reporters inexplicably standing in front of the twisted elevator. "Come with us," Sandino said, "We've got to find another way down." But they stared at him and continued to wait. Sandino shrugged and moved on. Reaching a branch in the hall, Pedrón turned into its dark tunnel.

"I'll be behind you. I want to find the whore."

"No!" Sandino shouted after him. "Leave it alone! It's better to get out alive!" But he had disappeared.

"Fool!" But Sandino pushed on, Kate behind him then Wills. The flickering red light of fire showed at the windows, plaster dust drifting down and covering them, and he thought they must appeared as ghosts stalking a dead place. He knew the stairs were there and persisted until he found them. Their entrance showed a black hole. The steel stairs, made in Bethlehem, Pennsylvania, were bolted together forming a complete unit, and when the lower floors fell away they had twisted but remained in place, secured at the floor top and at the bottom. Looking down at six stories of free-hanging, corkscrew stairs disappearing into the dark was an awesome experience. Others who finally had followed drew back, unable to comprehend a climb down into that dizzying space. Sandino put his foot on the first rung, and felt it move. "It will be easier in the dark," he said, "if we could really see we would never go." And he stepped down. "Wills, help Miss Kelly."

"I don't need help!" she said, stepping off after him. And it was just as well, Wills was terrified of heights and could barely force himself to take that first awful step.

Pedrón found his way to the end of the hall where Karen's room had been. He was puzzled as it grew lighter, then realized the entire end of the building was gone. He stood at the edge where the floor had broken away to drop six stories and saw the white limbs of bodies in the rubble. "Mother of God," he whispered and turned. As he did the hotel gave another desperate shiver, a tremor that shook it from top to bottom, sending off more wreckage tumbling into the piles below.

Starting back he had a thought—a hunch. Although The Grand was a first-class hotel, it had been built at the turn of the century when large bathrooms were placed strategically on each floor to be shared by the guests. He forced the door of the bathroom closest to her room and found Karen Sven floating in a big claw-foot tub. It was surrounded by chunks of heavy fractured marble and she was unconscious, bobbing with the motion of the earthquake-shaken water. "Mother of God!" he repeated, this time smiling.

As the others went down, the stairs swayed with their weight, turning like a vane in the wind and it was necessary to stop often and let them unwind. Standing suspended in the center of the ruined building was much worse than moving ahead. Eerie sounds came up; the sing-song pleading of a voice buried somewhere deep in the rubble; above, pieces broke off and dropped the full six floors to hit with a hollow thud below. Poised at the halfway point, Sandino felt as though he were Don Juan descending into hell—surely that trip could be no more sinister than this one.

Behind, he could hear Kate's breathing, but nothing to suggest panic. It annoyed him that she was brave. He did not want to accept a thirteen-year-old girl as fearless.

As for Kate, she was terrified, but would have rather jumped off those stairs than let Sandino know it. She controlled her breathing, letting it out slowly, counting as her father taught her. At six she had climbed a tall ladder on a dare and this was how he got her down. It never occurred to her she was being brave. The only thing she knew about fear was that you didn't show it. The earthquake had come almost as a relief—she had expected to be shot by Pedrón—instead the building fell down, as though God had meant it to. Being led out of the room she stepped over the body of the young man, his high, smooth forehead smashed in by something. She guessed God meant that, too.

Wills was near swooning; he was close to going catatonic. The only thing that allowed him to continue was keeping his eyes shut. Going down the swaying stairs he locked one hand on the twisted railing like a robot, descending as a blind man would. His mind had stopped functioning and for the moment he did not really know where he was. Fear had reduced him to one reflex—stepping down.

Finally they reached the bottom, climbing over rubble toward the direction of human sound from the street. Behind them fires started in the hotel kitchen and roared upward in the gaping flue created by the ruined building. Then overhead was an ominous rumble that preceded the collapse of the sixth floor.

Sandino looked back, fighting the impulse to break and run. "Damn! Where is Pedrón?"

Wills still not recovered, hadn't missed him. "Pedrón?"

"He went after that Norwegian whore. The fool!"

This baffled Wills. "What . . . how could that be?"

"It is, that's all." Now there was an unearthly sound, the shift of masonry followed by the screech of twisting iron girders— a ripping as pipe and wire was torn out by the roots. They looked up and saw the balancing act that was the top floor trip. It descended sending off a shower of dust then flinging bricks as projectiles.

They ran for their lives, plunging into the mob on the street. It had been their human sound they heard, a torrent of misery pouring out of the city. Sandino and Wills had to fight their way free. Using fists and elbows, then Sandino's gun barrel, they struggled to keep from being stampeded. Only his weapon and a uniform that was mistaken for *guardia* got them through.

With the consul driving the Packard at a walk, Magnusson and the music boy clearing the way, snaking the big car from the hotel basement to *guardia* HQ. The huge square allowed for manuevering and they got around the roadblocks. Puller was waiting with the Buick sedan and the squad of Marines.

"Come on! Come on!" he shouted, waving out the front window as the Marines piled into the two cars and stood on running boards. "Let me lead! I know the way out!" Siren moaning, he plowed through the mob, nudging some aside with the front fenders, the Marines using rifle butts on those who tried to climb aboard.

In the backseat of the Packard, wedged between Marines, General Butler looked at the man squeezed next to him wearing the wheel-in-chevron of an supply sergeant. "How did you get in a weapons squad, Sergeant. . . ?"

"Abrams, sir. Captain Butler told me we're going out looking for some fresh meat."

The general smiled. "He got that right."

Angel Ortez ordered the three companies into the boxcars. The engineer sighed with relief. He had kept the fireman stoking and they were ready to move at a minute's notice. When the last oaf was tucked into the cars he would steam out of this rotten place like the Twentieth Century Limited. A pox on soldiers and earthquakes.

The pickets started back, stepping over track and detouring around a rusty tank car. "That's it," Angel said, watching them with Sabar. "Let's go."

"We waited three hours—"

"I know."

"This place will be swarming with relief people, the Red Cross—I'm surprised there hasn't been a train in from Granada to reinforce the *guardia*—if we get trapped between here and Leon we risk the lives of these men . . ."

"*All right!* I said let's go!" Suddenly the pickets swung around and and the cocking of rifles was audible. There was movement—figures in the distance crossing the yard. "*Don't shoot!*" Angel shouted.

Three people stumbled toward them staggering with fatigue, the lead man waving his arms.

Sabar sucked in his breath. "*That's César!*" and leaping up gave a clear, wavering yell, a rebel salute he'd heard first at Ocotal. Running forward, both men met Sandino, exchanging *abrazos*, tears in their eyes, helping them gently back to the boxcars.

"Cesár," Angel asked, noticing Kate and instantly turning on his aristo charm, "who is this beautiful soldado with the red hair? Are we recruiting film stars now?"

"That is the American consul's daughter and if you are not careful she will shoot you as she did Pedrón."

"Is that possible?" Looking at Kate with admiration. "This little girl shot that bad man? Is he dead?"

"Not because of her—we lost him back in the city. It was his job to watch her."

"Ahh, that is action I volunteer for."

Kate looked at Angel Ortez, seeing the perfect teeth and knowing they were talking about her but not able to catch the rapid Spanish. He was blond and very good looking, and despite herself she smiled back.

At that moment there was a shout and they saw two cars approaching fast from the edge of the yards, dodging around the obstructions. One had a red light and siren going. "Oh my God," Sabar said, "It's that damn *policia* back with a friend! Into the boxcars! *Hurry!*" and they climbed aboard even as the engineer pushed the throttle ahead, sending back a jet of steam. Wheels spun, caught, and the train moved ahead, the sixty-nine-inch drivers beginning to pump.

Puller cranked the Buick around until it was parallel to the track and began pursuit, the Packard coming up fast behind him and to his right. They zigzagged around the upright block signals, missing poles by inches, veering sharply by sidetracked cars and sending passengers bouncing wildly as they hit the washboard edge of ties and closed on the train. In the back of the Packard, the general shouted over the roar of the engine and gravel rattling under the fenders, *"Music, give them a burst!* We're going to run out of yard!"

Standing and bracing himself against the windshield frame without glass, the music boy clacked back the loader on the submachine gun and pulled the trigger as Magnusson had taught him. The line of fire reached out past Puller's Buick, to beat out a pattern on the rear of the caboose. His aim had improved since the Rama drive and he took out the round, rear windows sending glass flying, tearing up the tongue-and-groove oak siding and whanging off metal parts. As the general predicted, they ran out of yard, coming up against a trestle abutment as the track passed on across a swamp. Brakes locked, they slid up to a dead end as the train gathered speed, acclerating on. The line of fire from the Thompson dropped off like a hose losing water pressure.

In the next instant Puller had reversed, shouting through the window as the Buick whipped past, *"We'll make up a train and follow!"*

"That young man is irrepressible," General Butler said, before he could catch himself.

\* \* \*

Those in the caboose were pressed flat to the floor during the machine gun attack. In the rocking boxcars, the heavily armed troops could not see past the mask of the caboose to shoot back at the automobiles coming head on, one blazing away. The officers endured it, making themselves as small as possible while the windows blew out in a shower of glass and big slugs tore through the tough oak.

Lying on the floor squeezed between bodies, Kate felt someone's arm around her, and turning her face, found it within inches of Angel Ortez. She frowned and opened her mouth to protest when he said, "*Bosque picotazo*," indicating the sounds of the bullets against the wood. She giggled; it did sound like a woodpecker. He continued to look at her, smiling, so close she could smell *chicha* on his breath. "*Tinto—muy hermosa*," he said, his eyes indicating her hair. Kate had made it her rule never to be stared down by anybody, but looking into his eyes at this distance was unnerving. She thought she could see her own reflecting in their irises. She turned her head and felt his hand gently squeeze her arm.

The firing dropped off and the sound of rails clicking came up as the train gained speed. Sandino rose up. "Is that it?" he said, then stood. Looking back down the track through the shattered windows he saw two cars falling away, growing smaller. His heart skipped—one was the Packard.

The officers were up now, gingerly brushing off the shards of glass and making jokes. "I have had friends see me off at the station, but this is too much!"

"Perhaps they were angry husbands after Angel."

"No, they would need a bus for that."

"Anyone hurt?"

Sabar Manzanares remained on the floor of the caboose.

"Sabar's taken a nap as usual . . ." Angel said, helping Kate up. "Come on Sabar . . ." In that instant they understood he wasn't getting up. Angel bent over him, lifting his head gently. He had been shot through the top of the skull, the bullet passing down his body while he lay flat. "Mother of God!" Angel wailed, clutching the dead man to him, hands smeared with blood. They all began to cry, the officers weeping unashamedly at their comrade's death. It reminded Wills of grand opera. You would certainly never catch hairy-chested Americans breaking down like this—the whole point of their ritual was not to show grief—except for the women of course. Wills was caught up in it, felt his own eyes fill with tears although he had never met the man. "It should have been me!" Angel cried in an excess of emotion.

*Yes*, Sandino thought, smoothing back Sabar's thin hair, *it should have been*. There was no shortage of brave men to go against the enemy, ah—but where would he again find a man who could add a column of sevens and knew how many rolls of toilet paper to order for three hundred men? It was a loss not easily replaced.

Kate was puzzled and disturbed by the open show of emotion. Like her first shock of violent death at Rama she found this kind of dying unacceptable, arbitrary—all the more frightening because it came on silent feet, striking without warning at the person next to you. There was something very sinister about luck and odds in war. Those who began as self-confident, believing in their invincibility, soon became superstitious and shrank back. A totem was made of survivors—and the men tried to stay close to them, step into their magic circle, take on their aura of protection. If there was a devil adrift in the land, Kate thought, then this was his way of showing himself. Looking at the weeping faces of the tough rebel officers made her uneasy, even at her grandmother's funeral no one hadn't carried on like this. True, she had cried when Calvin died, but crying over pets was accepted. She jumped as a spine-chilling yell went up from Angel.

"*MUERTE A TODOS LOS YANQUIS!*" and the others took it up, clenched fists raised in salute, shaking with anger. She saw that Wills was watching her. He smiled that slow smile of his and lifted his eyebrows.

"They're talking about us, Miss Kelly. Are you prepared to die for United Fruit?" He laughed. At that instant the noise dropped off and Angel heard him and turned, furious, eyes blazing.

"You laugh you son of a bitch?! Do think this is funny that a brave man was killed?"

"No, of course not, I . . ."

"You damn *maricon*!" There was a drawing in of breath at this ultimate Latin insult. Wills stepped back and stiffened but said nothing.

"Why aren't you talking now, big mouth?! No sick jokes or sneering insults?"

Sandino took his arm. "Angel . . ."

He shook it off. "No by God! I never liked this sneaking bastard, this writer who writes in our blood. He is a foul stink in the company of men!" And reaching over he slapped Wills hard across the face, knocking his glasses off. He blinked in near blindness and stepped back against the swaying side of the car. Angel drew his arm back to strike again and was struck from the side by Kate, who swung her arm up and slapped him across his face. He jerked his hand up in surprise and covered the spot.

"Don't you dare hit him again!" She pushed herself in front of Wills. "What kind of a brave thing is that with a car full of armed men behind you! Leave him alone!"

"Enough of this!" Sandino said, "No insult was meant to our dead comrade. Wills is under my protection!"

"Now perhaps!" Angel shouted, "but when we get off this damned train I'm going to cut his throat like a pig!" Embarrassed by the tide of emotion and the girl's defense he turned away, and the men looked elsewhere.

Sandino had had a problem controlling Angel Ortez from the beginning. There was no doubting his courage or the loyalty he inspired in the men. He was a born leader, but the difficulty was he wanted to be *the* leader. After the battle of Tamanindo which he, Ortez, had considered his great victory, he issued a proclamation to this effect. Sandino was displeased and ordered him to stop publishing proclamations on his own that gave him an "air of independence." After that Ortez acknowledged he was operating under Sandino. But Sandino knew at some point there would be a confrontation and, like the others who had tried to climb over his bones, he would have him shot.

Wills fumbled his glasses on. "Thank you, Miss Kelly, but I think I would have preferred another slap rather than having my throat cut."

"You would."

At that point the train brakes locked up, sliding along the track with a sound like a thousand fingernails scraping on a blackboard. Everybody went down, tumbled together and to her horror, Kate found she had fallen on Sabar's body. She pulled back, struggling against the others, and as she did saw that his holster was open and the handle of a small automatic protruded. She removed it quickly and tucked it under her uniform. "What's happened?" she heard someone shout.

# ELEVEN

## Casa Somoza

CHESTY Puller roared around the rail yard, braking the Buick, leaping out at the sight of lurking train personnel, chasing them down. General Butler was reminded of rodeos. "Lewis would have made the perfect bull dogger," he said. "He has a broken-field running style that could have only been developed dodging cow pies." Those of the rescue party and the dozen Marines sat and leaned on the Packard while the music boy topped up the radiator.

"He sure has got a lot of speed," Music said, "I bet he drinks a gallon of coffee an hour."

"If I thought that would do it, I'd feed it to the rest of this bunch," Magnusson said, giving the sleepy pick-up squad the hard eye. It was an odd group: a fat supply sergeant, two Okies from cooks and bakers, a feather merchant with iron-rimmed glasses and one private from Thiells, New York, who was skinny enough to be a circus freak. Another, who smiled without front teeth and had complicated tattoos, Magnusson suspected of being sprung from the brig because of the earthquake. The drill was, whatever you did in the Marine Corps, your first job was that of a rifleman.

Chesty came driving back with his captive train crew in the Buick. They looked very unhappy and only threats, and finally the lie that they would be reimbursed by Uncle Sam got them moving. A locomotive and tender was located, watered, and stoked up, while the Marines loaded the two automobiles on a fifty-foot flatcar. Planks were laid down and the Packard driven on, then the Buick, both blocked and tied down to stake pockets. The locomotive puffed up and was coupled, clanging, to the back. "We will push the warriors into battle," the engineer said, winking at the fireman who winked back, understanding that if the bullets did fly they would uncouple the engine and reverse down the track at full steam. The engineer was an expansive man, sly, with a leonine mane of white hair. As locomotive driver he was important and full of himself. His son-in-law was the fireman. The third member of the crew, the brakeman, was not related and it was his job to stand at the front of the flatcar and manage the brake wheel. As he released its ratchet chain he looked uneasily over his shoulder and was startled to see a machine gun being set up just behind him. If they began firing now it would be between his legs.

It had taken nearly three hours to make up the train and the general began to suspect stalling. Chesty Puller was busy shouting at people, so Butler walked back along the track to discuss it with the engineer. As he went past the engine's running gear, he tapped the nuts with his walking stick to check if they were loose, looking to see if grease cups showed signs of lube. He was not unfamiliar with trains, having on two occasions during the 1910 fracas been charged with their operation. The first time he opened this same line from Managua to Corinto. A naval commander, in command of the train had panicked when confronted by rebels in León and walked back with his troops. Butler took over the disgruntled Marines and sailors and pushed through, regaining their reputation and ruining the commander's, dubbing him "General Walkemback." He wrote about it in his book and Lowell Thomas had loved the story.

The second outing was rougher, breaking through to Granada in the heart of the rebellion and storming the fortified hills to Coyotede and Barranca. That had won the revolution for Díaz and the Conservatives. During the wild train ride, the general sat beside Lieutenant E. H. Conger, a Marine who knew how to run a locomotive. He paid attention.

H. Sanchez, the engineer, leaned out of his cab watching the general with suspicion as he tapped at the Walschaert's gear. By the time the man arrived below him he was ready with a smile anchored by the keystone of a gold tooth. *"Buenos dios mi generál."*

Butler smiled back. *"Maestro*—we are losing time, we must catch that rebel train."

"No worry," Sanchez continued in rapid Spanish, hoping to dazzle him, "that old teakettle ahead cannot get up enough steam to open a letter flap—we will catch them easy," he said, patting the side of the cab. "Very modern, the pride of coastline."

The general knew the locomotive, a Baldwin Little Pacific 4-6-2 built in the twenties and bought up for so much on the dollar when the Florida East Coast Line went belly up and defaulted during the Florida land bust. He saw the fireman bend down by the rear truck wheel shaking down the grates. Good. Engine speed would depend on maintenance. The general swung aboard smoothly, causing the engineer to swivel his neck around, offended that his space had been entered without a by-your-leave.

"Let's get under way, shall we?" he said, still smiling.

"Patience," the engineer said smiling back, "this is a complicated job and needs time."

"Complicated?" The general leaned forward and tapped the steam gauge. "Two-hundred and ten pounds to the square inch—correct. Water level topped up." He twisted a valve, "Air pump oil reservoirs full—I'd say we were ready." And reaching over he tugged the whistle in a deafening blast. The engineer jumped and before the general could lay a hand on the sacred throttle, eased it ahead.

At the sound of the whistle the rescue party climbed aboard the flatcar and the Marine squad frantically heaved on the sandbags they were piling up and clambered after them. As the engine sent out a steamy shudder and began to move ahead, Chesty Puller hopped on the stirrup step behind Magnusson. "Who in hell gave the order to move out?" His expression took on the familiar bulldog frown.

"I'd guess General Butler."

"Well, by God my people were still loading—I'd like to know just who in the hell is running this operation?"

"Why don't you ask him, Chesty?"

"What's he doing down here anyway? I heard he was retiring out. Nothing came through Panama lining out his command. I think he's in receiving and playing loose with my troops!"

"He *is* a general, and he's made the right moves so far."

"Yeah? Well then why haven't you people caught up with Sandino?" Chesty asked, and before Magnusson could answer he walked off down the car, swaying with its motion in a banty rooster strut.

"How about that Chesty?" The music boy said behind Magnusson, laughing.

"Are you talking about Captain Puller, private?" Magnusson snapped.

The music boy caught the icy inflection and it froze him. "Ah, sorry sir."

"You address all officers by their proper title. And you watch your mouth—this is not a Boy Scout Jamboree or a K of C clambake—and you are not a special aquaintance—you are not equal, and in fact, nothing. Now sharpen up, or by God, I will personally throw you off this train and you will walk back to the *Cleveland* with your bugle up your ass! Is that clear?"

"Yes sir!" he replied, bracing himself.

"I want you to go forward to the ammo boxes and personally grease every round. Move!"

"Yes, sir!"

The music boy moved. *Jee-zuss!* He thought, *Magnusson was hard to read, one minute he was your older brother, a buddy—next a D.I. It did not pay to be friendly with officers, they took advantage of you.*

Magnusson was annoyed at Chesty and taking it out on the music boy. He resented the slur on General Butler and himself for not coming to grips with Sandino. The entire U.S. Marine Corps and the *guardia* had been unable to find him in five years and they had been at it what? Five days. It was also galling that Chesty, with the same time in, had already made captain. He knew why—self-promotion, he was good at selling himself. He and Butler had a lot in common there, they made enemies by speaking up and being pushy, but by God, people knew who they were and snapped to. And here was Chesty instantly taking over the rescue party.

Not for the first time Magnusson wondered about his future in the Corps. He had considered himself dumb lucky to have arrived at lieutenant—pulled up through the hawser hole as they said—but he hadn't considered that it would take politics and social graces to advance to the top. He had neither. Would he end up as the world's oldest lieutenant? He knew officers that stayed in the same rank for years. If he didn't remain in the Corps what would he do? What else was he fit for?

He suddenly thought about Karen, coming to it like hitting a wall—seeing the arms and legs of bodies poking up out of the rubble piled under her room. What a hard way to go— remembering their only time in bed with such sweet sadness it caused his heart to constrict. Realizing it was his only experience in bed with a woman he could love. Now that she was gone it might never happen again—would always have the heightened color, the painful nostalgia that a dream took on. She was gone before he realized he loved her.

Sitting in the front seat of the Packard, the consul watched the rail yards fall behind, felt the undulating of the flatcar as it rode over the rise and fall of landscape, newly shaped by the earthquake. The familiar cadence of clicks came up and he knew this happened when the wheels of a train passed where rails were joined. Standard rails were thirty-nine feet—if you kept count you could calculate how far you had traveled. He tried to do this but his mind returned to its one obsession—his daughter, Kate. *Where was she now—at this moment? Has she been abused, hurt? Was it a mistake to pursue her with this wild posse? What would he say to Norma if anything happened to her? How would he tell Hilaria about Tomás's death?* The same questions repeated in an endless chain, the first replacing the last, going round and round. In his head he had been reduced to begging, making deals and promises to whomever he thought would listen; God, the devil, the U.S. Government—Sandino. He no longer wished for Sandino's death, and in fact began to picture him as an intelligent, benevolent leader, a man you could trust. If the consul had the power he would have promised to pull the U.S. Marines out of Nicaragua tomorrow. In imaginary conversations he agreed to reveal what state secrets he knew—betray the nation—anything if his daughter would be released unharmed. *Where was she now—at this moment?*

Leaving the rail yards at Managua, the Sandinistas had been tumbled to the floor of the cars when the train screeched to a stop in front of twisted rails. The troops had to get out and manhandle them back in place. After that, the engine went ahead like a man walking on tiptoes. Signs of the earthquake were visible in the countryside. They saw its frightening slash traveling like an arrow toward the heart of the city—fresh splits in the earth's crust. Sandino began to despair. They stopped a dozen times in as many miles to repair the tracks, move obstructions before the old engine with its funnel-shaped stack could move on, its puff an antique exhalation.

He had failed, been stopped from bringing the war home to

the politicans and exploiters; of laying its bloody head at their feet—rubbing Yankee noses in it. A great chance had been lost to press the revolution to a conclusion, of forcing them to all recognize his Army Supporting the National Sovereignty. This time an earthquake had stopped them—God's will? No matter, he had failed, his shout for attention would be lost in the cries of its victims. He had turned it around, telling the men, "This disaster clearly demonstrates to the doubters that divine gestures are guiding our actions. You should not tremble before these things of divine origin, precisely for the reason that our army itself has sprung from this invisible impulse." The simple troops, *campesinos*, were comforted by the grand sounding words, but the others, officers, knew better. The campaign was over. It had taken every last resource to put together the three companies for the attack. As it was, his poor troops went barefoot with too few arms to go around and precious little food. In his army no one was paid, troops or officers, and any recompense they received was taken in looting—with the failed raid there was nothing to take.

Again they would retreat into the mountains, back to El Chipote where the army would shrink to a skeleton, and he would be left a general without soldiers to carry on the paper war. Letters, speeches, begging requests to other countries who sympathized but gave nothing. Then—he had a thought—one bright spot in a dim landscape. *The girl.* The American consul's daughter. He still had her to bargain with and in the end she would be worth a dozen companies. She stood now against the swaying caboose wall with Wills, sullen, defiant. He didn't understand how a young girl could be like that; like an angry rooster. Was it being American? And she hated him—for what? Killing her donkey. It was typical that a spoiled rich girl would cry over a donkey when there were thousands of poor dying in the country every day. She had accused him of using Captain Sangre badly, well what was he to do? The stupid woman deserted and in the military you made hard choices. Still, in the back of his head he knew he had insulted Sangre because he was embarrassed by her bizarre behavior—never mind, it only showed what happened when women were allowed to behave like men.

After a long day's journey, the train slowed for a curious junction just outside León. It was dusk and to the east the mountains of *Los Marrabilos* sloped away, their rise marked by the hazy steps of terraces. Ahead the tracks funneled between two long, concrete buildings, suddenly drawing the train into a narrow enclosure. It was disturbing because it came at the end of a tame, open landscape. "What is this place?" Sandino asked uneasily as they entered the tunnel of buildings and it got suddenly darker. Thick walls rose four stories on each side; doors and window frames were missing and the place had the eerie look of an eyeless relic.

"It is called *La Casa Fantasia.*" Angel Ortez said, "It was to be a resort for the rich with the hotel—which you see here— right on the line so that passengers might disembark discretely to rooms. We are only five miles from León, and there was thought to be the need for such a place."

"A hotel for rich men's affairs," Sandino said.

"Something like that. At any rate the promoters went broke before it was finished and it is now a warehouse to store fertilizer."

"Perfect."

"At the far end, a small section is used for train people and telegraphy. We will want to check and see if the line is cleared for us at León to switch to the El Sause connection."

"What I am interested in is not what's ahead, but what's behind."

The train crept to a stop in front of a dimly lit area. A huge opening meant for a showpiece of a door contained a crude one transferred from a box car, complete with stenciled numbers. Sandino and Angle got down from the caboose and walked toward it. The troops shoved the car doors back and peered out. "Pickets to the front and rear!" Angel shouted, "The rest stay

where you are! Officers join your platoons!" The officers hopped
down and ran along the track. "I hope we can give them a night's
sleep before we go rattling into the mountains in this old crock,
César."

"That's all they've had."

"Listen, the fact that the raid was called off doesn't mean
they didn't risk their lives!"

"Well they came back alive. I would think they would want
to stay awake and enjoy it." Angel gave up.

Kate and Wills stood at the window watching them. They
had hung back after the hysteria with Angel Ortez. She felt the
chill of the place and hugged her arms to her body. "Why are we
stopping here?"

"To telegraph ahead. León is over the next hill—they'll
switch the engine to an extension there that will take us up to
Malpasillo and El Sauce."

"In the mountains?"

"Yes, from there we'll go on foot to Nueva Segovia and
Sandino's country."

"Once we're there no one will ever find me," she said,
staring off toward the shadowy rim of mountains.

"It would be difficult."

"Are you going to let them do that?"

"It's not up to me."

"You said we're only a few miles from a city—you must
know how to get there—you could take me."

"I couldn't do that."

"Why? You're an American!"

"Miss Kelly—Kate, try to understand. I'm a writer—a
journalist—I'm here on trust to report what I see. If I enter into
those events—help you escape—then I've lost my objectivity and
no one would believe what I wrote again. As a war correspondent
I must maintain absolute integrity."

"Would you do it if you were forced?"

He smiled. "How do you intend that?"

"With this." And she produced Sabar's little automatic.

The station master and several bedraggled railroad employees greeted Sandino and Angel, all bows and nervous smiles. "Welcome General Sandino! As ardent supporters we wish you military success and long life."

"An unlikely combination." The room was a cement box with form marks still in the concrete, an unfinished space meant to be the great hotel's elegant waiting room. In the hollow space their voices sounded amplified as through a drainpipe. Sandino brushed past the greeters to the telegrapher's desk. It was behind a crude chicken-wire enclosure, bare cables running down from an open window and kept in place by blue glass insulators.

"Are the lines open?" he asked the operator.

"Only as far as Mateare. We have no word from the capital."

"You come from there, General," the station master tentatively asked, "How is it with the city?"

"There is no city." There was a gasp from the others and he continued questioning the telegrapher, a spare man with an intelligent narrow face. "What about trains? How many are on the line?"

He picked up his clipboard. The top of the desk was stacked with papers and ledgers, the only open space around the key. "The U.S. Army Engineers sent a trainload of demolitions and firefighting equipment from Granada to arrive at Managua at nine-ten . . ."

"Sabar was right," Angel said, "we just got out in time."

"What else?" Sandino pressed forward.

"Only one other coming from Managua, it passed Nagrote two hours behind yours, sir."

Sandino looked at Angel, then back at the telegrapher. "How was it made up?"

"A locomotive pushing a flatcar . . . the dispatcher noted it was loaded with two automobiles and banked with sandbags. He said there were soldiers aboard."

"They're still after us," Sandino sighed, then straightened. He shook his head. "The Packard."

"Who?" Angel asked.

"A group from Bluefields. A Marine Lieutenant called Magnusson and Smedley Butler."

"Smedley Butler? You can't mean that old general of Marines?"

"So it seems."

"But he must command at least a brigade!"

"No, I don't believe so. But I would think they would be foolish to come after us with less than a company." He turned back to the telegrapher. "Did your man say how many soldiers he saw?"

"No sir. It flew by."

"Come on." And Sandino walked past the obsequious station personnel and went outside. He stood in the lighted doorway looking down the tunnel of unfinished hotel buildings on both sides of the tracks. Windows were at the second story level, small openings against the noise and smoke of the train. The heavy shadows cast by falling light gave the two facing buildings the look of fortresses.

"César, if they are only two hours behind, we better get the train going up the mountains toward El Sause!"

"No. They will only come after us," he replied, resigned.

"But . ."

"It's time to stand and fight them, Angel, to kill them once and for all. I'm sick of these dogs on my heels." He waved his arm down the track. "Have you ever seen a more perfect place for an ambush? If we arrange ourselves on both sides in these two buildings and they come down the center of the track we will have them."

Angel made a sour face. "Who was it said an ambush was a trap inside out?"

\*　\*　\*

Pedrón Altamirano had fished Karen Sven naked and unconscious out of the bathtub on the sixth floor of The Grand. Throwing her over his shoulder like a sack of beans he lowered her down the elevator shaft on a series of ropes and went after her. They were in the basement when the building fell and so survived. She came to, screaming, and he had to slap her.

"What's the matter with you for God's sake? You're saved! I pulled you out of this building! Me the hero!" He laughed. She looked at him with horror, could not understand his Spanish or what had happened. "Come on, Blondie, we've got to dig our way out of here."

He managed it and they squirmed onto a street filled with an hysterical mob; pushing out of the city, battling to stay on their feet. Pedrón had left his handgun on the sixth floor, and picking up a stout stick, began to batter his way into the crowd tugging Karen along. Naked, blond hair flowing back, her white skin gave her the appearance of a wraith; a spectral image, and people shrank back.

Pedrón was unfamiliar with Managua but he knew the compass points and went west toward the rail yards. As they passed out of the downtown zone, central to the worst damage, they came by side streets where the buildings stood relatively undamaged. In the front of one of these, a large sedan idled, its exhaust bubbling back. The two-story house was wood, cut to resemble stone and butted up to its neighbors with narrow windows and a door covered with heavy grill work. Its front was a closed facade, the interior arranged around a courtyard.

Pedrón could see the rear of the driver's head as he sat in the car and smoked. Turning in the street, he tugged Karen along, keeping flat to the buildings so the man could not see him in his mirror. Then reaching the car, he crossed over in two steps, grabbed the driver by the throat and slamming his head against the top of the car's door jamb. Opening the door, he tumbled out and Pedrón kicked him sharply again in the head. He wore the uniform of the *guardia*. "Get in!" he shouted to Karen, and opening the rear door, shoved her in the back. Behind the wheel, he put the car in gear and moved ahead in a jerking motion. He was no good with automobiles but if they were to reach the rail yards in time, then something had to be done. As he pulled away two *guardia* dashed out of the house followed by an officer.

"Stop! That is an official car!" When Pedrón continued they raised their rifles.

"No!" the officer shouted, "Don't damage that car! He can't get away, the street is blocked! Go after him!" And they began running.

Pedrón came up to a barrier where a brick building had collapsed into the street, blocking it. Cursing, he tried to turn the big machine in the narrow space, backing up on the sidewalk and cranking the wooden steering wheel around frantically. The car stalled and he jumped out as the soldiers reached him. Grabbing the rifle thrust at him by the first soldier, he knocked him down but before he could turn, the other man struck him in the side on the head with his rifle butt. He stumbled and was hit again and again giving the first soldier time to recover. Then together the two of them beat him to the ground with blows to the head and back—still it took minutes before he was quiet. The officer came up at his own pace, smoking, and drew a large automatic. "The fellow is a real bull!" one of the soldiers said, panting.

"Yes well, the bull hasn't been made who can stand up to a bullet in the brain." Cocking the weapon he placed it in Pedrón's ear, twisting it at an angle where it would not ricochet back. "Wait a minute . . ." he said slowly, taking the cigarette out of his mouth and bending closer. Shoving the toe of his polished shoe under his shoulder he tried to roll him over. "Come on you two! Dammit! Give me a hand!" Together they got him over on his back. "By God!" he said putting the gun away, I know who it is! Drag him in the house, Tacho is going to love this!"

"Hey, Captain Somoza!" one of the soldiers said, sticking his head in the car window and laughing. "There's a naked woman back here."

"Probably his whore—bring her along too," he said, barely giving her a glance.

The interior of the house was cool with the smell of *Piñole* masking cigarette smoke and faulty plumbing. It was semidark—shutters were closed and the electricity out from the quake. Captain Somoza walked down a tile hall that boxed the courtyard to a sitting room hung with heavy tapestry and dim portraits of someone's ancestors. A single ornate oil lamp was centered on a round parlor table filled with coffee cups and the clutter of papers. Several men sat around it smoking, their cigarette butts ground out on the tile floor, Latin style. All were in the uniforms of the *guardia* except Somoza's cousin Tacho.

At 33 Anastasio "Tacho" Somoza Garcia was only a few years older than his cousin from the country, but gave the appearance of being his senior. He was a huge man by Nicaraguan standards with a tendency to paunchiness that put years on. Mature and self-controlled, he somehow seemed the father or uncle at every gathering. He had a friendly face with a wide band of freckles across the nose and eyes slightly turned up, that were at once amused and penetrating. He radiated a hardy charm: the oily unction of a used car salesman, which he had been, or the glad hand of the politico which he was now.

His cousin saluted and couldn't help smiling. "Sir, amazing news! We've caught Pedrón Altamirano!"

"What?! Poco, are you sure?" This galvanized the table—the officers stopped talking and looked at him. The cousin was radiant, all eyes on him.

"Yes sir. I've studied his picture—and I caught a glimpse of him at Rama when we were in pursuit." The latter wasn't true, but reminded the group that he had recently been in combat with Sandino's bandits. After the fight at Rama, he had taken a chance and reported it directly to Tacho, whom he had met only once at a wedding. Tacho had been impressed with his push and had him assigned to his staff. As foreign minister and a relative he bumped him from sergeant to captain, just like that. When the earthquake struck, Poco drove his cousin to Managua and joined with the *guardia* and the Americans fighting the fire and setting up apparatus to help stricken civilians. Tacho's friends, the American minister Matthew Hanna and his wife, were away from the city, but the chargé, Willard Beaulac, said publicly that Anastasio Somoza had performed a great service for mankind. Of course he was also doing business. It was no secret that when the Marines went, he was likely to be the next *Jefe Director.* The ranking officers here today were loyal members of his claque come to pay homage.

Taco was beaming, "Well boys, it takes a lad from the country to catch a rat." They laughed. "If this is Sandino's machete man that is something—come on, we have to see this terror."

Chairs scraped back and they trooped out of the room. Tacho gave his cousin's arm a squeeze. "Poco, I can see it was no mistake to bring my Aunt Juanita's little boy to the big city."

"Rosita, Tacho."

"Of course." They went through French doors with the glass whited out, to an inner courtyard. It was bare with the exception of a single chair and a long narrow table stained with brown spots. The courtyard had once been open to the sky but was now crudely roofed over with a corregated tin roof visible underneath rough beams. What light there was came from around the imperfect joining of this addition. The space was meant to be banked with plants; now only the rings where they stood were faintly visible. The tile floor was a complex hexagon pattern that caused the eye to be fooled and repeat a line of squares, then reverse itself, giving the impression of movement. This confusing distortion sloped to a drain in the center where Pedrón lay naked. Two *guardia* soldiers sloshed him down with water, the blood from his beating swirling off, sucked down the drain. His feet were hobbled with a foot of rope between them and his arms tied behind, a broom handle shoved in the crook of his elbows.

"Get him up," Tacho said, "let's see if he's as big as they

say." Pedrón was jerked to his feet, swaying unsteadily and supported by the soldiers. "Well, what do you think? He's not that much after all." He was perhaps six inches shorter than Somoza, broad and hairy from shoulders to ankles.

"It's all that monkey fur," one of the officers said. They stood with Somoza smoking, several holding coffee cups.

"Do you know who I am, Pedrón?" Tacho said.

"You're the hair around a donkey's asshole." Pedrón answered, apparently not permanently damaged, and in control of his hatred.

Tacho smiled. "Well, that could be, but for the moment I'm the foreign minister, one of the people your boss Sandino gets all hot under the collar about . . ." He turned to the others. "Did you know I was born in San Marcos only a few miles from Sandino's home in Niquinohomo?"

"Really?" the officers said.

"That's right, we went to the same high school—but not at the same time . . ." He laughed. "It's just as well, or they would have called us Mutt and Jeff." Tacho was proud of his grasp of the American idiom and worked it in whenever he could.

Although his father was not a big landowner, a succession of good coffee crops had allowed him to send his son to the United States to study at Philadelphia's Pearce School. Here he developed the fluent English he was famous for. It was without accent and spiced with current slang. *Norteamericanos* thought they were talking to one of their own. It was the reason for his success with the American minister Matthew Hanna; the other was Hanna's young German wife who thought Tacho a smooth rhumba dancer.

"You're also a fuckin' toilet inspector!" Pedrón sputtered, trying for an original insult and repeating a popular slur.

"You've heard that? Yes, it's true, I once was a privy inspector for the Rockefeller Foundation. But I did it with such style, using a flashlight, like a baton"—he demonstrated, waving his hand in a graceful arc—"that they nicknamed me the

'Marshal.'" The officers laughed with him. "Do you think I'm ashamed of that Pedrón? That I pretend to be something I'm not? I've had my nose in shit many times, my friend. I've had a dozen different demeaning jobs, but here I am and there you are."

"You're here because your fat wife is that traitor Sacasa's niece."

This was not amusing. Somoza leaned forward, voice dropping to a whisper. "Listen to me bad man. You are not the only bandit to give the finger to the authorities. My grandfather Bernabé would make you look like a hairless pussy—they called him 'Seven Handkerchiefs'—you know why? Because that's how many it took to wipe the blood off his hands. Ha! When they finally hung him in Rivas there was a holiday and the widows of the men he killed stood in line a half mile long to spit in his face—can you match that? So don't act the bad man here. I have more of the bandit in me than you or that peanut Sandino—I'm the one who will walk away with it all." Pressing closer he said, "All of it!" Then straightening, he relaxed. "Enough nostalgia. Time for work. We here have all admired your *cortes*, Pedrón. Until you invented them, we were satisfied with simply whacking limbs off—but you've made an art of it. We'd like your help in perfecting the *corte de cumbo*." Pedrón got a very cold feeling in the pit of his stomach.

"We have a fellow here we're bringing along and we'd like your opinion on his work." He turned, smiling. "Poco, bring in the surgeon." Tacho grew quiet and looked into Pedrón's eyes, holding them, as his cousin's shoes clacked on the tile, crossing the room. He went out the door and in the silence his footsteps could be heard down the hall. There were muffled orders and the sound of shuffling following his return.

The officers in the room remained perfectly quiet, all of them watching Pedrón's face. When the surgeon came in they saw his eyes widen. He was a fat boy, round and soft as a girl with a small head carried to one side, apparently without benefit of a neck. One of his tiny eyes had a cant and looked permanently to the left. His mouth hung open, slack.

"*Bobo* . . ." Pedrón gasped.

"Do you think so? Yes, but an idiot savant—you don't have to worry, he knows what he's about. Pepe," Tacho said clearly to the surgeon, "show-us-how-you-slice-a-melon."

He carried a nearly round green melon in one hand and shuffling to the table carefully positioned it on the top. A drop of water glistened on it and ran off in a curved path. In his other hand he held not a machete but a double-edged *cutache*, with a blade that had been honed to a whisker's edge. Without preparation or command he commenced slicing the melon, his arm working mechanically, descending in rapid whacks, the blade never thumping into the table. When he sliced half the fruit he stepped back and Taco held a piece up, paper thin, the shadow of his finger visible on the other side.

"Remarkable, eh? You could read through it. How many slices of the brain like this will it take to kill a man? Pedrón, you should know." He set the piece down and his hand shot out, grabbing Pedrón by the hair, pulling his head to one side. He stood at arm's length, still talking in the same even, reasonable voice. "Witnesses have reported that your victims—our people—sometimes lived as long as a half hour with part of their brain cut away—let's go for the record—shall we? *Pepe!*"

And the blade came down on the side of Pedrón's head shaving away a slice as thin as the sample, hair still attached. A small piece of his ear also came went with it. "No extra charge for the shave and haircut." Tacho laughed.

# TWELVE

# La Fantasia

MAGNUSSON and Puller saw it coming from a distance.

"What in hell is that?"

"A place they call *La Fantasia*. It was going to be a hotel or something, there's a telegraph key there. León's just over the hill." It was nearly dark but light still hung on over the low range to the east. Orange rays slanted in, sending shafts running down narrow valleys to cross the tabletop of land.

The train was on a curve approaching the two buildings astride the track. From where they stood on the flatcar the rails seemed to disappear in their shadow. "Looks like the perfect place for an ambush," Magnusson said.

"Come on, you got ambush on the brain. Sandino is not going into action a couple of miles from the León garrison. Don't sweat it." But Puller turned and walked back along the length of the flatcar, swaying with its rhythm, keeping his feet as a sailor might, anticipating the roll of a ship. The men squatted where they could, backs against the sandbags, smoking with cupped hands, and gave him the eye as he went by. They had not seen what was ahead. Reaching the end of the car, he paused for a moment in front of the pilot coupling, gauging the engine's roll, then jumped to the platform above the cowcatcher, grabbing one of the angle braces. Regripping, he climbed to the side of the locomotive, and hanging on to the boiler rails, went along the catwalk inches above the drivers, the blurred pump of their piston sending up a shudder of vibration that made his feet tingle. Around him the aggregation of links, levers, and bars danced in monkey motion. Reaching the cab on the left side he swung in, and if he thought to surprise General Butler he was wrong.

"Well, Lewis, good to see you. Care for coffee? There's no shortage of hot water up here," he said, tilting his cup. The general sat in the fireman's seat with seven feet of backhead between him and the engineer. The fireman perched on his tender. The heat was terrific and the noise deafening. Puller crossed over to the engineer and shouted in his ear.

"Blast through that junction full throttle!"

The engineer shook his head. "No, there's a block signal." He was right, as they approached *La Fantasia* the semaphore flashed yellow for caution and they began to slow.

"Why not stop and put out flankers, Lewis?"

Chesty ignored him. He was not going to waste hours and let the rebel train get away while they pussyfooted.

Ahead, the three Sandinista companies were in position, weapons angled down from second-story windows. The results would be, they said, like shooting fish in a barrel. Sandino and Ortez stood in doorways each commanding a building. The engine's headlight could be seen down the track as the train slowed, silhouetting the shapes of automobiles on the flatcar.

Sandino sucked his breath in. *It was the Packard!* The same automobile that had dogged them all the way from Bluefields after the girl. *The girl!* He stopped and looked around. *Where was she?*

He shouted over at Angel, "Where's the consul's daughter?"

"The last time I saw her was with that writer!"

*Wills?* Sandino had an unpleasant thought. *Would he help the girl to escape?* He opened his mouth to shout at Angel, but he was already running back toward the troop train. "I'll find them!" Sandino knew if he did, Wills was a dead man.

Wills had smiled when Kate produced Sabar's small ornamental automatic. "Do you expect me to believe you would shoot?" They both stood in the dark caboose, pressed against its wall, hearing the sound of a train approaching.

"I shot Pedrón. He didn't believe I would, either."

That was uncomfortably true. "Kate . . ."

"I wouldn't shoot to kill you—maybe in the hand—which one do you type with?" she smiled.

"That is a terrible thing to say."

"If you like I'll shoot you in your integrity."

Wills smiled. "All right, I'll point you to León—but from there you're on your own."

"Let's just go!" And she pushed him toward the caboose door. Wills shrugged and went out on the narrow platform, swinging down to the track. As they looked toward the approaching locomotive they saw someone coming, outlined by the halo of its light. Kate turned and began running alongside the boxcars. "Come on!"

"*Alto!*" Angel shouted, drawing his pistol, but he didn't dare shoot, afraid of springing the ambush. Reaching the caboose he ducked between cars and made out the figure of Wills two cars ahead stumbling along. "Writer! Stop or I'll shoot!" Wills stopped, raising his hands as Angel ran up, grabbed him roughly, and slammed him up against the boxcar. "Where's the girl?!" Kate was nowhere in sight.

"I . . . don't know . . ." He didn't, she had been in front of him and as he turned to look back, vanished. Angel had his left hand around his throat choking him, jamming his head back against the boxcar. Then in a smooth motion he reached around and came up with a large knife. To Wills it looked like the kind chefs used to bone chicken.

When the flatcar nosed into the tunnel between buildings the men grew uneasy. "Jesus!" someone said, "It's as dark as the inside of a dog." Magnusson sensed their fear, loading his rifle with a grenade launcher, the long rod of a British Hale grenade, fired with a blank round. Around him he heard the others shifting and the sounds of clicks as safeties were let off.

"Easy . . ."

Pressed against the doorway, Sandino watched the locomotive continue toward them at a maddeningly slow pace, the big wheels turning over in quiet revolutions you could count, steam shooting out trackside to vanish in wet vapor. So quiet now the rasp of flange was audible on rail—then, the sharp snap of a single shot echoing down the tunnel of buildings. Sandino knew immediately that it came from the empty troop train and turned his head in that direction.

Then a sheet of flame erupted from the side of one building, followed simutaneously by broadsides from the other. At once bullets filled the air, smacking into sandbags on the flatcar, clanking off metal, whipping past some, tearing into others with that awful, unforgettable sound; the startled grunt; the drawing in of breath that signaled serious wounding. In that first murderous fusillade four men were killed and every man but one wounded, some grievously. In the buildings there was a second's hesitation while rebel bolts were worked, shells charged, and in that space, those of the rescue party who could, fired back. The surviving machine gunner, angling the Lewis gun up and spraying the concete, sent chipped pieces flying, spent slugs falling back in a curtain of dull thuds. Magnusson had launched his first grenade at moment of contact, lobbing it in a window to his left, then swinging it to one on his right—seeing the bright flash of ignition, the muffled *whomp* of explosion. The thing that saved the few was the extreme angle the Sandinistas had to bring their guns to bear on the flatcar.

In the cab, Chesty Puller was trying to drag the engineer up off the floor. "Reverse the engine!" Around them bullets shattered glass instruments and pinged off brass pipes.

General Butler reached across and threw the Johnson bar in reverse. "Allow me," he said, and the engine began to creep backward. As it did, the staccato beat of a heavy machine gun rattled on the rear of the tender. Two guns had been set up behind them, locked in for crossfire.

"Forward!" Chesty shouted, "Maybe we can break through!" And they went forward in a slow jerking motion as he hung from the side of the engine firing at the windows with the pump shotgun. Through the steam and smoke of gunfire he saw that they were blocked ahead by the stalled troop train. To his right, coming up, were the double doors of a loading platform. When they were opposite he shouted, "Stop!" Jumping across with a hiss of steam sending up a screen, he found the doors to the building secured by a huge brass lock and blasted it off with the shotgun. "Reverse!" The general backed until the flatcar was opposite the shattered door, and he leaped for it. "Fall back to the building!" At last the music boy got to blow his bugle, sounding retreat. A second later he was hit. With Magnusson and the BAR man covering, they dragged the dead and wounded inside.

It was a huge two-story space intended to be the lobby of the hotel and now stacked with fertilizer bags. Curling down from the far end were cast cement stairs that were to have been the grand entrance to the dining room. Windows and doors were bricked in, and the heat generated by the fertilizer was terrific.

"Cover that stairway!" Puller shouted, and in the next minute there was the scurrying of feet and men appeared at the top. At the burst of Marine fire they retreated back into the doorway connecting the rooms—then, a pause and the sound of a single rifle clattering to the floor. Next, a man stumbled backward into the opening, disembodied hands reaching out for him—but he fell, tumbling down the stairs, slow and limp, dead before he hit the ground.

At the bottom they stared at the body, face turned up, straw hat still in place. He was very young, with a twisted sisal belt and bare feet. "That's the first one I ever saw close up," someone said.

"Yeah? Then take a good look," Puller said, "this guy and his buddies just shot us to pieces!" Looking up, he saw Magnusson's eyes on him and knew what he was thinking: *It's your fault.* He had broken his own rule about blasting anything ahead that looked like an ambush. They couldn't do that to railroad property, but he should have stopped the train and sent out flankers like the old man said. That would have taken hours and he was pushing to catch up with Sandino's train. Well, they had.

It was true they were shot to pieces; some, two or three times. The music boy had been shot twice through the same leg, the right, one shattering his knee, the other through the muscle of his calf. General Butler was doing his best to bind him, tearing up his uniform shirt to cinch up tourniquets. There was a medical bag but it hadn't been located.

"Mother . . ." the music boy said, "Jesus . . . my mother . . ."

"She'll be proud of you son," the general said, thinking he was asking for her.

"No . . . Jesus she's going to kill me . . . she told me this would happen . . . I'd have been better off with the Poles . . ."

"Do you think so?" The general had no idea what he was talking about.

Richard Kelly, the American consul, sat staring at his left hand. His ring finger was gone—shot away, and so was the wedding ring—vanished. This seemed to him more ominous than anything that had happened yet.

They were all wounded in one place or another, some superficially, others with complications that would stay with them for life. They were all wounded but Magnusson. Bullets had passed through his uniform and hat. The holes were visible for all to see, but he hadn't been touched, not one scratch. They stared at him in awe.

Satisfied the Marines were trapped in the lobby, Sandino set up harassing fire. He was not going to attack a Marine entrenched position head on no matter how few men defended it. He made that mistake at Ocotal and would not repeat it. Instead, he walked back toward the troop train. Who had fired the shot that prematurely began the engagement?

With Angel Ortez choking him with one hand and ready to stick a knife into his belly with the other, Wills had done his best to resist, flailing out, twisting, but he was helpless as a combatant, and a knee in his groin pinned him to the side of the boxcar. *So much for witty, intelligent conversation* he thought, *and the skills to speak and write it.* There was not one bright, right word he could say to this simple young man that would persuade him that he should not be murdered because he laughed at the wrong time.

Rotating his eyes downward he caught a horrifying glimpse of the wicked blade being drawn back. Then, at the perimeter of his vision he saw something else; a perfectly white hand appeared out from the tracks under the boxcar holding a shiny, small automatic. While he watched, the gun was placed against the toe of Angel's right boot. The trigger was pulled, then he heard the sharp crack as it fired. There was a scream of pain and Angel released him. This was the shot that began the battle.

At the house in Managua they got bored with Pedrón. The officers watched for nearly two hours as he lurched around the courtyard, banging off the walls, the left side of his brain cut away. "He certainly wins the prize for marathon *corte* gourd," Tacho Somoza said, laughing. "If we could get him a partner, he would be a big hit at taxi dancing."

"Or as a dancing bear," someone else added.

The surgeon made two more paper-thin slices causing him

to lose total equilibrium, suffering the agony of repeated convulsions. He lay now in a corner curled in the position of a hemiplegic. He had thoroughly fouled himself and shook in spasms. The smell began to get to even the hardened voyeurs and they drifted out of the room one by one.

Captain Poco Somoza and his cousin Tacho, the foreign minister, left and went down the hall, both lost in their own thoughts, not talking. As they came past a narrow door, the sound of crying could be heard. "What is that?" Tacho said.

"There was a whore picked up with Pedrón. She is locked in there."

"Let's see her."

Poco unhooked the door and saw a naked woman crouched at the back of the small, windowless room. It had been a utility closet and with the exception of a bucket for waste was empty. She blinked against even the dim light. "Help me! Please help me!" she said in Norwegian. Tacho was immediately struck by the marvelous body, tall and lush at the same time. Despite the dirt, she showed elegant features and blond-white hair to her waist.

"What is that she's speaking?" Poco said, "German?"

"No—how do you know she was Pedrón's woman? She doesn't look like someone he would have."

"Well she was with him in the car—and naked." That was enough for Poco.

"Do you speak English?" Tacho said gently, bending over her anguished face.

"Yes! Yes! Help me!" She saw in his concerned, intelligent eyes the first sign of hope.

"Who are you?"

"Karen Sven, a Norwegian national! I was taken by that horrible man from my hotel . . . "

"Which hotel is that?"

"The Grand—I was staying there with a party from Bluefields—"

"The Grand?" Tacho was instantly alerted.

". . . General Butler, Lieutenant Magnusson . . . and . . ."

"What!" he exclaimed, galvanized at the mention of the famous American general.

". . . and the American consul—Mr. Kelly—they, we, were looking for his daughter . . ."

Tacho was horrified. *My God!* he thought, *The very people that supported me.* He turned snarling at his cousin, "You damn fool! Didn't you question her?"

"Nobody could understand her . . . and she was naked . . ."

Tacho took off his jacket and put it around Karen's shoulders, helping her up. "My dear lady, there has been a terrible mistake! What can I say to apologize? Please come with me!" Arm around Karen, he pushed past Poco without a word, but his look said it all. Stunned, Poco watched them go down the hall. His career had peaked and plummeted all in a few hours. Thinking about it, he now remembered hearing about a woman with General Butler's rescue party, someone hinting she'd been the whore of the mill manager. Were they the same? He could find out.

About dusk one of the lowly *guardia* privates came in the tiled courtyard to mop up the mess. He stayed away from the body in the corner, averting his eyes. They told him it would be removed and dumped on the pile with other earthquake victims later that night.

Pedrón heard the swish of the mop and opened one eye. He found if he kept the other closed, he could focus.

When Sandino walked to the troop train to investigate the single shot, Angel Ortez was sitting on the ground while Wills bandaged his foot. The consul's daughter was not evident.

"What happened?"

"The girl shot me in the foot," Angel said, chagrined.

Sandino had to laugh. "My God, will I have any officers left? Didn't I tell you to be careful?" He looked at Wills, less friendly. "How did she happen to be escaping, and in possession of a gun?"

"The gun was Sabar's," Angel said. "She must have taken it from his body."

Sandino continued looking at Wills. "And the escape?"

"She pointed the gun at me, César, said she would shoot—I believed her." He nodded at Angel. "She did."

Sandino had to agree this was true. "Where is she now?"

"Probably under the train hiding. She scurried off after the shot."

"All right, give Angel a hand and we'll send some men to look for her. She won't get far."

"Oh no!" Angel said, hopping up on one foot. "Dammit, she shot me and I'm going to find her!" He picked up his polished boot with the bullet hole aft of his big toe, and proceeded to cut the end off, using the same knife he'd been ready to stab Wills with. Tenderly slipping his foot in it, he was able to walk.

"All right," Sandino said, "but this time be careful or it will be your head instead of your foot that gets a hole in it." He turned, "Come on Carlton, I have business."

When the music boy came around from a dip into the unconscious he saw an amazing sight. General Butler's chest.

Ripping up his shirt for bandages, the general exposed a remarkable tattoo. It was the Marine Corps emblem; eagle atop the globe carrying the *Semper Fidelis* motto on a streamer grasped in its beak. The size was impressive—it covered his entire chest from sternum to rib cage. The garish colors had mellowed with age and a drift of white hair, but it was astounding—he was a living monument to his profession.

"Had it done as a tad lieutenant in the Philippines by a Japanese needle man. Took a while, I'll tell you, like putting a Bull Durham sign on a barn. Edith never cared for it, few women do—and I suppose staring up at a billboard for the Corps on your wedding night might tend to take the dew off your lily. At any rate I'll have it until I'm skinned." The music boy had drifted off and General Butler examined his wounds, knowing the rise of dark blood on the bandages was not good.

Chesty Puller and Magnusson conferred in muted voices, squatting in a position to move instantly. Bullets zinging in the open door chipped the concrete but everyone was behind stacked-up fertilizer bags, with the wounded in the middle, the dead laid out to the rear.

"There's a telegraph key down at the end of this building," Chesty said.

Magnusson looked interested. "Maybe they've cut the lines."

"Why? Sandino is in command. I'd keep that line open to know what the other guy was up to."

"How are you going to get there from here?"

"See that bricked-up doorway over there?" He indicated a wide arch on the north side of the room. "We could knock it down—I'll bet there's one in the next room and so on until you get to the building on the end."

"Maybe."

"I'll take a couple of men and we'll break through and get to that key."

"What if the place is full of Sandos?"

"Would we be any worse off than we are?"

Magnusson knew exactly what Chesty was doing. Although there had been no hint from him that he made a mistake by not stopping and flanking *La Fantasia*, he felt the heat. He was going to do what he did best to make up for it—he was going to be a hero.

Chesty stood up, ignoring the stray bullets, shouting at two of the nearly whole survivors; the painfully thin private from Thiells, New York, and the ex-prisoner with the crafty smile. "You and you! Yardbird and Bones! Fall in!" They looked at each other and followed as he marched them to the bricked-up doorway. "All right, turn to and clear this hatchway—I'll cover you." He jerked the Thompson submachine gun away from the yardbird.

Sacrificing two rifles, they pounded at the bricks with the butts forcing the barrel ends in as pry bars. The bricks came away easily, laid up with poor mortar. When a small hole was opened and there was no response from the other side they continued until Chesty could wiggle through. He lit a match and found an empty room. At the other end was another bricked-up doorway. They cleared this and entered a storeroom, filled with rolls of wire and boxes of insulators. At the far side, Chesty could see light through the cracks in a double door. Holding his finger to his lips he motioned the two ahead. The doors, made from the scrap wood of discarded crates, sagged on hinges and Chesty could see what looked like a screen door hook between the gap. Backing off, he ran at this, and using his shoulder as a ram, smashed his way through. The flimsy doors came away too easily and he windmilled into the room fighting to keep his feet. At the same time the submachine gun went off, chewing an erratic pattern in the cement floor and throwing up chips and dust. Two startled soldiers standing at the trackside door turned and brought their rifles up, but at the angled shower of cement and spent slugs they backed outside.

Chesty got himself straightened out and tossed the machine gun back at the yardbird. "Hold that door!" And searching out the telegrapher, he found him and the station manager under a desk. "Welcome sir!" The manager said in fair English, "We are all one-hundred percent behind the U.S. Marines."

"You!" Chesty said to the telegrapher, "Get up! You're going to send for me." The man reluctantly squeezed out from under the desk and got behind the key. "Listen carefully," Chesty said in Spanish, "You send exactly what I tell you—I can read Morse like Marconi." The man nodded and Chesty began to compose.

\* \* \*

Anastasio Somoza Garcia had bought the small house in Managua when it became apparent that his climb to power must be through the Nicaraguan *Guardia Nacional*. The house, purchased in another name, was only walking distance from the main *guardia* headquarters and *Academia Militar* at *Campo de Marte*. It was a private place where *guardia* officers could unwind and discuss politics out of the earshot of their American advisers. Gradually it came to be a place where secret interrogation and "punishment" was handed out. It became the focal point of *guardia* personnel and political supporters who believed their future lay with Tacho Somoza.

The house was also used for personal entertaining and Tacho reserved a large bedroom suite on the top floor for himself. It was done in the new Hollywood Deco style he admired and featured an Atwater Kent radio that picked up the American station in Panama. While he waited for Karen to finish her bath, he tried to relax in a *moderne* chair of stainless-steel tubing that would not give an inch to his large frame. He looked at his watch. He had promised his wife, Salvadora, he would meet with relatives in the city and make sure they were safe and cared for.

Somoza's greatest piece of luck had been marrying a Debayle, one of Nicaragua's most aristocratic families. They had got him through some tough times including a charge of counterfeiting gold coins in 1921. He thanked his lucky stars for this sweet woman, the mother of his two fine sons.

The bathroom door opened and Karen came out, wearing a silk Japanese kimono he kept on hand. He was impressed. She was even more beautiful than he imagined. He met her with tears in his eyes. "What a vision—like a movie star." Bowing over her hand, he kissed it.

"Hardly," she said, "I will never be the same, it's not every day a hotel falls in on you and you're carried away by a brute—I suppose I should thank him."

"I'm deeply sorry you had to suffer such horrors. I will never forgive myself for the callous way you were treated. I thank God you're all right."

"No," Karen said, smiling and knowing exactly what was expected, "It is I who must thank you . . ."

In the kitchen below, the "surgeon," Pepe, sat at a white metal table eating Wheaties. It was his favorite food, brought in by the case as a gift to Tacho from the American minister. He ate with his right hand, dipping it into the bowl like a bird's beak, scooping up the Wheaties and bringing them slurping to his mouth poised in a kiss shape. He was alone in the small room. The cook had long since departed along with the servants. Of the *guardia*, only Poco Somoza had the duty and was asleep upstairs in an extra bedroom. The *cutache*, cleaned and honed, lay on a chopping block by the door.

There was a shadow against the doorway and Pepe looked up to see Pedrón bent in a half curl watching him. He had a bloody rag wrapped around the slice into his brain, tied off so that it covered his left eye. He was unable to talk and dragged his left leg, but as long as he kept an eye covered he could focus and maintain equilibrium. Pepe looked at him with flat uncomprehending stare, eye canted toward the ceiling, and went on eating. Pedrón, bracing his one useful arm, the right, against the wall stepped in the room in his painful curl and picked up the *cutache*, its honed blade catching the light. Pepe followed this, still scooping in the Wheaties with his right hand. When he dipped it back in the bowl it was struck off at the wrist in one rapid stroke.

He gave a little cry and jumped back, staring at his hand floating in the bowl, staining the Wheaties red. He was puzzled and confused, how would he eat without that hand? When he instinctively reached in to retrieve it with his left hand, Pedrón struck that off, too.

\* \* \*

Poco Somoza lay naked on the top of the sheets, hot and worried. He had a difficult time going to sleep, concerned over his future after the terrible gaffe with the Norwegian girl. He finally drifted off and was instantly aware of a curious cold stirring at his crotch. His eyes popped open and he saw at his bedside a monster out of his worst nightmare. A thing bent into a crescent curl like some primitive species of man or ape. One eye gleamed in the light from the window and there was the wet shine of teeth. It mumbled in gibberish and in the half light he did not recognize the twisted figure of Pedrón—could not have imagined him alive in any case. The ghastly apparition held a sword under Poco's balls, bouncing them gently on the tip of the bright blade. Poco could only stand this for a second and made a grab for his parts with both hands. Before he reached them they had been cleanly removed by a swift lateral swipe of the sword.

A long, terrible scream echoed through the house but occupied as he was, Tacho didn't hear it. He had the bed hopping, actually inching it across the tile floor as his big body pounded home. He was in Elysian fields riding the top of his own dream, this one a match for his size, returning his thrust with hers—moaning with what must be pure Nordic abandon. It had never been this good and he increased the rhythm, threatening the integrity of the welds on the tubular stainless-steel bed.

Pedrón roamed the house dragging his left leg, his right arm hanging useless. Although he could think rationally he couldn't translate it into words that made any sense. Never mind, his machete arm worked fine. Then on the top floor he heard the sounds of passion. Moving crablike down the hall he stopped in front of the closed door and listened—thinking he recognized the woman's moans. He reached for the doorknob.

The telegraph wires had been cut but Sandino reasoned their message got through. His men counterattacked the station house but three Marines held them off for ten minutes then retreated through the narrow doorways. They were sealed in now, but time had run out. Reinforcement would arrive in a matter of hours.

"We're going to attack one more time and kill them," Sandino said. The men were in the building across from the Marine position. Their *cotonas* were ragged and filthy from the boxcars and most were barefoot, shoes being the mark of an officer. Their only insignia consisted of the ubiquitous red and black ribbon of syndicalism drooping on a straw hat or tied around the neck.

"Are the bombs ready?"

Dynamite bombs were made of rough bags of wet rawhide sewn around sticks of dynamite, packed with stone and iron to act as shrapnel. When the rawhide dried, it hardened like iron and was fused, ready to throw. Sandino counted on these to blunt the defense.

"Now let's finish this!"

The men began to clang the flat of their machetes against the cement walls, shouting over and over, "This is for Marines!"

Across the street the rescue party could hear the machetes ringing. "I guess we know what that means," Chesty Puller said.

Magnusson got up and moved among the defenders. All were hunkered down behind fertilizer bags, ammunition at hand, guns sighted in on the doorway. "If they get through," Magnusson said, "use your bayonets."

The consul couldn't believe his ears, *My God, bayonets.* He watched, horrified, as next to him, General Butler fastened one on the pump shotgun. A military issue, it had a post on the end of the short barrel. "It never occurred to me," he said, "but using a bayonet means that a man trying to kill you will be less than two feet away."

"That's why it's called hand-to-hand combat, Dick." The general said cheerfully.

At that moment a dynamite bomb came through the loading dock doors and exploded, sending homemade shrapnel against the floor and ceiling. Behind its reverberation was a shouted battle cry, a trilled *zagareet* that chilled the blood, then the Sandinistas charged.

Bare feet flapping, elbows out, they came on firing Krags and Springfields; Thompson submachine guns, old revolvers, and new automatics—all wildly pumping bullets, propelled forward by the fierce force of male macho and the soldier's faith that death and wounding will happen to others.

# *THIRTEEN*

# Managua

**M**AJOR Ross E. Rowell was awakened about 3:30 in the morning. He kept his eyes shut as Corporal Pulaski tentatively shook him. "Major, this telegram just came from Captain Puller . . ."

"No it didn't," the Major said, refusing to open his eyes. He was dead tired; there had been round-the-clock work parties since the earthquake.

"Well sir, it's signed by him and it sure sounds like his style."

"I thought the lines were down."

"They are, this came in at Mateare—a kid rode his donkey over with it."

"What time was it sent?"

"Ah . . ." He looked at the battered piece of paper. "At nine o'clock last night."

"Oh my God," Rowell said wearily, swinging his legs off the bed. Corporal Pulaski noted he was still dressed in a uniform as wrinkled as balled-up tinfoil. "In that case he must be dead by now." He read the message while the corporal bent down with an oil lamp. "Get your people on the line and start pumping gas, Ski."

"You going up there *tonight?*" Rowell just looked at him and he straightened. "Yes sir." He went out and took the light with him.

The major cursed and found his flashlight. All the power had been off since the quake hit yesterday morning. Actually, they had been lucky, the flying field was outside of Managua and suffered little damage—some tiles slid off the roof and the water tank ruptured, but none of the aircraft or their ancillary buildings had been damaged. The field was headquarters for the Marine Observation Bomber Squadrons VO-1M and VO-4M with Major Rowell commanding. It occupied what was once an experimental farm built by the Department of Agriculture in 1913 in an effort to introduce new crops to the country. It had failed when they couldn't get Nicaraguans to eat potatoes. The tubers still came up wild in the grass field and landings were judged by how many potatoes were hit. The record was twelve.

The building that housed officers and men was a pleasant enough *finca*, or farm house, of an even earlier era, joined to the operations office by an arcade. Major Rowell went down this open passageway to sleeping quarters housing pilots and observers. Like himself, they had been working in the ruined city fighting fires and were exhausted. "Wakie! Wakie!" Rowell said, lighting a large oil lamp that hung from the ceiling. There were groans of disbelief.

"Come on!"

"Christ!"

"Puller's got himself pinned down outside of León by the Sandos."

"What? How in the hell could he do that tonight? Jesus!"

"He's going for another Navy Cross."

Second in command, Christian Schilt was up and buttoning his shirt. Schilt was the Marine pilot who had won the Medal of

Honor at Quilali flying out the wounded after a battle with nearly 400 Sandinistas in January of 1928. He made ten landings and takeoffs on Quilali's main street under fire, ferrying the wounded back to the hospital. As the corporal said, "He walked apart." Tall and good-looking, he affected a pencil-thin mustache and a deceptive languorous style. "Where exactly outside León— Mexico City?"

"*Fantasia*, Chris—right on the Contino line, you can't miss it."

"Wanna bet?" somebody said.

Schilt looked at his watch. "We're going at first light?"

"Now. As soon the aircraft are fueled and armed."

There were raised eyebrows. They never flew at night and rarely in bad weather. It wasn't for lack of skill or courage, rather, those depression times meant that losing a plane made it unlikely to get a replacement.

"The moon is full up and all you have to do is follow the rail line to the target and back." When no one commented he said, "Chesty sent this message at nine last night. What was left of one squad and others he doesn't identify were under attack by three Sando companies. Now you know *he's* going to survive no matter who else is killed—do you want to be here when he comes around asking where you were?"

Fifteen minutes later, pilots and observers were in the operations tugging on the rest of their gear, drinking coffee and listening to Major Rowell go over the attack plan on a map that had been cut out of the *National Geographic*. It had an overlay to tissue paper with soft pencil markings on it.

"Puller says they are the east building—here at the far end, three spaces down from the station master. Do not, repeat, do not attack the train parked between buildings—you will recognize it by a flatcar carrying two automobiles . . ."

"What kind of automobiles?"

Major Rowell made a face. "The kind with four wheels."

"Is this Company M?"

"If it is there's only one squad left—no, it seems to be a rescue party for the American consul's daughter."

"The redhead?"

"You would know that, I don't."

They went outside where the planes were revving up. There were four 02U-1 Vought Corsair biplanes with the vertical striped rudders that identified them as Marine aircraft. As predicted, the moon was bright, with only a slight drift of volcanic ash mixed in with smoke from the Managua fires to obscure it; visibility was up to a thousand feet.

The pilots and their observers climbed into cockpits and it was no longer possible to talk over the roar of the engine. Like everyone else, Rowell was listening to the radial engines, hearing every tick of wrist pin and push-rod roller. The engines peaked and they began to roll down the potato field. Fully gassed and carrying bombs the lift-off extended over newly opened earthquake fissures. Rowell watched until their silhouettes crossed the moon. Then he went back inside.

Angel Ortez moved along the boxcars limping slightly. Every few feet he would stop and bend down, cautiously looking under the running gear, but could not find Kate. Straightening, he sighted down the tracks, rails shining in the moonlight. Had she begun walking toward León? He didn't think so; the landscape here was flat, uncultivated fields with no cover and he was sure he could have seen her. She must be lying out there waiting for him to give up the search. He squatted down, leaning his back against one of the wheels where he had a view of the track. He would outwait her.

Twelve feet above him, Kate lay out on the top of the boxcar. She had read once that nobody ever looked up, and it was true. Angel Ortez had circled the cars a dozen times and never did look above him. Actually, she felt bad about shooting him in the foot. Unlike Pedrón, whom she shot with no regret, she did kind of like Angel's looks, couldn't believe he meant her real harm. He was certainly pretty but maybe a little dumb. *That's probably why he resented Wills so much,* she thought.

She heard the frantic sounds of guns between the dark buildings, the flash of muzzles then the muffled *whomp* and explosion and billows of smoke. Then she raised her head hearing a new sound—airplanes!

Smoke had filled the room and it was no longer possible to make out distinct figures in its swirl. Next to him, General Butler was firing the shotgun into the choking, nasty haze and the consul followed with his birdgun, pulling the trigger until he realized the weapon was empty. As he fumbled with the shells a figure appeared out of the smoke above him, face curiously opaque in the diffused light, teeth drawn back showing missing molars. The consul looked at him, suddenly surprised, saw him swing back a machete, and did nothing, frozen. Then lurching across him, the general thrust his shotgun in a rapid jab, bayoneting the man under the left armpit. The consul saw the blade go in up to the hilt in the matted, moist hair. Saw him stagger back, astounded at the offense, grab hold of the gun, jerking it out of General Butler's hands, then disappear in the smoke as though he never existed.

As quickly as it began, the firing dropped off. The smoke was sucked out of the open doors—wisps following the retreating attackers until finally the room cleared and they realized the charge had been broken. Bodies lay where they fell and the anguished groans of the wounded came up. The defenders looked at each other. *Was this it? Was the attack over?* Then a swooping roar bounced sound waves into the room, actually blowing the smoke back in with its displacement of air. Next the rattle of machine guns coming and going in *wah-wah* distortion. "What is that?" someone asked.

"Corsairs," Chesty answered. He'd heard them many times.

So had Sandino. They had attacked as early as 1927 at El Chipote, shooting anything that moved, including women and children. He himself had been wounded at El Sarguazca. He had made a bad mistake assuming the rescue party had wired Managua or León for reinforcements—but he had never known the planes to fly at night. They had caught his men out in the open and slaughtered them.

Schilt had led the first strafing run, threading through the eye of the needle at rooftop level, careful to avoid hitting the train carrying the two cars. They came in low, catching the bastards out, nailing them between the building walls, one bullet doing the work of many as it zinged back and forth.

The pilots were merciless when it came to Sandino. In the beginning they had been careful about not hitting civilian houses or, God forbid, a noncombatant. But in October of 1927 one of their planes had been shot down on the Zapotillo ridge and the pilot and observer captured. Both had been hanged straight away, then mutilated by Sandino's men. Later a photograph of the pilot, Lieutenant Earl A. Thomas—neck stretched out, hanging from a tree, was published in Mexican and Honduran papers. After that there were no holds barred.

Schilt flew up the slot and banked over the enemy train stalled at the end of *La Fantasia*. Climbing, he would get altitude and begin this bombing run hitting the boxcars broadside. In the rear cockpit, the observer leaned over as they crossed the top of the cars and clearly saw a figure lying on the middle car. "You poor bastard," he said.

Kate watched fascinated as the first plane flew straight up the track between the buildings. Then a flashing, like sparklers, and in the next split second the sound of machine guns. It was on a line with her, propeller whirling and at the last minute the firing stopped and it zoomed up and over the top of the boxcar. As it did she twisted her neck and saw a figure lean out over the backseat and look down at her. On the plane's bottom wing were two star-in-the-circle insignia and big lettering: U.S. MARINES. She jumped up waving frantically. *"Hey! I'm here! It's me!"*

When Schilt reached two thousand feet he leveled off and

prepared for the dive. The others would continue their attack with the fragmentation bombs while he dropped the fifty-pounders. He half-rolled into a seventy-five-degree angle and began his near vertical plunge. To hit the target squarely the plane had to move straight down, without skidding to one side or the other. This took concentration and nerve—it was a hairy business to drop two thousand feet, then pull up within three hundred feet from the ground. Dive bombing had been invented in Nicaragua by Marine pilots and they had become very good at it. Face to the windscreen, eye to the sight, he saw a tiny figure on top the center car and aimed for it.

Angel Ortez grabbed Kate from behind. She stood, neck angled back looking up at the diving plane. "You fool! That plane is going to blow us up! Come on!"

She tried to squirm away, fighting him off. "No! They've come to rescue me! You better get out of here! Let go!" She swung on him but he neatly blocked it. Catching hold of her arm above the elbow, he dipped down and hoisted her over his back as she kicked and pounded with her fists. Fighting to maintain his balance on top of the car, his toe killing him, he managed to reach the ladder and half fall down the side. At the bottom he set her down and she still fought him. "Let go or I'll . . ." But she had lost the little automatic in the struggle.

"Listen!" he shouted. *"Listen!"*

And she heard it, the scream of an engine full out, the eerie awful whistle of a dive bomber at the second before bombs release. The rush of manmade wind preceding death by explosive. They began to run toward a pile of cast concrete columns left out in the field next to the track but they were a good fifty feet away.

The bomb exploded in a muffled *whomp* of a sound, hitting the cars midcenter and lifting them in a splintery crash of wood and metal, tearing the wheels off one and sending them soaring. The ground shook with the reverberations of the explosion and the smoke as dust from the disintegrating boxcars plumed out, obscuring the runners.

When the train went up, Sandino passed orders for the men to break into small groups and make for the mountains. The foothills of the *Cordillera de Los Marrabillos* began here and several days hard marching (or climbing) would put them in the department of Jinotega where they would regroup for the final leg to Nueva Segovia. The trick was to get across this open area and escape the airplanes. They could not now afford to wait it out in the protection of *Fantasia.* Reinforcements would arrive momentarily—it was time to cut and run.

Sandino stood with Wills in the doorway of the station master's house. The dozen men who would accompany him back to El Chipote were dashing out, one by one, running the gauntlet of strafing planes to the cover of rocks and trees several hundred yards away. When the last had gone, Sandino said, "You didn't see Angel again?"

"No."

He looked toward the train, boxcars burning fiercely, the outline of the old engine with its antique funnel was lit by the flames. "I can't believe he was killed. He is much too lucky for that. No doubt he'll be waiting at El Sause for the final climb to El Chipote."

"And the girl?"

Sandino shrugged his shoulders. "That's over. I hope she survived, but she'll be no use to us now—I suppose it was a lost cause with her from the beginning—she was too much . . ."

"American?"

He smiled, "*Norte* American. I admired her bravery and the truth is I admire many *Norte* Americans but like none of them."

"Present company excepted I hope."

"You're not an American, Carlton—you're an internation-alist—a man with feet in many camps. But we have been *campañeros* and I like your bad jokes."

Wills looked at him closely, seeing in those flat Indian eyes nothing that suggested parting but knew that's what it was to be. "*Adios?*"

"It's time for me to go back to the mountains and wait. I see now that it is not a raid on the capital or taking the consul's daughter that will end intervention—no, it's *time*—it's on your side. I've fought them for seven years and can go on another seven—can they?"

"And that's what you want me to tell them?"

"Tell them what you wish, but spell my name right."

They laughed and came together for a last *abrazo*—an awkward embrace of two singular personalities: one a Catholic, Mason, and mystic, the other forswearing all but *I AM* without invoking luck, God, or even fate. The provincial and the worldly merged, both brave with a sense that only they had the answers.

Then Sandino was out the door dodging across the open field. Wills last caught sight of him by the flash of an exploding bomb. Apt, he thought, the small figure lit against the long shadows of the mountain.

Kate Kelly and Angel Ortez lay tumbled together behind the pile of cement columns. Deafened by the exploding bomb, she had no recollection of the split second before the blast. Her legs and back burned with the prickling sensation of sunburn, her clothes had been blown into tatters, and the very air seemed compressed, pressing down at each new explosion.

Under her, Angel lay perfectly still, head against the side of the concrete column and she desperately hoped he wasn't dead. Twisting, she could see flames as the boxcars burned, feel the heat waves they generated; the engine glowed cherry red behind a leaping curtain of fire. Beyond, in the field the planes continued to dive, the bright flash of bombs exploding silently. It was a curious sensation—like watching a silent movie. At intervals between attacks, figures darted out running toward the distant tree line. Were they Sandinistas? Marines? She was confused and disoriented.

Near dawn the planes went away and she was startled by the distant, unmistakable moan of a train whistle. Her hearing had returned. She pushed up and looked down the tracks to the dark enclosure of *La Fantasia*. It was particularly eerie in the early light and absolutely still. Was everybody gone? Dead?

There was a stirring from Angel and he rolled over clutching his head. Blood had coagulated on his forehead where it had slammed against the concrete column, matting his hair down. Working his jaw to get his ears to pop, he saw Kate and smiled, his voice hoarse. "You're still alive, redhead?"

"I think so—what about your head—are you all right?"

"They say if you can find your head with your hand, it means it's not missing and you're all right. Besides, it made me forget my foot."

She blushed. "I'm sorry . . . I . . ."

"Never mind." There was another distant moan of train whistle, and she helped him get to his feet, both of them unsteady. "Thank you," he said, gently disengaging her hand. "Time to go."

Kate followed him across the field. Smoke drifted with them from the train fire and the unpleasant smell of explosives—cordite—came up. As they went past the gouged bomb craters there were bodies twisted and blown into the arrested position of sudden death. He paused to lift a rifle and bandolier of bullets from a boy who looked as though he were sleeping. "Juan Sacata," he said aloud. Reaching the tree line they could hear the hiss of the train slowing for *La Fantasia*. In the other direction a cloud of dust was visible up the tracks. "The *guardia* from León. We got away just in time."

Kate couldn't help wondering from whom?

The *guardia* company from *Fortin de Acosaco* marched in at nearly the same time as the train from Managua. The train had brought a squad of Marines, a hospital car and a major from General Logan Feland's brigade headquarters. While Puller and

Magnusson helped load the wounded they talked. The major was from the intelligence branch and felt like a lawyer at a funeral.

"Gentlemen, this is not going down well. Your timing is rotten. Five men have been killed and six so grieviously wounded that some are not expected to live. This at a time when the folks at home have been told the fighting was winding down, that Marine hides were not going to be exposed to bandit bullets."

"It was a well-laid ambush, sir—I walked into it." Puller had one end of a stretcher, Magnusson the other.

"We all did," Magnusson said, "None of us expected Sandino to attack so close to León." He saw that the man on the stretcher was the fat Marine with the QM rating. He was bled nearly white.

"You're sure it was Sandino?"

"Oh yes, sir. The station people actually spoke to him," Puller said. "And I'll tell you those Corsairs did a real job on his bunch."

"That is the only plus in this dismal business." They could all see the headlines. The battle would be touted as a routing of Sandino by Marine aviators who ". . . drove the bandit rats back in their holes . . ." The dead would be extolled as men who had volunteered to join the rescue party in search of the American consul's little daughter.

"What happened to Miss Kelly?" the major asked in a hushed voice. The consul could be seen poking through the still warm embers of the bombed train.

"We're not sure," Puller said, hurrying on, "her body hasn't been found and there's a good chance they took her with them."

"Then you intend continuing this rescue party?"

"Oh yes sir! Sandino is sure to head for the department of Jinotega. We're unloading the cars now to go after him. If we can beat him to El Sause and hook up with Company M, we can cut him off and give him the chop before he reaches El Chitone."

"You people are attached to the *guardia* and are General Matthew's problem—however, no regular Marine personnel—

those who can still walk that is—will be permitted to continue."
He looked at Magnusson. "What is your status, Lieutenant?"

Magnusson handed over a battered envelope. "I am under
oral orders from Colonel Wise. These are covering orders
authorizing my movements from three eight thirty-one to four
eight thirty-one."

*Authorizing assassination*, the major thought, but he said,
"Yes . . . yes," shaking his head. This was not the way it was
done. "All right I will report back to General Feland and you will
no doubt hear from our office." He looked toward the consul.
"Mr. Kelly will have to sort out his position with the State
Department on his own."

"What about General Butler?" Puller said, jerking his
thumb to indicate him, standing by the train talking to a Navy
Corpsman two cars down.

"General Butler is here as an unofficial guest of the State
Department. He has no assignment from the Marine Corps."

"Does that mean he's not in command of the rescue party?"
Puller asked.

The major looked at him as though he were simple. "Do
you want to tell him that?"

The general helped load the music boy aboard the train. He
had been unconscious for what—eight hours? His face drained
and ash gray, the black curls emphasized a waxed image. "What
are his chances?" He asked the corpsman, a navy petty officer
assigned to the Marine Corps.

"Not good sir. I doubt if he will make the trip back. Look at
his color. He hasn't any blood left."

"I did my best to tie it off, but most of the right knee is
gone."

"Looks like a 4-0 job. Don't blame yourself, sir, chances of
recovery from that kind of gun shot wound are not good in this
country—he's already septic." He had a pencil poised over a
clipboard. "Can you give me his name? He's not wearing tags."

The general opened his mouth, then shut it. Finally he had

to admit, "I don't know his name. We all called him Music. As I remember he was ships company on the *Cleveland*."

"That's good enough. They will know him." And he swung on board the train. "Thank you for your help, sir, good luck with the hunt." He dismissed this antique general who didn't know his own runner's name.

The train immediately began to back up in a hiss of steam; drivers skidding, reversing; locking up, then steady revolutions as they cleared the ominous buildings of *Fantasia*. The engine pulled one Pullman car with the wounded bound for the hospital in Managua. It was a bad time to be wounded. The hospital there was wall to wall with earthquake victims, the death rate, awesome due to lack of medical personnel and supplies. León was only a few miles away but blocked by the bombed train. They wouldn't clear it for three days.

Terribly shaken, General Butler stood and watched until the train disappeared. He had grown genuinely fond of the music boy and it shocked him to discover he hadn't even known his name. After the calamity of the past days climaxed by the violence of the battle, this lack of concern on his part, to not have *asked* his name—affected him the most. It was so—*pitiful*. Tears began to stream down his face.


"Who in the hell is that?" Chesty said.

Magnusson looked over his shoulder and saw a tall, thin man walking up the tracks toward them. He carried a fat suitcase and a little portable typewriter. His pongee suit was a mess, bloody and torn, looking like something a tramp would eschew. But Magnusson recognized the way he carried himself; head up, pince-nez glasses on the beak of an arrogant nose.

"Carlton Wills."

"Who?"

Reaching the officers, he took a handsome leather passport case from the bag. "May I ask who is in charge here?"

"I am at the moment," the major said, "And who might you be, sir?"

"Carlton Wills." He handed over the case. "You will find my accreditation from the newspaper guild, passport, and an introduction from Senator Burton K. Wheeler."

"Ah . . ." the major said, examining the papers, "the correspondent from *The Nation*."

"I know who this scissor-bill is!" Puller said, letting his breath out in an explosion of air. "He's the one who printed all those stories about Marines lopping off gook heads!"

Wills looked at him coolly. "As I remember there was a photograph of one of your officers holding a severed head. I certainly didn't take it."

"That's was somebody else's head! If you're so hot to write up atrocities, why is it we don't hear about the Sandos? Chopping up people and hanging pilots!"

The major handed the papers back. "Mr. Wills, you can hardly expect sympathy here among men you've maligned."

"Now wait a minute!"

"No, you listen to me sir, these men are soldiers sent by their country to do as they are told. To die for that privilege if necessary—and many have. If you disagree with that then take it up with those who sent them." There was a pause. "I suggest you clear the area and do not, repeat do not, avail yourself of government transportation." And turning his back on Wills he walked away, accompanied by Puller.

There was an uneasy silence and finally Wills said, "You're . . . ?"

"Magnusson."

His eyes widened slightly. "Yes, of course, Miss Kelly talked of you."

"Where is she?"

"When I saw her last—she was by that train." He turned and pointed. "I don't know about now."

"You didn't look out for her?"

"Believe me, she could look out for herself."

"Maybe you better tell her father that. He's the one searching for her body."

"Yes . . ." Wills met his eyes, ". . . you're right." And he walked toward the consul. Magnusson watched him go, spitting audibly.

Richard Kelly turned at his approach, startled by his sudden appearance, then recognizing him. "I know you . . . !"

"Carlton Wills, Mr. Kelly."

"But how . . ."

"I stayed behind when Sandino pulled out . . ."

"My daughter!"

"I don't know what happened to her sir—my guess is she was taken away by the Sandinistas."

The consul followed his gaze toward the mountains, his shoulders slumping, rubbing his forehead with his bandaged hand. "Then she's gone again . . . they've taken her . . ." He turned back to Wills. "They didn't hurt her . . . abuse her?"

"She was well—thin but healthy I believe. Certainly her spirits never flagged, quite the contrary, she was very, ah . . . aggressive."

"Why would he do that? Why would that man take a young girl and risk her life in all this . . ." waving his hand to include the battle scene.

"It was Sandino's idea that he show her his side of the struggle . . . he intended no ransom . . . just, well, education."

"*Education?*" the consul said incredulously.

"He wanted to convert her to his cause, but it was impossible—she was difficult from the beginning—insulted him."

"I'm glad to hear that—I'm proud of her."

"I did my best to mediate between them, but you must understand my position was that of an observer—a neutral. I'm terribly sorry . . . I know you think that because I'm an American I could have . . ."

"You're not an American," the consul said softly.

Wills looked up quickly, then turned. "Excuse me." Walking away he was surprised at the level of hurt he felt. He had explained it badly. There was no reason to justify his actions to anyone—but as he thought this, he knew it was wrong. It was the second time today someone had said he wasn't an American. First Sandino, now the consul. He *was* an American. In going against public opinion to restate the ideas of freedom he had risked his career and his life. Intervention in the name of greed was not what the Constitution was about. But in defining it from the left he was now identified with the current enemy—what he said or wrote was immediately suspect.

He had lost objectivity. What was the good of being read by only the people who believed you in the first place? He had been polarized, made ineffective by his own propagandizing. He believed he was being fair and telling the truth—but whose truth? He knew very surely that he had to change this if he was going to be believed about what was happening in Nicaragua.

But how?

# FOURTEEN

# El Sause

ALL that day they climbed into the mountains. Up through valleys that were humid and fecund, sheltered from the sun by a canopy of dense leaves. Insects were ferocious and progress wet and difficult. Finally at several hundred feet above sea level signs of cultivation began and they caught glimpses of coffee plantations and buildings. Angel made a wide swing around these, traveling parallel to the trails and moving quietly. Once she heard voices and a woman's laugh but they kept going, climbing and gradually the stands of trees outdistanced habitation and it actually got a bit cooler. By late afternoon when she was ready to drop they stopped.

There was water, a stream running in rivulets over mossy rocks and forming a shallow pool before it continued. Bugs skittered on its surface and it smelled of ripe vegetation. He skimmed the top with his hand and they drank. Then soaking the blood off his head and untangling his hair, he fell back next to her exhausted.

They were quiet a long time, then she asked, "Where are we going?"

"El Chipote."

"Is that where you're from?"

"Oh no," he said, smiling. "It's the roost of Indians, bandits, smugglers—and of course Sandinistas—people who have little respect for boundaries or laws. To the North is Honduras and on the other side, the Coco River. Up there they have had their fill of persecution by both Hondurans and Nicaraguans. They love Sandino for saying 'No more!'"

"You don't look like one of them."

"Who?"

"One of Sandino's kind."

"*Kind*? Well, I'm not an Indian or part of one if that's what you mean. My family likes to think they can trace their line back to Aryan establishment in Spain by Teutonic barbarians in the fifth century—Ortez y Guillew."

"Is that true?"

"Of course not. But it's a way to explain the blond hair. They will tell you they were here in the fourteenth century with old de Cordoba to settle León. No doubt what happened was, they immediately began to fight among themselves and stalked off to establish Granada so they would have somebody nearby to hate. My family are good haters."

"But if they're, you know, Spaniards and all—what do they think of somebody like Sandino?"

"They hate Sandino, but then they don't like anybody who isn't related. In our family it's not important who you fight or what for—just as long as you do. They are holdovers from the old way; Spanish settlers who were corrupt, indolent, and believed everyone else culturally inferior."

"And Sandino is going to change that?"

"Perhaps. He is a man who comes along only once a century. The Indians and mestizos believe in him utterly. So do I. It is a rare thing in this country to find a man who wants nothing for himself but the welfare of his people. We serve him with unquestioned obedience."

"I can't believe that shrimp is a great man."

He looked at her. "Does a man's size count for brains or bravery? Is a fox less brave than an elephant?"

"Is it brave to kidnap girls?"

He laughed. "If I had seen you first I would have kidnapped you myself."

She blushed and stammered, "You know what I mean. I . . ." But it was hard to stay mad at someone who looked at you with goo-goo eyes.

He laid a hand on her arm. "Of course I do. It is a misfortune of war. Believe me I won't let any harm come to you. Make a wish, redhead, and I will fulfill it."

"You know what I'd like?"

"Anything." His voice was soft.

"Something to eat."

It was one thing he couldn't conjure up.

The Packard was unloaded from the flatcar, looking, Chesty Puller said, "Like two tons of swiss cheese." It had sustained dozens more bullet holes, ventilating the sides and ripping up tufts in the leather upholstry. "I'll tell you," Puller went on, examining the holes, "if a fella was musical he could play a tune blowing on these like a piccolo."

"It runs anyway," Magnusson said. It had kicked over on the first crank which was more than could be said for the Buick. Leaking oil under the pan told the story there—the block had been cracked. "Let me ask you something, Chesty—what good is a car going to be anyway? As I understand it there's no road up to El Sause."

"Yeah, but there's a new railroad line, Mag. It goes all the way—narrow gauge—you can ride the ties like it was the Lincoln Highway."

"What about trains?"

"No sweat—unless of course you should happen to meet one coming across that long trestle over the Estero Real."

"That's reassuring."

General Butler appeared, wearing a new shirt supplied by the *guardia* reinforcements. He had salvaged his cutout, tin-can stars and fixed them to the collar. He took the salute from the two officers. "Ready to get under way?"

"You're going with us, sir?" Puller said, eyes big as if surprised.

"Of course I am—I put together this rescue party and I intend seeing it through until the young lady is recovered."

"Oh well, sir—it's just that where we're going is the high country—all uphill. Four or five thousand feet until your breath comes short and your heart pounds like a bass drum—it can konk out up there—that's true."

The general cut him off. "Have you got a heart problem, Lewis?"

"Why no sir, not me but . . ."

"Well neither do I. I appreciate your concern, but keep it to yourself. If the time comes on any march where I can't leave the men behind I will turn in my cordovan puttees." This was a strike at Puller's *guardia* outfit. "Now, let's shove off. Where's the consul?"

"Just coming back from sickbay, sir."

Richard Kelly could be seen walking up the tracks from where the train puffed away carrying the wounded back to Managua. He wore a fresh bandage on his left hand tied in a sling around his neck. With his black beard, straw hat, and ragged clothes the general was reminded of Civil War veterans he'd seen as a young man, stooped and weary from one too many battles. When he reached them, the general said cheerfully, "You're looking fit, Dick—how's the hand?"

"Oh, fine . . ." he replied, looking up from other thoughts. He sat down on the running board of the car, holding his hand out awkwardly.

"Well now I'm sure it is but I don't think you'll want to drive, do you?"

"I'll drive sir," Puller said, "I know the way."

The general looked at him still smiling. "Now there's the kind of soldier I like—a man who's ready to do anything in a minute. I'll bet you can cook too, is that right? I'd like to put in my order right now for corn pone at evening mess." Chuckling pleasantly to dispel any notion this might be a slur on Puller's Southern background.

"You get the corn and I'll pone it, sir." Puller smiled back with equal insincerity.

"Here comes Wills," Magnusson said.

"*What?*" Chesty spun around, "By God he's got the nerve of a carpet salesman!"

The general examined him. "So that's Wills? Yes—I believe I ran across him at a rally in New York for the relief of Sandinistas."

"Yeah? And you know who they relieved themselves on."

Wills stopped squarely in front of the group and set down his heavy bag and the portable typewriter. "Captain Puller, I wonder if I might have a word with you?"

"No."

This took him back despite his cool demeanor. "Well then . . . who?"

The general thought he resembled a bird of prey. The beak; eyes bright with intelligence. Caught in a circle of hostility, he showed no apprehension. The general liked that. "May I serve you sir?"

Wills turned. "Smedley Butler?"

"General Smedley Butler," he said, smiling.

"Well, *general*, to put it short—"

"That would be a departure in a writer."

"Perhaps—but I would like to travel with you as a correspondent . . ."

"What!" Puller said, dumbfounded, "*What?*"

Wills turned back to him. "Captain Puller, you accused me of not giving fair representation to the Marine Corps—of maligning you . . ."

Chesty began choking, "I'll . . . damned . . . if I . . ." But he couldn't get his breath and Magnusson pounded him on the back.

"I report what I see—if you people think me unfair then take me along on this patrol—let me see for myself your side of the events."

"The Marine Corps does not take writers on combat patrols in Nicaragua Mr. Wills," the general said, remembering that when a representative of Cecil B. De Mille's office called asking to shoot footage of "Marines in Jungleland" flares went up at Eighth-and-Eye.

"Then how does the American reader know what is really happening? Is it any more unfair for you to disseminate information than it is for me to report on Sandino?"

"You've got a point sir, but that is official policy."

"Really? Is this 'rescue party' official? Do Marines now go into battle in a Packard?"

"Marines will go into battle in whatever will carry them," the general said, "Is it less patriotic to die in a Packard rather than a Ford?" He smiled.

Wills had to smile back at this piece of capitalist logic. "No I suppose not. D. H. Lawrence certainly went to war in a Rolls."

"Why not let him go sir?" Magnusson said, leaning against the car, arms folded. They all looked at him.

"Yes," the consul said bitterly from where he sat on the running board. "Let him write the end to the story."

"Assuming he's still alive," Chesty said recovering and warming to the idea.

Remnants of Sandino's three companies were spread out in small groups heading for El Sause. Sandino himself had moved all day with a dozen men including an old comrade from Ocotal days, Carlos Salgado, who Carlton Wills had said looked exactly like the Indian head on the American five-cent piece. Since then his nickname had been "Cinco." An experienced guerrilla, he was familiar with the area and suggested they cross the railway trestle over the Estero Real "It will save hours of climbing, *jefe*— down into the gorge, then crossing the river and back up."

"I agree." Sandino was anxious to make El Sause by tomorrow where they could rest and find boats for the ride upriver to Nueva Segovia and finally El Chipote.

The trestle was nearly a thousand feet, a delicate span of bolted angle-iron thrown across a deep gorge by American know-how for the Pacific Railway. It held a narrow one-way track and it was an awesome experience to walk—a good two hundred feet above rocks and river below. Although Sandino and his companions certainly accepted danger as part of their lot, they proceeded gingerly across it in single file, seeing the flash of the river far below between the ties at their feet. Wind tugged at their uniforms and they were eye to eye with soaring birds.

When they were more than halfway across and committed, Sandino stopped, backing them up. "What is that sound?"

They froze listening and heard the distinct sound of a motor; could actually feel a slight vibration from it on the track. "Is that a train?" one of the men said, anxious to be told it was not.

"No," Cinco answered, "Trains only run three days a week, then early in the morning. Not today."

"Well, it's something," Sandino said, "and it's getting louder, it must be close behind us—around that bend in the mountain."

"It sounds like an automobile," Cinco said.

"Is that possible?" another asked.

"Oh yes," Sandino answered.

Carlton Wills and General Butler were discussing education. Wills was astounded to find the general had attended no college, naval or war. He had not really graduated from high school.

"I'm probably the only general in the United States without a degree of any sort." He sounded proud of it. "When the *Maine* blew up in Havana Harbor in February of ninety-eight I was just sixteen and joined. Congress had increased the Marine Corps by twenty-four second lieutenants and two thousand men for the period of the war and I got one of the lieutenant's commissions."

No doubt with the help of his father, Wills thought, but he said, "Then you've been involved with Latin American policy from the beginning."

"I've also served in the Philippines and China . . ."

"Well then you know that in China, Chiang Kai-shek's revolutionary army has a unit named after Sandino."

"The Chinese have odd taste—they also eat fish lips."

It was necessary to speak loudly because of noise coming up from the tires hitting the ties. They had left *La Fantasia* early that same morning, taking only enough gear for the fifty-mile trip to El Sause. The Packard pulled out around the wreckage of the rebel train and followed the dirt road to León where they hooked up with the rail extension to the northeast. Puller had been right about riding the rails, Packard wheels fit nicely around the narrow gauge tracks, running along on the ties. But it was rough on the tires and they had already blown in two. Fortunately the Buick tires were nearly the same size and strapped to the back mount.

By late afternoon they approached the halfway mark to El Sause; the trestle over the Estero Real. Puller was driving with Magnusson next to him. The general sat in the back with the consul on one side, Wills on the other. As they bumped along feeling every hump of tie, climbing up valleys between mountains, Wills continued the interview. He found General Butler an outspoken subject.

"Wills, do you think you and your Bolshevik friends are the only ones who believe it wrong for the State Department to use

Marines as personal troops? Many of us in the Corps do so also. I made a speech in Pittsburgh last year where I said our government had used strong-arm methods to elect the president of Nicaragua when I was down here the last time in 1912. Well, the secretary of the navy, Charles Francis Adams, sent for me and I stood on his grand carpet while he sat at a desk big enough to house a depression family and chewed me out—saying he was acting at the direct order of our president, Herbert Hoover."

"Is that right."

"Oh yes. At the time I was senior ranking officer in the Marine Corps—a major general and next in line for commandant. When it came time to appoint this premier job, they reached halfway down the list and picked Benny Fuller—a brigadier general! So don't tell me about the penalties of speaking up! But also understand that I am a soldier and go where I'm pointed. I will defend U.S. citizens anywhere on earth and I will chase a man who would kidnap a little girl to his grave."

Wills turned to the consul. "It must give you confidence, Mr. Kelly, to have a major general commanding a three-man rescue party."

The consul looked at him, seeing the half smile. "It will only take one of us to kill Sandino."

"Bridge coming up," Puller said, slowing. A gorge dropped off in a steep tangle of green to a river that took on the perspective of a miniature railway model.

"Are we going across that?" Wills said, diverted from the interview by his morbid fear of height.

"Oh yes, sir. And I'll tell you it's one hellofa view. It must be four hundred feet straight down to those rocks." Seeing Wills's face, Puller began exaggerating. "Makes you wonder how that little spidery bridge can hold you up."

Looking straight down the tracks, Magnusson saw that they were clear—but were they? It would certainly be the right place to lay charges. He said so.

"They're not going to blow this bridge," Puller reassured

him, "All the good things in life come over this line for the interior; booze, cards, newspapers, and genuine U.S. ladies' brassieres. Now you'd think in this hot country women would go around, freed up, so to speak. No way. Every girl child from the time she sprouts nubs is strapped in a harness. You've never seen such gearing up—outfits that look like ammo slings—criss-crossed with stitching and straps that might hoist a mule—"

"That's really interesting, Lewis," the general said, "but what about the bridge? Is it advisable for Magnusson to climb down and see if its wired?"

"Forget it sir, if Sandino blew this bridge the locals would lynch him tomorrow and our troubles would be over." Putting the car in low gear he edged out on the trestle, the initial push from land to midair was like the launching of an aircraft. The view was spectacular. The big car filled the track and looking over the side gave the impression of traveling on thin air. As they continued there was the feeling of give as the trestle sprung beneath them.

"It's moving . . ." Wills said in a strangled voice, lips and eyes compressed.

"Yeah, that's right. Listen, come across it on the train and you think your galloping. Those engineers who built it must have done a couple of wrong slides on the slide rule."

"*Stop!*" Magnusson shouted.

"What?" But Chesty put the brakes on very gently and they came to a shuddering stop, engine idling roughly, Motor-Meter climbing.

"Something wrong, Lieutenant?" the general asked, twisting his head and looking down the track. The consul unlimbered his double-barreled shotgun, wondering if Magnusson had spotted a sizzling fuse, and what in the world they would do if he had.

Magnusson took his rifle and climbing over the front seat, stepped between the general and Wills. "There's somebody hanging on under us," he said quietly. Bracing his hand on the spare tires and jumping down to the track, he went quickly along looking down through the openings between the ties. At movement, he shouted in Spanish, *"Su nombres!"*

His answer was a shot that zinged up through the wooden ties and sheared off a creosoted splinter, flattening itself on the rail with a ringing sound not unlike a dinner bell. He fired back at a flash of dirty white cotton and leather gun belt.

In the Packard, Chesty stepped over the front seat carrying the submachine gun, and put his foot squarely on Wills's notebook. "Excuse me sir."

The general passed him climbing the other way. "I'll stand by to drive if necessary."

"Aye aye!" Puller said, out of the car and running up the track. Kneeling down next to Magnusson, he shoved the barrel of the Thompson between the ties and began firing at a blur of movement. There was a terrific racket as the bullets clanged off the bridge.

Magnusson held his hand up and the firing stopped. "You know," he said looking down, "I wonder what we're doing to the bridge?"

Puller drew back. "You don't think we could hurt it, do you?"

"It might be the kind of thing where if you hit it just right it would go down—like a kick behind the knees."

Chesty peered between the ties. There had been no return fire and from his narrow angle of vision he saw no one. "We can't hit a damn thing from here anyway—they're climbing down out of our line of sight—we might as well break off."

They got back in the car and Puller changed places with the general. He put it in gear and drove off the trestle. On the other side they jumped out and ran back to the drop-off, looking down at the panorama of river cutting a meandering path through dense green jungle. No one was visible.

"They've skinned out," Chesty said. "My guess is that bunch was on the point—out front. It's twenty, twenty-five miles to El Sause. We're going to beat them there in plenty of time."

"Company M will meet us?" the general asked, joining them with the consul.

"Oh yes sir. I wired Billy Lee from León like I said. They check the key at Jinotega twice a day when we're laid up from patrol. He'll be at El Sause with two squads."

"Are you talking about Lieutenant *William* A. Lee?" Wills said, recovered from his acrophobia but standing well back from the edge of the gorge. Chesty knew why he was asking. Lee, his second in command and acting company commander while he was away, was the focus of more atrocity stories that any other American officer in Nicaragua.

"That's right," he answered.

Angel Ortez heard the distant sound of gunfire and stopped, listening. When the rattle of an automatic weapon cut in he guessed others must be running into *guardia* patrols from Jinotega. He had avoided the rail line and stayed on a straight-ahead compass course that was direct but grueling—totally out of the way of house and village—or the chance of finding food. He had promised the redhead a meal ahead but in the meantime they had to button their shirts to their backbones as the poor did.

They were nearly halfway to El Sause and he had to admire her stamina. She'd stayed up with him all day, stopping only when he did. They were resting now, and as he watched her, back against a tree, eyes shut, he found it hard to believe she was as young as they said. She had a woman's body, and in the torn clothes he was very aware of skin—actually seeing the dot of a nipple once—and he was sure, a glimpse of red hair down there. *Whoee!* He sucked his teeth. Maybe this was not the time to think about such things but he couldn't help it, she gave him iron in his pants.

He shook her gently, "Come on redhead, time to go—we're almost there."

She tried to get up but sagged in slow motion. He reached out to help her but she brushed off his hand. "Leggo, I just slipped."

Kate was utterly exhausted but would not admit it. She guessed she had lost at least another ten pounds and wondered if there would be anything left of her when this was over—maybe a grease spot like Little Black Sambo. *Over?* She had reached a point where she didn't believe it would ever be over. Those Marine planes back at the train had tried to *kill* her. So much for being rescued. She went with Angel willingly because she trusted him to take her to safety. She had absolutely no idea where she was and followed blindly.

"It's all right," he was saying, "let's rest a bit more—I'm tired too. Here, lean against me . . ." And she did. He stroked her tangled hair. "What a color, I've never seen anything like it. You know if we had little babies I'll bet they would all be redheads. Can you imagine a house full of them running around like . . . *picamaderos*—what is that in English?"

"Woodpeckers."

"Yes! Woodpeckers! A whole houseful of redheaded baby woodpeckers!"

She almost laughed, then minutes later, fell into an uneasy sleep.

It was nearly dusk when they finally sighted the house—a log cabin built in the universal way of knotched logs and chinking. Windows were small, almost gun ports and the door sturdy, studded with bosses. It sat in a clearing surrounded by pine and could have been straight out of the Canadian woods. The most arresting thing about it was a huge Union Jack tied on the roof. Angel left Kate in the brush and walked into the clearing where he still might have a chance to dash back. There was always the possibility the wrong people were about. Although he held the rifle barrel down, it was cocked and his finger was on the trigger. He called out, *"Jorge! Jorge Williams!"*

There was a long pause and the door opened cautiously. "Who's that?"

*"Guero!"*

"General Ferrara?" This was a nom de guerre Ortez had used in the Matagalpa region.

"That right, what's happened to your hospitality?"

George Williams opened the door and hustled out. He was a big man, fat, with a balding head balanced by a beard. British, he had been the manager of the San Albino gold mine. This was the very same mine Sandino had worked at as assistant paymaster in 1926 before beginning his career as a revolutionary. Williams was married to an Indian woman and known to be sympathetic to the Sandinista movement despite the looting of the mine—Sandino had occupied it in 1927 and actually had extracted ore and minted gold coins. George Williams had stayed during this dangerous time and won the respect of the rebels. He was allowed to live among them, and displayed the Union Jack on the roof, hopefully, to discourage Marine aircraft.

"Angel!"

"Jorge!"

They met in a noisy *abrazo* and Jorge held him out at arm's length. "Good God boy! What's happened? You look like the bloody dogs have been at you!"

"What? Me? No this is the way they dress in Managua now that Sandino has passed through."

"You've been in the capital?"

"They called it an earthquake but actually it was Sandinistas kicking Moncada's ass."

Jorge gestured toward the house. "Come on in! Tell me about it!"

"First I want you to meet my traveling companion—wait here."

A minute later he returned with Kate. Jorge was horrified. The appearance of a white, redheaded girl alarmed him. No matter how dirty and ragged, he knew immediately she did not belong with Angel. "Who is this?" he asked in a hoarse whisper, as though Kate was incapable of speaking for herself.

Angel smiled, obviously pleased with the effect she had

caused. "I would like to present Miss Redhead Kelly, the daughter of the American consul . . ."

Jorge looked around as though they were standing on a corner in downtown Managua. "Come in the house—please!" Herding them toward the cabin, Kate let herself be supported by Angel, stumbling along in the stiff-legged shuffle of those ready to drop.

Inside Jorge guided them to a table and Kate slumped in a chair. "I would give just about anything for . . ."

"Forgive us, Jorge—we have not had the chance to eat. Our progress was *rapido* as they say in Spanish." He smiled and lowered himself tenderly in a chair, sore foot out.

Jorge shouted for his wife and she appeared from behind a handloomed drop that separated the sleeping quarters. She was a serious-looking Indian woman, young, with hair skinned back tight enough to slant her eyes. Three small children of stair-step ages peered shyly out from behind her. She went to pots on an iron stove and began to dip the contents on wooden dishes. "No! Not those—the *good* dishes!" These were in a polished mahogany corner cupboard with bull's-eye glass doors. Stepping up to it, she carefully took out Queen's ware dinner plates in the water lily pattern.

The cabin interior was an odd combination of roughly sawed logs, pounded clay floor, and elegant English furniture. The floor was covered with an oriental carpet, the oil lamps had beaded silk shades, and windows were hung with silk drapes. Books sat everywhere, the desk stacked with old issues of magazines and papers, suggesting voluntary confinement—exile.

"*Gauco pinto!*" Angel said as the heaped plates were put in front of them. "Spotted rooster, Redhead. What a treat."

"To your health," Jorge said, pouring off a homemade wine and raising a cut glass. He settled back to watch them eat, sipping the wine and puffing on a half-bent briar.

George Williams had walked the tightrope as a foreign mine boss in a politically explosive country. He had bet his future on the Sandinistas and because of it the Americans suspected him of complicity, seeing to it the mine stayed closed. If the Marines did not leave soon the company would be ruined. The taking of the American consul's daughter was insanity. It would give them an excuse for more punitive raids and bombing. He watched the girl as she ate, obviously ravenous; they must have starved her. He hoped to God she hadn't caught any of the dozens of deadly fevers that infected the place. Before she could finish eating, her head dropped toward her plate and he called quietly for his wife to lay her down, speaking in an Indian tongue even Angel had trouble with.

When she was settled behind the curtain, the two men relaxed back, Angel working the kinks out of his arms and puffing up a cigar. "How goes it, Jorge?"

"The same. The mine is still closed."

Angel raised his eyebrows. "Not because of César."

"No, the Marines 'persuaded' Mattison to cut the main drivebelt, then for the sake of safety—so they said, they took away the mercury and destroyed the explosives and cyanide. A damn curious operation for people who came here to protect American and foreign property."

"It's almost over. They will be out of here by next year— after the thirty-two elections at the latest."

"By then it may be too late for a lot of us."

"What about the *guardia*?

"It's not like the old days with Major Floyd—this "M Company is literally a bloody terror. Besides Puller and Lee there is a one-armed officer named Gutiérrez that would give Pedrón a run for his money."

"That I would like to see."

"I imagine you will."

The Packard pulled into El Sause after dark, finding its way through a rudimentry rail yard and past stacks of pine telegraph poles ready for shipping. The town consisted of one main street with wooden buildings, many of log construction and the occasional false front. There were crude signs offering meat, "medical healing," and an arrow pointed to a deserted branch of the Pentocostal Church. There was not a single light to be seen. The place seemed empty; walks deserted, animals absent.

"You can be sure Lee is here," Chesty Puller said, driving down the one street, headlights off accompanied by the flapping of a rear tire ready to go.

"You're sure, Lewis?" General Puller asked from the rear seat.

"Everybody has gone to cover, home saying novenas for the bandits. This is a real Sandinista town. If they call El Jicaro 'Sandino City' then this is the next closest thing. When we come into this place you can feel the hate come up like heat from the sidewalk."

"Have you been jumped here?" Magnusson asked, examining the buildings for movement.

"Not in town, it's a kind of a neutral zone. Noboby wants to shoot up the consumer goods. The thing about it is, you know everybody here is out to get you so you don't have to worry about shooting innocent bystanders."

"That's comforting," Wills said.

A single unraveling telegraph wire was stretched on irregular poles along the street, and where it dipped into a dark building Chesty pulled up, stopping the car. The shine of a river could be seen further on through the lacy foliage of willow trees the town was named after.

Chesty got out, arming the submachine gun, pulling the cocking bolt against his leg to muffle the sound. "Let's all be *very* careful, weapons on the cock, and watch your ass. Mag, I recommend the trench cleaner—if it comes to action it will be from the hip."

"I thought you said the place was neutral?"

"Well . . ."

The building was a long rectangle without windows. It

offered no clue to its purpose other than the smell of fermentation. Puller went under a sagging porch and pushed open the door. When there was no challenge he entered, Magnusson behind him, Wills and the consul next with General Butler bringing up the rear, holding out the other pump shotgun. They did their best to look casual but alert. To the left on the inside was a dark alcove with a telegrapher's key and no operator. Directly ahead a long narrow room was lit by one dim oil lamp. Its pale light showed several figures sitting at the back, faces cut off by its arc.

Wills thought it resembled nothing so much as the saloon sets of western movies. Not the current crop of sanitized quickies, but the silents of sobersides William S. Hart whose personal image of Old West reality was a quirky mix of Mexican-Indian culture overlaid by a classical theater background; Hamlet as Billy the Kid.

There were rough tables, chairs kicked back, cigarette butts ground out on the floor and nasty stains. To the right was a bar. Not the classic variety seen in movie sets, but a simple, greasy plank set on saw horses. The drink was held in lopsided crocks behind flour sacking tacked to the front of the plank. It was a combustable local brew that fermented while you drank, served up in whatever container you brought. There was actually a picture hanging behind the bar. Wills couldn't be sure in the murky lighting but it seemed to be a likeness of Dolores Del Rio, fan to face, hip cocked. A poster, no doubt brought in from some distant, worldly place. Then, for just a second he glimpsed a woman at the far end of the room, spit curls and bee-stung lips—a whore! My God is was cowboy heaven!

"Is that you Chesty?" The voice had a pleasant drawl and a smile in it.

"That's right Billy."

A man got up and ducking the lamp came in view wearing a *guardia* uniform. Thin, with a long face and shoulders hunched in the stoop of a tall man in a small place. He had an engaging smile, shy and illuminating.

"This is Lieutenant Lee," Chesty said, introducing them. "Lieutenant Magnusson, General Butler, the American consul Mr. Kelly, and a writer."

Lee shook hands with each stopping at the consul. "I'm sure sorry about your little girl, sir. But you can bet we're going to do our best to get her back."

"Thank you for risking your lives."

"Well we do that anyway, don't we? But when it comes to children we can't do enough."

Wills was terribly disappointed. Expecting a monster or at the very least a brute—what he got was a Sunday school teacher. Lee looked like the ideal Westerner, a woodsman, the perfect scout leader. With his diffident way and lopsided, likeable smile he was the poor man's Gary Cooper to Wills's movie Westerns. Wills didn't know it, but Lee came from Massachusetts.

"What is the situation, Lieutenant?" the general asked.

"Well sir, two squads are in place at the river covering the approach to the town. Weapons are laid in and all we can do is wait."

"You're sure they will come this way?"

"Oh, I think so, sir, they always do." This was said with the conviction of a man who knew. "Polly here will stand watch and sing out when they get up to it."

Another man stepped into the light and Wills found his archtypical villain. Policarpo Gutiérrez was a Nicaraguan lieutenant who had lost his left arm in the 1927–28 campaign against El Chipote. He was a small, stocky man with a handsome face arranged in sharp planes and hooded eyes, flat and deadly. A clipped mustache cut straight across a mouth that didn't smile. Like Lee he wore a *guardia* uniform, with laced up boots and suspenders supporting a web belt with holstered automatic and ammunition pouches. He held a Thompson submachine gun in his right hand.

"This is the command post then?"

"Yes sir. We're only a hop, skip, and a jump from the front lines." He smiled. "That automobile can get us there in a wink so why don't we relax and wait for Polly's signal? My guess is they will come through at first light."

"This is an ambush?" the consul asked uneasily.

"I'd like to believe that sir, but everyone in this department is a spy for Sandino. They'll be waiting out there to warn him."

"What I'm concerned about is my daughter—if she should be with this group—how will your men know not to shoot her?"

He smiled, exuding confidence. "Well sir, these men are expert shots and they will be on the lookout."

"If General Sandino knows you're waiting for him, why would he try and get past you?" Wills wanted to know.

"If he doesn't get on the river here he'll have to go miles out of his way on foot—clear down to Esteli. He leaned over the bar and extracting several dusty bottles, set them on the table. "Say, how about a Coca-Cola?"

Two hours before dawn Sandino arrived at the outskirts of El Sause. Others had joined him and they were now about twenty-five in strength. As the descent through the tight jungle trail was made they knew the river was just ahead and across it, El Sause's main street. Coming closer, a young boy and two men were seen hunkered on the side of the trail waiting. They pointed out the location of Company M and said a big automobile had come in town carrying other soldiers.

Sandino thanked them and asked that *pipantes* be brought up. They would run the river in the canoes as soon as the men rested. There was no question of looping the many extra miles around the town to pick up the river at Esteli. Everyone was hungry and exhausted. They would sleep a few hours and take their chances slipping by the *guardia*. They had done it before.

At nearly the same time at the cabin in the pine grove, Angel Ortez was saddling two of George Williams's big mules. There was a twelve-mile ride to El Sause and he wanted to arrive there at daylight when there was the best chance of finding someone to paddle them upriver. He had waited until the last minute to wake Kate Kelly. When she came out, ducking under the fence he got a surprise. She was scrubbed, her hair tied into a mass of curls, and wearing a dress that must have been given her by Jorge's wife—probably her best, stitched in the moon patterns of the Amerindian tribe.

"*Muy bonita*, Redhead! You look like a real Indian princess! Jorge, would you believe this girl is a Yankee?" Williams cinched up on the latigo hitch, pounding the animal to expel its breath. He smiled but was not inclined to comment. His hope was the girl would remember decent treatment under his roof—that is if she survived.

Kate was interested only in the mules. Recovered after nearly twelve hours sleep, she approached her mount gently, kissing him on his long gray nose. "Just my luck," Angel said, "the girl I love is a mule kisser."

Williams held the mule while Kate swung up in the saddle. "I wish you good luck, Miss Kelly. Try to remember we do our best here to survive no matter what the politics."

She looked at him puzzled and Angel said, "Don't worry Jorge, I will keep her safe. Thank you *compañero*. The mules will be sent back from El Sause—especially the one who has stolen my redhead's heart." He mounted and kicked the animals ahead, leading off into the woods. Behind them Kate could see Williams's Indian wife and three little kids standing in the shadow of the doorway. She waved.

"This is the writer who made you famous, Billy." Puller said, drawing on his warm Coke.

"Is that right? I never thought to get in the papers." He smiled at Wills with a sly glint in his eye. They all sat at one of the rough tables in the bar directly under the circle of lamp light. It was hot and still despite the altitude because there were no windows in the room to let in air—or dynamite bombs. Outside,

Lieutenant Gutiérrez stood watch on the porch, waiting for the flashlight signal from the river bank that would indicate contact with Sandino.

There was a plate of *nacatamal* on the table. This was the Nicaraguan version of the Mexican tamale, meat wrapped in a pungent leaf like a corn husk. Next to it was a loaf of bread and Magnusson tediously removed the meat from the *nacatamal* and spread it on a slice of bread.

"Well," Puller continued, popping one of the lip-mummifying *salsa de chiles* in his mouth, "It's all those interesting atrocities you get up to—what was the last one we read about?"

"Come on, Chesty."

"I remember. After stabbing prisoners to death, 'the crazed gringo' then used the bloody knife to cut bread and made the troops eat it. Isn't that what it said?"

"Damn!" Magnusson said, "I thought that was ketchup!"

There was laughter around the table and Wills smiled along with them. "There are fantastic charges on both sides. But the facts are, there are photographs of your men holding severed heads."

"You won't give up on that will you?" the consul said.

"I only know about one head," Puller said, "mine. Sandino has put up a proclamation offering five thousand *cordobas* for it."

"It's worth at least twice that," the general said. "I'd get up ten for it myself."

"You've got to understand sir," Lee said very seriously, "a lot of our people—theirs too, are Indians right out of the trees. They tend to get excited in battle."

"I find it difficult to tell the difference between who is the savage." Wills answered stiffly.

There was silence and a sliding of feet under the table. Wills knew once again he had gone too far. And, he sighed, at table full of heavily armed men, none with his interests at heart.

Finally General Butler leaned in. "Sir, in guerrilla warfare only the aggressive and ruthless may expect to survive. These officers are eminently qualified on both counts—as is your friend Sandino."

Then, they were aware of the shrill sound of Lieutenant Gutiérrez whistling through his teeth. Chairs were kicked back and they ran for the car, bursting through the doorway and piling in, Gutiérrez on the running board. As they roared off, rear tire flapping, they heard gunfire. It was to be the last engagement for the rescue party.

# FIFTEEN

# El Reposo

SANDINO paused at the riverbank waiting for just the right light. Six of the native canoes, *pipantes*, were drawn up at intervals ready to go—men waiting to push off and paddle for their lives. From experience they knew going at night was more dangerous; a white wake on the water was highly visible from the near shore and if they fired, the flashes of gunfire would identify them as targets. When the sun rose in the east and its rays cleared the mountains they shone directly on the opposite riverbank—that was the time to push out and paddle frantically—clear the several-hundred-yard bottleneck in front of town, make the turn in the river, and when it widened, be safely away.

On the other shore, Company M waited. The two squads composed of thirty men strung out for maximum crossfire with six automatic weapons and twenty-four rifles, four of them with grenade launchers. The men, mostly Indians, were eager for combat and literally had to be held back by the sergeants. This most successful of *guardia* formations, Company M had become the first real threat to Sandino's guerrilla bands in North and Central Nicaragua.

For all of his bluster and self-advertising, Chesty Puller understood bush warfare. His operation was simple: maintain two highly mobile patrols with one held in reserve at Jinotega ready to jump off if the other got in trouble. The key was freedom to move in any direction at any time. They had no set defensive position and could be deployed rapidly to a threatened sector. Local Indians were recruited for his command and although they could be dangerous, there were few equals for endurance, loyalty, and combativeness. They respected him and as his fame grew many came into Jinotega asking to join, calling him "The Tiger of the Mountain."

"Now!" Sandino whispered, and the first canoe entered the water, men running alongside like the crew of a bobsled, launching it at full stride, hopping aboard, digging the paddles in and stroking furiously.

The morning sun cut over the mountain with the sudden brilliant illumination of a stage set. The shoreline was caught in its flare and the men tugged down hat brims, squinting and holding a hand up for shade. At the far end of the line an Indian BAR man slipped on a pair of dark glasses with white frames. He had traded a jaguar skin for these and they were his proudest possession, setting him apart from his trible and giving him the nickname "Ojosnegro." He lay prone behind the awkward weapon, barrel supported on a tripod and in that instant saw the hull of a low boat skimming the water, paddlers hunched over. Putting his shoulder against the butt he fired on full automatic, the weapon jumping. The canoe got past him but his action alerted others and they were ready for the next target.

It was this gunfire that the rescue party heard as they tore down the main street of El Sause in the Packard. Sliding the big car to a stop at the riverbank, Chesty cranked it around broadside and Lieutenant Gutiérrez jumped off, kept his feet, and began directing fire as the next canoe shot by. It stayed close to the far bank and was not an easy target in the rapid rush of the river. Underwater rocks created confusing eddies and the paddlers remained nearly out of sight.

But Ojosnegro was ready this time; locked in he let off the BAR on its full cyclic rate of five-hundred rpm, catching the center paddlers and chopping them up. The canoe veered toward the center of the river and was suddenly swept around the turn.

Puller gunned the car ahead following it, bumping along the bank, riding over brush and rocks, cutting across the spur of land and arriving at the curve of river the same time as the canoe. A man in the bow gripped the sides riding it out, as another in the stern dug his paddle in, steering into the sudden increase of swift water. The car came to an abrupt stop at a tangle of stumps and it seemed in the next second the canoe would be out of sight, lost behind a screen of jungle. Magnusson stood, Springfield resting on the windshield, and fired. The man steering slumped over and the canoe whipped around the bend, disappearing. Puller and the general were out of the car together, hitting the ground in nearly the same stride, racing side by side up the bank. As they came through the brush the canoe was visible veering toward the shore out of control. The man in the bow raised a pistol and fired. As he did, both pursuers returned fire, Puller with his service automatic, the general with the trench cleaner. The sound of the shots overlapped and the man dropped. Chesty splashed in the water, waded out and pulled the canoe toward the shore.

Angel Ortez and Kate Kelly had heard the burst of gunfire at nearly the same time as the rescue party, and spurring the mules ahead gained a hill overlooking the town and river. Catching a glimpse of smoke from the *guardia* position, Angel dismounted.

"Don't they ever stop shooting at each other in this place?" Kate moaned, pulling her animal up behind him.

He handed her the reins. "Hold on to your friends,

Redhead, and stay back." Taking the Krag rifle he went cautiously toward the crest of the hill where he could best observe.

The canoes had accelerated past the *guardia* in a matter of minutes, very much like ducks in a shooting gallery, Sandino thought. Of the six, four skinned by—made it. The other two had faltered, been holed and swamped, perhaps half the paddlers escaping toward the far shore. The dead would be carried miles downriver, snagged on sand banks and tree stumps. Clearing the curve, Sandino looked back and saw a flash of the Packard between the trees. His heart jumped. The superstition that had grown in his mind was confirmed. The car was pursuing him— and unless he could do something about it he would never get away.

The *guardia* kept up a heavy fire at Sandinistas climbing up the far bank and Gutiérrez immediately organized pursuit, commandeering boats. At the curve of the river the rescue party was examining the man killed in the bow of the canoe.

"Looks like you got him with the pump, general," Magnusson said, as they ascertained wounds in the way of hunters.

"I don't know," Lee said, "that doesn't seem right—look at that spread—that's nothing that would kill a healthy man."

"Maybe it was a heart attack," Magnusson said.

Lee rolled him over. "Where were you aiming, Chesty?"

"Side of the head—profile." Puller stood aloof, not contesting the kill.

The general watched all this like a marksman whose bull's-eye was in dispute—a hair out of the black. Lee bent closer, hand on the dead man's face twisting it to the side. "Would you look at that! By gosh, Chesty drilled him through the ear! Right in the opening of the ear!"

They all leaned in and it was true; there was the seared entrance of a bullet hole to prove it, showing very little blood and nearly invisible.

"That's got to be the greatest field shot I ever saw!" Lee said,

"He shot that bird from twenty-five yards, running at a canoe going full speed! Damn!"

Wills thought the discussion typical of hardened soldiers no matter what side—totally impersonal. That the body had minutes ago been a living, breathing human being was not considered; it had become a thing; a piece of meat. For the general it meant something else entirely. He saw it as symbolic of the end of his career. Thirty years ago roles would have been reveresed; *he* would have made that shot. That he had not told him more clearly than Puller's loud voice it was time to step aside, let the young lions take over—or in this case, tiger.

Directly across the river on the hill, Angel Ortez watched the group. He had instantly recognized Wills even from this distance. There was no mistaking the glasses perched on that nose. Angel was lying prone, Krag rifle steadied against a rock. The Krag was a Norwegian idea that didn't survive the twentieth century, purchased by the U.S. Army in 1892 and made obsolete by the Springfield in 1903. The remainders had been palmed off on the *guardia* as its "official rifle." It did have one advantage, a long barrel, that made it reasonably accurate. At this range Angel would have no trouble hitting Wills. He loaded it through an odd trapdoor arrangement, the closing stroke of the bolt pushing the first cartridge into the chamber. Then, he was ready.

"We'll leave the car here with a couple of men and cut across the river after those Sandos that got away," Puller said, standing in the group of officers and noncoms, General Butler listening with the others. "Lieutenant Gutiérrez will take one squad upriver in canoes to pursue the main force and we will connect at Esteli tomorrow night."

"God willing," Lee said.

"Any questions?"

Wills put his hand to his face to brush away a fly. "If I have a choice I'd like to go with . . ." And he was knocked off his feet by the impact of a bullet striking him. The sound came in the next instant and a puff of smoke from across the river indicating a low-powered cartridge. They dropped and began firing back. Chesty shouting orders in Spanish over the din. "Gutiérrez, get your people upriver—now!" and in English, "Billy! Take one squad and cross over!"

On the hill, Ortez crawled backward with incoming rounds clipping brush and overhead branches above him. When he got down the slope of the hill he took the reins of his mule from Kate and mounted. "We can go now, Redhead—fast if you like." And they let the animals out as much as they dared along the tangled trail. The sound of firing could still be heard.

After a long run with the mules blowing they slowed and Kate asked, "Did you cause all that?"

"They must have seen me." He knew better than to tell her he had killed Wills.

"I thought I heard you shoot first."

He sighed. This girl was sharp. "It just sounded like that." He changed the subject. "The town is full of *guardia*, we'll have to ride all the way to Esteli now."

"Oh good! I'd rather do that anyway," she said, patting the mule.

It meant many extra hours and if they were closely pursued the animals would have to be pushed hard. It was bad luck to miss the boats and Sandino. It occurred to him that César would not be happy with Wills's death either. He had warned him off— still, what was Wills doing with the *guarida*? He never trusted the son of a bitch, and even Sandino had not trusted taking him on to El Chipote.

He realized Kate had fallen behind. Slowing, he looked back. "Come on, Redhead, give your sweetheart a talk, we've no time to waste."

"Something's wrong with Carlton."

"*What?*" That stopped him.

"My mule, he's holding his foot up."

"Oh."

He got off and walked back to where she stood examining the animal's small hoof. Please God, he asked, don't let this beast come up lame. Clamping the hoof between his knees he saw immediately the rubbed end of bayonet thorn in the groove next to the frog. "Damn!" He got out his clasp knife and with some effort worked it loose while Kate snubbed him down. The wound bled and the animal would not put its full weight on the leg. Angel sighed again. "Let's get the saddle off. You can ride up behind me."

"Oh no! I'm not leaving Carlton behind!"

In his mind, Ortez wondered if this was heaven-sent punishment for killing Wills. He ground his forehead. "Redhead, we must go and swiftly. You can't ride this animal. See— he's lame."

"I'm not going to leave him here for something to eat!"

"But we . . ."

"You go ahead, I'll stay with him." He now recognized the signals; chin up, the back stiff—there was no way he was going to persuade, or force her to do what she did not want to do. "See if he'll walk behind you."

She led him off, coaxing and patting, and he hobbled along slowly, probably no more anxious then they were to be left in a strange place. "That's it poor baby, come on." She eased him along at a snail's pace.

This would not do. If the *guardia* were close after them they would be caught in no time. There was one alternative, leave her with the animal, as she suggested and make his way alone. But he couldn't do that.

"Head wound?" Puller asked, standing to one side as Magnusson worked quickly trying to staunch the flow of blood. Wills lay on his back where he'd fallen, covered with blood. Further up toward the main street the *guardia* were crossing the river in every manner of boat requisitioned from the locals.

These citizens appeared after the firing had quieted, coming down to the river to count Marine and *guardia* dead. Several stood around as Magnusson worked over Wills.

"No, he got it in the hand—through the palm. He must have grabbed his head when he went down. He'll make it."

"Sorry to hear it."

Wills was conscious, staring up at Magnusson, still in shock. He couldn't believe he'd actually been shot. After all the weeks—months with Sandino's army and not a scratch—now to be shot by one of his own, while with the hated *guardia*. It would not make good copy.

Magnusson was having trouble with the hand. The old 8-mm slug had torn through the palm, taking with it all sorts of nerves, bone and tendons. The hand was already constricted into a clutching position and he doubted very much if it would be useful again. He saw Wills looking at him, eyes asking the universal question of the wounded. *How bad is it?*

"You right-handed, Wills?"

"Ah . . ." Finding it hard to make the words come out, ". . . left . . ."

"You're going to be in good shape then."

Magnusson finally got the blood stopped and they found one of the Pentacostal converts in town who agreed to nurse Wills until he could be taken out, back to León. As he was lifted up to be carried to her house, close by the river, Puller leaned over and said, "Looks like your buddies nailed you, writer."

Wills looked at him, trying to focus without his glasses, "Yes . . . I guess . . . they did . . ."

"Well don't worry about it—you're in good hands now. We won't let them get your head."

General Butler and the consul stood by the river watching the *guardia* cross over. The general was curiously subdued, and the consul wondered if he were tired—worn out. He was not a young man and had been keeping ahead of all of them. "Are you feeling all right, sir?"

"What? Oh yes, of course. It's just, well I was thinking about Lewis and I raced to see who would kill that fellow in the boat first."

"Yes?"

"And I wondered if I had it in me to do killing anymore. No matter what they say, no soldier can ever adjust to violent wounds and death. The worst of it is to command, of course, to put men in harm's way. After ten thousand casualties at Cold Harbor in twenty minutes Grant is supposed to have admitted he made a mistake. Can you imagine spending men like that? It's a young man's game. When you get old your conscience grows as long as your ears."

The consul didn't know what to say. "Maybe you're just tired sir—you have a right to be. Why don't you wait here, rest, until we come back?"

The general laughed. "Did I sound like a weak sister? Oh no, I said we would find that young lady and I want to be there when we do."

"Would you look at those two crying on each other's shoulders." Chesty said, as he and Magnusson went by. No wonder you haven't been able to catch up to that little girl with those two anchors around your neck."

"I notice Sandino got past your bunch. He must be halfway to Esteli by now."

"We'll catch the bastards, don't you worry about that."

"I'm not worried about anything, Chesty—tell you what—I'll take those two anchors, you take your squad and I'll bet you a month's pay we find the girl first."

"You're on, Swede!"

Several miles downriver Sandino motioned the canoe in, and they cut toward the shore, hopping out and easing it up at a sandy spot. Sandino gestured for Carlos Salgado, Cinco, to accompany him and they walked a short distance up the bank.

"Carlos, there is something I would have you do for me—a personal thing."

"Anything, *jefe*."

"Since we left Bluefields we have been pursued by this automobile, this immense Packard—do you know the kind?"

"Wheels as big as well covers and two front windows?"

"Yes. Now we know it is impossible for such an automobile to go in the jungle and travel up mountains and rivers of our country—am I right?"

"I would think so."

"This one has done it. I have had a dream about it and in it this machine appears at my death."

"Hmmm." Cinco was impressed. It was known that Sandino was a superstitious man—who else would be a Catholic *and* a Mason? But then that was something that was appreciated by Indians, a man who knew what made the moon move, the sun come up, and Yankees bleed. "What would you have me do?"

"Go back to El Sause, find that automobile, and kill it."

When they crossed the river, the two parties broke up. Puller, Lee, and the *guardia* pressed along river trails looking for signs of Sandinista paddlers who had escaped the ambush. Chesty reasoned that the first caught could be persuaded to give information about Kate Kelly. She would be highly visible, certainly seen by the troops. He believed she had to be with Sandino himself: An important hostage would be carefully guarded. When he found Sandino he would find the girl.

Magnusson explained the split to General Butler and the consul, carefully chosing his words. "Sir, with your permission we will break off from Captain Puller's company and proceed on our own."

"Why is that, lieutenant?" the general asked, suspecting this had been Puller's idea to get rid of him.

"Well sir, with two groups, one taking the river trail the other going over the mountain we stand a better chance of making contact."

"That's all?"

"No sir, I believe I have a different slant on this and Puller doesn't agree."

"That recommends it to me at once."

They climbed the bank up toward the hill opposite the town. The going here was relatively easy, bushes beaten flat by locals who used it as a shortcut to the main trail, a notch in the valley beyond. The general liked to think that in the disagreement with Puller, Magnusson had remained loyal to his "command" of the original rescue party. This push and shove of ambitious officers was an old game to him and he had survived many a bloodless coup. But he was cautious, not willing to give it his blessing until he knew what Magnusson was up to. When they reached the hill he asked, "Just what was the contention, Lieutenant?"

"Wills, sir. When I thought about it, it seemed queer the sniper would pick him. The man had a clear view from this hill and could not mistake him as a civilian—or the rest of us as military. Why didn't he aim for one of the officers? I would. Unless of course he deliberately went after him."

"Why would he do that?" the consul asked.

"Maybe he was recognized and they were afraid he would give us information we could use against them—the number of officers by name, how many casualties they had taken—routes— military information."

"Yes . . ."

"If that was the reason, then the only person to my mind who could give the order to kill him had to be Sandino himself."

"You don't think he was in the canoes?"

"No one identified him."

The general turned and looked back down at the river. They were now at the apex of the hill, above the spot where Wills had been hit. "I suppose it could have been a diversionary tactic—the canoes down there to draw fire so Sandino up here could escape over the trail."

Magnusson found the sniper's position pressed in the mashed-down grass. The rock that his rifle rested on was still in place. "Here's the shell case." He held up a spent brass case. "Eight millimeter, sir, a Krag."

"I never liked the gun," the general said.

They followed the path of beaten-down grass and arrived at the main trail. Like others in the countryside it had been worn down by centuries of use, a serpentine shape snaking over mountains, enclosed on both sides by rampant growth—not the wet steamy jungle of valleys and rivers—but huge trees of smooth skinned ceiba and dark mahogany pressed together with silvery matapalo. Below, their roots were entwined and exposed against the bank of the trail, a trough cut by endless rainstorms surging down its escape route. Above, a canopy of leaves and troops of screaming white-faced monkeys.

"Here's where they joined up." Magnusson said, examining the dig of hoofs and droppings.

"Horses," the consul said, instantly thinking of Kate's donkey.

"Two. You can see where they dug in and galloped off—and not long ago—they can't be more than a few hours ahead of us."

The consul was discouraged. "But, if they're on horses we're never going to catch them on foot."

"Oh yes, Dick," the general said. "He who travels fast travels on foot. In this kind of country its best to stay close to the ground. Horsemen make splendid targets, they tend to bunch up on a trail like this and trying to get a contrary animal off into the heavy brush is a job. We can actually move faster on foot then they can."

They had a chance to find out. Moving along the trail on the point, Magnusson set a pace; a brisk double time, thirty-six inch steps, one hundred eighty per minute. He was reasonably sure the quarry would not double back for an ambush, but kept a wary eye, trusting his ears to pick up the warning sound of birds or monkeys. They would double-time a mile, walk a mile, rest every hour for ten minutes.

In the center, the consul labored to keep up, his breathing coming heavy. There was no way he could lag behind men who were out to rescue his daughter, and the truth was, he felt physically better than he had in years, understanding for the first time the meaning of "field life" and comrades at arms.

At the rear the general was in his element. Famous as a serious hiker who chewed up thirty miles before lunch, he stepped out to his own tune; marches made through North China to the beseiged cities of Tientsin and Peking in the Boxer Rebellion; slogging across Cuba, the Philippines, and Haiti. Marching at the head of a division of Marines in the Pennsylvania countryside, off to reenact the Battle of Gettysburg for the amusement of President Warren G. Harding and the nation.

Marching had been his life, legs measuring off the miles at the head of the troops—and, on this last one, bringing up the rear of a three-man rescue party, in God-knows-where-Nicaragua. Well, if it was the last then let it be, he was still a Marine marching in the company of a few good men. Yes.

Near dusk Angel Ortez and Kate turned off the trail. He stopped periodically to listen but heard no telltale canteen clanking, metal on metal, coughs, shouts—the sound of troops. He convinced himself that they were not being followed; that Company M had gone after Sandino downriver. A quarter of a mile off the main trail was a clearing where many other travelers had stayed. The ground had been worn flat and there were the signs of old campfires. A spring had been laid up with rough stones and near it on a large rock someone had written: EL REPOSO. Hobbling the mules where there was some grass, Angel hoped that by resting them overnight, the lame one would recover and they could make up the twenty miles to Esteli tomorrow. Taking off the saddles, they left the animals to feed on what they could find and walked back to the spring carrying a pack. Laying his rifle at hand and positioning himself to face the narrow entrance trail, he sat next to Kate and they shared tortillas, wrapping them around bits of last night's rooster.

"Are you married?" Kate said, apropos of nothing.

"What? A young boy like me? Of course not."

"I don't believe you—you're the kind who is always married and has girlfriends."

"*Yo?* Me? Never! Before becoming a famous general I was studying for the priesthood—taking vows to the church, swearing by the Holy Father and baby Jesus that I would never touch another girl—unless of course she was a redhead."

She laughed. "You're terrible, you'll never go to heaven talking like that."

"What do I want to go to heaven for when I can look at you?"

"Hooey."

"*Hooey?* What is hooey?"

"Insincere—hooey."

"Hooey Long?"

She giggled. "Huey. How do you know about him?"

"I'm very educated about the United States, I know it is a country where they play miniature golf, bridge, and Tarzan the Ape Man is in the funny papers. I also know if you married me you would be a happy redhead."

"I'm only thirteen."

"All the better! We could have lots of babies fast, then still be young with them."

"I hate babies; they're smelly and their heads bob around."

"Our babies' heads would never bob around—not with your stiff neck." And he reached up and gave her neck a tender squeeze."

She ducked her head, pulling away. "Cut it out!"

"You don't like to be touched? I know, I bet you're *consquilloso*, right? What do they call that in English?"

"Ticklish?" And he suddenly dug his fingers in at both sides of her waist. "Stop it!" She jerked her elbows down squealing with laughter, "No, please, don't do that!" and then grabbed his leg above the knee. "Let's see how you like it!" They rolled on the ground, laughing, tickling each other. It was a time-honored thing people did who both wanted to touch each other without admitting it. It was harmless fun.

Magnusson stopped where the animals had turned off the trail. Kneeling, he waved the others forward. "They're in there," he whispered, indicating the path into the woods. It was dusk but there was still enough light to see by. He leaned closer. "With your permission, General, I'll flank them on the right," swinging his arm in an arc, "you on the left . . ."

"Agreed."

He looked at his watch. "Five minutes to get in position—if we have to fire I better lead off sir, followed by you." He turned to the consul. "You're going to hear us if that happens, Mr. Kelly."

"What do I do?"

"First, go down this path very carefully about a hundred yards and wait out of sight. If any of the Sandinistas try to escape your way—shoot—but first be sure it's not the general or me."

"Yes . . . I'll be careful." His heart was speeding up, his hands clutching and reclutching the double-barreled shotgun slippery with sweat. "What if Kate's in there?"

"I promise you sir, I won't fire if there is any chance of hitting Miss Kelly. If that seems likely we will fall back and wait our chance."

The general nodded. "Don't worry, Dick, I've got a good feeling about this—we're going to connect this time!"

The general and Magnusson moved off down the trail in opposite directions to cross into the woods. The consul watched them go very apprehensively then went up the path keeping to the side, staying with the warp of shadows as he'd seen Magnusson do. He desperately hoped no one would try and escape his way and he would have to shoot. There was no way of knowing, especially in the confusion at *La Fantasia*—but he didn't think he'd killed or wounded anyone yet. He didn't want to do that.

He stopped, arrested by a faint sound. What was it? Human? A high-pitched, distant trill vaguely familiar that suddenly broke off. He began to move faster forgetting caution and passed the hundred-yard mark Magnusson had set out.

Then he was in an open place. Above, a break in the canopy of leaves let the last flat light in, casting everything in a curious monochrome. At the far end of the clearing against trees he made out the movement of animals; mules grazing. Next, to his left, another movement—a muted thrashing of legs; a gasping sound he knew to be Kate's.

A man sat astride her, head bent down, the shine of teeth visible in the half light. The consul walked close to be sure he wouldn't miss and aiming carefully, pulled both triggers of the double-barreled shotgun. The blast blew the man off of Kate, taking most of his head.

Magnusson heard it, knew the sound was the consul's shotgun, and began to run, holding the Springfield out to break his way through the brush. At the other side of the apex the general did the same. They both knew that something terrible had happened.

Kate scrambled up screaming, splattered with Angel's blood. Scooping up the Krag rifle, she jumped over his body, and ran after the mules. Startled by the gunfire, they had bolted into the woods. Behind her she heard her name called frantically, *"Kate! Kate!"*

She stopped, whirled around, holding the rifle out. In the failing light she saw a bearded man in ragged clothes, limp straw hat casting shadows over a face she didn't know. "Who . . . are you . . . ?" She said between gulping sobs, tears running down her face.

The consul was astounded by his daughter's appearance. The red hair was unmistakable but . . . she was thin, appeared taller than he remembered . . . a woman. "Kate . . . it's your daddy . . ."

"Oh no," she said fighting down the gorge in her throat, "Oh no! My daddy wouldn't do that!" and she raised the gun.

In the next instant a man broke through the trees to her left and she swung the gun toward him, hesitating, "Magnusson? *Magnusson!*" Then dropping the rifle she ran to him, throwing her arms around his waist, head against his chest crying bitterly. "It . . . is . . . you . . ."

Magnusson tentatively put one arm around her, patting her back. Looking over her head at the consul he raised his eyebrows, but the consul's eyes were cast down.

## SIXTEEN

# El Chipote

MAGNUSSON arrived in Esteli late the next day. He had crossed over to the river and found an Indian to paddle him the twenty miles for fifty cents U.S. He thought the price reasonable and the Indian thought it enough to get married on.

He stepped off at a slippery shoreline below complicated docking: One-lung power boats and beached canoes were wedged into a turn in the swift river that was Esteli. Walking up past squatting Indians and mestizo boatmen he got the eye. He was a Marine, thin but broad at the shoulders carrying himself with self-confidence, campaign hat cocked over pale eyes, rifle carried loosely, a faint smile saying approach-me-at-your-risk. He did not veer off and they did not contest this. American or not they recognized macho when they saw it. As for Magnusson, macho in Swedish was called *karakar* and had something to do with the size of your balls.

The main street was a bit more lively than El Sause,

boasting a hotel with a veranda; a sweep of tin roof that fronted the muddy street; tables and chairs elevated on warped boards. The hotel was called the Beau Rivage after the owner's one visit to Martinique. Magnusson found Chesty Puller and Billy Lee sitting here facing the river drinking pisco and Coca-Cola respectively, weapons at hand, backs to a protecting angle of porch.

"Well, Mag," Puller said, "alone?" He gave him the bulldog grin.

"That's right."

"You left the rescue party behind?"

"General Butler and the consul went back to El Sause."

Puller couldn't keep the grin back. "Who was carrying who?"

"No, they went on their own feet."

"I'm glad to hear it."

There was a pause, and Chesty pushed the pisco bottle across. "This is not too bad—but don't smoke around it."

Magnusson waved it off. "They don't have beer?"

Billy signaled and immediately a waiter appeared, took the order, and snatched a beer from a nearby table, startling the occupants. Magnusson looked at the label. "I don't believe I've heard of Baby Jesus Beer."

"Bad translation, Mag, it's something like, 'Brewed in a Manger.'" He was still smiling.

"Oh."

"You didn't find her?"

Magnusson took a long draught of the beer then wiped his mouth. Reaching very slowly in his back pocket he drew out a wallet curved to the shape of his body, a handmade piece of shipboard leathercraft. While Puller and Lee watched, affecting casual interest, he withdrew a square of paper, unfolding it in a maddeningly slow movement. At last he produced a spring of hair, bouncing the bright red curl daintily between thumb and forefinger.

"Son-of-a-bitch!" Puller said, slamming his fist on the table and jumping the bottles. "You did it!" Reaching over he smacked Magnusson on the shoulder. "God damn you, you fucking hero! You always were lucky!"

"God bless you," Lee said in his missionary style, holding up his Coke in salute.

Kate Kelly had been hysterical and clung to Magnusson. It had taken a great deal of gentle coaxing by the general to get her calmed down and finally accept the fact she had been rescued. This was a totally different girl than he remembered, thin and wired like she was plugged into an electrical connection, jumping at the least sound. She had gone back with the general and her father to El Sause to catch the Friday train to León, but Magnusson saw that it would be a long time before she forgave the consul for shooting her escort.

"Do you know one of Sandino's bunch with blond hair?"

Puller and Lee looked at each other. "General Ferrara."

"Who?"

"Angel Ortez y Guillén—he usually operates in the Matagalpa department—he's a good man."

"Well, he's a dead man now. The consul shot him."

They sat and thought about this a while. Wondering how a dashing, courageous officer who had escaped death many times could be shot down by a civilian with a bird gun.

"What about Sandino?"

"He came through here just a few hours before us—about noon. Picked up horses and headed out toward Madriz—he's on a straight line to Nueva Segovia and El Chipote."

"What are you waiting for?"

"We're not going after him."

"No?"

Puller dug in his shirt pocket and took out a crumpled paper, smoothing it out on the table with his hand, giving it a final slap. "This was waiting for us on the key from Matthews. What it says is—cease pursuit and return to Jinotega for reevaluation—what it means is, the government has decided to pull back from a confrontation with Sandino. They haven't been able to nail him after six years so they're going to ignore him."

"Anything about me on that?"

"No, but my guess is you'll be hearing from old Tempo through Panama very shortly. The losses we took at *La Fantasia* have just hit the stateside fan and people are screaming 'Get out!'"

"Finding the consul's daughter should help."

"I doubt it. Stories filed from Managua suggest she went with Sandino 'willingly' to learn about 'Nicaraguan problems.' Others say she was a kind of wacky kid on a 'joy ride.' The State Department is not commmenting, which translates into 'Goodbye career' for Kelly. They were not happy that he took off on his own to chase after her."

Again there was a long silence. As they sat on the veranda of the hotel watching a traffic pattern of donkeys, mules, and carts, Lieutenant Gutiérrez rode up on a handsome mule, dismounted, and tied it to a table leg, using his one arm dexterously.

"You're still going after him, Mag?" Puller asked watching Gutiérrez.

"Oh yes, until notified otherwise."

"You don't know the country up there."

"I'll have to learn it."

"I've got an unofficial idea."

"That's the best kind."

"Gutiérrez is from that neck of the woods. He lost his arm up there at El Chipote and you might say he is reasonably rabid on the subject of Sandino. As long as we're this close I don't know why he shouldn't be given a Forty-eight to visit the old home town."

"I would appreciate that."

"Listen, if we can't get Sandino, I hope you do."

"I'll bring you back his head."

"Thanks, but I'll be stateside. I've been assigned to the infantry school at Fort Benning."

"Army?"

"Well, I can't do anything about that."

"Shoot!" Billy Lee said.

By early morning Magnusson and Gutiérrez were moving up the San Rafael del Norte range. Here the mountains would rise to five thousand feet at El Chipote (the bump). As the mules climbed, the air became drier and the vegetation thinned out. Unlike the lower jungle trails it was an ideal place to ride and they made good time. Passing through a stand of ocote pine, Magnusson caught a flash of mountain partridge, and heard the rapping of woodpeckers. On the mile-high plateau at on the top of the mountain clouds brushed the trees and the jeweled quetzal flew between limbs enveloped in orchids. It was cool but never froze.

They rode in silence and at noon stopped to rest the mules and eat. Conversation was carried on in Spanish and was stiff.

"Sandino will stop first at San Rafael del Norte," Gutiérrez said.

"Not El Chipote?"

"You must understand El Chipote is not a place but an idea in the heads of *Norte* Americans. There is a mountaintop called this but Sandino's people—his army is strung out all around us." He nodded his head toward the woods. Gutiérrez had met him this morning out of uniform, wearing the traditional white cottons and a wide hat. Magnusson took the hint and reluctantly left his campaign hat behind for a Panama, putting a native rain cape over his uniform shirt.

"Why San Rafael?"

"His wife, Blanca, works there on the telegraph." What passed for a smile occurred; a rapid riffle of his mustache. "Major Floyd got her the job thinking it might help him get to Sandino." There was a pause while he drank from a skin full of water, wiping his mouth. "The only thing that will get to that dog is a bullet in the head."

Magnusson didn't like Gutiérrez's eyes. They were hard to look in; flat with hate, never changing, hooded like the eyes of violent men he had known, a mask that prededed ferocious attack. He had heard Gutiérrez's story from Chesty.

On New Year's Day 1928, Lieutenant Merton Richal was moving a column of *guardia* toward Las Cruces hill, six miles northwest of Quilali. The point was led by Lieutenants Bruce and Gutiérrez, and at the approach of the hill the Sandinistas ambushed them, opening up with a hailstorm of bullets and dynamite bombs from above. Bruce was killed at once and Gutiérrez stood his ground as the other guardsmen panicked and ran. He was struck repeatedly with machete blows to his left arm and with it dangling, finally fought his way out. He lived now for one thing, the killing of Sandino.

Magnusson thought he better get something straight. "Lieutenant, I have direct orders to kill Sandino. What that means is I am to have the first shot if he is encountered. If I miss—or killed—you may act on your own."

Gutiérrez nodded. But Magnusson was not sure this meant he agreed, perhaps only that he understood. He knew better than to insult him by demanding a firm answer and had the uncomfortable feeling that when it came down to it, the man would shoot him in a minute if it meant killing Sandino.

Sandino rode into San Rafael del Norte that same day, avoiding the people of the town. They were in a difficult position—on the edge of the sword as they said. Although Sandino and the Defending Army of the National Sovereignty had their support, frequent visits by the *guardia* tempered endorsement. As in all war zones there were spies and traitors created by the violent surge of politics and old rivalries. Sandino understood this and took only six trusted men with him into town. The rest would continue on to the current "El Chipote" higher in the mountains behind the town. But tonight he wanted to sleep in the house of his wife.

Sandino made an important decision around this time. He was going back to being a husband, and he hoped, a father. In the years of his campaigns he saw little of his wife, Blanca Arauz y Sandino. He was not willing, he said, to risk her precious life to the terrorist attacks by Marine aviators. This had not been so with his mistress Teresa Villatoro who had been hit in the forehead on El Chipote mountain during an aerial bombardment. When he decided for family and hearth she had gone back to El Salvador with her young son. He no longer wore the ring of San Albino gold with a tiny fragment of her bone mounted in it, but kept it tucked down in his vest pocket.

Blanca lived in her parents' small frame house at the outer edge of town. It was set against the mountains on a dirt road lined with ocote pine trees. As he rode up to the door his men spread out, taking up positions to block both ends of the road. As he dismounted, he found twelve-year-old Guillermo Martez waiting for him. They had met before.

"Well Guillermo, how goes it?"

"Ready now to join your army, General."

"As I remember you were eleven."

"No, thirteen, sir," he answered, lying.

"Well another year in school."

"Schools are closed!" He said this as though Sandino should know better. And it was true, incredibly, President Moncada had closed all public schools because the budget for the *guardia* had grown so high that something had to stand aside. It turned out to be education.

"Let me think about it."

Guillermo produced an old .36-caliber Colt cap and ball pistol, holding it up by its walnut grips with both hands. "Look at this general! It was my uncle's!"

"Venerable—loaded, I hope?" He pushed the barrel away from his stomach.

"Yes sir, all I have to do is cock it."

"Not now," he said, laying his hand on the boy's thumb. "Why not find Sergeant Fernando and let him assign you a job?"

"*Viva Sandino!*" and the boy ran off, his life complete.

Sandino went up the stairs to the porch and opened the door to the house. Inside Blanca waited patiently with her niece Angelita Gonzalez Arauz, whom he was particularly fond of. They embraced and with tears flowing sat in the tiny parlor while he told them of his long dangerous trek from Bluefields. He played down the narrow escapes and bloody battles making it amusing and never once mentioning the consul's daughter.

It was early evening when Sandino finally took his wife off to bed. Angelita had cooked *la cena* and he listened while the two women talked on about family. The Arauz, Blanca's parents could not stand Sandino, politically or socially. In the beginning he brought their two sons, Blanco's brothers, to his camp and gave them work as secretaries. They had so infuriated him that both fled to Jinotega in fear of their lives. When Sandino was expected in town, the in-laws were absent.

Now as husband and wife lay in bed whispering together, Sandino talked about having a son. Blanco was thrilled. "We'll call him Augusto!"

"Well . . . " He was pleased. "Chico for short."

"Yes! Chico! Oh my love you make me so happy! You know today I saw a beautiful rainbow appear in the west—that's a really good omen!" And she began laughing. "You will never get shut of me again! Good-bye telegraph key! Good-bye tapping out others good news! I'm going to be the full-time wife of General *papasito*! And I want my own gun—yes! A beautiful one with a mother of pearl handle that you can teach me to shoot so that I can knock the eyes out of Yankees!"

Sandino knew that he was a lucky man. His beautiful wife adored him despite the terrible years of absence where death waited at every turn of the trail and, he must admit, other loves. No matter, that was over, good times were ahead. He sighed, closing his eyes, remembering if you went to sleep thinking a happy thought you would wake up happy. Suddenly he thought of the Packard automobile and his eyes popped open.

Carlos Salgado—Cinco, reached El Sause at nightfall. He was met by two young men who headed up the Sandino *voluntarios*. They uncovered weapons and two dynamite bombs. The Packard was parked by the river, they said, in front of the shack of Amalia Donaldo, the old woman who was nursing the Yankee. The Indian guardsman whose job it was to stand watch was drunk under the shack.

"This is the plan," Cinco said, as they walked toward the river keeping to the shadows and stopping to listen every few yards. "I will creep up to the automobile, put these bombs under its belly, and light the fuses. Then when they explode the Indian will rush to see what has happened and we will shoot him. After that we go in the house and kill the Yankee."

They liked the killing part but were troubled about the Packard.

"Why would anyone want to explode such a marvelous machine? Why not just steal it away?"

"Because," whispered Cinco, "this machine is *magico, encantado!*"

Eyes widened. "How could that be?" they whispered back.

Cinco was enjoying fooling these two simple country boys. He had a reputation as a story teller and something of a mystic. In his tribe he was called *brujo*. He didn't answer and waved them on. Working their way closer they crawled the last distance and lay behind a rack of fallen trees. The Packard was visible, standing in front of a shack raised several feet on poles above the river. A rickety set of stairs bridged it to the muddy ground.

The two boys looked at the car in a new way; it now seemed even bigger and the huge drum headlights faced them, silvery reflectors winking as eyes. They repeated their question, "How . . . could this automobile be *magico?*"

"This machine came all the way from Bluefields and the *costenos*—now how did it do that?"

They looked at each other. "Why, on those big wheels."

"There are no roads for those wheels to roll on across that country. Not through the jungle and mud. No automobile has ever done it before—how did this one?"

That stumped them. The two had never been further than León and knew certainly there was no road to that town from El Sause. "The railroad," the brighter one said, "It came on the tracks!"

Cinco made an exasperated sound, "Trains travel on tracks—not automobiles! Do you think those rubber wheels would stay on skinny rails?" They agreed this was not likely. "Listen, I have been sent to kill this machine by General Sandino himself—it has been following him. Where he goes—it goes. If we do not stop it, it will be his death." Saying this, he twisted the fuses of the two dynamite bombs together, cutting them to give himself time to place them under the car and get back. Finishing, he fished a battered cigar out of his pocket and lit up, filling the air with smoke. "Remember, when it goes off and the Indian comes running, be ready to shoot him."

He climbed over the dead tree and, staying below the drop in the river bank, cut across until the car was a shield between himself and the shack. Walking in a crablike crouch he reached the driver's side, wiggled under the chassis, and placed the two bombs below the gas tank at the rear. When it went off the gasoline would add to the explosion. Puffing up the cigar, he placed the ember against twisted fuses. They caught.

In the shack, Amalia Donaldo slept soundly in her hammock. The Indian guardsman had begun drinking the minute he saw the rest of the company disappear downriver. He now lay flat out on the wet ground under the raised floor. Mouth open as he snored, each intake of breath drew in hovering gnats.

Carlton Wills was on a rough pallet in one corner of the single room. He had not been able to sleep since his wounding.

The hole in his right hand felt as though it had been reamed out by a hot iron and kept up a furious throbbing pain. He was not sweating and his skin burned to the touch. Still, he believed the nurse had done what she could to keep the wound clean. It was borne in on him that you didn't have to be shot in the head or stomach to die. A simple thing like a bullet in the hand could kill you in this climate, and in fact most of the deaths in combat came as complications of what at first seemed a minor wound. If he could just last until the train came up on Friday and took him back to León his chances of survival would double.

As he lay staring at the unshaped logs that made up the rafters his mind spun forward, then back, repeating over and over the events of the last weeks. Bluefields . . . Rama . . . up the river and to La Libertad . . . across the mountain to Managua . . . the earthquake . . . the battle of *La Fantasia.* Each episode of conversation with Sandino . . . Kate . . . the Norwegian Karen . . . Angel . . . Puller—Smedley Butler, all of these were replayed again and again—images called up flashing on the screen of his mind and remembered verbatim— well, no doubt he had colored some, altered others that were too painful to deal with. *At least,* he thought, *I am still being honest even though I may be dying.*

One thing that appeared to him and remained was Magnusson's face. He saw it hovering above him, concerned and anxious as he struggled to stop his bleeding hand. It was a miraculous thing. This man whom he treated with contempt, thought of as an example of everything he hated in the military—who no doubt despised him in return—had tried to help him. He began to understand the bond between soldiers in combat. No matter what their disagreements, the wounding of another was attended to like a sacred ritual, each man depending on the other for help at that terrible moment when it happened to *him.* There was no stronger bonding.

Then, just for an instant he was reminded of the Fourth of

July. A breeze drifted in through gaps in the wooden siding and brought with it the familar smell of burning punk.

At that moment the Packard went up with a terrific bang, a huge hand slap echoing and heard miles away. Exploding upward, it lifted the rear end of the car a full four feet off the ground. Gasoline was ignited next in the muffled *whomp* of a fireball, lighting the riverfront in an eerie glow. Every door on the Packard was blown off and seats reduced to ash, springs twanging red hot through the air. The extra tires lashed to the back were projected straight up, the last, mounted on one of the large red wheels, spun counter-clockwise reaching a height of nearly fifty feet.

Cinco and the two *voluntarios* shouted with delight as the automobile exploded. It was a marvelous thing to see, destruction on an intimate scale that everyone could appreciate. The glare of the fire lit their excited faces and they looked forward to the next step, the killing of the Indian and the Yankee.

The steel wheel, shedding its tire, slowed, arced over, and started down, picking up speed. Catching a flash of red, one of the boys was on his feet followed by the other. Cinco was still looking up when the wheel rim struck him in the chest, killing him instantly and driving his body six inches into the soft ground.

In the shack, Amalia Donaldo tumbled out of her hammock and hit the floor screaming. Scrambling for a hidden crucifix she stayed on her knees praying to the patron saint she had renounced for the Pentcostals.

Wills pushed himself up from the pallet, feverish, face wild, and staggered across the room to the open doorway. The door had been blown off and the shaky steps were missing. Under the house the Indian didn't wake up, although the insects that hovered over him had been cleared by the sear of heat from the explosion. Wills braced himself against the door jamb and watched the car burn. It was in profile, body already vanished in the furnace of flames. At the glowing core, the skeleton was perfectly outlined: radiator, engine, steering column, transmission, drive shaft, and rear end—tied together by the circle of steel wheels. He was reminded of naked chassis in automobile ads revealing the inner working of the machine, and under it copy extolling its virtues. It occurred to him that the slogan of the Packard Motor Car Company was "Ask the Man Who Owns One."

They arrived at San Rafael del Norte at midnight, April 3, 1931. Magnusson had to admire Gutiérrez's skill as a guide. Granted it was a remote, sparsely settled mountain wilderness, but the man had brought them through without meeting another single person. He was convinced their presence was undetected as they approached the town, swinging wide to make their way to the Arauz house through the grove of ocote pine.

Tying up the mules, they proceeded cautiously on foot. Once they saw the flare of a match and the outline of a sentry at the north end of the road. This was encouraging, making it likely that Sandino was visiting his wife. At only fifty yards from the house they stopped. It was just across the road and Magnusson would take up his position here. Gutiérrez with the heavy Browning automatic would continue on another fifty yards to dig in directly in a line for converging fields of fire. When Sandino appeared (if he did), Magnusson would kill him and while Gutiérrez pinned down the guards, take the body out. He knew this would be extremely difficult and the chances of success small, but he had faced even greater odds in Haiti and brought Charlemagne Peralte's body back. This was essential if his followers were to believe he was really dead.

Magnusson certainly didn't think of himself as an assassin. That was somebody who killed unarmed civilians—heads of state, presidents, kings, and the like. He was a soldier and soldiers killed other soldiers—that's what they did. He had never shot an unarmed man, a civilian, or a noncombatant. The purpose of the job was to shorten the war, perhaps end it and save lives. After Charlemagne's death the trouble with *caco* bandits evaporated. It was hoped, with good reason, that with Sandino gone the

Defending Army of the National Sovereignty would wither and die.

It was dark with only a sliver of moon, but the night was so clear at this altitude that he could make out details of the house. It was unlikely that Sandino would be up before dawn so he had several hours to wait. It was very pleasant here, the pine needles were thick under the trees and he burrowed down into their sweet smell, his rifle resting on the thorny branches shed by the tree. Waiting, thoughts he had managed to resist in the frantic days of the rescue party began to crowd in. Once again he went over the story of his brief encounter with Karen Sven. At each retelling it gathered color and the terrible conclusion brought such a pang of loss; such frustration that he felt empty, defeated. He knew he would never, ever meet such a woman again and that he had lost her after the miracle of finding her—it seemed perverse, cruel. He had known her barely a week and she was gone. What stuck in his mind was the utter finality of seeing the tangle of arms and legs in the rubble below the hotel and wondering which were hers.

At the first touch of dawn above mottled mountains things began to stir. A rooster crowed close by and the piney squirrels began to chatter, tails batting in warning at his presence. Guards rode in from each end of the road and gathered in front of the house. Magnusson was surprised to see only six men and no automatic weapons. They were saddling another horse now and loading pack animals, joking and laughing. There were coughs and puffs of smoke from cigarettes. He put his face against the cool stock of the Springfield, once again counting off the yardage to the porch; estimating that the speed and direction of the wind was from the rear. Range fifty yards, wind at five miles per hour at six o'clock.

Then the door opened and Sandino stepped out. Magnusson recognized him instantly from descriptions and newspaper photographs. He was small, shorter that he had been led to believe, dressed in a Mexican getup and carrying a large sombrero. As he paused, hand on the doorknob, talking to someone inside the house, the sights were squarely on his left ear, and Magnusson's finger began to ease back on the trigger. At that moment a woman's profile appeared in the doorway, lips pursed.

Magnusson was stunned. She was beautiful and in her expression he saw love and delight, face lifted to be kissed. He hadn't thought of Sandino as a man who would be loved by a beautiful woman. It was a shock to find him capable of tender, romantic emtions. He remembered only the rhetoric and savage fighting. That this woman was lovely disarmed him, and although she looked nothing like Karen, he felt a pang of remorse. He raised his eyes from the sights, then heard a sound and turned.

A young boy stood over him holding out a heavy old pistol in both hands. He aimed down the barrel and his hand wavered with the weight of the weapon. It was ludicrous and Magnusson smiled. As he did the boy pulled the trigger, the gun fired, and the ball stuck him directly in the left eye. His luck had just run out.

# SEVENTEEN

# La Calavera

THE Marines were gone from Nicaragua. Elections had been held in 1932 as promised and the Liberal candidate, Juan Batista Sacasa, was the new president with Anastasio Somoza *Jefe Director* of the *Guardia Nacional*. But Sandino still held the mountains, stronger than ever and there was the real possibility that he could galvinize the country, destroy the weakened *guardia*, and impose his terms from the capital. In December, Sacasa wrote a conciliatory letter, asking him to come to Managua and discuss peace. He agreed, saying, "Intervention was the enemy, it has been defeated."

A plane was sent for him, and February 2, 1933, he said good-bye to Blanca in San Rafael del Norte. They stood on the same small porch of the Arauz house where the failed attempt on his life had taken place two years earlier. Although this was the culmination of all his struggles—a summons to power—he was gloomy, pessimistic, superstitions constantly picking at him.

"I woke up today feeling romantic and tragic," he said, "I think we have to make peace in the next five days or I'm dead."

Blanca was appalled. Finally pregnant, she patted her stomach. "Come on *papasito*, don't make us cry. I beg you in the name of little Augusto, let's do everything possible to make him and ourselves happy."

"Yes . . ." he said, "we all want to be happy but some of us must die for it." She cried for hours after he was gone, feeling they were in the grip of some terrible force over which they had no control. Her mother said it was the Masons.

The plane landed in Managua about noon on the same field Marine squadrons had flown out of to attack Sandino at the battle of *La Fantasia*. They were gone now, sorely missed by the *guardia* and potatoes were spudding in on the runway. The government had tried to keep his arrival quiet but word got out and a crowd pressed forward as the plane taxied up to a waiting *guardia* formation. Propeller noise died to a whine and when the door clacked open there was silence. Then, Sandino appeared in the doorway wearing his rough field dress, a bandanna in the colors of syndicalism at his throat, a heavy revolver swung low on his right hip, and a sombrero in his right hand. He looked the rural, the *campesino*, and some thought, the bandit. Elevated by the step and rising above them he at once seemed larger than life.

They stared at him, wondering if this could be the hero they waited for. In that instant a *guardia* lieutenant saluted and offered his hand to the guerrilla general. "No," Sandino said, coming down the steps, "an embrace; we are brothers and I bring you peace." They came together in an *abrazo* and the crowd went crazy, sending up shouts.

"Sandino! Sandino! Sandino!"

Followed by the cheers of the crowd he was escorted toward a car President Sacasa had sent to carry him to the palace. Before they could reach it another large sedan roared on the field and cut them off. The crowd drew back and the escort shifted their weapons, but when the rear door sprung open, General Somoza got out and threw his hands up in welcome. Not to be upstaged, he embraced Sandino and they waved to the crowd arm in arm. Somoza had come to personally invite Sandino to ride with him to the presidential palace.

Sitting in the back of the car they seemed an odd pair; the enormous bulk of Somoza, six-foot-six and already showing a weight gain that would be ongoing, wearing the full uniform of a major general—next to him, Sandino, minute, subdued, dressed as a rural. Somoza, in his ebullient style, never let the conversation falter, talking and laughing over friends they had known in school in Granada, speaking of lodge work—for by another strange coincidence both were Masons. As they went along the streets of Managua crowds cheered them, shouting "*Viva Sandino! Viva Sacasa!*" and Somoza was reminded of his place in the order of things.

Inside the palace there were more embraces from President Sacasa, and the party proceeded to a room in the west wing. Here a protocol of peace was discussed and at ten minutes before midnight, signed by both leaders. General Sandino agreed to an amnesty and the disarming of his troops. In return his demand would be met for military and political control of a huge new department that would stretch from El Chipote to the west coast.

The next morning before leaving for the north, Sandino told the press that he felt no bitterness toward his former enemies. "I have nothing against the North Americans personally," and he read a letter sent to the *New York Herald Tribune* offering condolences to the families of the Americans killed in Nicaragua. The American liberal press responded by calling him a true patriot in the tradition of Washington and Bolívar.

The *guardia* was furious with the treaty. Instead of being allowed to finish off Sandino, the dog was to retain an armed force of one hundred men called "Emergency Auxiliaries." Not only that, but regular Sandinistas would turn over their arms to the government—not to the *guardia*! Somoza told the president that he would not be responsible for the consequences if this happened.

He repeated this at lunch to the new American minister, Arthur Bliss Lane. "This treaty is an intolerable insult to the *Guardia Nacional* and would place them under Sandinistas in the northern departments. "My men want to proceed at once against Sandino."

They were eating lunch in the dining room of the new *Grande* hotel, or as it was now called, the *Gran*. It was a building in the current international style; "parched with modernity" critics said. They ate at a table watched over by waiters and Somoza's bodyguards. Lane was being very cautious with comments. "I think you must proceed with extreme care, General," he said, separating the *chiles* from his salad. "It would be a tragedy to plunge the country into a civil war over this—no one would profit."

Somoza shrugged. "My feeling exactly, but I don't know if I can hold back men whose honor had been insulted. They are furious and demand action."

Lane had grave doubts himself as to whether Somoza really had control over his men—any more than Sacasa had control over Somoza. He had information that *guardia* troops in the north were seeking any pretext to attack the Sandinistas. "Promise me you won't you do anything while Sandino is in the capital confering with President Sacasa."

Somoza smiled over his chicken *mole*. "I promise not to move without first having your approval." He wiped his mouth and bent closer. "If you would merely wink your eye," and he demonstrated, "I would lock him up."

Lane was horrified. "No, no! That would be the worst thing you could do!"

Somoza shrugged and went back to his chicken. "Not the worst."

Sandino's army was officially disarmed at San Rafael del Norte on February 22, 1933, but only three hundred and sixty-one weapons were gathered by government agents from eighteen hundred troops. The *guardia* was adamant in demanding *all* weapons be turned over to them. Nevertheless, President Sacasa officially accepted the disarmament and declared the protocol of peace in effect. Somoza was left to try and contain the hotheads in his command.

During the year there was more violent push and shove between the *Guardia Nacional* and Sandino's men in the northern area. It culminated in the ambush and killing of five Sandinistas herding livestock at Yali.

Sandino traveled twice more to the capital to discuss the increasing difficulties with Sacasa. He arrived for the last time on February 16, 1934, almost a year after his triumphal ride to the presidential palace. He brought along his father, Don Gregorio, his mother, his brother, Socrates, and the generals Juan Pablo Umanzor (who had taken Angel Ortez's command), and Francisco Estrada. All were alware of the danger of coming to the capital and apprehensive. But Sandino told them this would be a final "family effort." They would be safe in his friend Sofonías Salvatierra's house—after all he was Sacasa's minister of agriculture and labor.

But the talks went badly. By now the positions of both sides had hardened with Sacasa trying to mediate from the center. Sandino met with the Magnagua press and made matters worse by announcing that, while he still upheld the peace, he would never surrender to the "unconstitutional" national guard.

Somoza knew then he had to act.

*La Noticia* had reported a gathering of *guardia* officers from all over the nation. Commanders had arrived from as far away as Bluefields and Puerto Cabezas. The paper was unable to come up with the reason for the secret meeting but there were many sinister conjectures and people wondered what was going to happen next.

So did Somoza. He sat in the office of the *Jefe Director's* house torn with indecision. Three officers had just left with an ultimatum: Either he give the word to kill Sandino or they would do it without him. One of the men was Major Policarpo Gutíerrez. Somoza hesitated, and finally agreed to meet with the others within the hour and give his answer. He didn't hesitate out of compassion for Sandino, but for the consequences of his murder. He himself very well could be swept away with the first retribution—as the one who ordered it against the president's wishes—he could be the next to go.

There was a tap at the side door and he knew it could only be one person. "Yes?"

The door opened and a woman paused in the opening, "They've gone?"

Somoza got up, "Yes, yes, please come in, darling."

Her blond hair was pulled back from her forehead and held by an emerald clip at the neck that matched her errings. "We're still going out?" As she crossed over, the long satin dress moved with her body in a shimmer of palletted accents. They kissed tenderly.

"Yes, of course, I have one meeting, then we may go."

She smoothed his hair back. "What is it Tacho? What's wrong?"

"Sandino, of course." And he broke away pacing nervously, confiding in her as he always did. "Officers were just here— Policarpo and two others—the *guardia* demands that Sandino be killed—tonight. I must give the order or . . ."

"What did you say?" She held her breath.

"If I give the order against the wishes of Sacasa and the Americans I risk everything—if I don't, the *guardia* will proceed without me and I may never gain their control again." He stopped in stride and turned to her. "What would you do?"

Karen's memory of Sandino was vivid. She had no trouble bringing up the image of his face at Rama when he ripped her dress down and threw her to that monster Pedrón. It still made her shake when she thought of it; that this macho little man with his wife and mistresses should have done this because she had not admitted she was a whore infuriated her. He was the epitome of men who demanded purity from their wives and came to her bed asking for the most demeaning acts.

Somoza was watching her face; it showed nothing. "Well what do you say, shall we off his head?" He was smiling even then.

"You've said he was popular, that even the people here in the city shout his name."

"For the moment, but that will change, they still believe him to be the savior . . ."

All she would have to do, she told herself was say yes, kill him and it would be done. Awful revenge for the ultimate insult. *But then*, she thought, *was having your dress torn off and being chased around by a brute the reason to kill a man?* "If you kill him now, when the people think he is a savior, he will remain that in their minds. No, I think it would be a mistake."

"Yes . . ." he said, ". . . it's true we would have to live with his ghost." He turned and retrieved his hat from the desk. "Now, I will get my meeting over with and be back in minutes— where are we going tonight?"

"To a recital by that Chilean poet, Cardenas."

"Good God! I would rather face a firing squad—perhaps I should changes places with Sandino." And laughing he went out the other door where his bodyguard was stationed.

Together they walked to a building in the *Campo de Marte* military compound. Inside sixteen men waited, all sworn to secrecy; officers from chief of staff General Gustavo Abaunza to sublieutenant César Sanchéz. When the door opened conversation broke off and they looked toward Somoza. Cigarette smoke swirled to the ceiling, hovering around an overhead light in a green tin shade. Its circle fell on him and he radiated confidence and perfect control. This was a relief to his admirers who had been uneasy with his vacillation of the past few weeks. "Gentlemen," he said in a clear powerful voice, "I have just come from a conference with the American minister Lane who has assured me that the government in Washington supports and recommends the elimination of Augusto César Sandino."

A cheer went up and they crowded around their chief shaking his hand and pledging support no matter what the circumstances. It wasn't until much later that they realized the speech he had just made was a complete lie. When they calmed down a unanimous vote was taken to kill Sandino that night. To share equal responsibility they then signed a resolution dramatically called, "The Death of Caesar."

President Sacasa had arranged a farewell party for Sandino at the presidential palace and he arrived in his friend Salvatierres's car with his father Don Gregoria and Generals Umanzor and Estrada. They were met by Sacasa and ushered in to dinner. His son and daughter would join them with General Portocarrero.

Despite the tension and unspoken fears, Sandino was in good humor and kept everyone amused with war stories, talking about a Carib prisoner of war he had assigned as cook and very nearly executed because the man had made a terrible flan he was convinced was poisoned. His Blanca had saved the poor devil's life by eating it herself. As he went on about his beloved wife his eyes filled with tears and his mood changed. She had died in childbirth while he was away and the boy they hoped for, "the adored Chico," was a girl.

Then for the first time he mentioned the American consul's daughter. Speaking quietly and describing her red hair and fierce eyes, telling how she had defied him to the end, never bending. "I don't understand this in a young girl," he said, "certainly the female is to defend her young but the man is master—everyone accepts that, even the Bible says so. Is it because she was rich and spoiled? Thinking herself an American and me an inferior? Was it because she was unable to comprehend her personal danger?" He turned to Maruca Sacasa, the president's young daughter, "What do you think?"

It was most unusual for her to be included in the heavy conversation and she blushed. Then, without having time to equivocate, said honestly, "I think it's simply because she was brave."

"Yes," Sandino said, nodding his head, "there is no scientific evidence to prove that men are braver than women—it may be possible."

At ten, President Sacasa gave Sandino a farewell embrace and accompanied him to the car. Sandino, his father, and Salvatierres took the backseat with generals Estrada and Umanzor in front with the driver.

Coming down Tiscapa hill from the presidental palace, they approached *Campo de Marte* at the bottom and the sentry post, *El Hormiguero*. The lights came up on a stalled truck with a group of soldiers trying to push it. A sergeant signaled the car to stop and a *guardia* corporal walked over casually carrying a Thompson submachine gun. Both Estrada and Umanzor drew their weapons.

"Damn! I smell a trap!" Umanzor said.

Sandino shook his head. "No, no, put those away, I'm sure it's just a delay—easy."

The "corporal," Major Delgadillo, placed the machine gun on the windowsill of the car. "You are under arrest. Drop any weapons to the floor of the car—now!" Sandino nodded and the guns were dropped. "Now get out of the automobile."

"Why are you doing this?" Sandino said with real surprise, "We've just come from the president's house . . ."

"Move!" He urged them toward the sentry post. Sandino saw Delgadillo's ring.

"You're a Mason! So am I, as is General Somoza—why, he embraced me and gave me a signed portrait." He laughed. "Well, it might not be a work of art—but we three are brothers—call him, let him come and tell me to my face what the problem is! Go on!"

Troubled by this unexpected plea to Masonic brotherhood,

Delgadillo left them under guard and went to call the new *Campo de Marte* theater. Tonight's recital was its opening performance. He returned to say he had been unable to get a message through. "I'm sorry, now please get into the truck."

"What about my father and Minister Salvatierres?"

"They will remain here, the rest of you get in the truck— now!"

"Are you obeying the orders of the president of the republic?" Salvatierres demanded.

Sandino answered for him, shaking his head, "No, *guardia* orders—let's go." And he climbed in, General Umanzor and Estrada after him. There were no farewells.

With the three squatting in the back of the truck surrounded by *guardia*, Major Delgadillo climbed aboard and banged on the roof of the cab ordering the driver ahead. Bumping along the road, Sandino tried to catch the eye of the soldiers but they would not meet his, staring off into the night and hanging on. They looked no different than his Sandinistas, the same simple faces; doing what they were told, ready to follow whoever led. The major had his back to them, looking over the cab roof to the dark road ahead. It was his ambition and a few others like him they served.

Ten minutes later they slowed and turned into the woods near the airport. Following a lake road, the truck came to a deserted spot called *La Calavera* (the skull). A curious landscape, with the humps of smooth rocks breaking the surface of scrubby grass. The three Sandinistas were ordered out and sat casually on one of the rocks while the machine gun was set up. The lights of the truck were full of them and they could hear the metallic sounds of the weapon being armed.

Still the optimist, Sandino reassured the others that his father would be able to contact Somoza before it was too late. Then he heard a car drive onto the field and stop. He stood, and shading his eyes against the glare of the light, could make out the shape of a large open phaeton. His mouth dropped. *It was the*

*Packard.* At that moment he knew it was over. The car door clicked open and a man got out, walking toward him. Squinting into the light he saw that he was tall and angular in a rumpled suit, Panama squared above his eyes. When he stepped past the flare of lights and stopped in front of him there was a patch over the left eye.

"General . . ."

Sandino looked closely into the one pale eye. "You're Magnusson."

"Yes."

"I should have known you'd be here . . . it all comes together now." He sighed in relief, superstitions meshing.

"I had nothing to do with this."

Sandino shrugged. "What does it matter, the girl told me you would kill me, and in the end, she was right."

"I came to say good-bye and tell you I was sorry to hear of the death of your wife."

"You knew her?"

"I saw her . . . once."

There was a pause. "You're no longer in the military?"

"No, a civilian—I'm back in the States—working."

"Really, at what?"

"I run a shoe store . . ." He smiled.

Sandino was puzzled. "Shoes?" then he went on, "What of the consul's daughter? Is she still the troublemaker?"

"She sent you this message." He took a worn letter out of his jacket pocket and handed it over.

Sandino read:

> . . . and when you see General Sandino tell him
> I've thought a lot about him since I've been back. I
> read everything I could and listened to lots of
> people talk about Nicaragua. I still don't believe
> what he did was right, but I see now he was
> honest, he did all those things because he believed

it was for the people. I guess he's one of the few
good men there. Tell him I forgive him about
Calvin.

Sandino looked up. "Who was Calvin?"
The donkey."
"Oh . . . may I keep this?"
"Yes, of course."
A sublieutenant stepped out of the lights nervously gestur-
ing. "It's time."
"Just a minute," Sandino said.
"I'm sorry . . ." he said, firming up, "*now*"
"Don't ask anything of them, General," Estrada said next to
him, "let them kill us and get it over." He tossed a package of
cigarettes at the lieutenant. "Here, keep these as a souvenir,
*cachorro.*"
On the other side Umanzor took off his neckerchief and
handed it over. "And this can be your diaper."
Sandino searched his coat pockets but found nothing. "I
would like to give you something Magnusson, but . . ." Then
digging down in his vest pocket he found the gold ring encasing
the fragment of bone. He pressed it in Magnusson's hand. "It's
better you should have this than these dogs, it was meant for
someone I loved."
Magnusson turned and walked out of the lights, passing
Major Delgadillo who, unable to face his fellow Mason, kept his
back to him as he raised his arm and fired a single shot in the air.
At his signal the machine gun opened up with a sustained burst,
a crackling sound that reverberated through the moist night.
Magnusson got in the open car and motioned the *guardia*
driver ahead. Next to him Carlton Wills wept openly, head
thrown back against the seat. The car, a rented 1932 Cadillac
pulled out of the *Larreynaga* camp and past the lake in the
Zacarias hospice. Once on the main road it headed toward

Managua. Wills got control of himself. "Did . . . he ask about me?"

"Yes," Magnusson lied and he handed over the gold ring. "He sent you this."

Going beyond the presidential palace the car slowed at Salvatierres's house. The front of it was riddled with bullet holes and there were several bodies in the street. A squad of *guardia* stood around on the broken glass holding automatic weapons. The car stopped and Major Gutiérrez came over and bracing his one arm on the car's windowsill, looked past Wills to Magnusson. "Well?"

"It's over."

Gutiérrez slammed his fist on the sill. "Then we got him at last!" It had been Gutiérrez who had brought Magnusson out of El Chipote. Driving Sandino's bodyguards off with the BAR, he had carried him back to the mules and strapping him on, rode back to Jinotega. They had been unable to save his eye but fortunately the old pistol hadn't been loaded with enough powder to kill him.

"What happened here?" Wills asked.

"They chose to shoot back." He indicated two bodies stacked by the front door. "Sócrates Sandino and Salvatierres's son-in-law Murillo—General Lopez got away, but he was wounded and we'll catch up to him."

"What about these?" Wills gestured toward the civilian bodies in the street, one a ten-year-old boy.

"Bystanders," Gutiérrez said. "They were crossing the street at the time."

There was a silence and Magnusson leaned over and handed back the pass. Only Gutiérrez could have done that for him, and in his own way he suspected the man thought of him as a friend. "I'm in your debt once more."

Gutiérrez touched the brim of his cap. "Think of it as gesture from a man with one arm, to a man with one eye."

# EIGHTEEN

# Valhalla

THE *guardia* driver delivered Magnusson and Wills to the new *Gran* hotel. It sat fresh atop the ruins of the last, piles of rubble still not completely cleared away. All along the block buildings had been erected on the same fatal spine of earth. It was as though builders believed the earthquake a thing that wouldn't dare strike again in their lifetime.

They went through the lobby already abuzz with rumors of terrible happenings, to a special table reserved at the back of the bar. This time the decor limited itself to murals in abstract animal designs. Magnusson and Wills sat down and General Butler asked, "They've killed him?"

"Yes sir."

"You were able to give him the letter?" Richard Kelly said, sitting next to the general.

"Yes. He asked about Kate."

"What did he say?" Kate Kelly sat in the place of honor.

"He wanted to know who Calvin was."

"Oh."

There was a silence. "It was a rotten way for the thing to end," the general said. He had organized the reunion of the rescue party, making all the arrangements and hiring the plane to fly them down. Major Chris Schilt was the pilot, and like others at the table he was dressed in mufti. The plan had been to meet with Sandino the next day and present him with one of the enamel pins the general had run up. It was a miniature of a Packard wheel.

Kate Kelly was fifteen now and very different from the fat girl who had ridden Calvin up the bluff in Bluefields. She had remained thin, and with her remarkable red hair and white skin was very beautiful. She no longer wanted to be a Marine but had not forgotten Magnusson. He still filled her dreams and each year she ticked off their difference in age: When she was eighteen he would still only be thirty-eight.

He looked even more handsome with the eye patch—melancholy and heroic. Although they had never once carried on an intimate conversation, he now called her Kate and smiled on occasion. She knew there was an unspoken thing between them that each secretly felt.

Norma Kelly had been totally against her daughter going back to Nicaragua. They lived in Boston now where Dick had taken over his father's investments. She thought it mad to revive that ghastly time, but Kate was obdurate and she came to believe it might clear the air between father and daughter.

In the end she had flown down with them against her instincts, feeling the old fear the minute they arrived in the country. She begged off tonight's reunion of the rescue party, saying she was not part of it. While they acted, she waited.

A young man with dark curly hair and a starter mustache limped to the table carrying a bottle of champagne and glasses. Sitting down, he positioned his stiff leg out. "Hey—the bartender has heard Sandino was murdered."

"That's true, Music," Magnusson answered. "He got the firing squad."

"Damn! Ah, excuse me, Miss Kelly, but that's not the way it was supposed to turn out." They couldn't agree more. It was one thing to pit your skills on a battlefield—but a firing squad was for criminals and traitors—it was below contempt. "I suppose I should hate him for what happened to my leg—but hell, he didn't ask me to join the Marine Corps and he sure didn't ask me to come down here and fight him." After his wounding, the general made sure he got the best of care and when he recovered bullied him into going back to school. After intense tutoring and a push by Lowell Thomas they got him into Harvard. He was going to be a lawyer, he said, to defend the general's big mouth.

Champagne was poured. "Gentlemen, shall we toast those who are not with us?" The general held his glass up. Wills watched them silently.

"To Tomás!" Richard Kelly said, glasses clinked and they drank.

"To Doctor Bruder!"

"To Captain Edd!"

"And let's not forget all those poor devils who fought at *La Fantasia*." And the bottle went round again.

"Just a moment," the general said, taking a cable out of his jacket pocket. "This came from Lewis Puller—he's commanding the mounted detachment at the Peking Legation."

"Wouldn't you know it! The Horse Marines," the music boy said, "That's just about perfect for him, with all the horseshit he shoveled. Whoops—excuse me Miss Kelly."

The general ignored this. "He sends his salute and reminds Magnusson that when he returns to the States he expects a discount on Buster Brown shoes." They laughed.

"To Chesty!"

"And Billy Lee!"

"I think it's time you looked to those above you," Chris

Schilt said, "As I remember you got us up at four in the morning to save your bacon."

"If there's anything more arrogant than a Marine on a horse it's one in a plane," Magnusson said, and they raised their glasses.

"To arrogant aviators!" someone shouted and they drank.

They laughed again and the consul asked, "Is that all? Have we missed anyone?"

Wills had not taken part in the toasts and finally said, "Although I was with you on that last leg to El Sause I certainly don't qualify as one of the rescue party—quite the opposite—but I would ask that we toast the quarry."

There was silence, then the general said, "Yes, I'll drink to him as a worthy enemy—they're rare these days."

All the glasses but Schilt's went up.

"To Sandino!"

Kate wondered if she should offer a toast to Angel Ortez. But she knew this would be wrong. She had come to accept his death as inevitable. If he had seen her father first—they would be toasting him tonight. She looked toward her father and smiled; he brightened and smiled back.

There was a pause after this and when it looked like attention would turn to other things, Magnusson said tentatively, "Have you forgotten Karen Sven? She was with us from Rama to Managua . . ."

"That's right," the consul said.

"Who?" Kate whispered to her father.

"Of course," the general agreed, "a lovely lady."

"Karen Sven is alive." Wills said, "She lives right here in the city."

Magnusson's jaw dropped. "*What* did you say?"

"She calls herself Karen de Seville now."

"But . . . before I left I searched the records . . . talked to people, there was no trace of her—they told me she was probably buried in an unmarked grave!" Magnusson was stunned.

"There's a reason for that," Wills said, "She's under the protection of General Somoza."

They all looked at him. *"Karen Sven?"*

"Yes, our Karen Sven. Gabry Rivas, editor over at *La Nueva Prensa* told me about it. She's seen with him around town at all the best places his wife isn't likely to be. He keeps a house for her in the park at La Loma. She's his mistress."

Magnusson suddenly stood up and smashed his hands down on the table, jumping the glasses off in a crash of glass. *"Oh no! Oh no! He's not going to get away with this too!"* he shouted. Everyone pulled back in amazement. They had never seen Magnusson in one of his Nordic rages. In the bar the conversation dropped off and people turned to stare. By coincidence the bartender was the same man Magnusson had beaten over the head with the parrot. He quietly went out the side door.

"I'm sorry," Wills said, confused for once, "I had no idea that you . . . ah, thought that much of her."

"Oh yes," Magnusson said, shaking with fury, "And I'm going to take her out of there—where is it?"

Kate was puzzled and hurt. No one had told her about this . . . Karen . . . and Magnusson. She couldn't believe he had *time* to fall in love while he was trying to rescue her. And he was so shy and solitary, so straight and . . . pure. How could he be in love with a woman that was somebody's mistress? What hurt most was the fact that he hadn't waited for her.

"Where is it?" Magnusson repeated.

"Magnusson—it's right in the middle of exclusive *guardia* housing. There are sure to be soldiers around the place."

"Why don't you take this a step at a time," the consul offered, "perhaps if you wrote to her . . ."

"I'm going over there and I'm going tonight—now! Where is it?"

"I'm telling you there's no way you can get her out of there without a small army."

The general set his glass down, making a face at the bad champagne. "Well . . ." he said, "there's always the rescue party."

As they came out of the bar, Kate waited for Magnusson by the glass doors. "I'm going to say good-bye."

"What?" He was looking after the others hurrying through the lobby.

"Mother and I are leaving by boat at the end of the week."

He was flustered. "Well, I . . . expect we'll see each other again."

"I hope so, but Boston and San Diego are at opposite ends of the country."

"Yes, well . . ."

She held her hand out. "Good-bye, I'll never forget you."

He touched her hand and was gone, heading off after the rescue party. She doubted if he even heard her. As she watched his tall figure disappear out the door she knew that every other man she met would be measured against him.

Karen Sven de Seville was dropped off at the La Loma house after the poetry recital. Tacho apologized for not accompanying her home, pleading urgent business. *Urgent indeed*, she thought, *taking her to the recital had been his alibi*. Coming out of the theater the word had already spread of Sandino's murder. The *guardia* compound was a little world unto itself; special privileges created to put distance between the people and their protectors. Most of the women here were expensive mistresses and girl-friends. It was not a place you took your wife.

The house was a modern Spanish colonial with an over-hanging balcony along the front supported by heavy, adzed timber. Windows were small, elaborately barred with iron curlicues and inset initials. There was a bright bulb to the left side over an attached cubicle housing a *guardia velador*. As Karen stepped out of the big car, he saluted and she went up steps bordered by huge coyol palms that cast the feathery shadows of their leaves on whitewashed walls. At night, in this park setting, surrounded by tall pines, it had a romantic aura; a created effect. Across, and down the facing slope was the shimmer of the lake.

The door was opened by the houseman, another armed *guardia* regular and she passed him without a word, high heels clacking on the tile of the hall and up the curved stairway. At the top a maid bowed but she waved her off and went into the bedroom alone, shutting the door. It was done in the Hollywood style Tacho loved so much: lavish use of satins and chrome incongruously applied to a stuccoed and beamed room. Across the south wall were French doors that led to the balcony, again swagged in satin and roped by silk cords. Karen was indifferent to this. She had grown up in the red velvet overkill of bordellos and was immune to bad taste. If it was white or gold it was enough.

She slumped at a lacquered dressing table and looked into its round mirror, hand supporting her chin. "God!" she said aloud, "He did it." It had been a leveling blow. Just when she imagined she had some small power over him, he had done exactly the opposite of what she suggested. Not only was Sandino shot, but from what she could gather from excited whispers, six or seven others. It was so pitiful, so depressing that she ached. Tacho was an enigma: charming, funny, beautifully spoken, and she had to admit, an ardent lover. He was also a man capable of *anything*. It was almost better to know evil as in Pedrón than find it smiling at you in bed. He was also generous and protecting and she at last had the security she dreamed of. What she must do, is stop thinking of herself as the power behind the throne and be content as a mistress. Looking in the mirror there was a face above hers. Startled, she spun on the stool and there he was, standing in the fold of drapes by the glass doors, looking like some foolish swashbuckler out of the movies.

"Magnusson!" They crossed the room together and met in an embrace. When they parted she gently touched the eye patch. "Oh, my poor hero, what have they done to you?"

"I love you, Karen," he said, having had the time to practice his lines.

"Of course you do—and I love you—but why are you here?"

"Why . . . I've come to take you away—back to the States."

She laughed. "My brave Viking, how do you intend that?"

"Out those doors—leave it to me."

"What then? Are you still in the military?"

"No, I live in San Diego. I'm in business—I have a . . . shoe store."

She laughed until her throat caught. "Come with me." She led him to a closet taking up one wall. Sliding the doors open revealed a solid tapestry of dresses, the shimmer of sequins, silk, satin, some trimmed in fox. They were arranged by color, the shadings drifting from white and the palest violet to the bold slashes of prints. "Could you buy me these?" When he faltered she towed him to the dressing table, jerking open a drawer, "Look at this," she said, holding up a bracelet, "How many shoes would you have to sell for this?"

"This is junk—I . . . we love each other."

She cupped his face. "And what does that matter? I've sold love all my life, do you think I would leave rich love for poor love?"

"But . . ."

"My hero, you are hopelessly romantic. They say women are, but it's men with their idealized notions of love and impossible expectations—the foolish belief that they can rut their way into paradise." She smiled. "For you it would probably be Valhalla."

She was slipping away. Here in front of him was the love he believed dead, gone forever. The beautiful thing he imagined never to see again and found. A dream answered—and she was slipping away.

"Come on now, go before they hear you." She lifted her head up, closing her eyes. "Kiss me one last time."

Magnusson hit her hard on her raised chin and caught her as she fell.

The Cadillac had pulled boldly up to the front door with the consul driving, the music boy next to him, and General Butler in the back. The *velador*, seeing the expensive car and well-dressed gentleman, came out of his cubicle and walked over, touching his cap. "Can I be of service, *jefes*?"

The music boy showed a large automatic, smiling. "You sure can fella, just keep your hands where I can see 'em and back into that guard shack." Getting out carefully, he maneuvered him into the small room, taping his hands and feet, slapping a piece over his mouth. While he did this Magnusson had stood on the back of the car and jumped to the balcony railing.

The houseman heard the automobile idling and looked out the front window. Suspecting the *velador* to be drunk or asleep, he hurried out the door and down the steps to the car. "I'm sorry gentlemen, the *velador* should be here—are you friends of General Somoza?"

"No," the music boy answered behind him, jerking the man's pistol out of his rear pocket, "friends of the groom."

There was a low whistle and Magnusson appeared on the balcony above them carrying Karen Sven. He carefully lowered her down to General Butler standing on the backseat. Then swinging over the rail he dropped in beside them.

As the car pulled away with Karen unconscious between them, the general was alarmed. "What happened to the poor girl?"

"Fainted from the excitement, sir."

The escape had been planned to the minute. Before driving to the house in La Loma they had reconnoitered the airport road and found a spot opposite the runway where the car would have access. The barbed wire was cut and the post marked. Then, circling to the airport buildings, Major Schilt was dropped off and the car continued on.

In the flight office, Schilt found the sergeant in charge of the *guardia* contingent and handed over his papers. They were in order and the sergeant, young and literate, was impressed with Schilt's rank and the big Ford Tri-Motor. But he thought it odd he would be coming out to the field at this time of night; the plane was scheduled to take off tomorrow.

"Flying down here we had trouble with the starboard engine," Schilt explained, "I've been worrying about it and I think I know what the problem is. I'm going to run the engines up and check pressure lines." He handed the sergeant a bottle of champagne. "Here, for your trouble." And waving, he started for the plane. The sergeant set the bottle down and followed him outside. The soldiers lounging in front of the small airport office watched them walk toward the plane.

The Ford Tri-Motor sat to one side of the field, too big for the hangars. A monoplane, with a huge wing area and three big radial engines, it was popular with airlines for being rugged and able to get in and out of rough fields. It was all metal, carried ten passengers, and showed Pan American colors. The general had borrowed it from his friend Juan Trippe for the cost of the gas.

When they reached the tail, Schilt cautioned the sergeant, "Better not come any closer or you'll get blasted by the propellers." Continuing on alone under the wing, he pulled out the chocks, hoping the man would not find this suspicious. Then opening the low door, he hooked it back, and waving again, went up the one step and forward to the cockpit.

When he started the engines in their proper sequence, the wind blast drove the sergeant back and he walked around the plane to where he could stand and watch Schilt in the yellowed cockpit windows. He had been stationed at the airport long enough to know when they took the blocks out from under airplane wheels they were getting ready to fly. He was hesitant to confront an American officer but felt something was wrong. He undid the flap on his holster and felt to see if the automatic was cocked.

Schilt saw the move and began to sweat. He revved the engines up, then backed them down to give the impression of testing. When twenty minutes had gone by, the sergeant walked close and shouted up to him. Schilt cupped his ear, shaking his head, and the man began to point vigorously back to the office. At that moment Schilt saw the lights of the car flash on the road bordering the field. Pushing the throttle forward and using the right engine, the plane roared forward swinging to the left, forcing the sergeant to drop to the ground as the tail came around. When the plane continued, he jumped up and ran for the truck, shouting at his squad. *"Prontamente, con preteza!"* They threw their weapons in and piled aboard as he started off in a squeal of tires.

Coming up the road the consul adjusted his speed to match the Tri-Motor taxiing parallel on the field. The idea was to cross over where the wire was cut, come alongside the plane, slow and stop together—long enough to get aboard, then take off leaving the car. No one had counted on the truck and it was coming up fast.

"I'd give a lot for my double-ought-six," Magnusson said. The only weapon at hand was the Colt automatic.

"Get ready!" the consul shouted. The mark on the post indicated the opening in the fence coming up and he cut the wheel over, bouncing the big car across the berm and onto the field. They accelerated, came under the plane's wing, then both began to slow. Before they stopped, Magnusson was out the door with Karen in his arms, crossing and lifting her into the low doorway. The general next, helping the music boy, and last, the consul grabbing the car keys, jumping out and running for the door.

The truck was closing at fifty yards, and soldiers, resting their Krags on the top of the cab, began to shoot. The consul could hear the bullets whip by, grooving into the metal—then the rattle of automatic fire. He was in the door now, legs still half out when Schilt shoved the throttle forward, swinging the plane to the right, notched rudder wagging, tail wheel crossed up, propeller blasting back a cloud of dust and gravel from the edge of the runway. The truck ran into this and swerved, the sergeant very nearly hitting the Cadillac. When he got straightened out the Ford Tri-Motor was acclerating down the end of the field and lifting off into the nighttime skies over Managua.

As they began to climb, the general settled in his cane seat up front and got out the *Philadelphia Inquirer* to finish the crossword puzzle. Behind him the music boy sighed, and head resting on his hand, went to sleep. Across the aisle, the consul, still panting from his exertion, watched the lights of the city below.

In the back of the plane Magnusson held Karen Sven in his arms, looking into her supine face and worrying if he'd hit her too hard. Then, when they began to change course toward the Gulf of Mexico, she came around. The first thing she saw was his face close above hers. Bewildered, she looked past him out the windows and saw fluffy clouds. They seemed to be floating. "Where . . . are we?" she asked.

"Valhalla," he answered smiling, in one of his rare attempts at humor.

# Epilogue

ON the high ridge of the Cordillera Entre Ríos between Honduras and Nicaragua is the peak of Cerro Mogotón. At 2107 meters it is one of the highest spots in Central America—more than a mile and a half up. The nearest town is Ocotal 30 kilometers away. It is a place so high and remote that the jaguar hunt above the clouds. Air is thin, game scarce and the wind constant. It is not a place where you expect to find anyone.

On the west slope below sheer cliffs where the pine begins, a camp was tucked into rocks, invisible even from a few yards away. In its narrow enclosure mules grazed on tough mountain grasses, rear legs constantly elevated by the slope. Here, under weaving branches and ragged ponchos a man sat eating, his back to the opening of a cave. Using a tortilla as a scoop he chased beans around a metal plate. A worn rifle lay beside him and in the recesses of the cave a woman cooked, smoke, rising up through the natural chimney of rocks, was dispersed by the wind.

There was a shout from below and canting his head in a peculiar way and squinting out of one eye, he saw his son laboring up the slope leading a mule. A gringo rode it. "Who in the hell is that?" he shouted over the sound of the wind. Angry.

"He's been asking for us in Ocotal."

"You fool! Why bring him all the way up here? Why didn't you kill him down there?"

"He says he's a friend."

When the gringo got off the mule he recognized the parrot's beak, and despite a scraggly beard and wire glasses hooked behind his ears saw the arrogant, whimsical expression. "By sweet Jesus! It's the writer!"

"Pedrón." He walked up the last angle of slope and sat next to him. There was still the massive frame Wills remembered but he was thin with a gray-streaked beard and a right arm he had to move with his left. "It's been some trouble finding you, General."

"Why in God's name would you want to?" He continued eating, finishing off the beans with a swipe of his finger.

"You're the last Sandinisto, Pedrón. All the others are dead or converted to good citizens."

"The idiots let themselves be disarmed and killed. At Guiguili the *guardia* slaughtered more than three hundred— women and children included. It was their own damn fault."

"Somoza is in full control now. Sacasa will be lucky to live his term out."

"You know," Pedrón said, pausing and looking up, "I almost had that lard ass. After they broke their machetes on my skull trying to do a decent *corte gourd* I killed two of them and heard Somoza behind the bedroom door going to it with a woman—but the door was locked and in my condition I was lucky to get away."

"You're the only one left to lead the revolution."

"Don't be silly. I haven't got the words and if I did I can't write. César was the end of it."

Wills bent forward, animated with a zeal that made Pedrón tired. "Let me be the words, Pedrón, we can build it again!"

"What have you been smoking? Here's my army," he said, sweeping his one arm back. "My daughter Rosa, two no-good sons, and some old farts that kill Indians with rocks."

"People will remember Sandino; we'll start with that!"

Pedrón laughed, shaking his head. "It would take fifty years, writer."

*Sacasa was allowed to stay in office until 1936 when the* guardia *deposed him and elected Somoza president. He continued the facade of reelection year after year, then in 1956 was assassinated by a poet.*

*Nicaragua was handed down to his sons. Luis became president and Anastasio, "little Tacho,"—a West Point graduate—took over as* jefe *of the* Guardia Nacional. *The family remained in power up to July 19, 1979, when the new "Sandinistas" overthrew them, eight years short of Pedrón's fifty years.*

*At Somoza's death many remembered Franklin Roosevelt's famous remark about him: "He may be a son of a bitch, but he's our son of a bitch." But few had heard his 1934 epitaph for Sandino.*

*"If I had been a Latin American," he said, "I too would have taken up arms against the intervention."*